THE CURSE OF ASI

UTKARSH SHARMA

Leadstart
INKSTATE

ISBN 978-81-948044-8-2

First published in India 2020 by inkstate Books
An imprint of Leadstart Publishing Pvt Ltd

Sales Office:
Unit No.25/26, Building No.A/1,
Near Wadala RTO,
Wadala (East), Mumbai – 400037 India
Phone: +91 969933000
Email: info@leadstartcorp.com
www.leadstartcorp.com

Editor: Vaibhav Pathare
Cover: Nitin Ingale
Layouts: Victor Patali

Note from the Author

Growing up in a Hindu family, Hindu epics fascinated me from a very tender age. The earliest stories I can remember listening to were that of Mahabharata and Ramayana. My love for stories only enhanced with my age. It might be a story I heard from one of my school friends, about his summer vacation or a story I read from one of my school library's old, worn-out books. The source didn't matter. I would be all ears and eyes because I would find them interesting.

History was another thing I would stay up long nights for, researching, and reading. From reading about the illustrious history of the Maurya Empire to researching how Queen Victoria's descendants, currently or once, ruled Germany, England, Denmark, Sweden, Spain, and other European territories, I came to understand that most of the fictitious stories we come across were once or are derived from factual reality.

I've taken inspiration from the time in Indian history when wars among mighty kingdoms were common and frequent. To it, I've added a sliver of Hindu epic, Mahabharata. The fusion I got is what you will read in this story of 'Curse of Asi'.

I have tried my best to not tell, but show you this story. And my editor has helped me to smoothen and enrich it, getting the best out of it. We both have tried our best to present this story to you with no mistakes. But if you come across any bump on the road during this journey, feel free to contact me with the same.

I would hope that you enjoy reading the story of 'Curse of Asi' as much as I did writing it.

Utkarsh Sharma

Contents

Dramatis Personae

Yashvasin Yuvan
A trusted member of the Akshobhyan army. An excellent swordsman.

Maharaja Brihadratha Akshobhya
The current ruler of the Akshobhyas, the greatest empire in the whole Bharatvarsh.

Maharani Drisana Akshobhya
The Queen of the Akshobhyan Empire, she is married to Brihadratha Akshobhya.

Senapati Aagneya
The current commander of the Akshobhyan army. A disciple of Senapati Yayati.

Senapati Yayati Yasah
A former commander of the Akshobhyan army.

Mahamantri Brahmanand
The chief advisor of Maharaja Brihadratha. He is also the former deputy chief justice. A post from which he resigned due to his increasing age.

Mahapradhan Ganakarta
Prime minister in the Akshobhyan council.

Mahamatya Acala
The Finance minister of the Akshobhyan Empire. He is also the current deputy chief justice. In the past, he was involved in small criminal schemes. But because of his intellect, he was granted a post in the Akshobhyan council by Maharaja Brihadratha.

Nrchakshu Yudhvan
He is the leader of the 'Angrakshak' panel of the Maharaja of Akshobhyas. He is also the last surviving member of the esteemed Yudhvan clan.

Rajkumar Dvij Akshobhya
Crown prince of the Akshobhyan Empire, he is the eldest son of Maharaja Brihadratha and Maharani Drisana.

Rajkumar Adhirohah Akshobhya II

The youngest son of Maharaja Brihadratha and Maharani Drisana. Named after the greatest Akshobhyan King, Samrat Adhirohah Akshobhya.

Yugant Yasah

The only child of former Senapati Yayati Yasah. He was adopted by Maharaja Brihadratha after Yayati's death. He shares a strong bond of brotherhood with Rajkumar Dvij. He is also the successor of Senapati Aagneya as the next commander of the Akshobhyan army.

Raja Samrendra

Ruler of the Kingdom of Rajkot, in the region of Saurashtra, which pledges direct allegiance to the Akshobhyas. He called for aid from the Akshobhyas when he found his kingdom in chaos and peril.

Aatreyya Aarosh

Member of a three men vigilante group. His family was slayed by Akshobhyan flag bearers. Hence, he joined hands with Kalki and Nichakra to bring down the Akshobhyas.

Nichakra

Another member of the vigilante group. He spies in the palace of Rajkot for Kalki.

Kalki

Leader of the three men vigilante group. He plans to bring down the Akshobhyan Empire.

Samaharta Deenabhandwe

Revenue collector in the Kingdom of Rajkot. He is corrupt and manipulates the tax imposition rates.

Shulkadhyaksha Kadamba

Officer in charge of the royal income in Rajkot. He is the master-mind behind the illicit increased rates of taxes of import and export.

High priest Chandak

A priest in the Kingdom of Rajkot. He is also the leader of the peaceful protesters of Rajkot.

Hanan

A young man who wants to fight against the corrupted officials of Rajkot and seeks help from Kalki.

Annapala Bhadraka

He is the head of the food and grain department in Rajkot. He was one of the ministers who were kidnapped by Kalki's associates.

Pattanadhyaksha Nrrat

An officer of the port. He was another minster who was kidnapped by Kalki's associates.

Prakrant

A spy of Mahamantri Brahmanand.

Maharaja Drshkrit

Maharaja of Kuru Kingdom, one of the allies of the Akshobhyan Empire. He is the son-in-law of Maharaja Brihadratha Akshobhya.

Maharani Aarunya

Queen of Kuru Kingdom, married to Drshkrit. The only daughter of Maharaja Akshobhya and Maharani Drisana.

Maharaja Vira Advaitya

The current ruler of the Advaitya Kingdom. He broke the peace treaty with the Akshobhyas. After allying with the Varunyas, he declared war upon the Akshobhyas.

Maharaja Jatsaya Varunya

The current ruler of the Varunya Kingdom. Along with the Advaitya, he too declared war upon the Akshobhyas.

Bhagiratha

Commander of the Advaitya army.

Vrishank

Commander of the Varunya army.

Raja Ijay

Ruler of the kingdom of Pataliputra which pledges direct allegiance to the Akshobhyas. He joins the Akshobhyas in the war against the Advaityas and Varunyas.

Anns

Son of the commander of the Pataliputra army. He replaced his father as the Commander of the Pataliputra army against the alliance of Advaityas and Varunyas.

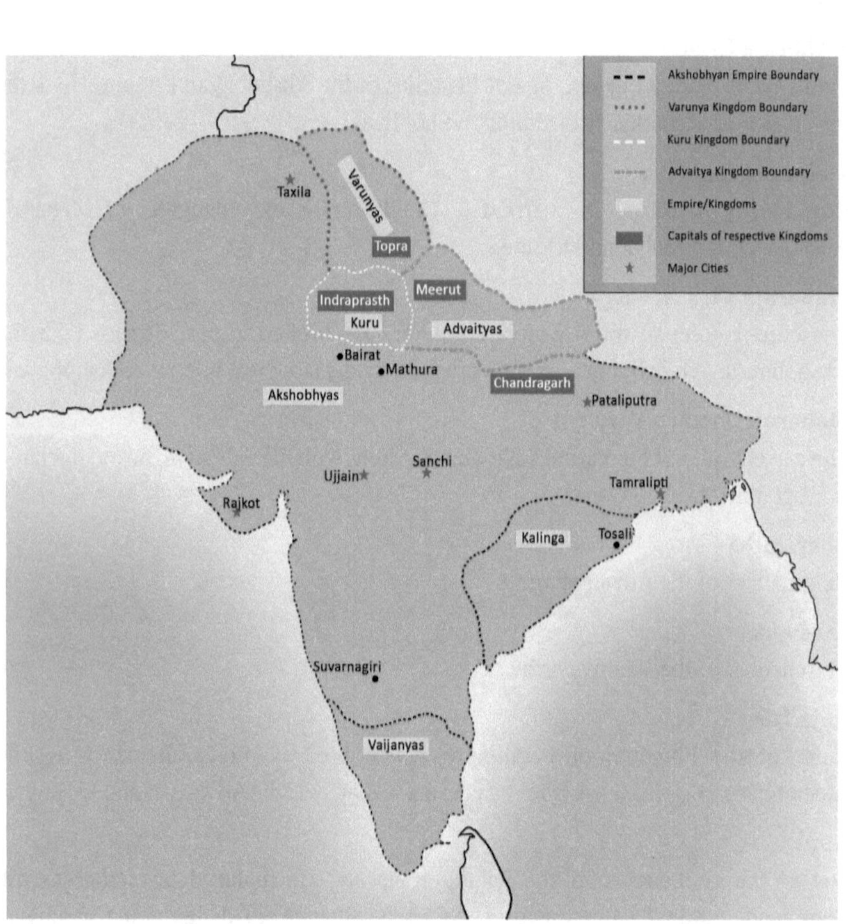

Akshobhyan Empire Boundary
Varunya Kingdom Boundary
Kuru Kingdom Boundary
Advaitya Kingdom Boundary
Empire/Kingdoms
Capitals of respective Kingdoms
Major Cities
Taxila
Varunyas
Topra
Indraprasth
Meerut
Kuru
Advaityas
Bairat
Mathura
Chandragarh
Akshobhyas
Pataliputra
Sanchi
Ujjain
Tamralipti
Rajkot
Kalinga
Tosali
Suvarnagiri
Vaijanyas

PART 1

THE FIRST WAR OF CHANDRAGARH

The alliance of the Rudras, Rudraveeryas and Shatabdas was the first to break into the territory of the Akshobhyas and proclaim upon them a war in their capital, Chandragarh. Nerves of steel were required to step into the Akshobhyan boundaries with cruel intentions against the royal family in heart, let alone declare open war against them. Such courage or, as some would say, madness was required to as little as disdain the rulers of Akshobhyan Kingdom not only because of their vast army who, since the inception of the Akshobhyan rule, hasn't lost a single war but also because of the rumoured revered weapon of gods whose existence, some say is a myth, whilst the others believe to be true, lie within the vicinity of the wonderful architectural marvel of the Akshobhyan palace in Chandragarh.

The 'ASI', otherwise simply known as the weapon of the gods was believed, by many people, a 'hearsay' whose reach in the ears of the people of Bharatvarsh and the people who live in the lands beyond, was the work of the servants of the Akshobhyan family who after their years and years of pumping fuel into the crossfires of rumours, only to never let it douse, have finally established a sense of apprehension in the hearts of the enemies of the Akshobhyas. The spree of the battles and wars won by the Akshobhyas followed next. Which only added strength to the 'hearsay'. As a result, the Akshobhyans stood invincible. The base of the rumour could never be confirmed either. Many Rajas of the kingdoms serving the Akshobhyas wanted to rest the surge of inquisitiveness within them by simply asking Maharaja Brihadratha, the ruler of the Akshobhyan Empire, about the strength of the rumour. But the little fear and massive reverence for the king never let them ask the Maharaja, fearing that it may be taken as an insult or somehow taken as a question which asked the

Maharaja and the long history of the Akshobhyas about their true capabilities. As a result, the truth about the ASI was enslaved amidst the walls of the royal palace of Chandragarh. Only a handful of the members of the council of the Akshobhyas knew the truth. I am one of them.

And hence, challenging the Akshobhyas to war, that's too within the vicinity of their own empire was no mere task of either the faint hearts or some foolish lunatics. We, the council members of the Akshobhyas, couldn't take in lightly either. For the first time since the foundation of the Akshobhyan rule was laid, an army of the enemy reached the borders of Chandragarh. Without saying anything further, one can conclude that the Akshobhyan capital was in a state of peril, be the rumour of the ASI true or not.

The north, east and west provinces that lied near the borders of Chandragarh were very strong in terms of military protection. If the army of the enemy had tried to reach Chandragarh from any of those directions, they have had to trace back from the same route for it was impossible to attack and defeat the armies of those vassal Kingdoms without giving the Akshobhyas enough time to fight the enemy army at those particular provenances, away from the land of Chandragarh. It wasn't that the kingdoms coming under the rule of Akshobhyas in the south of the empire lacked the strength to stop any enemy intervention. Comparatively, they were more vulnerable than the others and the massive army with which the allied enemy forces marched, made it difficult for them to provide any hindrance. Moreover, the attack was sudden and well planned. Clearly, it must have taken years of patience and strategic planning to come up with a calamity of this scale. Even though the south region is more vulnerable, it has its benefits for us. The Ganani River flowed through the land of the Akshobhyan Empire in layers, south of the capital. The enemy army has had to cross what was the most treacherous path of the river. It would've been impossible for them to do so if they had marched any different time. But they had done their homework. The water in the Ganani level drops to its lowest at this time of the year, with another two months for the first shower. But one hindrance remains constant throughout the year. The southern edge of Chandragarh provides an elevation advantage to the Akshobhyas. After the border, there's a hundred and fifty feet drop to acres and acres of barren land. This particular piece of land has not seen a single drop of rain since ages. Even though there are tunnels to provide easiness to commute if one wants to, which is rarely the case, from Chandragarh to the barren land

and back, most of them had been blocked a couple of days before for obvious reasons. Only a few remained open. Most people doubted while predicting the outcome of this war. I, on the other hand, didn't. It was obvious for me who would turn out to be victorious.

The army of the Akshobhyas and the allied forces met in the middle of the barren piece of land, otherwise known as Vandhyabhoomi, miles away from the border of inhabited Chandragarh. Separated by some distance, both sides looked prepared to take arms.

I was sitting on my horse, heavily armoured. Maharaja Brihadratha in his shining armour rode his horse in front, being closely followed by Senapati Aagney.

There was a moment of extreme silence on the battlefield. Hundreds of thousands of some of the most ruthless and strongest soldiers in the whole Bharatvarsh stood in the Vandhyabhoomi in the state of quietude. Apart from the light blowing wind, nothing could be heard. Under the extreme sunlight, the helmets of the soldiers shone like a mirror, reflecting rays of light everywhere. From heaven, it must look like a rare treat for the eyes, thousands of shining stars in broad daylight. I shifted my eyes towards my left, over a soldier in the infantry. A drop of sweat rolled down from his temple to the side of his neck as he gulped in angst. My eyes shifted over the soldier standing behind him. His eyes were glittering with excitement and a broad smirk on his face made him look like a warrior in the tales of the legends. It is both tragic and prestigious for a soldier to be associated with war. Especially this one when the stakes were so high. But the atmosphere changed when the conch was brought in the Vandhyabhomi which was about to turn into a battlefield.

The steady soldiers became restless. A fire ignited in their eyes which could be doused only by blood. Shields were banged together, spears stomped on the ground giving rise to a mammoth cloud of dust. The thunderous sound on the battlefield was deafening. Maharaja Brihadratha rode his horse horizontally along the line of our soldiers, getting them psyched up with chants of patriotism and declaring them as the heroes of Chandragarh. The army on the other side was as ready as the Akshobhyan army to rage war. And what followed after the sound of the blown conch was total annihilation.

On the 12th day, I made my way across the battlefield, passing through countless lifeless soldiers. Slayed. Butchered. Some missing a limb. Some without a head. Some with only an inch of life inside them, lying motionless, asking themselves the meaning of this predicament. The soil underneath my feet was drenched with blood. The smell of blood and corpses filled the air with an atrocious intensity. The clashing of swords mixed with the sore screeching of the injured was sufficient to fill the heart of a mere mortal being with the highest sense of fear and trepidation.

'They have roughly 11,000 men remaining, Senapati Aagneya.'

'What about the cavalry and war elephants?' asked Senapati Aagneya.

'Their war elephants have all been slayed. And about 300 enemy cavalries remain in the battlefield.'

It was quite appalling to acknowledge the fact that out of 100,000 soldiers only 11,000 were left. Almost 90,000 were butchered in 12 days, not including who fought from our side. The military strategy of Senapati Aagneya was unmatched in the whole Bharatvarsh. No wonder we suffered from much fewer casualties than the allied enemy forces.

'The war is almost over. Ask the infantry to get in position for the 'garurd' formation. We'll end this war before the sun sets.' Said a determined Aagneya.

Garurd formation was one of the most lethal formations ever designed. Mahamantri Brahmanand is credited for designing this formation with the assistance of former Army commander of the Akshobhyas, Senapati Yayati. It was first used during the '5 nations war'. The speciality of this formation is the number of enemies that can be killed in quick successions. Garurd formation had a pivotal role in our victory in the '5 nations war'. Senapati Aagneya must be agitated enough already to be using this formation.

The soldiers were commanded to regroup and to get into the formation. After getting the marching orders, in no time, the Akshobhyan army attacked the enemy head-on with the 4th and 5th infantry forming a double-layered circle around the remaining enemy infantry. What followed next was a clear massacre. The fear could be seen in the enemies' eyes now. They knew their end was near. The horror in their eyes was too big to not notice. Thousands of men butchered in a few seconds. It was bloodshed. The greatest war in the history of

'Chandragarh' was nothing but massive bloodshed. With nowhere to go and after offering much resistance, the remaining 5000 men surrendered. All 5000 of them were taken as prisoners. Another victory was added in the illustrious history of the 'Akshobhyas'. The Akshobhyan soldiers were celebrating this exceptional victory by singing, chanting, and praising the king and this prestigious land of 'Chandragarh'.

The soldiers of the allied armies were being taken to the dungeons when a soldier approached me.

'Maharaja Brihadratha has ordered for your presence in his camp.'

'Go on. I'll be there in a moment.' I said.

After singing another victory song with the soldiers, I headed for the Maharaja's camp.

Inside the camp, Mahapradhan Ganakarta and Mahamantri Brahmanand were accompanying Maharaja Brihadratha beside the wide table placed at the centre of the camp. I greeted them separately before walking towards Maharaja Brihadratha.

Maharaja Brihadratha didn't look ecstatic about the victory. Maybe he wasn't very pleased with the cost we had to pay for this victory. He wanted to talk to me alone. Instead of asking the revered ministers to step out, I followed the Maharaja out of the tent. He took a few steps towards the Vandhybhoomi before halting. Maharaja Brihadratha was staring at the battlefield with a composed face. I stood there without disturbing the silence that surrounded us for a couple of minutes. The scene of the battlefield wrenched my heart. I was overcome by strong emotion, but kept my nerves firm and stared at the physical resemblance of pain until Maharaja Brihadratha finally spoke.

'What do you see in front of us?' he asked in a firm voice.

Trying to control my emotions, I finally spoke.

'I see someone who will never return to his home. I see a father who won't be able to see his daughter. I see a son who won't be able to take the blessings of his parents anymore. I see a brother with whom I won't be able to laugh anymore. I see a victory. But no victors, sir'

Maharaja Brihadratha stared gravely at me for some time. I didn't give an answer that he hadn't expected. He almost knew me inside out, after so many years of my service to him.

'You still amaze me, Yashvasin Yuvan.' He said before turning his head away towards the battlefield.

'Record the complete statistics of the casualties in the war. I want the report by tomorrow morning.' Continued Maharaja Brihadratha.

'Affirmative, sir.'

'And one more thing.' The Maharaja said just before I was about to leave.

'Never change. You have the heart of a poet. We rarely get to see a poet among the soldiers. Never change'

I received his message with a warm smile.

'On the other hand, I'll give you the previous records for your reports myself. They're inside the camp. Come with me.'

We walked inside the camp again, where Maharpradhan Ganakarta had already assembled a stack of papyrus records.

Maharaja Brihadratha was loosening his armour as I collected the records from the table behind him. I removed my helmet to have a clearer look at the records when Senapati Aagney entered the camp with an unexpected guest. Brought in chains was Raja Rachit Rudra of the Rudras. One among the three rulers leading the allied army force against the Akshobhyas. He was a strong man, with a physique of a beast. Just as he entered, he looked at the direction of Maharaja Brihadratha. It was at that moment I realized the graveness of bringing him inside the Maharaja's camp.

'You, Bastard!' He exclaimed as he pushed five soldiers, holding him, away but not before stealing a dragger from one of them. He came running towards the Maharaja, who was in a clumsy position removing his armour.

'You took everything away from me!' He screamed at the top of his voice.

Senapati Aagney was left behind. There was no way he could stop the mad Raja of Rudras.

I stepped in front of the Maharaja, swiftly, and noticed a calm and confident smile on his face.

'Now die!' Rachit yelled.

I removed my sword from its sheath and in one swing slit open Raja Rachit's throat before he could come near Maharaja Brihadratha. The man in chains fell on his knees as the dragger came loose from his grip. He tried to say something, but only blood slurred out.

'What did you do?' shouted Senapati Aagney.

I looked at the astonished Senapati in acute wonder.

'Fulfilled my responsibility towards my king, perhaps.' I said.

'You stepped in front of the Maharaja and saved him from a mishap, that is brave and very loyal of you, but you need not kill him. He was the last surviving commander of the allied army.' Senapati Aagney said as he looked down at the lifeless body of Raja Rachit.

'Why would you even bring him inside the Maharaja's camp?' I asked. My voice reflecting my inquisitiveness and rage.

'Maharaja Brihadratha's orders.' He replied.

Maharaja Brihadratha removed his armour and stepped in front.

'Yashvasin did what was necessary.' He said while placing his hand on my shoulder before looking down on the dead ruler of Rudras. 'You need not worry about him, Senapati Aageny. Every enemy associated with this war is either dead or behind the bars. The war is won.'

Senapati Aagney ended his protest and ordered the soldiers to take the lifeless body of Raja Rachit away.

'Now if you may allow councilmen, I have got to work on a report.' I said while giving a glance to everyone in the room before turning towards the Maharaja and asking his permission to leave. I picked up my helmet and the stack of papyrus records and left the camp. I was about to head back to Chandragarh but the Vandhyabhoomi called out for me.

There was still time for the sun to set and a group of soldiers was already preparing to give the final rites to their fallen brothers. It was agonizing to watch the great warriors of 'Chandragarh' fallen. Back into the warmth of the land, they swore to protect.

The sterile land, which had forgotten how to yield a soul from its depth was ready to take thousands of them inside its womb. The land which remained unproductive for so long now has become a graveyard of the unburied. The land which once remained barren now had a small stream flowing across it. A small stream, deep red in colour. Maybe promising to wash the sins of the dead away. Maybe not being a symbol of life, but a messenger of death itself. But not for so long. The ferocious eyes which once had flames in them now were motionless as those strong limbs which were once ready to tear all the hindrances. The funeral rites were given to all the soldiers who fought bravely for their motherland. They were being cremated. And in seconds the whole battlefield was ignited with thousands of yellow flames. Flames so big, trying to grasp the sky.

The sun finally touched the earth and slowly began its journey of descending into nothingness. I watched the sky as it started to change its shade from blue to a lonely shade of pink. At the far horizon, what remains of the bright yellow sun, started to become a lot deeper, maybe it was trying to match the shade of those thousands of flames on the battlefield, before finally descending completely. We, who were destined to survive this horror to live on to see many of those again, stood still. Asking ourselves what did we do to deserve this and what they didn't?

The sun was long gone and it was all dark, but the flames were still so big, still touching the night sky as if 'life' was transcending from one end to the other. We all remain at the battlefield giving our final respect to our fallen brothers until the thousands of them joined the millions of others in the night sky.

❖

PILLARS OF AKSHOBHYAS

More than a couple of months passed since the war between the allied forces and the Akshobhyas took place. The dejection and sadness among the citizens due to the loss of their men in the war lingered in Chandragarh. But the capital state was in peace. A state of tranquillity and contentment was returning in Chandragarh. Time will eventually heal everything. Time may prove to be wicked sometimes. But in solitude and distress, time is that compassionate companion that resolves every difficulty.

Chandragarh was not only the home of the most powerful dynasty in 'Bharatvarsh' but was also one of the most beautiful cities in the whole country. It was covered with Simha Forest in the north and Ganani River in the south. Samrat Mahadhyata, the founder of the 'Akshobhyan Dynasty', founded this city with his younger brother and the greatest ruler in the history of the 'Akshobhyas', Samrat Adhirohah. The brothers fought against the rulers of 'Chandraketugarh', the 'Karnapratapas'. After winning the war, Chandraketugarh was divided into Chandragarh and Ketupradesh for better administration by the two brothers. The present city of Chandragarh was prospering more than ever in every field of art. Maharaja Brihadratha acknowledges and understands the importance of education and art in every aspect of life. In his reign two universities were established in the city of Chandragarh, attracting students to come from different corners of the world to learn art, economics, and strategies. Mahapradhan Ganakarta and Mahamantri Brahmanand were the chief architects of this ever-prospering city under the rulership of the previous ruler and father of Maharaja Brihadratha, Maharaja Sarvyoni. Today Mahapradhan Ganakarta and Mahamantri Brahmanand are the most respected people in Chandragarh and one of the elite pillars behind the expansion of the Akshobhyas in 'Bharatvarsh'.

All the matters of immense importance are first checked and verified by Mahapradhan Ganakarta and Mahamantri Brahmanand before getting presented before the Maharaja.

Mahamantri Brahmanand, who was also the chief advisor of the king, is known for his immense knowledge in the field of economic policy, military strategy, and politics not only in 'Bharatvarsh' but also in the land beyond. He was the chief advisor of Maharaja Sarvyoni too. He is revered by all the citizens of 'Chandragarh'. Even Maharaja Brihadratha acknowledged his importance in every matter. Not a single matter was considered by Maharaja Brihadratha without the consultancy of Mahamantri Brahmanand. Mahamantri Brahmanand was one of those few people in Chandragarh who would do everything in their power for the well-being of the kingdom. Such people were seen a few times in the history of the Akshobhyas. But it was because of them that the Akshobhyas now ruled more than half of the 'Bharatvarsh'.

The Akshobhyan Empire has produced the strongest warriors, cleverest minds, and most loyal workers. Today, the empire stretches from Gandhara Mahajanapada in the north to Suvarnagiri in the south and Tamralipta in the east to Saurashtra in the west. Covering more than 4 million square kilometres. With no distress among any of the conquered states, the support that the empire gets from the citizens made the empire strongest and most powerful in the competition. The relationships of the Akshobhyan Empire with foreign lands were healthy too. Mainly because they all were associated with trading. Major exports from the Akshobhyan Empire included silk, textiles, spices, and exotic food. Trade has been flourishing in the last ten years since the appointment of Uddanda as the foreign trade minister. Due to his clever tactics and foundation of easy and economically feasible roots, trading with the Greeks has never been easier.

Another thing that the Akshobhyan Empire is famous for is its judiciary system. The first constitution and judiciary system was laid by Samrat Adhirohah. But it was the 5th emperor of Chandragarh, Maharaja Prataparat, who made certain amendments in the original constitution and judiciary system to give a more rightful insight in justice. Whole 'Bharatvarsh' revered and acknowledged the judiciary system of 'Chandragarh'. Law and order were also followed by everyone in the capital. Maybe because the tolerance against even the pettiest crime was negligible and heavy penalty was given for the crime. Mahamatya Acala, the finance minister of 'Chandragarh', is presently also the deputy chief justice of the city. He followed Mahamantri Brahmanand after the chief advisor asked the king for permission to leave the post. With the increasing age, Mahamantri Brahmanand found it difficult to accommodate and give justice to all the responsibilities he had upon him. Hence, he retired to being only the chief advisor of Maharaja Brihadratha.

Mahamatya Acala was a middle-aged man who doesn't have a very admirable or revered past. But he excelled in finance and had a keen interest in the judiciary system of the city from a very young age. Although he has been, in many instances, labelled as corrupt and capricious and, hence, was opposed by many council members when he was nominated for being the finance minister of the capital. Even Mahamantri Brahmanand asked Maharaja Brihadratha to give his action of appointing Mahamatya Acala the finance minister of Chandragarh another thought. It rarely happened that Maharaja Brihadratha had taken decisions that Mahamantri Brahmanand had opposed. This being one of them. Maharaja Brihadratha did appoint Mahamatya Acala as the new finance minister of the capital, to everybody's dismay. Although there have been some rumours about Mahamatya Acala receiving generous compensation from the merchants at the Ganani River for allowing them to trade in a quantity of spices more than the quantity mentioned in the official papers so that they won't have to pay the higher tax. But these rumours were never proved to be true. And the judiciary system was getting respect from the citizens, more than ever. Hence Maharaja Brihadratha was a proud king. Even Mahamantri Brahmanand had to give in. But he still had his doubts that Mahamatya Acala would prove to be fatal for the kingdom in the long run. Mahamantri Brahmanand kept information about everything that was happening in Chandragarh. Whether it was happening behind closed doors or out in the front. There wasn't a single thing that Mahamantri Brahmanand wasn't aware of. He had his secret messengers spread all over the capital city. Hence he had his men keep an eye on the finance minister.

The Shooras and Jaitharas

I was approached by Nrchakshu today. He gave me a scroll with a royal stamp on it, indicating it was coming from the king himself. Instructions were to deliver it to Mahamatya Acala. It was a Friday morning, which meant that Mahamatya Acala was in the court. Therefore, I headed towards the court.

The court building was in the east. A direct passage, guarded by many armed soldiers, was made for the officials and nobles, from the royal palace to the court and back. But even though the message was from the King himself, and so was of paramount importance, I opted to take the longer path through the residential area of the common folk of Chandragarh. It was a pleasant morning and I didn't want to hush it up with any rapid activities. Moreover, I was assured that I would reach in time, anyhow. After walking a while south of the palace, I took a left turn from the old, deep well which lies on the right edge of the three-way. The water of the well remains cold and unharmed from the outer impurities due to the tranquil shade of an old and gigantic banyan tree that overlooks Chandragarh through its long and tall branches. The tree has been in the city for as long as I can remember. It was here when I was born and, maybe, shall remain long after I return to dust. A wide and busy passage passes between the many huts of the commoners. I took that passage. People were up and busy with their work. A couple of stray cows mooed with their head held high. Children, jolly and happy, found themselves indulged in their fun activities. A bunch of them, sons and daughters of people I knew, came rushing towards me with their mischievously smiling faces. I was expecting a prank to be played on me. Instead, they offered me corn. At first, I refused their generosity but eventually gave up on their kindness and accepted their gift. Munching on the corn, I carried on. The passage grew narrower after I walked past the huts and cottages. Straight ahead, I could see Chandragarh architecture in all its glory.

The court building showed the pinnacle of architecture in Chandragarh. It was as magnificent as it can get. With an increasing belief and growing respect among the people of Chandragarh for the judiciary system, Maharaja Brihadratha reckoned to build this splendid piece of architecture.

The Entrance gates were alone 20 feet tall, which roared even while getting slightly ajar. As the supporting pillars on the main entryway of the building were two gigantic statues of Samrat Adhirohah and Maharaja Prataparat. The two kings of Chandragarh who established and further shaped the judiciary system of the city, respectively. After sharing a brief company of the two rulers in the entryway, I took the walkway that appeared. The walls on either side of the walkway were decorated with huge picture frames. Portrait frames of all the loyal and influential officials and warriors the land of Chandragarh had seen. Many great and revered personalities had served the Akshobhyas and, hence, many portraits adorned either wall. The walls were divided into sections. Sections depicting the time under a specific ruler of Chandragarh. Starting with Samrat Mahadhyata, the sections followed to the present reign of Maharaja Brihadratha. Mahamantri Brahmanand, Mahamatya Acala, Senapati Aagney, Mahapradhan Ganakarta, and all the former Mahamantris, Mahapradhans, and Senapati's had their enormous portraits nailed to the wall. There have been some council members in the past who eventually proved to be disloyal and treacherous. Such members were also marked in the Akshobhyan history in a particular fashion. Just like the perfidious council members, who were removed from their respective positions and the capital, leaving a dark mark on their family name, their picture frames were removed too, leaving a black dense mark on the wall. Signifying their disloyalty towards the throne of Chandragarh. The section under Maharaja Brihadratha's reign had that mark too.

The walkway led to a staircase.

The building was divided into two parts. The upper part was reserved for all the financial matters of the whole empire. Messengers and statistician, from all over the empire, would bring information regarding the financial statistics of all the states being ruled by the Akshobhyas. Export and import information too were kept at the top atrium, which was always crowded as a result. The same was the situation of the lower part of the building, where the court was established on Fridays. On Fridays, all the major issues of Chandragarh were addressed and resolved. Today's case was regarding a dispute between two tribes. The dispute was over a section of land which was sold to them by a deceitful landlord a couple of months ago. The landlord's whereabouts were unknown since he left the city of Chandragarh a month back. I made my way through the crowded hall in the direction of Mahamatya Acala. But before I could hand him the scroll, he had already climbed the podium and had made himself comfortable in the 'Nyaymurti Pathika'. So I decided to hear the case out. I stepped aside and stood alongside Mahamatya's aangrakshaks.

The large hall with a capacity of 10,000 people was getting overcrowded. Almost all the members of both the tribes were present in the courtroom. A tumult of shouting and speaking broke out among the tribes. It was chaos until Mahamatya Acala raised his right hand without lifting his eyes from the papyrus record in front of his desk. The quietude that followed next showed the respect that the people of Chandragarh had for him. Mahamatya Acala, after carefully reading the records from the papyrus, lifted his eyes to examine both the tribes which stood on either side of the court.

'The representatives of both the tribes shall come forward now.' said the Mahamatya.

The first one to come forward was a member of the Shoora tribe. A rather young representative for a tribe so old and important. His name was Narottam. Narottam's father was the previous representative and head of the Shooras. Shooras were Vaishyas. They were farmers who were affected by the recent famine.

'Long live the king!

Long live Chandragarh!'

He said as he came forward.

'I am Narottam Shoora. The representative of the Shoora tribe.'

Mahamatya Acala gave him a long, steady look. After carefully examining the young representative, Mahamatya Acala shifted his eyes towards the other tribe.

The representative of the Jaithara tribe stepped forward. He was an old man nearing his seventies.

'Long live the king!

Long live Chandragarh!'

He said as he stepped forward. He was rather rigid for his age. He stood firmly as Mahamatya Acala began examining him too.

Vajranakha was the head of the Jaithara tribe. And was leading them for 22 years now. The Jaitharas were one of the oldest inhabitants of Chandragarh. In fact, they have been here when Chandragarh and Ketupradesh were in a union. They have a long history of building temples around Chandragarh. Even today most of the Jaitharas are in the profession of building and renovating temples in the capital.

After a couple of minutes, Mahamatya asked the representatives to put their cases forward.

'State your case, Narottam Shoora.'

'We Shooras have long been farming on our ancestral land happily. But due to the recent run of famine, the land we farm upon became barren. All the members of the tribe, as a result, discussed the numerous ways in which we could tackle this major problem. As you know, Mahamatya, we Shooras still depend upon farming to earn our living. So we decided to buy a new piece of land. We approached Padmakar, a landlord. Some of our tribe members used to work on his land to make ends meet. We presented him with an offer which we knew was less for the piece of land we discussed on buying. But after we promised him to pay the remaining payment after the harvesting period, Padmakar accepted and sold his land to us. The same land which the Jaitharas are claiming to be theirs. We are poor farmers, Mahamatya, and can't afford to relocate or tackle this new problem. Therefore, here we are. Justice is all that we seek, Mahamatya. Justice is all we seek.'

Mahamatya again, after carefully listening to Narottam, examined him. Narottam felt a bit self-conscious, because of Mahamatya's continuous staring. After a couple of minutes, Mahamatya Acala asked Vajranakha to step forward and to state his case too.

Vajranakha came forward with a high head and was very much confident too. He was undaunted by the huge crowd and the officials that were present in the court.

'Mahamatya Acala!', said Vajranakha in a thunderous voice.

'41 years ago, I and my clan members were appointed with the task of building the divine temple of Lord Rama. North of the holy Ganani river. The temple has become a symbol of sanctity and virtue in this capital city. This is who we are Mahamatya. Jaitharas! One of the most eminent craftsmen and architects not only in Chandragarh but in the whole 'Bharatvarsh'. Vajranakha roared.

'And our history of building holy temples of the gods dates long back. Even before the Akhsobhaya dynasty came into existence.'

Mahamatya's eyebrows shot up listening to Vajranakha speak without any agitation or dread.

'In this dispute over this piece of land....'

Vajranakha paused for a split second and caught the representative of the Shoora tribe in the corner of his eye before continuing again.

'Both Jaitharas and Shooras agree on the fact that we have been swindled by the immoral Padmakar. And, ergo, we agree that he should be caught and punished as soon as possible too.'

Both the tribe members acknowledged Vajranakha's words by shouting and chanting against the landlord Padmakar.

'Punish the deceitful!'

'Imprison Padmakar!'

Protested both the tribes.

Mahamatya Acala was, for a second, caught in the moment, forgetting about the case, he could not help but wonder and praise Vajranakha's skilful oration. Vajranakha was, somehow, able to bring the voices of the two tribe members, who were going against each other for several weeks, into unison.

'And so Mahamatya...' said Vajranakha in a booming voice which again brought the court into a standstill.

'This brings us back to the topic of the dispute. To whom the land belongs?

We Jaitharas bought the land nearly at the same time as the Shooras, as we know now. We bought the land to manage the increasing number of people in our clan by building new homes on that land. And because it is a question about the residence of our people, I would request you, Mahamatya Acala, to have your say and to finalize a decision regarding the ownership of the land.'

Mahamatya Acala's eyes were again on the papyrus records on his table. After not getting any response from the deputy chief justice of the capital, Vajranakha tried to draw his attention again.

'And that should be all, Mahamatya.'

Mahamatya Acala's eyes finally raised. His eyes went from one corner of the court to the other examining both the tribes and their representatives in between, eventually retiring to the records in front of his desk again.

'Dandnayak Dardanos…' Called the Mahamatya without lifting his eyes from his desk.'…. is ordered to start the search of the culprit Padmakar. Dandnayak is ordered to bring the culprit back to the capital city in three weeks.'

Dandnayak Dardanos bowed and asked Mahamatya's permission to leave the courtroom to work on the search operation rapidly. After getting the permission, Dandnayak Dardanos, with his five men, marched towards the exit of the courtroom.

Mahamatya Acala, giving a final glance to the records, looked up again.

'Maharaja Brihadratha has bestowed the power of justice on me, to make impartial and unprejudiced decisions about the important cases of this mighty city of Chandragarh. But this case sees two ancient and important tribes of Chandragarh, fighting for a land which is by all right their own. Making this case too big and important for me to decide on. Hence, three weeks from now, this case will be brought in front of Maharaja Brihadratha. Three weeks from now, Maharaja Brihadratha will make the final decision on the ownership of the land and will also see that Padmakar gets his punishment too. Till then, this court is dismissed.'

Upon hearing the final words of the day from Mahamatya Acala, both the representatives of the tribes acknowledged the decision by bowing to the deputy chief justice and the finance minister of the capital. The Shooras and the Jaitharas both then made their way towards the exit in a systematic order. After updating the records, Mahamatya Acala too stood up from the 'Nyaymurti Pathika' to make his exit. I greeted him as he stepped down from the podium by bowing to him.

'Yashvasin Yuvan! The man who showed utmost valour in the most recent and furious battle of Chandragarh!' he gushed.

The Mahamatya changed his position. He stood stiffly, with his arms crossed and chuckled with amusement. 'I wonder what brought you here, Yuvan.'

I removed the scroll from my waist cloth and extended it towards the Mahamatya.

'Something of utmost importance, perhaps' I said with a gracious smile on my face.

Mahamatya's eyebrows lowered as he saw the scroll in my hand.

'Coming directly from Maharaja Brihadratha, huh?' He acknowledged with a sense of graveness in his voice.

'Yes, Mahamatya Acala. A message from the Maharaja himself.' I said as I handled the scroll to him.

'Do you know what this is about, Yuvan?'

'No, Mahamatya. I received it from the young leader of the Maharaja's aangrakshak squad and was asked to deliver it to you as soon as possible.

'Nrchakshu isn't it? That young lad. I wonder what Maharaja Brihadratha sees in him. That lad must have some calibre and character perhaps, you see? It isn't every time that Maharaja goes against Mahamantri's decisions.' Mahamatya Acala rebuked in conflict.

'Perhaps, sir.'

'Do you know him personally, Yuvan?'

'No, sir. I don't.'

'Very well. I would like you to keep a soft eye on him, anyway. With the history he has, one never knows.' He sighed as he patted on my shoulder.

My eyebrows shot up and I nodded in agreement with a grin.

'Ah, you sly!' Mahamatya understood the meaning of my expression. 'Mine is an entirely different case. With the history I have no one needs to worry a bit.'

Keeping the stature of Mahamatya Acala in my mind, I didn't say anything. I just received his words with a warm smile.

'I shall now go, Yuvan. A lot of work awaits me at the finance office. It's not an easy task being both the deputy chief justice and finance minister of the capital, you see.' Mahamatya Acala burst into laughter as he made his way to the finance office with his aangrakshaks.

The courtroom was all empty. After a couple of minutes, I too made my way back to the royal palace.

There was a lot of work still left to do. After all, the crown prince of Chandragarh was returning from his six months stay in the western extent of the empire.

There was a lot of work that still required my assistance.

The Prince's Homecoming

Preparations were commenced since the early morning. Even before the first rays of the sun fell on the newly deposited dew in the widely spread farms of Chandragarh, only to add more radiance to the already joyous city which was ready and long awaiting the return of their crown prince. The whole city was covered with the sweet scent of flowers. As if the spring had arrived early this year in the capital city. Flowers, matching the colours of a rainbow, were brought directly from the royal gardens of Ketupradesh in huge quantity. Citizens of Chandragarh were as ecstatic as the royal family of the Akshobhyas. From the experienced but weekend eyes of the elders to the big innocent eyes of the future of the capital, all that was reflecting was pure joy and happiness. The city was blissful and was awaiting the arrival of Rajkumar Dvij.

Months ago, the western extent of the empire suffered an imbalance. The region of Saurashtra saw disputes among the many inhabitants of the kingdom of Rajkot. The dispute turned into a riot that took a violent turn. In the riot two high officials of the kingdom of Rajkot were abducted from their respected home late night. They went missing for some time until one day when their butchered bodies were found in an aisle near their residences. The riot went out of hands and forced Raja Samarendra, king of Rajkot, to ask for help from Maharaja Brihadratha. Mahapradhan Ganakarta consulted Maharaja Brihadratha about this situation. He told Maharaja Brihadratha that this could be a good opportunity for Rajkumar Dvij to prove his worth and therefore advised Maharaja to send his son to control and stop the riots in Rajkot. Maharaja Brihadratha too saw this as a big occasion where the crown prince could not only prove his worth but could also further develop his statecraft tactics. After hours of consultation, Rajkumar Dvij was commanded by the Maharaja to set for the kingdom of Rajkot.

Rajkumar Dvij, since his childhood, has always been interested in the fields of statecraft, economic policies, and military strategies. Since his younger days, he would always try to eavesdrop on the discussions held in the royal courtroom among the highest officials of the capital city, only to increase his knowledge about the current affairs. Mahamantri Brahmanand was always seen clearing and answering the little prince's doubts and questions regarding statecraft. Whereas whenever Rajkumar Dvij would see Senapati Aagney, who would remain preoccupied most of his time, in a little enforced leisure, he would rush to him only to ask him about any new military strategies. Rajkumar Dvij was not only loved and cherished by the officials of the Akshobhyan Empire but was also adored and respected by the citizens of Chandragarh. The little prince would always accompany his mother, Maharani Drisana to her weekly visit to the Temple of Lord Rama, north to the Ganani river. Maharani Drisana would provide support and charity to the indigents by the hands of Rajkumar Dvij.

Being taught by the likes of Mahamantri Brahmanand, Mahapradhan Ganakarta, and Senapati Aagney, Rajkumar Dvij excelled in every aspect. He was also an excellent swordsman. On the eve of his 21st birthday, Senapati Aagney presented him with a sharp double-edged sword. Rajkumar Dvij became so excited that he challenged Senapati Aagney for a duel. Although the rules of the Akshobhyas inhibits any official to pick weapons against a member of the royal family, Rajkumar Dvij was too excited that a duel was conducted behind closed doors between him and Senapati Aagney. I and a couple of assistants of Senapati Aagney were the only ones, apart from the crown prince and Senapati Aagney, who knew about this duel. And we were ordered by the crown prince never to talk about that duel in front of anyone. Or else it would prove fatal for us. And that's why I can't reveal the winner of that duel now. Maybe I will a little later. Although the result was quite surprising and the duel was one of the best I've ever witnessed. Believe me, one would not want to have a duel with either Senapati Aagneya or Rajkumar Dvij.

And that's why Rajkumar Dvij was the ideal crown prince. One who is excellent with swords and other weaponries, one who knows everything there is to know about statecraft and one who has vast knowledge about military strategies. I won't be surprised if, in the next few months, the capital would conduct 'Rajyabhishek' of Rajkumar Dvij.

Mahamantri Brahmanand advised Maharaja Brihadratha to let Yugant Yasah accompany Rajkumar Dvij on his expedition to the region of Saurashtra. Without any more consultation, Yugant Yasah was commanded to travel with Rajkumar Dvij.

Yugant Yasah was the only son of the former Senapati, Yayati Yasah.

Maharaja Brihadratha took Yugant Yasah under his care when he was only eight years old. He was brought up just like a prince. Being also taught by the likes of Mahamantri Brahmanand and Senapati Aagney, Yugant Yasah too excelled in statecraft and military strategies. He was also an excellent swordsman and was untouchable with his spear skills. Rajkumar Dvij and Yugant were brought up together. The bond between them was as strong as a bond between brothers. Yugant being four years older than Rajkumar Dvij always looked down at the latter as his younger brother. Just as Rajkumar Dvij was considered to be the ideal crown prince, Yugant was also destined to be the next Commander-in-chief of the Akshobhyan army. And that's why, I reckon, was destined to follow his father's footsteps. Yugant is most likely to be the successor of Senapati Aagney. It can be said that the future of Chandragarh and that of the Akshobhyan dynasty was already written. And written so well, it was in safe hands.

Rajkumar Dvij and Yugant Yasah's journey to the kingdom of Rajkot bore fruit. After only a month from their visit, the riots stopped in the western city. But the apprehension among the citizens was just too big. With Yugant Yasah in charge of finding the real culprit, the army and investigators of Rajkot got down in brass tracks to solve the mysterious rise of aversion among the citizens towards the kingdom. As the investigation went forward, it was found that a group of vigilantes were responsible for the violent outburst. Yugant Yasah saw to it that the vigilantes got the punishment they deserved. But even after six weeks of punishing the culprits, the tension among the citizens didn't vanish. Therefore, after analysing that difficult predicament, Rajkumar Dvij had a convention with Raja Samrendra and other high officials of the kingdom of Rajkot. In the convention, Rajkumar Dvij declared that he'll be supervising a detailed investigation of the state affairs. Even with several high officials opposing the decision of Rajkumar Dvij, Raja Samrendra had no choice but to give in. Weeks into the thorough investigation, which also included some sessions of Rajkumar

Dvij and Yugant Yasah's direct interaction with the citizens of Rajkot, Rajkumar Dvij was able to track the corrupt officials responsible for the riots in the city. Yugant Yasah again saw to it that the corrupt officials were punished too. After a month of reviewing, Rajkumar Dvij and Yugant Yasah were assured that the city will now be in peace.

The special moment for which everyone was waiting, finally arrived in Chandragarh. Rajkumar Dvij and Yugant Yasah, accompanied by half a dozen horsemen, finally arrived in the capital city. Children, with cheerful laughter, started chasing the horsemen as soon as they entered the boundaries of the city. The crown prince with his companions crossed the Ganani river and made their way to the Palace through the city market and the houses of the citizens. Bringing a smile on the face and a sense of beaming joy in the heart of every citizen they encountered on their way. Joining the children, in their pursuit to the palace, were now the adults who too wanted to see the welcome ceremony of the crown prince. Moreover, it was more likely that Maharaja Brihadratha, in the joy of his elder son returning home, would become quite generous.

Rajkumar Dvij and Yugant Yasah were welcomed by the royal family and the high officials at the premises of the Palace. Everyone present there felt a degree of admiration for the two. I rushed towards them to get a hold of their horses' lead line as they stepped down. Rajkumar Dvij, with his glittering eyes, couldn't resist shedding a tear as soon as he saw Maharani Drisana. But realising the essence of the situation he reassured himself and with Yugant Yasah sauntered towards Maharani Drisana. Maharani Drisana with a radiant smile on her face welcomed them both with a proper Hindu ceremony. Just as they touched Maharani Drisana's feet to take her blessings, a shower of flowers on the three of them made the environment livelier and more beautiful. The whole courtyard burst into laughter, surrounding everyone with contentment and delight.

'Now, now! If the mother has given her blessings, can the father give his too?' gushed a rather proud father.

Rajkumar Dvij turned his eyes towards the source of the voice. Maharaja Brihadratha was standing there with his arms wide open to greet his son. Rajkumar Dvij embraced his father.

'You too Yugant! Come here and hug me.'

Yugant Yasah too rushed towards Maharaja Brihadratha. Maharaja Brihadratha was the proudest in the whole country. Holding Rajkumar Dvij and Yugant Yasah he was satisfied that the Akshobhyan Dynasty would only prosper.

After Greeting all the officials present in the courtyard, Rajkumar Dvij felt an absence. He turned towards Maharani Drisana.

'Where is Adhirohah, mother? Does he not want to meet me?'

'He should be with Mahamantri Brahmanand, studying the history of the dynasty. He wants to outsmart you, Dvij.'

'Well, then he ought to study harder.' Sighed the crown prince.

'But couldn't he take some time off his studies to greet his older brother?' he asked.

'Adhirohah might be fully unaware that you have arrived. He was waiting for your arrival since morning too. I'll send someone to fetch him.' Replied the Maharani.

Maharani Drisana then called for me and asked me to inform Rajkumar Adhirohah that Rajkumar Dvij has arrived.

Rajkumar Adhirohah is going to be 10 in a couple of months. He is a very bright child and had these magical powers of captivating everyone with his eyes and sweet words. The little prince encounters no problems in making acquaintances and friends and so is loved and cherished by everyone in the palace. Rajkumar Adhirohah had this honest trait of speaking what is in his mind without any fear or hesitation. It was alright to be not afraid because he was the youngest child of Maharaja Brihadratha, but even while speaking to his father he shows no hesitation and represents his thoughts in the form of words as it is. Being quite attached to his mother, Rajkumar Adhirohah, when not having lessons with Mahamantri Brahmanand, is always seen with his mother. The young prince has affection towards everyone. I am also the one who shares a special bond with him.

'What are your ambitions, Rajkumar Adhirohah?' I once asked him.

'I have only one ambition.' His arms were in a cross now on his tiny chest.

'And what is that, Rajkumar?'

The prince formed a fist on his left hand and thumped it into the air

'To outdo my namesake. I will outdo all the achievements of Samrat Adhirohah,'

I couldn't help but giggle in amusement after listening to the heroic talks of the juvenile. Seeing me laugh, the young prince snapped.

'You laugh too much,' He brought his eyebrows down. 'I'll ask the Maharaja to have you in handcuffs and put in the black room. Where you'll be spooked by spiders and other insects.'

'Mercy, my lord! Please don't tell Maharaja Brihadratha about this.' It was both comical and adorable to see the young prince all red. I untied a piece of red cloth that Maharani Drisana had given me earlier and extended it towards the angry prince.

'Please accept these sweets as a token of my apologies.'

Rajkumar Adhirohah, still full of rage turned away. With the corner of his eye, he took a hint of the sweet in the red cloth. After noticing that the sweet was his most favoured one, the young prince forgetting all his anger took the cloth from my hand and gulped all the sweets one by one.

'Alright, I'll forgive you. But promise me you'll bring me more sweets tomorrow.'

'Surely, your grace. You are so merciful!'

I took Rajkumar Adhirohah's words that day in humour, but the young prince is determined to follow his ambition of outdoing the greatest ruler in the Akshobhyan history, Samrat Adhirohah. The prince has been taking lessons from Mahamantri Brahmanand for quite some time now. Last week he also went to see Senapati Aagney and asked him to teach him about weaponry and to Mahamatya Acala to ask him some questions about the judiciary system of the city of Chandragarh. Even now he is with Mahamantri Brahmanand.

And so I went back inside the palace, following Maharani Drisana's orders, to search for Rajkumar Adhirohah and Mahamantri Brahmanand.

Akshobhyas' Secret

After asking as many as five palace guards, I was told that Mahamantri Brahmanand was seen accompanying the young Rajkumar to the chamber of historical artefacts. Rajkumar Adhirohah is now almost 10 years old. Mahamantri Brahmanand must have reckoned that it was time that the little prince should know about the rich heritage of the Akshobhyan Empire. After all, the prestigious history of the dynasty is illustrious and renowned across the entire country and also in the lands beyond. Even though Rajkumar Adhirohah must have learned a great deal just by listening to his family and other high officials, over time, praising their motherland, the previous great rulers, and their heroic tales. But a Rajkumar should know his dynasty's history in-depth and maybe it was the right time.

I hastened towards the chamber of historical artefacts and after acknowledging half a dozen of the guards' salutes who were guarding the chamber, I went inside. The architecture of the chamber was rather intriguing. On the upper half of the wall at the right was an aperture which was the only place through which light could enter the chamber. But with the help of multiple reflecting surfaces laid inside the chamber, all the artefacts could be seen as clearly as possible. The chamber had tables and heavy shelves supporting historical artefacts. The chamber was divided into three main sections. The first section was of the Akshobhyan royal family. Portraits of the family members adorned the wall. The first portrait was of the founders of the Akshobhyan Empire, Samrat Mahadhyata, and Samrat Adhirohah. The stretch contained portraits of all the prince, kings, and queens that the Akshobhyan Family has had over the years. The table that laid in front of the wall contained some memorabilia of the royal family members. From the 'pichangatti' gifted to Maharaja Nagbhushana by the Satavahanas of the middle east after they agreed to become a part of the Akshobhyan empire to the toys of Rajkumari Dhyuthi, daughter of Maharaja Prataparat, who later became the Maharani of the Kaishoriyas. The middle section belonged to the papyrus records of some of the brightest minds the city of Chandragarh has ever witnessed. In that section, the last occupied space belonged to Mahamantri Brahmanand. It contained some of his ideas about statecraft and his early attempt on poetry. It may come as a surprise to many people who have known Mahamantri Brahmanand, that in his early years when Mahamantri was far from state politics and was yet not a world-renowned strategist, he tried his hands-on poetry. Mahamantri Brahmanand still admired poetry. Years ago when it became widely known, throughout the capital city, that I wrote poetry in my spare time, thanks to the then notorious prince, Rajkumar Dvij, who just 'happened to stumble' upon my record of poetry before making it public by sharing it with the palace guards, officials and eventually with Maharaja Brihadratha and Maharani Drisana, Mahamantri Brahmanand used to call me weekly to have a secret session of poetry recitation. Where we both used to share our vision in the form of verses. Mahamantri is truly full of secrets. Some of them, I would like to know. The third and final section belonged to the military equipment having historical significance. It was divided accordingly to the different reigns of kings in which those weapons were used. The table had spears, swords, arrows, and bows which were used in battles of immensely important to the dynasty's history. On the wall, in that section, was a cabinet made of glass. It had edges made of gold and corners decorated with diamonds. Two rubies, the biggest, I've ever seen. Both were embedded on either side of the golden crest on the lower half of the compartment. The crest that read.

'The sword of Samrat Mahadhyata'

The cabinet contained the personal sword of the founder of the Akshobhyan Empire. The sword was all glory and prestige. It had a handle of gold, casted from the mines of Indraprastha. And in the middle of the handle was a shining sapphire which was presented as a gift to Samrat Mahadhyata by the King of Greece back in the day when Samrat Mahadhyata was considered as a force to be reckoned with. The edges of the sword still looked sharp and, in the middle, an engraving was done. 'Akshobhya' in Sanskrit was engraved with a couple of roaring lions on either side. The sword was made in the latter half of his reign and was never used by Maharaja Mahadhyata in actual combat. It was more of a show material, even though it could cut through the enemies' chest like a paper. He used to carry it around the palace mostly, to the court meetings or the other chambers of the palace. But he never used it in an actual war.

I ran my eyes across the chamber but couldn't find Rajkumar Adhirohah and Mahamantri Brahmanand. The guards on the entrance told me that Mahamantri Brahmanand and Rajkumar Adhirohah left the chamber a few minutes before my arrival and headed towards the northern part of the palace.

After wondering for a while, it just hit me where the Mahamantri might have taken the young prince. Alas, it was time for the prince to know about the most valuable entity of the Akshobhyas. The entity of immense importance and historical value. It was time for the prince to know about 'Asi' and its curse.

The Weapon of Gods

As directed by the soldiers guarding the chamber of historical artefacts, I headed towards the northern section of the palace. It was recognized as a quiet and secluded area by most eyes. With only a storeroom in that sector, it was hardly ever visited by the guards or other residents of the palace. They all reckoned that the storeroom had nothing to offer. And it would seem just like that. But I and only a handful of other trusted associates of the Akshobhyan family knew that the old, filthy storeroom bore the factual truth about the supremacy of the Akshobhyan Empire.

After making sure that no one was around, I entered the storeroom. Just like any other basement, every corner of the room was obliterated with huge cobwebs. With only a hint of light entering the secluded room, it was difficult to make way across the other end. I tried to reach the other end and, in the attempt, knocked over an old table lamp which scattered over my foot, injuring my toe in the process. Blood started to pour out of my left toe. I limped towards the other end and reached out for a shelf, at the centre of the wall which was covered with dust. To the left of that shelf was an old portrait of a young prince. I could never make out who the prince in the portrait was, neither did I ever ask anyone. I didn't want to compromise the confidentiality of this place in any way possible. If one observes, the portrait might be all covered with dust but the bottom-right edge of the frame would seem to be comparatively cleaner. Why? I tilted the frame towards the left by applying a suitable force at the same place. The right bottom edge of the frame. Behind the portrait was a loosely attached brick that goes four inches inside the wall when gently pushed. I pushed the brick with the utmost care. To the right side of the shelf, with a huge thud, a brick door, formed from the wall, became isolated from its attachment. With blood still oozing out from my toe, I hobbled to the right and pushed the isolated door, with my shoulder, in the right direction. The door shifted and opened a passageway in the process. The passageway was dark and only a few initial steps were visible. It was pitch black in there. Towards the right of the passage were three unignited torches and, on the left, there was a shelf with two rocks. I scratched the rocks over the torch. A few sparks were generated from the rattling of the rocks. In a few seconds, I was able to ignite the torch. The stairs were visible now and I made my way downstairs. Leaving a trail of blood drops, I limped downstairs until there were no more stairs left and an aisle appeared. After walking for a few more seconds, strolling now, across the aisle, I saw Rajkumar Adhirohah and Mahamantri Brahmanand in a hall which was lit by huge flames in each corner. Four gigantic iron statues stretching over 10 feet in height, dressed as warriors were placed in the middle of the faces of the walls. Each statue had a sword, probably six feet tall. The statues represented the first four rulers of the Akshobhyan Empire. Samrat Mahadhyata, Samrat Adhirohah, Maharaja Bhairava, and Maharaja Nagbhushana. All the statues were facing a glass cabinet as if they were guarding the entity kept inside it. Inside, was the secret of Akshobhyan power and supremacy. Inside the cabinet was the Asi.

Mahamantri Brahmanand and Rajkumar Adhirohah were standing between the cabinet and the iron statue of Samrat Adhirohah and were facing the glass cabinet. Mahamantri Brahmanand, with a deep smile on his face, was staring at the Asi. The little prince was juggling his eyes between the cabinet and the Mahamantri and was curious about the captivating power of the entity inside the cabinet that was making Mahamantri Brahmanand stare it for so long. Confused between the Mahamantri's deep smile and his continuous gazing, Rajkumar Adhirohah tried to concentrate on the glass cabinet too. He saw the reflection of the huge flame on the glass mirror and then saw his reflection. But swerving the images away, he tried to concentrate on the entity inside it. I was still at the edge of the aisle and reckoned it would be best not to disturb the student and his master as of now. I felt a little hesitation in eavesdropping on their conversations.

Still gazing at the Asi and with his hands crossed behind his back, the Mahamantri finally spoke.

'So, tell me, young prince.'

Rajkumar Adhirohah's eyes shot up.

'What do you see?' he asked.

'A sword, Mahamantri. An old sword inside a glass cabinet.'

Still, with a smile on his face, Mahamantri's eyes fell upon the young prince who was still looking inside the cabinet.

'And what kind of sword is this?' He questioned the little prince again.

Rajkumar Adhirohah scratched his head with his left index finger.

'Come on now, Dear Adhirohah. I know you've been asking Senapati Aagney about weaponry for quite some weeks now. You should be able to answer my question.'

After giving it a lot of thought, remembering all those evenings he had spent with Senapati Aagney and then observing the detail of the sword, the little prince's face lit up with joy and he answered the old Mahamantri with utmost enthusiasm.

'It's a khanda! A double-edged Khanda!'

'Excellent, Rajkumar Adhirohah. Now tell me what is written on the crest below, will you?'

Rajkumar Adhirohah bent down to have a clearer look at the text written in Sanskrit on the crest.

'Aa…Sss…Eeee? 'The prince formed a 'v' from his index finger and thumb of his left hand and placed his chin on it, supporting the elbow of his left arm with his right hand.

'I've heard this name before, Mahamantri. I've heard elder Brother Dvij and elder Brother Yugant talk about it once.'

Mahamantri was now again looking at the double-edged khanda kept inside the cabinet. The pupils of his eyes were reflecting the image of the Asi which was glittering because of the light of the flames falling on it from every corner of the room.

A bug crawled upon my bloody toe and bit it. I managed to jiggle and toss the bug away.

Now facing the little prince again, Mahamantri spoke.

'Today I'll be telling you about the Asi. Its history and its significance.'

With resolute eyes, Rajkumar Adhirohah leaned in.

'The tale of the creation of Asi goes long back to the time when the Devas approached Brahma, the creator of the universe, to help them in their fight against the evil Asuras. Brahma after hearing the protest of the Devas agreed to help and protect them from the immoral Asuras. Brahma, along with the Devas and many Maharishis, descended to the Himalayas to perform a pivotal Havan. Amidst the Havan, form its huge scattering flame, a mighty and terrible giant arose. The giant had skinny and long limbs and had teeth so sharp that they could pierce into anything.'

Rajkumar Dvij was now listening to Mahamantri Brahmanand with his eyes wide open.

'The emergence of that giant created a drastic surge in the environment.' The Mahamantri continued. 'Heavenly spheres of fire begin to descend on earth with exceptional speed. Volcanos erupted; the oceans swirled. A vigorous gust of wind blew everything away. Brahma declared that the creature that he has conceived from the flames of the Havan for the destruction of evil and restoration of Dharma in the world, is Asi. The Asi was then covered with a large, uncontrollable, fire and it eventually took the form of a blazing double-edged sword. Handling the sword over to the Devas, Brahma said to them, that whoever held Asi will be assured a victory in any war. The devas used the Asi in the war against the Asuras and ensured their victory.'

'But, Mahamantri, how do we Askhobhyas have the Asi with us?'

'I am glad you asked that, Rajkumar Adhirohah. After Brahma gave the Asi to Lord Shiva to punish the evil and to restore Dharma, Asi was given to Lord Vishnu by Lord Shiva. Lord Vishnu handed the Asi to Rishi Marichi, the cosmic creator, and one of the Saptrishis. Over time, the Asi saw many owners. From Manu, son of the sun god, to his own son Ikshvaku. From Maharaja Bharat to Bharadvaj Brhaspatya, the Asi went through many hands before playing a pivotal role in the Mahabharta.'

'And how was that, Mahamantri?' asked the curious prince.

'Bharadvaj Brhaspatya gave the Asi to his son, the great Guru Dronacharya, preceptor to both the Kaurvas and Pandavas. With Asi in his hands, Guru Dronacharya was invincible and provided a great deal of grief and distress to the Pandavas. He caused a stir in the battlefield slaying everyone that came in his way. Anxious, Lord Krishna came up with a scheme to stop Guru Dronacharya from causing further distress in the battlefield. Which could have been done only by disarming Guru Dronacharya.'

'He asked Bhima to slay an elephant named Ashvathama. After slaying the elephant, Bhima then went to Guru Dronacharya and claimed that he has slayed Dronacharya's son, Ashvatama.' Said the young prince with a hint of enthusiasm.

'And where did you learn that?'

'Mother told me. She tells me the story of Ramayana and Mahabharta every night before I go to sleep. She told me that out of his grief for his proclaimed dead son, Guru Dronacharya dropped his weapon and went into Sadhna, where his soul left his body to search for the soul of his son in heaven. And his corpse was later beheaded by Draupada, the commander-in-chief of the Pandava army, as a revenge for killing his father Drupada, the king of Panchala. So that his soul could not return to his body. Is that correct, Mahamantri?'

Mahamantri acknowledged the little prince with a smile.

'When Bhishma was on his death bed of arrows, Nakula, one of the Pandavas, out of curiosity asked him about the strongest weapon that was ever created. Bhishma told him that Asi, the weapon created by Lord Brahma, would make its holder invincible. After the death of Guru Dronacharya, the Asi was taken by Krpacharya, one of the Chiranjivi. Krpacharya gifted the sword to Nakula. From Nakul the sword went to Parikshit, the Kuru King. The Asi then saw Parikshit's son, Janamejaya and Grandson Satanika as its owners. But after Satanika obtained salvation, the weapon went back to Krpacharya. He kept the Asi with him until its rightful owner would come to claim it, Son of Dronacharya, Ashvathama. Another Chiranjivi.'

'But mother told me that Ashvathama was cursed for his inhuman deeds by Lord Krishna. Ashvathama attacked the womb of Uttra, wife of Abhimanyu, with a Brahmashtra. Lord Krishna cursed Ashvathama that till eternity, he will roam in the forests with blood and puss oozing out of his injuries and will cry for death. But death will never come to him. His body will also suffer from a host of many incurable diseases and that he will live in total isolation without any human contact. With so many injuries how can one use the sword, Mahamantri?'

'With the answer to your question, I will also tell you how the Akshobhyas got their hands on the Asi.'

Rajkumar Adhirohah was now clearly jumping with excitement.

'Long before when Samrat Mahadhyata became the ruler of Chandragarh and conquered almost half of the Bharatvarsh, he with his younger brother, Samrat Adhirohah would perform daily sadhana in the Simha forest. After the Sadhna they would come up with solutions to the problems they used to face in those days. Problems of providing justice to their clan and other residents of Chandraketugarh form the corrupt officials and sinful landlords. The problem was that their king was ignorable and immoral. So, they decided to have a riot against the king and to remove him from that position. The question was how? And to discuss that problem the brothers shall perform Sadhna in the forest and would later try to find a solution. One fine day a silhouette appeared among the distant trees of the forest. The brothers, noticing the silhouette of a humped and rather an old man, questioned its purpose of visiting them. The silhouette asked Samrat Mahadhyata and Samrat Adhirohah whether they were the Akshobhyan brothers who were standing up against the deceitful king of Chandraketugarh. The brothers presented themselves as the stated brothers and stepped forward to get a clearer view of the silhouette. The silhouette said that he would help them in fighting the immoral king and then disappeared into the woods. The silhouette would make regular appearances and would advise and help the brothers to plan and execute the riots against the king but without ever revealing his identity. One day before the raging war against the king of Chandraketugarh the silhouette appeared in front of the two Akshobhyan brothers. According to the legend, he was an old and ill man with a humped back and many spores on his body, with blood and puss oozing out of them. He offered the older brother a sword, a double-edged khanda, and asked him to use it in the war tomorrow. With much hesitation, after knowing the actual outward form of the silhouette, Samrat Mahadhyata accepted the sword and used it in the war. The Akshobhyas were victorious and the king was overthrown from his power. After the war, the brothers would go to the Simha forest every day but the old man was not seen by them. Samrat Mahadhyata used that sword in all the battles that he fought and was victorious in all of them. Even after several years, the brothers would regularly visit the same spot in the Simha forest to perform Sadhna. One fine day they encountered the same old man again, with his same poor condition. The brothers offered him to take him to a Ved, but the old man declined their generous proposal. He congratulated the brothers on their victory and told them that they would make a happy and peaceful kingdom for the people. When Samrat Mahadhyata offered the sword back to the old man, the latter asked the Samrat to keep it as a gift. When Samrat Mahadhyata asked the old man about the exceptional fortune that the sword brought for him, the old man told the brothers that the sword was not ordinary. He stated that the very same sword made Guru Dronacharya almost invincible in the battle of Kurukshetra. The same sword was specified as the greatest weapon ever created by Bhishma on his death bed of arrows. It was the Asi, the weapon created by Lord Brahma himself. Bewildered, the two brothers gave an amused glance to each other. But the old man provided a caution to the brothers. He told them that the Asi should always be in their hands, near them, or else the empire they dream to build will only perish. Samrat Mahadhyata lifted the sword and both the brothers looked at the sword in total amusement. As soon as they turned towards the old man, he was gone. Vanished into the darkness of the forest. The brothers would continue their daily routine of performing Sadhna in the same spot of the forest, but the old man was never seen again. Samrat Mahadhyata and Samrat Adhirohah went on to win many wars and battles during their lifetime. And till today, the Akshobhyan dynasty has never lost a war.'

Rajkumar Adhirohah juggled his eyes between the Asi and Mahamantri Brahmanad, still bewildered that he was standing next to such a historic and powerful weapon.

'But Mahamantri, how can one be so sure that it's the power of a double-edged khanda and not the ability of those many eminent minds and warriors, that Chandragarh has seen over the years, that has won us so many wars and made us the capital of power in the whole Bharatvarsh?'

The old Mahamantri burst into laughter, amazed by the reckoning calibre of such a young mind. Rajkumar Adhirohah gazed at the Mahamantri gravely, still expecting an answer.

'One can never be sure, young prince. And we can never doubt the ability of those great minds and heroic acts of those great warriors who gave us the Chandragarh we know as of today. The Asi may be superstitious, but one can't deny the outcomes that we have seen since the beginning of the Akshobhyan era which has been achieved since Samrat Mahadhyata received the Asi. For god too only help those who first help themselves.'

Rajkumar Adhirohah was now gazing at the Asi curiously, not satisfied with the answer of Mahamantri Brahmanand.

'And what about its curse? What is the curse of Asi?' He asked without swerving his eyes from the sword.

'Ah! The curse of Asi!' The Mahamantri could be seen enjoying stating the facts about Asi to the young Rajkumar.

'To answer your question' continued the Mahamantri 'I shall tell you an anecdote. During the reigns of Samrat Adhirohah, the country prospered in all lengths. Not only the people of Chandragarh and Ketupradesh, but the people of every other nation and kingdom that were won by Samrat Adhirohah were content and pleased with Samrat Adhirohah as their ruler. As the extent of the Akshobhyan Empire grew, the number of ecstatic people also increased. But a turn of events disturbed the tranquillity of the Akshobhyan Empire. It happened when Samrat Adhirohah and his army prevailed over the mighty Kingdom of Gandhara in the north, one of the Mahajanapadas. It was a hard-fought battle. The geographical state and the treacherous Indus River between the army of Akshobhyas and the kingdom of Gandhara brought many struggles. But with the weapon of Brahma in the hands of Samrat Adhirohah, the Akshobhyan army was invincible. While Samrat Adhirohah was still there, examining the newly acquired kingdom carefully, with the Asi, Maharaja Durajaya of Tamralipata tried to attack the Kingdom of Chandragarh. Even though Chandragarh still had a vast army to protect it, former Mahamantri Banabhatta saw the city of Chandragarh vulnerable against the mighty army of Maharaja Durajaya. Mahamantri Banabhatta had no choice but to ask for help from Maharaja Lakshanya of Indraprastha till Samrat Adhirohah could return with his army. Even with the reinforcements from Indraprastha and the armies of the four nearby conquered states, it appeared as if the end of the Akshobhyas was near. The army of Maharaja Durajaya was three times the combined army of Chandragarh. And even with Samrat Adhirohah's army, it seemed as if the war will never be won. The reinforcements did their job of holding the army of Maharaja Durajaya until Samrat Adhirohah finally arrived with the army of Chandragarh which recently conquered the Kingdom of Gandhara. Defending Chandragarh with the help of exhausted soldiers against the army three times in strength seemed to be beyond the bounds of possibility. But the words of that old acquaintance in the forest of Simha echoed in the ears of Samrat Adhirohah. He was determined that with the power of Asi and the trust of Gods, he shall protect his Kingdom anyhow. With fewer soldiers left, Samrat Adhirohah jumped into the battlefield himself alongside the commanders of the Akshobhyan army. And as stated by that old humped man, the bearer of the Asi did become the victor, yet again. Against all odds, the soldiers of Akshobhyas were able to defend themselves against the ferocious army of Tamralipata. But it only happened because the Asi was back in the land of Chandragarh, the capital city. As the old man said, the Asi should always be in the hands of the ruler of Chandragarh. The Asi should always be in the city of Chandragarh, or else, this 'unconquerable' Kingdom may not remain indomitable. And that is the curse of Asi.'

The young prince shifted his balance to his other leg.

'So that's why the Asi has been kept here in this secret chamber? Because of its immense importance?'

'Yes, Rajkumar. This secret chamber was built under the direct commands of Maharaja Nagbhushana to safeguard the Asi.'

'And how many people know about its whereabouts, Mahamantri?'

'Only a handful of officials and some trusted soldiers have this classified information. And you now are one of them.'

The little prince's eyes sparkled.

'After seeing your resolve of becoming a responsible prince, I suggested Maharaja Brihadratha that the secret of the power of Chandragarh should be revealed to you.'

The little prince ran towards the Mahamantri with open arms and embraced him.

'I promise, Mahamantri. I will become a responsible and moral prince.'

The Mahamantri ran his hands over the soft hair of the prince. Being immersed in the conversation between the Mahamantri and Rajkumar Adhirohah, I failed to notice that half a dozen of bugs were now crawling around my injured toe until one of them bit around the wound. I jiggled my foot in pain again to sway the bugs only to notice that both the Mahamantri and Rajkumar were looking at me. After my act as a madman, jiggling my legs, I tried to soften the unpleasant predicament by bowing in front of my audience who still seemed to be dazed and confused. Rajkumar Adhirohah and Mahamantri Brahmanand exchanged glances. Mahamantri Brahmanad eventually broke the awkward silence.

'What brings you here, Yashvasin?' The old Mahamantri broke into laughter before continuing again.

'Were you eavesdropping our conversation?' He realized the gravity of his question and subsided his laughter with a grave look.

I was overcome by lassitude and felt a kind of languor in the confined air of the chamber.

'Maharani Drisana asked me to inform Rajkumar Adhirohah about the arrival of Rajkumar Dvij. He has....'

Before I could have finished my sentence, the ecstatic Rajkumar jumped with exhilaration and grabbed Mahamantri Brahmanand's hands.

'Mahamantri, will you please grant me the permission to leave?' There was a wide smile on his face which wasn't going to subside any time soon.

Mahamantri nodded with a grin and the little prince rushed away.

The little prince saved me from further embarrassing questions from the Mahamantri.

The Mahamantri walked towards me, looking straight into me through my eyes, stopping a foot away from me.

'Make sure the blood trail you left has been carefully washed.'

Saying this he walked past me. I stood still, in the same position until the heavy footsteps of the Mahamantri faded away.

Last of The Yudhvans

It was just another start of the day in the city of Chandragarh. The sun rose above the horizon, its hue illuminating the morning scenes in the city. The call of the hornbills echoed in the Simha forest. The Koel sang her way into the Palace garden. The morning light sparkled on the pious water of the Ganani river as if stars shinning in a cold winter night sky. The fishermen of the Rhyuoli tribe made their way to the Ganani River whereas the Shooras were deeply consumed in labour on their newly acquired land. Chants of mantras could be heard from the dozen of temples in Chandragarh. The soldiers were practicing their fighting skills in the akhadas. The Clashing of their swords could be heard even from the outskirts of the city.

I was the first to reach the royal practice arena and started ghost fighting with a Bhala. I wasn't even out of my breath when I heard someone clapping behind me.

'Always the first to arrive at the practice sessions, eh? You must have become the best warrior till now.' Yugant yasah stated in a rhetoric way while tightening his waistcloth. Rajkumar Dvij was just behind, near the weaponry table. He was swinging and weighing some swords.

I tried to laugh it off.

'Certainly not the best, sir.'

Rajkumar Dvij picked up a Bhala and without looking tossed it to Yugant Yasah. He caught it in mid-air and started swirling it.

'Are you ready, Yuvan?' Yugant asked me while dancing with the spear at the edge of the arena.

I acknowledged with a nod and a smirk and got into an embraced position.

'Very well, then.' Yugant jumped and revolved mid air and with all the momentum he gained, swished his Bhala and aimed for my head. I resisted the attack by placing my Bhala above in a horizontal position and, after the impact, rolled backwards.

I think I forgot to mention this before, Yugant was the best fighter in the city of Chandrgarh with a Bhala. He excelled in fighting with the long weapon. Every time he picked up a Bhala it was as if the weapon was a part of himself. His mere movements with it were a treat to watch. The way he turned and spun the Bhala around his body with such velocity was mindboggling.

He was still gloating his exceptional skills with the Bhala while walking around the edge of the arena. Rajkumar Dvij was still checking out the most appropriate sword he could use. He gave a glance at Yugant and shook his head, chuckled, and uttered "Show off" under his breath.

I picked up and dusted off myself. Yugant, holding the spear with both of his hands, sprinted towards me. I stepped aside just in time and gave a strong peck on his back with my spear, just before tripping him with my left foot. He fell face-first on the ground and broke his spear into two. I thought he'd be annoyed. But he took the knock light-hearted.

'All this practice is paying off, huh?' He was getting giddy. He ran towards me again with his one arm in the air. He opened his fist and cried. Rajkumar Dvij shot another Bhala at him and he caught it. Few feet away he swept the spear underneath me. I leaped, but it wasn't enough. In a swift move, after sweeping the spear, he too spun around uplifting himself and kicked me in the chest while I was still in the air. I was pushed out of the bounds of the arena and my spear fell a couple of feet away from me. Yugant Yasah caressed his long hair which was falling on his face, behind his ear.

'I thought you were good with spears, Yuvan.' Yugant teased me sarcastically while extending his hand. I grasped it and stood up.

'He is the best with swords, Yugant.' Said a familiar voice from behind. Rajkumar Dvij, Yugant yasah, and I turned towards the source of the voice. It was Senapati Aagney. He gestured towards Rajkumar Dvij to join him in the adjacent practice arena.

'A couple of minutes. You won't last more than that in a duel with swords against him.' He challenged Yugant.

Yugnat chuckled. And strolled towards the weapon shelf. He picked up two swords and tossed one towards me. I caught it and smirked before asking Yugant whether he was sure about this. He didn't utter a word and before we knew, our swords were clashing.

Senapati Aagney and Rajkumar Dvij were having a duel in the adjacent arena. I noticed them whispering to each other.

'So, what are Yuvan's chances?' The crown prince asked while being in an embracing position.

'I was serious, Rajkumar. Yugant doesn't stand a chance against Yashvasin Yuvan.'

The Senapati threw himself towards the Rajkumar. Swerving the attack away with his sword, he shoved the Senapati with his shoulder.

'Then I would like to watch their duel without any disturbance. Is that alright, Senapati Aagney?'

'Very well, Rajkumar.' And they both started watching our duel.

Yugant was getting agitated as I was not giving him any openings. He gave his previous move another try. He swept the sword underneath me. But this time I was able to move more freely because I wasn't carrying a long and heavy spear. I just moved aside, lifting my left leg and thumped on his sword with the same leg. Yugant tried his best to glide his sword away from beneath my feet. But was unable to do so. I thumped his forehead with my sword's pommel. He rolled backwards and uttered a yelp, leaving hold of his sword. I pounded upon the hilt of his sword which got suspended in the air. I caught it and tossed it in front of Yugant.

'Anytime when you're ready.' I tried to provoke him.

He tried to feel the size of the bump on his forehead.

'So, we're taking it to the highest level? So, let's get down to brass tracks. Shall we?'

Our swords clanged together repeatedly as Yugant tried to get into a spree of bows. I was playing it defensively. After several spoiled counters, frustration was taking over him.

'Don't play, Yuvan. Just finish the fight now!' exclaimed the Senapati from the sidelines.

I glanced at him and noticed there was another person who stood there behind the Senapati and the Rajkumar. It was Nrchakshu. The head of the Maharaja's angrakshak panel.

Yugant sprinted towards me, planning to shove me. I swiftly stepped in his direction in a split-second. He could not judge the decreasing distance between us. He rapidly tried to shove the sword in my stomach. I stepped aside and took hold of his arm. Bumped him in the face again with my elbow. He lost his grip on the sword. I kicked on the back of his knees and he fell on his knees. And pulled his arm behind his back and hustled him. He fell on the ground with his face covered with dirt. He punched the ground in exasperation and tried to recover by turning himself up again, only to find my sword inches away from his throat. Out of his breath, he stared into my eyes in disbelief. I gave him my hand and he grasped it to get up. Not forgetting that he was a member of the royal family, I bowed in front of him after our bout.

'At least I am better with the spears.' Yugant tried to sound upbeat.

'You surely are, sir.' I replied modestly.

Turning back towards their arena the Senapati called for the crown prince.

'So, shall we continue now, Rajkumar Dvij?'

Rajkumar Dvij shifted his weight to his other leg and seemed to be in deep thought. He juggled his eyes between Nrchakshu and me, eventually stopping at me.

'How about another duel, Yuvan? You will fight Nrchakshu now.' His eyes shifted towards the self-possessed Nrchakshu.

'Is it alright?' He asked Nrchakshu.

Nrchakshu bowed down to acknowledge the Rajkumar's proposal.

Nrchakshu was the last surviving member of the Yudhvan clan. The clan was once famous for their barbaric yet exceptional fighting skills. One of the oldest clans in the capital city, they were held in high esteem. Nrchakshu now served as the leader of the Maharaja's Aangrakshak squad. It was quite perplexing considering his age. He is only three years older than the young crown prince. Even to be the Aangrakshak of the King one has to go through the superlative regime. And to be the leader of that squad is, in short, the highest level one can achieve. Maharaja Brihadratha has always shown a deep regard for Nrchakshu. For what I've seen, Maharaja Brihadratha has gone against Mahamantri Brahmanand's advice only twice. One was during the appointment of Mahamatya Acala as the finance and judiciary minister of the city and the other was giving Nrchakshu the designation of the leader of the Angrakshak squad only after a year he had become an Aangrakshak.

Nrchakshu picked up a sword and jumped into the arena. Even though he was adored by our Maharaja, he wasn't a member of the royal family. It meant; I don't have to hold up against him. Even though it is a practice session. I was delighted, anyhow. He swung his sword in the air a few times. I chortled under my breath and got into the position too.

With my sword horizontally in front of me, I leaped towards him. He glided his sword against mine. I turned around with my elbow above and tried to knock his face up. He ducked down and threw himself away from me. I looked towards the sound of the applause. It was quite a crowd now which surrounded us. The sun was over the horizon. Its rays fell on Nrchakshu's bulging arms which were holding the sword firmly. The sweat on his arm in the bright sunlight glittered like morning dew deposited on the crops. He was about to pound my face with his right fist but I blocked the impact with my left arm. Next thing I knew an impression of the pommel of his sword was against my right temple. The crowd, that surrounded us, was now erupting. I reckoned about giving them something more to cheer about. I rubbed the blood oozing out from my temple with my wrist cloth and walked towards Nrchakshu, who seemed to be very grave. Few feet away from him I jumped towards him. With a loud cry, I gave him a blow as I descended downwards. He blocked it with his sword. But the blow was so heavy that he was pushed down on his knees. He quickly recovered from it. I gave him a dozen heavy strikes from my sword to defend. He almost defended himself perfectly. But the last of my strike was too heavy for him to handle and his sword slipped from his grip. The crowd was cheering my name now. I gave a glance at Senapati Aagney and Rajkumar Dvij. Senapati Aagney was smiling and Rajkumar Dvij looked to be a little disappointed. I strolled around the edge until Nrchakshu picked up his sword again. I was enjoying this practice duel. I didn't have to hold back. Nrchakshu brought down his sword on me. I swiftly stepped aside and the crowd burst into laughter. He attempted to land another blow on me but only found his sword clashing against mine. I was getting a little too excited. I never boasted about myself for being the best swordsmen in the city. But this fight was somewhat special for me. I've heard and watched Nrchakshu fight with bravery. It was now time to measure his bravery and sword skills. But he was rather getting desperate.

'Come on, soldier! Don't you call yourself the member of the esteemed Yudhvan clan with that losing mouth of yours.'

The crowd became silent. Maybe I went too far. But I wanted to.

Listening to this he sprinted towards me and landed a heavy blow on me. Our swords clashed as I yelled again.

'Oh, come on! You've got to be kidding me, soldier! Young girls of your clan used to have more strength in their arms.'

Dead silence surrounded us before I laughed, agitating Nrchakshu. He was getting influenced by it too. It could be seen on his face. He was hot red. He was desperate, infuriated, and helpless too. My little scheme was working so well until my stupid mouth questioned his service towards the king.

'Is this how you're going to defend our King?'

Yes. I said that and regretted a few moments later.

Our swords clanged with each other for a few seconds before I kicked him in the stomach. But he stood still. It was like he didn't even feel the impact. He embraced it and got a hold of my leg and swung me to the side. I managed to gain balance mid-air and landed safely. I looked up and there he was bringing his sword on me, I pushed myself backwards in an attempt to save myself from that strike. But he kept on coming. Somehow, I managed to pick myself up. I was still on one knee before he pounced upon me. He stepped on my lap with one leg and brought the knee of another leg against my face. Against my fucking face. It all went pitch dark for me. Next thing I remember, I was on a bed and a

Vaidya was checking my pulse.

❖

A TALE OF TREACHERY

The council members were meeting the Maharaja in the royal assembly room. It was a weekly gathering where Maharaja Brihadratha would listen to the reports of the council members. Statistics and different matters were shared and discussed in this weekly based meeting. Military expenditure, foreign trade income, financial statistics, judiciary cases of paramount importance, taxes, royal treasure status, and other such details were some topics which were discussed with Maharaja Brihadratha and Mahamantri Brahmanad in this gathering. Mahamatya Acala, Senapati Aagney, foreign trade minister Uddanda, the crown prince, and other eminent members of the council were all present. I was given the initiative of keeping a record of all the matters that were discussed. Today's meeting was just like any other. Income generated through taxes were discussed, Uddanda asked for permission from Maharaja Brihadratha to allow trade via sea route with the Bantu farmers of the Western African region, Yugant Yasah spoke about a minor rebellion outbreak in the city of Tamralipta in the east, Mahamatya provided numbers for the overall expenditure of doing repairs in the court building. It has been some years now since Rajkumar Dvij too started attending these meetings. Maharaja Brihadratha wanted his son to learn and gain some experience in the current affairs of the state. After all, Rajkumar Dvij was the crown prince. Occasionally, Maharaja Brihadratha would also ask for the Rajkumar's advice in some matters. He wanted to encourage the prince as much as possible. Even though the crown prince will always have eminent minds to advise him regarding any matter once he becomes the Maharaja of Chandragarh, Maharaja Brihadratha wanted his son to become the ideal ruler. That would mean that Rajkumar Dvij should be able to make crucial decisions on his own. Rajkumar Adhirohah would follow Rajkumar Dvij's footsteps in the near future too. That's a certainty. Judging by his enthusiasm and will power, he would outsmart most of his ancestors. I've seen the upbringing of both the Rajkumars' very closely. Maharaja Brihadratha and Maharani Drisana surely have done splendid work on their kids.

The meeting lasted for a little more than a couple of hours. The Maharaja appeared to be grinning cheerfully. I submitted the papyrus records to Mahamantri Brahmanand to place them in a cupboard at the corner of the assembly hall to lock them in. Maharaja Brihadratha stood up to conclude the meeting. He asked Senapati Aagney, Rajkumar Dvij, and Yugant Yasah to stay in the chambers. All the other members asked the Maharaja's permission to leave. In the end, I too turned around towards the exit. I was about to exit the assembly room when Maharaja Brihadratha shouted a call.

'Not you, Yashvasin. You're coming with us.' He said cheerfully.

'Where?' I asked in a rather fainted voice.

Maharaja Brihadratha bent to pick up his sword which was resting against his seat.

'To the Simha forest. For hunting. Why do you think Aagney, Dvij, and Yugant are present here?'

'I am sorry, my king. But there are some matters of immense importance that require my supervi....'

Maharaja Brihadratha interrupted in between.

'You're always working, Yashvasin. Now that I think of it, I always find you associated with almost every important matter in the state. You're a very busy man. Take some time off.'

I tried to present my case in front of him.

'But, sir...'

'It's an order, Yashvasin.' Humour vanished from his voice for a moment.

'No possibility of going against the order now. Right, Yashvasin?' Said someone from the remaining lot.

I acknowledged with a smile.

There have been some complaints from the citizens of Chandragarh about an ambush of tigers strolling outside the Simha forests a month ago. The complaint wasn't taken that seriously until last week when one of the farmers lodged a complaint and reported that his cattle were butchered by those free-roaming tigers. Also, it has been almost a year since Maharaja Brihadratha last went on a hunting trip. And so, it was decided to hunt down those beasts. Although the number of tigers in the ambush was not certain it was reported by some eyewitnesses that there were four to five in numbers. Although they weren't sure because it was late in the night when they saw them strolling in the outskirts.

Maharaja Brihadratha, Rajkumar Dvij, Yugant Yasah, Senapati Aagney, and I were accompanied by 10 bowmen and 10 soldiers who were on foot. And of course, Nrchakshu was also present. Not the Aangrakshak troop. But only the leader himself. The Maharaja didn't want to take a crowd with him to the hunt and so ordered the rest of the troop not to come. The Maharaja took his place on the giant 'Balrama'. A gigantic elephant gifted to him by the ruler of Ujjain for sending reinforcements in their time of distress. It was the biggest creature I've ever seen. Maybe the biggest anyone has ever seen. The tamed beast was unbelievably tall and his tusks stretched over six feet. It was well suited for hunting trips. The elephant trumpet as its mahout tickled behind its enormous ears to make it stand up. Maharaja Brihadratha was jolly happy. More than a year since his last hunting trip. Rajkumar Dvij was reluctant to go. But who can go against the Maharaja's orders? We all sat on our respective horses and headed towards the dense woods.

The Simha forest was home to many native beasts and birds. We were welcomed by an obnoxious troop of baboons. Their grunting and barking came to us as some warning. They followed us, hopping from one tree to another for about a kilometre and then retreated all of a sudden. Strange voices always surrounded us. As they say, the forest is always alive. About half an hour later we saw some movements in the nearby shrubs. The soldiers slowly approached the rustling bush and the bowmen had stretched their arrows. A grunting wild hog came out of the bush. Wagging his head around rapidly. The bowmen rested their bows. We were about to move forward when an arrow thrust into the wild hog's head. All heads turned into the direction from where the arrow came. Rajkumar Dvij was still holding the bow.

'Don't waste your arrows on pity animals, Dvij. Save something for those cattle eating beasts.' The Maharaja said, trying to be strict.

We continued our search for the ambush of tigers. A flock of great hornbills flew by us. Their uncanny call was not so pleasing to the ears. I noticed a black kite relaxing over a branch, overlooking every movement in the forest. The sunlight was entering the dense forest in lozenges shape, getting mostly blocked by the trees. It was a pleasant day. Although it was quite humid in the forest. The pleasant sound of the koel found us everywhere as we moved forward and onwards. We were enjoying its melodious voice until we encountered a rotten carcass of a buck. It was the deed of the tigers. They must have attacked the deer a few days ago, judging by the fetid carcass. We now had a clear direction to follow. Another hour of exploring the forest didn't take us near the beasts we were looking for. Instead, we stumbled upon an old place that was marked by an engraved stone sign. It was the place where Samrat Mahadhyata and Samrat Adhirohah used to perform Sadhna. It was a cleaned surface and had two separate rectangular stones on which the brothers used to perform Sadhna. The engraved stone sign was set over there by Maharaja Nagbhushana.

'We shall set our camp here and rest for a while.' Commanded the king.

We have been walking in this dense forest for some hours now. And this humid climate wasn't making it any better. A little rest was required. The soldiers began to set a camp for Maharaja Brihadratha. The Mahout gently kicked behind Balrama's ears again and it bowed down. The Maharaja descended from the elephant. Nrchakshu helped the king to get down carefully. The elephant trumpet again and rolled over in joy. The Mahout patted its stomach as the Maharaja looked at the cheerful elephant, over his shoulder, with a smile. He then went inside his camp which was carefully set up by the soldiers and Nrchakshu stood at the entrance. Guarding the Maharaja. Senapati Aagney, Rajkumar Dvij, Yugant Yasah and I handed over our horses to the soldiers who took them by their reins to a big tree and tied them there loosely. Allowing them to graze while we rest.

Senapati Aagney, Yugant, and I sat down under the shade of a banyan tree. The Rajkumar was staring at Nrchakshu while standing against the same tree.

'What does he see in him?'

Our eyes turned towards the Rajkumar.

'What does my father see in him?' He continued. 'He is always praising him. Like his son.'

He picked up a leaf from those few on the ground which had fallen from the tree. He looked at the leaf for a while and then started rotating it from its leafstalk.

'He's quite a swordsman. Maybe that's why.' I said.

Everyone looked at me and burst into laughter, picturing the day I was stomped into unconsciousness by Nrchakshu. The crown prince chuckled to himself.

'Yeah. Maybe that's why.' The smile on his face faded away by the course of his reply.

Senapati Aagney tried to cheer him up.

'Don't be stupid, Dvij. We all know that Maharaja loves you more than anyone.'

'I know that. But still. I mean… the way he looks at Nrchakshu. It's like he is always so proud of him. This sense of proudness… I've never seen his eyes shine bright because of my deeds.'

'Oh, Rajkumar Dvij! Stop talking that rubbish and sit here.' The Senapati said.

The Rajkumar threw the leaf back on the ground and made some place for himself near us.

'It's just Nrchakhsu's unfortunate past that gains him much affection from the King.' Senapati Aagney continued. 'He was only a year old, still, an infant, when your father took up his responsibility.'

'The last surviving member of the Yudhvan clan. The mightiest clan there ever was. It was a pity that they faced their conclusion in such a manner.' Yugant said while picking up some pebbles from the ground.

Rajkumar Dvij was gazing at the ground. Swinging lightly to either side. He stopped his movement and looked at Senapati Aagney.

'I've heard about the Yudhvan clan massacre a few times.' He said. 'But how could a clan so valiant get wiped out entirely? Most of the infantry at that time came from the Yudhvan clan. They were born warriors. What was so mighty that took them down altogether?'

'It was an invasion, from what I know. Right, Senapati Aagney?' Yugant asked while aiming for the distant tree and throwing pebbles at it.

'An invasion. A tale of treachery.' I said while gazing at the surrounding trees, not giving much attention to the conversation.

Senapati Aagney glanced at me and then sighed.

'Yes. It was indeed treacherous.'

'Can you tell us, Senapati? I've always been curious about this case. I've asked the Mahamantri about the Yudhvan clan a couple of times. But he never gave me a detailed explanation about that night when the Yudhvans became the target of mass slaughter.' Rajkumar looked at the steadily standing Nrchakshu, guarding the entrance of the Maharaja's camp before finally turning to Senapati Aagney again.

Yugant and Rajkumar Dvij's eyes were steadily looking at Senapati Aagney, waiting for his reply.

'Very well then. I'll narrate you the events that lead to that unfortunate event. But for that, you will need to know a little back history about the Yudhvans.'

Everyone looked at each other. I remained impassive throughout the whole talk. Yugant and Rajkumar Dvij nodded at each other. They both leaned in and said in a unison.

'Tell us!'

Senapati Aagney gave a brief smile before getting grave about the tale he was about to tell the two young lads. And so, he began.

'The Yudhvans were residing in Chandraketugarh long before Samrat Mahdhyata and Samrat Adhirohah first came up with a notion of a revolt against the remorseless ruler of Chandraketugarh. After the war was won, the brothers acknowledged the audacity and nerve shown by the Yudhvans who were loyal to their ruler and hence fought against the Akshobhyas. The Yudhvan clan was treated with utmost respect since that very day. No clan has provided more brave and skilful warriors to the Akshobhyan army than the Yudhvan clan. As time took its course, the Yudhvan clan too increased in number. They were given a new establishment by your grandfather, Rajkumar Dvij. Maharaja Sarvyoni.'

Rajkumar took a quick look at Nrchakshu again who was still standing steadily.

'Their new establishment...' The Senapati continued. '.. was by the Simha forest. Keeping in mind the increased number of the inhabitants of their clan, that was the only suitable place. The Yudhvans were delighted and lived there happily without any complaints for a long time until the reign of Maharaja Brihadratha commenced.'

Senapati Aagney scratched his temple with his right index finger and took a deep breath before continuing again.

'At that time Raja Sahasrajit was given the responsibility of handling the affairs of the kingdom of Zeerat by Maharaja Sarvayoni during his final days. Hence Raja Saharajit was the ruler of Zeerat. Before his appointment, the Zeerat kingdom used to come directly under the command of the ruler of Chandragarh. Because this Simha forest is the only thing between the land of Chandragarh and Zeerat, previously no other ruler found any difficulties to command Zeerat simultaneously. But with his deteriorating health, Maharaja Sarvayoni feared that too much responsibility would burden his young son, Maharaja Brihadratha. Raja Sahasrajit and Maharaja Sarvayoni were close friends. That's why he appointed Raja Sahasrajit in that position. But terrible times encircled the Akshobhyan Empire after the demise of Maharaja Sarvayoni. And tough times require tough calls.'

Senapati Aagney pointed a finger towards Rajkumar Dvij.

'One thing about your father, Rajkumar Dvij, is that no one has a better understanding of a person than him. Maharaja Brihadratha has this unique ability to know people's calibre, intent, and potential by sight.'

'No wonder he went against Mahamantri Brahmanand's decision and appointed him as the leader of his Aangrakshak panel.' Rajkumar Dvij said while looking towards Nrchakshu.'

'Well, that being said...' Senapati continued. '.. Just after his

Rajyabhishek, Maharaja Brihadratha took some heavy decisions which were not much supported by the council members. The Akshobhyan Empire had become vulnerable after the demise of Maharaja Sarvayoni. That's why Maharaja Brihadratha had to take some grating decisions. He replaced some officials with new ones. Appointed new representatives of several captured states. Even though most of his decisions were harsh, they were accepted eventually by the high officials. One such jarring decision was the removal of Raja Sahasrajit from his power and to appoint a new representative for the Kingdom of Zeerat. Which was not taken so pleasantly by Raja Sahasrajit. At the same time…'

Senapati Aagney was disturbed by the grunting of a baboon, sitting on a branch of the same tree under which he and his audience were sitting. Yugant Yasah threw one of his pebbles at him and forced the baboon to disappear into the darkness of the forest. Senapati Aagney watched Yugant dusting his hands off before continuing again.

'At the same time, a member of the Yudhvan clan came under the attack of a wild black bear. Which was reportedly the fourth time that a member of the Yudhvan clan has been in contact with a wild animal. They complain about the matter to the King and asked for a reallocation. Somewhere away from the Simha forest. This was the first time that their peace was disturbed since they were shifted near the forest by Maharaja Sarvayoni. Their case was scheduled to be represented in front of the Maharaja the day after the misfortune occurred.'

The Senapati bowed his head for a few seconds. The two young lads looked at me, asking me what happened to the Senapati. I reassured them and asked them to give their Senapati some time.

'I was the head of the infantry during those days. Your father, Yugant...' He said while lifting his chin towards Yugant Yasah. 'Yayati Yasah….' A smile shot upon his face as he recollected his memories with Senapati Yayati. 'The greatest warrior I've seen… He was the Senapati at that time, as you all already know. He was with me the night before the Yudhvans were to assemble in the King's court to represent their case. Just after the case, the Maharaja was also supposed to pass a decree which would see Raja Sahasrajit step down from his throne of Zeerat. It was quite late. The moon was complete and was right above us in its full glory, shining with the stars. Senapati Yayati, Maharaja Brihadratha, and I were present in the royal assembly room and were discussing the events that were supposed to take place the following day. It was then a messenger with an arrow pierced into his back, almost falling off his horse, arrived at the gates of the palace. He was immediately brought to us. He handed us a scroll before he was taken to the Rajya Vedya.'

A moment of silence followed before Senapati Aagney uttered his next words. He looked at his left and refrained for a moment. I stared at the Senapati with my eyebrows low. The Senapati hesitated for a moment after his eyes came in contact with mine but decided to go on.

'The scroll was from Rajkumar Akshaj, son of Raja Sahasrajit. The scroll contained a warning. It said that Raja Sahasrajit has proclaimed a war against the throne and has sent his whole army through the Simha forest to attack Chandragarh. Maharaja Brihadratha ordered Senapati Yayati to assemble the army. There was no time, so we headed towards the Simha forest with all the soldiers that could be gathered. But it was too late. What lied between the Simha forest and the palace of Chandragarh was the residing place of the Yudhvans. Before our army could've reached there, the damage was done. It was four hours before dawn. The whole Yudhvan clan was in deep slumber when the army of Raja Sahasrajit marched in from the Simha forest. They slayed everyone. We were too late to arrive at the scene. Even though we were able to control the revolt, we were not able to save the Yudhvan clan.'

Rajkumar Dvij and Yugant Yasah were in full shock. They were looking at the Senapati with their eyes and mouth wide open.

'By the dawn, the revolt was controlled. Hundreds were butchered and hundreds were sent behind the bars. The Akshobhyan army was standing distressed and was looking straight ahead at the hundreds of butchered bodies of the Yudhvans. The only sound that was heard was of the rustling of the leaves and the blowing of the wind. Everyone was paralyzed with shock. They remained over there for some time, trying to let everything sink into them. After some time the crowd started to fade away. Eventually, it was Senapati Yayati, I and Maharaja Brihadratha who remained. We were all standing there in anguish when we heard a sound. A sound other than that of the wind. It was Senapati Yayati who approached the sound. It was coming from the ashes of a hut which was set ablaze hours before. It was a cry. From the wreckage, Senapati Yayati picked up an infant who was crying his heart out.'

Senapati Aagney with a smile again on his face looked at Nrchakshu.

'It was Nrchakshu. The last surviving member of the Yudhvan clan.' The Rajkumar muttered in a low voice.

Senapati's eyes turned towards the crown prince.

'Yes. It was Nrchakshu. And what we witnessed that night was nothing short of a miracle. Maharaja Brihadratha was dejected. He took all the blame on himself. A tragedy of such intensity to happen only months after he became the King of Akshobhyan Empire, was due to his lack of administration is what he thought. That's why he is too close to Nrchakshu. He reckons Nrchakshu as his responsibility. He saw to it that Nrchakshu received the best education. He saw to it that Nrchakshu was trained by the best fighters. He saw to it that Nrchakshu would grow into a man he is today.'

Rajkumar Dvij's downcast eyes showed that he was dispirited. Nrchakshu's back story was appalling.

'Does...' Rajkumar Dvij's eyes tried to look into Senapati Aagney's eyes. But after several tries ended up looking at Nrchakshu only.

'Does he know all about himself?' Rajkumar Dvij asked Senapati Aagney.

'Just before he turned 16, I told Nrchakshu about his past. Mahamantri Brahmanad was there accompanying us. And to be honest, Nrchakshu took it very well. The lad was as firm as a tree trunk. And when I offered Nrchakshu to tell him the names of his father and mother, he refused straightaway. He told me that he doesn't want to be bothered by his past. And that the amount of knowledge that I provided was sufficient for him. Some real nerves were shown by a 16-year-old that day. Even today, he doesn't let his past trouble him. In any way'

'Senapati Aagney?' Yugant asked in a low voice.

'I am sorry, but I need to ask this. What happened to Raja Sahasrajit afterwards? How was he punished?'

'He wasn't.' the Senapati sighed.

'Rajkumar Dvij stood up swiftly and questioned the Senapati.

'How is that possible, Senapati? The punishment for treason against the crown is death to the culprit and banishment of his every descendent. But Raja Akshaj, Raja Sahasrajit's son is now the vassal of the kingdom of Zeerat. It doesn't make sense.'

The Senapati then tried to explain.

'The next day the Maharaja's special troop went to the kingdom of Zeerat for imprisoning the iniquitous Raja Sahsrajit. But he was already dead before their arrival. He had died that early morning from natural causes. Meanwhile, his son Akshaj was imprisoned the previous night by Raja Sahasrajit for sending a messenger to Maharaja Brihadratha to warn him about the revolt. So, you see...' The Senapati shrugged his shoulders. '. it makes perfect sense.'

'The following day Akshaj was felicitated by Maharaja Brihadratha here, in our capital city and was also declared as the new liegeman of the Zeerat, the vassal kingdom of the Akshobhyan Empire. If it wasn't for Akshaj, the palace of Chandragarh could've been under direct attack.'

'I... I don't understand.' Rajkumar Dvij spoke to clear his mind.

'Are we still talking about the same avaricious Akshaj? I know him quite well. He would even sell his kids for a chest of gold. It's a little too difficult to accept that the city of Chandragarh owes him for his such generous act.'

'I know it's hard to believe, Rajkumar Dvij. But this is the truth. Yes, I know it too that he is a gluttonous, gold worshipping idiot. But when it comes to showing loyalty towards the crown, you will find him at the front of a queue.' Senapati Aagney said.

Rajkumar Dvij's eyes caught me staring into the darkness of the wilderness.

'What's your say about all this, Yashvasin? What do you know about all this?' The agitated Rajkumar asked me.

'I don't know, prince. I didn't join the army until a few years after this incident.' I replied.

'Oh, is that right?'

'Yes, my prince. Even I've heard Nrchakshu's story from Senapati Aagney.' I replied with a smile.

Maharaja Brihadratha was out of his camp. The soldiers were preparing to leave on his command.

'Quite a rest we had. We shall all get going now.' Senapati Aagney said.

Our horses were delivered to us by a couple of soldiers. Maharaja regained his comfort over Balrama. Yugant Yasah and Rajkumar Dvij took up some pace and left me and Senapati Aagney behind. We strolled the forest for two more hours until the sunlight started to fade away. This hunting trip was almost a failure. We were not able to spot a single tiger in the Simha forest. If Senapati Aagney would not have implanted a story in Rajkumar Dvij and Yugant Yasah's mind, it would've been a total failure from some people's perspective. Alas, Maharaja Brihadratha would be delighted. Maharaja Brihadratha ordered a retreat and we all headed towards the palace. It was almost dusk when we exited the dense woods of the Simha forest. The lamps were being lighted as we entered the palace. The moon was up. Between the silvery-spelled moon illuminating the sky with millions of glimmering stars and hundreds of ignited lamps, the palace was nothing short of a prepossessing sight. Senapati Aagney and I were the last ones to enter the palace. The Maharaja was already pacing up the stairs of the Palace and Yugant Yasah and Rajkumar Dvij were handing over their respective horses from their reins to the stableman. I noticed Senapati Aagney being lost into the enchantment of the cast spelled upon us by the almighty artist in the form of these lifelike paintings. He was smiling while gazing at the millions of stars above us.

'That was quite an intriguing story you told, Senapati Aagney.' I said while descending from my horse.

Senapati's smile faded away in a split second.

'Do you have any point there?' He asked without swerving his eyes away from the night sky.

'Nothing specific, maybe. I was just wondering. What would one get if he mixes or manipulates a truth by adding a hint of lies in it? A lie or an intriguing story?'

Senapati Aagney's eyes turned towards me. They were as grave as a lion's, ready to pounce on his prey.

'Not a truth. Definitely not a truth. Isn't it, Senapati Aagney?' I stated the obvious as I watched my horse being taken away to the stable.

'Get to the point, Yashvasin.' He said while descending from his horse.

'My point, sir, is simple. If one lies on truth, too often, he gets confused between what is true and what isn't.'

Senapati's eyes widened with amazement.

'Nothing to worry, sir. Mahamantri Brahmanad is just honest with me. And I am loyal towards the King. So, there is no need to worry.'

Senapati Aagney took a sigh of relief as he watched me walk away from him.

PART 2

<hr>

KALKI

Shivering with cold, I made my way to an old cottage located on the outskirts of the city. The double layer of blankets was of no good. A little past midnight and here I am, riding my stupid horse. Maybe it isn't the chilly wind blowing deep at night which is causing me to tremble. Yes. Quite certainly it's the fear of that old imbecile. He asked me to meet him in the cottage just after dusk. But what does that old imbecile know about the hazards of spying in the Raja's palace? All he does is provide orders. That's it! He remains a silhouette and we are the ones jeopardizing our lives. He should be thankful to the gods that our ambitions are the same.

I was already late but the stars tonight were too fascinating to just walk by. I pulled the reins of my horse to slow it down and just looked above. I am telling you, our saviour or not, but that almighty is a true artist. I stepped down from my horse and decided to take a walk instead. The time I was walking while gazing at those countless lights above and praising the artist, my mind was clear and calm. No regrets of the past. No frets about the future. I felt more than just blessed. Miles ahead of the nearest civilization and miles behind my fated expedition. In the middle, I just wanted to stay. I just wanted to lie down and count the countless. At this moment I just wished to stretch my arms and slumber. But this foolish horse won't let me rest. He gave his head a shake a couple of times and neighed until my eyes were no longer gazing at the night sky but staring at his hideous head. I sighed and jumped on my horse. Kicked and pulled the reins and the horse was running again. We could not take rest now. Being so close to our ambitions. Years and years of working with that old imbecile should not go in vain. I can't stay with him much longer. Neither can I stay outdoors in this cold night anymore. I shrugged tightly behind my horse. The only good thing about this 'otherwise good for nothing' horse is the level of pace it gains. It has saved my life a couple of times. It has also taken an arrow for me. Just behind his neck. Good for him. Or else he would've been counting his days in a stable in the countryside. Quite a good chain of apprehension we have here. This horse fears me and I fear that old imbecile who must be dozing off by now in his rock chair in that old cottage. I am quite sure that the old cottage isn't as old as that 500-year-old imbecile. But god is he strong. Strong as a dozen of wild beasts. Although a quiet and calm folk, one would not want to see him fierce. I have witnessed him fighting and oh god does he know how to fight.

The woods started to get thicker and I could see the smoke rising from the distance. There's a reason I call him an old imbecile. Does that fool wishes to jeopardize our hideout? He might just set ablaze the woods and cry out our plans, to the citizens, for their beloved kingdom. Yes. Indeed, we are here only for the betterment of this place but, you see, we're the artists ourselves. We're drawing a bigger picture here. A picture which is dearer to me than any of the Almighty's.

The smoke emerging from the cottage was quite low and because of the wind blowing from the direction of the city, the smoke too was blowing in the other direction. Maybe the old man wasn't so stupid. This smoke could not be seen by anyone who was not at least a couple of kilometres away from the cottage. I stepped down from my horse and tied it down. The lazy horse went to sleep at once. The cottage had seen its good days. It was as fragile as it gets. That old imbecile is sure to laugh in his afterlife once this cottage crumbles with us inside it. Quite a death that would be. A chill went down my spine as a gust of cold wind blew from the other direction. I shrugged my shoulder, rubbed my hands together, and rushed inside the porch. I knocked on the door gently a couple of times. With no response from the other side, I slammed the door and it swung open. It was dark inside. A candle on an old filthy small table, kept in the centre was the only light inside the room. It was faintly lit and could go out any time. With the first step I took, the candle went to blowing fumes. Coal-black inside. I remember there was a torch in the other room. Stumbling and fumbling I went to the other room. I traced the torch by hand which was by the wall. I took it out from its case. Even though there wasn't any light in the room, it was pleasantly warm inside here. I turned around and tried to light that torch. After giving multitudinous tries with my trembling hands the room was illuminated again. The fire was a treat to the cold eyes. I turned around to place the torch in its case on the wall again. The light from the torch illuminated a face covered with scars and white beard and hair. My heart skipped a beat and my legs started to lose their strength. I was drenched with cold sweat and was able to trace one of the sweat drop rolling down my back. My grip on the torch got loose and from my shaking hands, the torch commenced its journey to the dark dusty wood floor beneath. It will be dark again in a blink of an eye. The scarface was getting covered in darkness as the torch began sinking into nothingness. Just when the face was not visible anymore, the torch was halted into its journey. Halted and raised again to the level of my face. He grabbed my right hand and placed the torch in it. His formidable face was visible again.

'Keep your hand steady.' He said in his heavy voice.

I gulped and gave a nod.

'Come to the other room. And get the torch with you. Try not to drop it this time.' He said as he made his way to the other room.

I assumed my state of complete apprehension for a few seconds. After a couple of baffling seconds, I went to the other room. I heard a squeaky sound going high and low in frequency with every alternative second. After placing the torch in its place, I saw it was him, shifting his balance around his rock chair.

'You are late, Aatreyya.'

I was staring at the fumes which were still coming out from the blown-out candle.

'Aatreyya…I said you were late.'

Grey in texture they were coming out in waves, changing their shape with the interference of the slightest of change in the wind.

'AATREYYA AAROSH!'

I came back to my senses immediately. I looked at him, frightened. His red eyes were glaring death. My legs never felt such a level of weakness until tonight. He stood up from his chair. Tall and strong as a mountain, he approached me. My blanket came loose and it fell on the floor as I took baby steps backwards.

'Are you out of your senses, Aatreyya?'

I hit the wall of the cottage on my journey towards the back. He was standing close to me. I could feel the warm air coming out of his nose. But I dared not. I dared not to look into his eyes.

'I am... I am just tired. I got you your list... our list. It was a tiresome task. But I did it.' I said with a trembling voice. I tried to calm my mind by picturing the night sky outside. But somehow those millions of stars in the constellation took the shape of his red daunting eyes, which I could not deal with right now.

He stepped back and walked towards his chair, not without giving me a death stare. After taking his place on the rocking chair again he knocked the table on his right side twice. Immediately, I rushed towards him and took out a scroll tucked between my waistcloth. Keeping the scroll in the table, I stepped back. His eyes were on me through the entire process. He juggled his eyes slowly between me and the scroll.

'How is Nichakra doing in the city?' He asked while opening the scroll.

'He is doing a splendid job, sir. He is keeping a careful eye on the people listed in the scroll. He has bribed the junior courtiers to sell him any information regarding the people listed. Ironically, the corruption business in this state is going to come back haunting the chief architects of the very same business.'

He nodded without diverting his eyes from the scroll.

Nichakra was the third member of our small group. He has been residing in the city for a year now, collecting information about the palace and the officials working in the palace. Raja Samrendra is an honourable king. But he is dewy-eyed. He trusts his officials so much and gives them the freedom to such an extent that they have become corrupted. Our first step in drawing the grand picture is exposing such officials. After months of spying and information gathering, Nichakra was able to fabricate a new image for himself in the hearts of some officials and was able to generate a list of the corrupted officials taking advantage of the citizens. Slowly and steadily we have to influence the people and somehow have to make them realize the lies that their leaders and rulers have been telling them. We need to ignite a fire in the hearts of the citizens. And from that fire, we will paint our glorious painting.

Nichakra and I were the children of the same past and destiny. Both of us had suffered from the same furious fate. Our clan and families were slayed. Our city looted and our childhood destroyed. Although we commenced our journey of redemption and vengeance from different sources, our destination is the same. Our ambition is the same. To bring down the Akshobhyan empire.

I belonged to a family of farmers, residing in the outskirts of the city of Tosah. Ours was a family of five and I was the youngest of the three brothers. I was still young to help my brothers and parents on our farm. But was determinant every day to assist them in any way possible. But my peers won't let me help. It was one fine day. A day like any other when a change occurred in our lives. My brothers were already in the field and my parents were about to leave the house. I was adamant at that time to leave the house too and to assist my brothers in the harvesting of the crops. But my parents, as usual, restrained me from coming. They left the house for the farms leaving me behind all alone crying. I cried a lot and eventually fell asleep. I don't remember how long I remained asleep. I woke up to the sound of chaos outside my house. The roof of our hut was covered in yellow flames. I rushed outside only to witness a battalion of soldiers slaying my town folks and setting fire to the huts. Panicked, I hid in a haystack. I pressed my hands against my ears and tried my best to not pay attention to whatever was going outside. After an hour when it was all quiet, I peeked outside. The soldiers were gone. I stepped out only to witness the butchered bodies of my town folks. I roamed around like a madman, screaming, crying for my mother. I rushed to our farm and saw the lifeless bodies of my parents. A few yards away one of my dead brothers lied alongside someone who was missing his head. Maybe that someone was my other brother. Maybe not. I turned around and rushed back to my hut and closed the door behind me. I closed my eyes only to get tormented by the images of the dead towns. I remained inside for the whole day. The next morning, when I stepped outside, I saw a flag. The same flag which the battalion of soldiers was carrying with them. I picked up the flag and made my journey towards the city of Tosah. Over there I found that the flag which I was carrying belonged to the Akshobhyas. It was simple then. At the age of 12 years, I swore to avenge my family, my town. I set out for the city of Chandragarh. It took me some time to reach the city of Chandragarh. I travelled through many cities and kingdoms. Took odd jobs. Met a lot of people. And just before my 14th birthday,

I was in the capital city. I was there at last but with no means, no ways, and no direction. I had no idea how to make my dream of vengeance a reality. It was there I met two men. We got into talking and I stayed with them for a few days. Eventually, I revealed my motive for coming to this city. They ultimately revealed themselves to me and told me that they shared the same motive. They took me under their care. Taught me, trained me to become a warrior. It has been 15 years since that day and here I am. Miles away from the city of Chandragarh but closer to my ambition more than ever.

I stood there without making any noise until he had completed reading all the names from the scroll.

'Have you read all the names mentioned in this list?' He asked.

'Yes. I have, sir.' I replied firmly.

He got up from his chair and walked towards the wall where the torch was. Picking up the torch, he turned around and walked to the fireplace. I rushed towards the fireplace too and from the adjacent shelf picked up a few wooden logs and threw them into the fireplace. He was watching every moment of mine. After I was done, he bent down and lighted the wooden logs from the torch. He then extended his arm towards me and I got hold of the torch. Giving the scroll a final glance, he threw it into the fireplace. We both watched it crumble into itself, its edges turning glowing red until it finally turned into ash. He turned towards me and placed his heavy left hand on my right shoulder. And told me the next part of the plan.

'You will meet Nichakra tomorrow again. I want you to deliver a message to him.'

'And what is that message?' I asked curiously.

'Tomorrow when you will meet Nichakra you will tell him to deliver scrolls secretly to all the officials which were mentioned in this list.' After saying this he lifted his hand from my shoulder and turned around with his hands back. He started walking back and fro.

'And what message those scrolls will contain?'

'A warning.' He said while stopping for a moment and glaring at me.

'A warning to all of them. To stop practicing illegal deeds or else they have to face their conclusion. As simple as that.' He said gravely.

'And also…' He continued. '… Ask Nichakra to give more attention now. Ask him to check their response after they heed the warning letters.'

'But, sir..' I said with a squeaky voice. '… I don't reckon that the corrupt personals will leave their foul habits behind after they receive only an anonymous warning letter.'

He chuckled before bursting into a round of laughter.

'Oh, Aatreyya! You're a silly man. You want to be an artist but you lack vision. How will you draw a grand picture with such a doltish vision of yours?' After completing he burst into another round of laughter.

'Oh, you'll see, Aatreyya. You'll see. Eventually, they will have to surrender.' He continued. 'You'll leave tomorrow morning. And don't come back to this cottage. I won't be here either.'

After strolling for a while, he retired to his chair.

'There is a case of greater importance that requires my attention now. I will see you three days from now in the city. I will be there to initiate the next part of our plan.'

'Alright, sir.'

I placed the torch on its case by the wall. I picked up my blanket and made my way to the exit door. But I was stopped by his heavy voice.

'Before going, Aatreyya, make sure that the fireplace and the torch are blow out. I hate fire.' He said while resting on his chair with his eyes closed.

I nodded and went to the fireplace to extinguish the fire. I walked by the exit door and was about to extinguish the torch too, but an important question arose in my mind.

'What should we sign under the warnings, sir?'

He opened his eyes.

'Write my name under those warnings. The name undersigned should be Kalki'

I nodded again and extinguished the torch as I left.

THE MARKET PLACE

I was resting below a banyan tree. Half a dozen other town folks were surrounding the tree too and were sharing a laugh.

'Samendu… Yes. It was Samendu.' One of them said.

'What is so interesting about Samendu?' The other one asked.

'His wife, friend. Last night he came back to his home late and was drunk. So, his wife shouted at him from the window and didn't open the door.' The first one replied.

'Oh, please. How can you be sure of this? Samendu lives ten huts away from you. How can you possibly know this?' Another person asked.

'Because his hut is located on the way to my farm. In the morning when I was going to my farm, I saw him sleeping in the stable.' The first one stated his case.

Listening to this everyone roared with laughter.

'Not only this…' He continued. '… I even heard him murmuring to his cow while half asleep and he was so drunk that he was referring to her as his wife.'

He even tried to mimic the Samendu guy.

'Oh, my sweetheart. You look so pretty when you're angry.'

And everyone burst into laughter again.

I was getting irritated from their pity talks. So, I got up and started walking away from the pleasant shade of the banyan tree. Another reason for my exasperation was this bloody pain in the ass Nichakra. There was no trace of him or whatsoever. Moreover, the crowd here at the marketplace was horrendous. I could still hear those imbeciles laughing behind. That ass Nichakra said he would meet me here. Since the past hour, I am continuously scanning the crowd looking for him and still no sign of that pretentious bastard. I was getting edgy. Impatiently, I started walking through the market place between the crowded passages. I saw earthen pots in one of the markets. Dozens and dozens of earthen pots. Oh, it would be so good to relive my frustration over those earthen pots. Taking advantage of the crowd, I kicked one of the pots which scattered over the ground into multiple pieces. The shopkeeper came out from the premises of his market yelling and screaming on the top of his voice but I was already lost from his sights into the crowd. Ah! It was a stress reliever. I certainly would try this again once that shrieking shopkeeper is all cool again. I was feeling just fine until these little fuckers came along my way. I hate kids. More than the Akshobhyas. More than that despicable Brihadratha. They started circling me, hopping, and holding hands. I tried to shoo them away, but they started whispering to each other and then burst into their irritating squeaky laughter. Desperate in their company, I brought them a doll from the very next market. As soon as they got their filthy hands on the hideous doll, they scattered away like pearls from a broken necklace. I was feeling indignant now. The day was getting worse and worse.

A little far away, I could see a cloud of dust rising from the carriage coming towards us at a very high speed. I walked towards the passage connecting the main road and stood by the edge. The speed of the carriage dropped and eventually, it stopped. It was a beautiful masterpiece. A craftsmen's splendid work. One could tell only by the look of it that only rich people, filthy rich people were entitled to ride such a carriage. From it, descended the Shulkadhyaksha (officer in charge of the royal income) and the Samaharta (revenue collector) in their royal and clean clothes. Their golden necklace stretched till their knees. All the nine fingers in the hands of the Shulkadhyaksha had an expensive ring each to accompany them. The greedy smile of the Samaharta exposed his golden tooth. They were both full of smiles and laughter as they stepped down from their carriage. Samaharta Deenabhandwe's office was on the other end of the market place. The passage between the markets was so narrow and so densely crowded that he had to leave his carriage behind every day and had to compromise to plain walking. Both Samaharta Deenabhandwe and Shulkadhyaksha Kadamba were revered by the citizens of Rajkot. Meanwhile, the tax ministers had the least of affection towards them. They both used to try their best to stay away as much as they can from the indigent natives. Now, that's ironic. These fat fucks have earned their fortune by robbing these poor maggots. Imposing fake tax rules and misusing the power bestowed upon them by Raja Smarendra. What's queer is that these people have no idea that they are being looted by these pretentious noblemen. Both the citizens and ruler of Rajkot are dewy-eyed. Well, as the quote goes, "The Maharaja is like a father to his citizens". Like stupid father like stupid children.

The townsmen gathered around the Samaharta and Shulkadhyaksha and started praising them. Sensing the decreasing space between the people and their costly clothes, Shulkadhyaksha Kadamba, while wearing a fake smiling mask in front of the foolish citizens of Rajkot, swiftly addressed his guards to encircle and escort them to the office. Even though Samaharta Deenabhandwe shared the same feeling of untouchability, his job made it difficult for him to keep away from the unwelcomed company of the residents. After all, he was the tax collector. Causally waving to the crowd, the tax officials made their way to the other end of the market place. The crowd after some time lost their interest and got indulged in their activities. It won't be a while until they will be gathering around again. Oh, won't that be a treat to watch?

Deenabhandwe and Kadamba were outside of their office when a merchant came riding along with his horse. I was still standing on the edge of the passage connecting the main road. The handsome horse was stopped by his owner just at the intersection. The merchant stepped down from the horse. A white Marwari stallion. He ran his hands over its shiny hair. Patted it good for a while and then tied it down. I joined him and soon we were both walking towards the office of Deenabhandwe.

'Sorry, sir. But aren't you dressed too much for a merchant?' I asked Kalki.

'For a merchant who has to establish successful trade connections in 5 cities coming under the rule of Brihadratha Akshobhya? No. I am well dressed.' He replied in his regular firm voice.

'But, sir...' I asked with a little reluctance. '...Nichakra is still not here. Won't that be a problem?'

Kalki took a good panoramic view around him. His tall and strong physique made him stand out from the crowd.

'He'll be here when we need him. Don't you stress on that.' He said while running his hands over his silky grey hair coming out from his royal red turban.

I nodded. We were standing at the front porch of the office. We stood there for a few moments. Kalki was deep into his disguise now. Acting like a merchant, he was analysing the architecture of the office with some interest.

'Quite shabby for an office building.' He remarked while we were still standing before the entrance door. Deenbhandwe and Kadamba were clearly in our sight.

The building was a big room. Only one big room which was attached to two small chambers at either right corners. In the middle was the desk of Samaharta Deenabhandwe. He was handling the revenue collection records to Shulkdhyaksa Kadamba. Two soldiers were guarding the entrance of the office. We maintained some space between them and us. It wasn't long enough until the venal eyes of Samaharta Deenabhandwe fell upon us. Well, his eyes caught the light getting reflected by the enormous ruby stone on Kalki's ring. He poked the Shulkadhyaksa with his elbow, with his eyes still on that ruby, and asked him to pay attention to the wealthy looking merchant. He then shifted his eyes towards Shulkadhyaksha Kadamba and came up with that excited and greedy smile. Shulkadhyaksha Kadamba was a man who could keep his nerves. Fooling him won't be much easy. But there is always a weakling among a group of inviolable who would place his companions in peril in a state of endangerment. Deenabhandwe was that weakling. We were just supposed to target his nerves and expose them. That would be so delightful to witness. When the whole crowd would turn against these officials and eventually towards the King. I was almost jumping with excitement just by thinking about it. The Samaharta ran towards the new merchant in the town. He started cursing the guards outside the office for not allowing us, the gentlemen according to him, to enter.

'It's alright, sir. They weren't blocking our entry. We just arrived here.' I said.

'Oh, is that right?' He said with that greedy smile still on his face.

'Surely your avaricious senses directed you towards us as fast as they possibly could.' I murmured.

'Sorry?' He said with a little amusement. 'I could not hear you properly.'

Kalki interrupted.

'We were told that we could find the Shulkadhyaksha and Samaharta of the kingdom of Rajkot here.'

The acquisitive smile on Deenabhandwe's face grew wider.

'Let me introduce us to you, gentlemen.' He said while welcoming us into his office.

'I am Deenabhandwe. I am the Samaharta. While this gentleman here…' he said while pointing towards Kadamba. '… He is Shulkadhyaksha Kadamba.'

The Shulkadhyaksha greeted us with a gentle smile.

'And what purpose brought you, gentlemen, here in our city?' asked the Samaharta with a sense of hospitality.

Kalki then introduced us.

'My name is Shikharhi. I am a merchant.'

He then pointed towards me.

'And he is Swayambhu, my apprentice. We have come here to establish a trade connection.'

The Shulkadhyaksha walked towards Kalki and stopped a few steps away before firing up a question.

'Can you tell us a little more about your expertise in trade?'

'Well, I have been into the trading business for over 40 years now. I've successfully established trading points in five other cities. We export spices to Tibet, Greece, and Arabia. And we import textiles from the same countries. Silk, you see? We import the finest silk made by the Tibetans; you see.'

Samaharta Deenabhandwe's eyes shone brighter than ever. He knew that a new rich merchant in town meant only one thing. Money.

'Why are you two gentlemen still standing? Please take a seat. I'll fetch you some water.' He said and went to one of the adjacent chambers to fetch water from an earthen pot for us.

Kalki continued.

'I want to set up a trading point here, in Rajkot. Textile export would boom here. And that's why I have come here, in front of you two gentlemen. For a merchant's license.'

Deenabhandwe handed us a glass of water each. And offered us some spirit which we gently declined.

Shulkadhyaksha Kadamba still had his doubts.

'It's not that I don't believe you two gentlemen, but as an official procedure, I would like to see your merchant licenses from other cities where you've set up your trading points. Also, your official trading permit from the Akshobhyan Empire.'

'No problem, Shulkadhyaksha. If the official procedure demands it, you must have it.' Kalki said and then turned towards me.

'Swayambhu, provide the documents to the Shulkadhyaksha here.'

I went forward and handled all the requested documents. Shulkadhyaksha looked at the documents with utter interest. Safe to say that Kalki has his connections. Good connections throughout the country. He must have forged a bond with the officials throughout the country over the years. No wonder we got the license and permit so easily. God, I wish I knew more about Kalki. Nichakra and I are his closest companions and even we don't know much about him. After carefully examining the documents a wide smile, similar to that of Deenabhandwe appeared on Kadamba's face too.

'Alright, gentlemen.' He said while handing back the documents. 'Let's talk about license fees and trading tax.'

A knock on the door caught our attention. I was almost unable to hide my amusement after what I saw next.

'Raja Samrendra has ordered all the soldiers to assemble in the palace's premises.'

The Samaharta and Shulkadhyaksha stood up in haste.

'Is there an emergency?' Deenabhandwe asked the soldier standing at the door.

'No, sir. He just wants to deliver a special speech to all the soldiers of Rajkot.'

'Alright. That's alright.' Deenabhandwe nodded.

Yes. It was Nichakra disguised as a high-rank soldier. For the second part of our plan, there needed not to be any unnecessary interferences when the crowd confronts the tax officials. With the soldiers guarding the premises gone, the window of opportunity will shrink moment after moment. So, we need to be fast now. The Shulkadhyaksha cleared his throat to gain everybody's attention. He led us to our seats. We were sitting on the other side of the table and were facing Deenabhandwe and Kadamba.

'The license fees, here in Rajkot, is the same for merchants, traders, and craftsmen. It's…'

'50 gold coins!' Samaharta Deenabhandwe interrupted the Shulkadhyaksha. Deenabhandwe sure was drooling with greed now. Kalki's eyes shot up after listening to this. From now on everything that has to be said and done by us, should be dramatic. Kalki's voice gained the loudest decibels. We were required to gather the attention of the crowd outside the office.

'50 gold coins? Isn't that too much for a mere license, Shulkadhyaksha?' Kalki asked Kadamba, in a high pitch voice, who was staring gravely at Deenabhandwe for quoting such a high fee.

'That's…That's the new fee imposed recently by the King. You see, the state has suffered some pretty serious backlash in the department of trade in the recent past. To compensate for that loss, strict rules are established now.'

'That's justified.' Kalki nodded. 'I've paid 20 gold coins previously for licenses in different states. But it is justified.'

I took a glance at the door. No one was there. I guess it will take more summon some crowd here.

Deenabhandwe and Kadamba's eyes met and it became awkward. The smile was gone from Deenabhandwe's face and he mostly kept his head low from that point on.

'From this year on, new merchants also need to pay Hiranya and Pranaya because…' This time Shulkadhyaksha Kadamba was interrupted by a raging Kalki.

'This is horrendous!' Kalki said by banging his hand on the table in front of him. Samaahrta Deenabhandwe, who was sitting with his head bowed down, shot up in amusement.

'Utter Rubbish. That's what this is.' Kalki continued. 'Rajkot hasn't been in a state of distress or emergency for many years. Why would the king demand me to pay Pranaya then?' A few people were now looking from the outside and were questioning each other if they knew what's happening.

'That's not entirely true, sir.' Kadamba tried to reassure Kalki. 'It's classified information, but a man of your stature should know this. Rajkot has been fighting somewhat of an economical fight for the past few months. Our king, Raja Samrendra is very compassionate. He weekly donates heavily at the temples. Even though it's a very pious deed, the royal treasure has suffered a lot from this.'

Kalki was still fuming, but he tried to overlook everything. God, is he a good actor. This guy always amuses me. I was trying hard to hide my smirk. This was just so good.

'You're making it difficult for me to set up my trading point in Rajkot, Shulkadhyaksha.' Kalki grunted.

Shulkadhyaksha kadamba was alarmed. He knew that he could not afford to lose Kalki as a merchant.

'Well, if you insist I…I.. .. I can help you with the Hiranya. We can provide you some concession on that.' Kadamba said.

'That would be great.' A smile suddenly flashed on Kalki's face.

I again took a glance at the door. The people were gone. We have to do something quickly.

'Now let me tell you about the import and export tax.' Kadamba's eyes were now on the table on a papyrus record from which he was reading.

'The Prabeshya...' He continued reading. 'that is your import tax would be 50%'. Kalki was red again. Kadamba was still reading from the record and therefore could not see the expressions on Kalk's face. He went on stating the tax fee.

'...And Nishkramya, that is the export tax would be 55%.' After completing his sentence, he looked at Kalki who was bristled on his statement.

'Is this a joke? Is this a fucking joke, Shulkadhyaksha?' He stood up from his place. 'This is a loot. 50% tax? Are you out of your puny mind, you imbecile?'

Now both Kalki and the Shulkadhyaksha were fuming with anger. Shulkadhyaksha stood up from his place too. He was about to throw some insults on the disguised merchant when he heard people murmuring at the door. The crowd had started gathering outside the office. The Shulkadhyaksha kept his cool.

'It's not I who have made the tax rules. The king and his advisor have imposed tax laws. You should know that.' He said.

'Tax laws imposed by the King of Rajkot?' Kalki asked rhetorically.

Without wasting any moment, Shulkadhyaksha rolled out a scroll with the royal stamp from Raja Samrendra and handed it to Kalki. Kalki read it with utter amusement.

'What rubbish is this?' Kalki raised his voice yet again.

'Don't tell me oh, a merchant that you can't read.' A gush of laughter ran outside. Kadamba continued. 'It's the decree that enforces the tax laws in Rajkot. Raja Samrendra has himself signed this.'

'But according to Mahapradhan Ganakarta of Chandragarh, every state coming under the rule of Akshobhya should abide by the tax laws decreed by Maharaja Brihadratha.' Kalki said. The laughter outside stopped at once. The crowd standing outside the office was amazed and bewildered. Murmuring could be heard yet again.

Shulkadhyaksha saw red. He didn't know that the merchant he was dealing with would know such facts. He underestimated the reach of the merchant's knowledge. Alas, he had established successful trade connections in 5 of the states coming under the rule of the Akshobhyas.

'Yes... Yes.... that is true' Kadamba said while wiping off the sweat on his forehead with his shaking hands. '... That was three years ago. Since then Raja Samrendra has launched a new set of tax laws for Rajkot.' He said with a feverish smile. Samaharta was almost out. He knew that they were now exposed. He was trembling with fear, imagining how his kids will feel when their father will be hanged publicly.

Kalki sighed and shook his head.

'In that case, Shulkadhyaksha... I would never set my trade here in Rajkot.'

Sulkadhyaksha Kadamba was relieved. The dejection of losing a rich client was nothing against the satisfaction of not getting exposed.

Kalki turned towards the crowd.

'What your king has done by implementing newly increased tax laws, going against the decision of Mahapradhan Ganakarta, is nothing but an act of treachery against the crown. The crown of Chandragarh.' Kalki sighed and shook his bowed head again.

The crowd was dead silent. They were living a lie. All of them were paying taxes which were more than double the original tax they were supposed to pay. Kalki raised both of his hands with his head still bowed.

'Only God can save Rajkot from the wrath of the Akshobhyan army.' He said.

The dead silence of the crowd was broken by a woman deep into the crowd. She screamed at the top of her voice. Which followed a turmoil. Everyone was screeching, squawking in amusement. Inside the office, the Samaharta had already passed out. The Shulkadhyaksha rushed towards Kalki and fell into his feet. He held his right leg with all his might.

'It isn't the King! It isn't the King! It's us! We were looting the people. We came up with this menacing plan. The king doesn't know about this.'

'I know.' Kalki gazed down at him and grinned. 'I, Kalki, know everything.'

Kadamba's face was white. He should've given more attention to the warning letter he had received. He stood up and ran towards the chamber from where he took out two bundles of gold coins. He then rushed back towards Kalki who was enjoying the bustle outside. Kadamba offered the money to Kalki, but Kalki was unfazed.

Kalki looked at me and gave me a sign. Leaving one passed out man and one distraught man in the office behind, we left the place. Amidst the crazy crowd, we made our way to our respective horses and after giving a last glance to the turmoil, we headed back to our place. The plan was successful. Now we have to wait till dusk to initiate our next plan.

The sun was still above the horizon. Nichakra joined us a few meters away from the market place. We weren't in disguise anymore. Everything from now on will be in the light. The cottages and huts of the people were north of the market place. We were on our horses. It was yet another chilly night. We made our way to the town and saw a group of people sitting around a fire. They were the old and important people of Rajkot, discussing today's turmoil. We left our horses behind and caught the eyes of some people. I rearranged my blanket over my shoulders and turned towards Kalki and Nichakra who were staring at the people sitting around the fire.

We started walking towards the circle formed by them. In doing so, we caught everyone's attention.

'Isn't he the merchant from this morning?' were the whispers surrounding us.

Our footsteps, the whispering, and the crackling of the fire were the only sound audible other than the chirping of the insects. We stopped before the people sitting around the fire. With our footsteps, the whispering of the other natives too stopped. The old and important people sitting around the fire rose and faced us. For a few seconds, the crackling of the woods in the fire was the only sound that could be heard beneath the stars. One of them, who also seemed to be old enough to be their chief, walked towards us through the dozen of them.

'I know you.' He said. 'You're undoubtedly the merchant who came this morning'

I looked at Kalki and Nichakra who were unfazed and were looking at the old man without blinking.

'I am Chandak.' He continued. '.. the high priest. And what is your name merchant?'

Kalki, with his eyes closed, shook his head slowly.

'I am no merchant. I am more of a social reformer.' He looked around himself and addressed the people standing around him in a high voice.

'A crusader. Fighting against the corrupt rules and officials. Fighting for innocent people. Fighting against the ill power bestowed in the deceitful hands of unprincipled. I am Kalki.' With this, he caught the attention of a few more ears.

'What you saw today, in the morning, was a small act carried out by me and my disciples to expose some dishonest people in your city. People who are taking advantage of your innocence and the powers handed to them by your King.'

A voice, from the small crowd that has now gathered around us, spoke out.

'The King is devious! The King is devious!'

While another one called for the King's hanging.

'Hang the King! Slay the King!'

Chandak rested his hand on Kalki's shoulders.

'We the people of Rajkot were so blind from our King's love that we didn't even reckon questioning the state about the hike in taxes, a few years ago. We should've known that behind his regular charity was a scheme so deceitful.'

Kalki caught Chandak's hand from his shoulder and held it between both hands.

'It isn't your King, old priest. Your king is just and merciful.' Kalki said. The whispering started again. Everyone was confused and were unable to understand that why would Kalki defend their King.

It was getting tedious now. Moreover, I was unable to withstand Kalki's cheesy acting. Those holding of hands, trying to win people's trust. Ah! These morons had no idea that we were going to use them for our greed. Fucking morons. They don't have a clue.

Kalki continued.

'The only fault in Raja Samrendra is that he is too dewy-eyed. He trusts his officials to such an extent that the latter feels no disregard in cheating their own King. It is your officials. People like Samaharta Deenabhandwe and Shulkadhyaksha Kadamba conned all of you, the people of Rajkot into believing that the tax rates had been increased by the King.'

'But how could the King not know? He is the King! How can the King be so deluded?' asked another old man stepping out from the crowd.

'The governing body of your Kingdom has been spoiled rotten to its very core. Even the officials working closely with the king are disloyal. That's why Samaharta Deenabhandwe and Shulkadhyaksha Kadamba carried on this deceitful scheme without any fear for so many months. They fill their pockets from the extra gold earned by the increased tax. But in the official records, the tax percentage established by the Akshobhyan King is only included. Moreover, whenever an honest man went ahead to expose the corrupted, his honesty and loyalty were brought for a few gold coins.'

Everyone was amazed by the extent to which they were getting betrayed for so many months. And I was amazed by the extent of solidity shown by Nichakra. The bastard has not moved even an inch since we got here. Here I am, trembling because of this cold. And here is this bastard who was having no effect of the cold or whatsoever. Some resilient dick he is.

A young man stepped out from the crowd and walked towards Kalki and Chandak. He bowed in front of them and with joined hands questioned Chandak.

'What are we supposed to do now, the high priest? Even though our King is merciful to donate gold coins from the treasure, the doubled taxes are troublesome.'

Chandak looked at Kalki and showed a glimpse of a faint smile on his face.

'I do not doubt the righteousness of this man. Now only he can tell us what our next step should be.'

'Raja Samrendra has always given the citizens of Rajkot the highest priority. If he is informed about how his kingdom is suffering from morose and agony, he will surely take some serious actions. That is why I reckon that the high priest along with other ctizens should present this issue in front of the king directly. We can count on Raja Samrendra to understand the problem and reach a solution.'

High priest Chandak nodded with a smile.

'Tomorrow morning, we shall go to the King to plead our case.' He said.

All the townsmen acknowledged to Kalki's proposal.

The night was getting deep as some townsmen retired to their huts. We greeted the remaining as we left. The fire dampened as we walked away from it. The decreasing sound of our footsteps was the only sound audible other than the chirping of the insects.

❖

THE RIOT

High priest Chandak and a dozen other experienced men accompanying him were ready to set off to the palace to greet Raja Samrendra. I, Nichakra, and Kalki were watching them from a few hundred feet away, watching them leave for the palace. We stayed beneath the pleasant shade of the tree for another hour before making our appearance. We walked our horses to the town where the younger and comparatively more passionate townsmen were waiting for their elders to arrive from the palace. We were greeted by Hanan, a young fellow with a wild spirit. Kalki opened the conversation with him by asking about the whereabouts of the high priest, Chandak.

'Has the high priest already left, son?' Kalki asked.

'An hour ago, sir.' Hanan replied. 'We are still waiting for his arrival.'

Kalki with his brows raised looked at the absence of the older representatives, with a sense of anxiety, and made sure that Hanan was observing his expressions.

'What's the matter, sir? You look a little tense.' He asked Kalki who was still rummaging for a glance of the elders of the Kingdom.

'I can't see any elders present today here.' Kalki said. 'Where are they all?'

'All our elders are accompanying the high priest to the palace, sir. Isn't that what you asked for?'

Kalki took a step back and opened his mouth in disbelief. I wonder where he has acquired such exceptional acting skills. This old imbecile must have been associated with a Tamasha company in his younger days.

'Are you saying that only the elders have gathered near the gates of the palace, Hanan?' Kalki asked the young chap.

Hanan was now worried and was starting to understand the predicament. Of course, the officials won't let them meet the king directly. Hanan feared the way his elders must have been treated by the guards of the palace who would be following the orders of the corrupt officials.

'The officials would take every possible measure to ensure that the high priest does not get any chance to interact with the king.

'We should leave for the palace at once.' Kalki said while shrugging Hanan's shoulders.

'Get everyone you can, we need to hurry!'

In just a couple of minutes, people in hundreds assembled outside and were ready to march towards the palace. Just as we planned. With Hanan leading the way, we headed out. Kalki, Nichakra, and I maintained our distance from the front of the marching crowd. We found ourselves amidst the raging passionate people who won't hesitate to start a riot if their elders are treated poorly. We walked for some minutes and could see the high priest still standing at the gates of the palace, trying to talk to the guards. The mob increased their speed. Still, a few meters away from the palace gates, the mob saw a guard shoving the men waiting outside the gate of the palace. This caused a surge in the mob. It wasn't long enough when the same guard kicked one of the high priest's counterparts. Seeing this the mob lost it all. Everyone started cursing and shouting. They increased their pace and with full throttle rushed towards the gate of the palace. I too commenced running but was held back by Kalki.

'Our work here is done.' He said with a smirk on his face.

I looked at him and acknowledged with a smile. And then I looked at the mob thrashing the gates of the palace. It was hard to say whether that guard got inside the palace in time or not. But if he didn't, he'd surely be dead by now. I could see a curious Raja Samrendra peeking from the gardens of the palace. He was taken back inside by his guards on the command of his commander. Every piece of our plan was falling in the right place. Our conquest of turning the people of Rajkot against their ruling body was a success. After pleasing our eyes for a few more minutes to the scene in front of us, we headed back to our hideout to discuss our next move.

By the evening the city of Rajkot had become a huge mess. The royal offices were set on fire and the idols of the king were vandalised. There was no stopping now for the people of Rajkot. They have lost it all. Late in the evening, we went to the city to analyse the situation. Not that it was required now, but we made more attempts to win the already won trust of the people. Hanan approached us the same evening to discuss some grave issues. He was accompanied by men of almost the same age as his. He was infuriated and wanted to take extreme measures to improve the situation of Rajkot. He declared that he will be establishing a group of vigilantes and asked Kalki to be the leader of the group. We weren't a bit surprised. This whole thing was so easy. I didn't know on whom I should laugh more. On these halfwits asking us to lead them or on our fortune which was being so kind to us. Anyway, Kalki didn't turn down their request and asked Hanan and his accomplices to wait until we come up with a plan. He told Hanan that this is a delicate situation and that he doesn't wish to jeopardise the safety of anyone in the city. And so, said that it would take up some time to come up with a plan. Hanan showed some signs of being impatient but ultimately agreed to wait. After examining the condition and mindset of the people of Rajkot we turned our heads towards the local tavern to have some wine and to take care of some certain business. It took us half an hour to walk our horses to the local tavern. We sat on a table in the corner at the end. We ordered our wine and until the arrival of our order, no one uttered a single word. I was about to have my first sip of wine when a man glided his way into our table. He was a tall dark man with a round belly. His face was hideous and so was his smile. Almost half a dozen of his teeth were missing which was made worse by a scar stretching horizontally from one temple to another.

'Have you brought my gold, boss?' He said while stretching his cunningly nasty smile.

'I didn't ask you to kick the old man, Thanga.' Nichakra said while loosening a small sack of gold from his waistcloth. He tossed it in the middle of the table.

'There's always a room for improvisation' He said while extending his hands to grab the gold sack. 'Isn't that right, sir?

It was exasperating. Sitting there looking him smile, being surrounded by his filthy aura and to witness his total lack of responsibility. I just couldn't take more.

'It was an act of sheer folly. Don't you understand that, asshole?' I said while raising my voice a little.

He frowned as he heard me say. It changed his attitude. Who were referred to as 'Sirs' moments ago, were nothing but a group of bandits for him now.

He banged his hand on the table, catching everyone's attention in the tavern. A risk we couldn't take.

'Listen to me, you fuck!' He said pointing his finger of the other hand towards me. 'I did what you asked for. I took a great deal of risk for your bunch of maggots.' He was now pointing his finger towards Kalki.

'... For some gold.' Kalki said while starring deep into the eyes of Thanga, gravely yet calmly.

'You can have your gold back, old man! But I don't think you would like to jeopardise yourselves. I know your pursuit. And I am no ordinary soldier.' Thanga raged.

Nichakra sensed the eyes looking at us from other tables.

'Calm down, Thanga' he said with a smile on his face. 'We acknowledge your work. You did a splendid job.' Nichakra addressed a boy at the counter and asked him to bring the biggest jar of wine they had, for Thanga. The jar arrived and Thanga was all happy again. His hideous smile was back.

'You're the only one here who knows the importance of a man like me.' Thanga said before gulping down the liquor. 'Your associates are just a bunch of baboon asses.' Saying this he burst into laughter.

In just 10 minutes he had finished the biggest jar of wine they had at this local inn. Nichakra signalled at the counter for another jar. Thanga consumed alcohol in large gulps.

'The liquor here meagre in quality. They can't get me, the great Thanga, under influence.' Hiccupped the man who was in an advanced state of inebriation.

Thanga was clearly under the influence and was wagging his head from left to right continuously. His eyes were closed but his grin was larger than life. Nichkara looked at Kalki from his shoulders and gave him a nod. Kalki leaned in towards Thanga and whispered.

'You do realise that you are a wanted man, right?'

Still, greatly under the influence, Thanga opened his eyes.

'Wanted by the beautiful women of Rajkot? Yes! I know!' He said giggling.

'Everyone saw what you did to the old man today, Thanga. Every resident here in Rajkot is thirsty for your blood. Do you realise that?' Kalki said again.

'I do…I do…. I do...' Thanga said with a string of hiccups. 'But I don't worry about that. I know you guys will protect me from them.' Thanga was all jolly now. No one could have wiped out that smirk from his face.

'And why will we protect you?'

The smile dissolved from Thanga's face. He stopped wagging and leaned in towards Kalki.

'Because I know your secret, Ass hole.' He said with steady eyes.

Kalki leaned back and assumed his original position. Thanga too resumed wagging his head and his mouth was revealing the six missing tooth again. We all remained silent and just kept looking at Thanga for a couple of minutes. After that Kalki gave me a nod. Kalki and Nichakra left me in the company of this drunken bastard. I knew what was to be done now. I ordered the inn's special red wine. One for me and one for my new friend.

'Can you handle another drink, mate?' I asked him with a cheerful smile while our drinks arrived.

'Don't you know who are you talking to, scoundrel? Bring on another jar. Nothing can intoxicate me!'

'Very well then.'

The tavern was almost empty. Apart from the young boy in the counter cleaning glasses, my new friend and I were the only ones inside. I stood up and from my waist cloth I drew out a blade. Thanga's sleepy eyes were now wide open. With swift movements, I thrusted the blade in his throat multiple times

His head fell on the table with blood oozing out from his throat. I drank my red wine at once and slammed the glass on the surface of the table. I took his glass and poured his wine on the table and some on the floor. With the back of my right hand, I wiped my mouth and stepped towards Thanga's dead body. I cleaned my blade by rubbing it on his back and tucked it inside my waist cloth again. After giving his lifeless body a final look, I walked out of the tavern.

The Ploy

The flame was swaying heavily from left to right. At a leisurely pace, it started to assume a steady position. The heavy swaying turned into light side-to-side movements. Eventually, it stood still. It stood still for some time. Calm and patient. With a thud, the door swung open. With Nichakra entered a gust of cold wind. Forcing the flame to dance again.

Nichakra was panting when he entered the cottage.

'Except for the Samaharta, no one is ready to give in their evil practices.'

Kalki, who was strolling inside the cottage before the arrival of Nichakra, closed his eyes and took a long deep breath.

'Were you certain to send the final warnings to all of them?' He asked as he let out the air.

'Yes, Kalki. Of all the warnings sent, only Samaharta Deenabhandwe has agreed to stop his malpractice.'

'They'll get a new captain for their vessel.' I said while swinging back and forth on my rocking chair. 'They will fire him and appoint another Samaharta.'

'Better fired than…'

'So, it is certain then.' Kalki interrupted Nichakra. 'We expected this, didn't we?'

'So, what's next?' A puzzled I asked Kalki.

'From here you to have to execute the rest of the plan.' Kalki replied.

I stood up from my rocking chair. With a sombre smile on my face and my arms spread in scepticism, I started juggling my eyes between Nichakra and

Kakli. Kalki saw me in my distraught state and walked towards me. He placed his heavy right hand over my shoulder to assure me.

'I have some important business to take care of in the mid-east. Some allies that I have to meet. Don't worry, Aatreyya. I'll be telling you what needs to be done. Moreover, you'll be having Nichakra's supervision. It will be just a couple of months. Nothing more. You just have to make sure that the fire ignited inside the hearts of the people of Rajkot doesn't douse.' He said.

I was a little calm now. 'So, what's the plan?' I asked in a soft voice.

Kalki leaned in. 'Here's what you have to do....'

OLD TREE AND A WELL

'Why would he abandon us in such dire times? Our mission is at its last juncture. Why would he leave now?' I asked Nichakra while scratching my teeth with a straw. 'My main concern is that he has another group of men whom he trusts more than us. Otherwise, why won't he tell us his true purpose of visiting the mid-east of the country?' I was able to scratch out the piece of meat stuck between my teeth from last night. I spat it out.

Nichakra, who was walking ahead, stopped and turned towards me. I continued with my whining.

'Why won't he believe us? Haven't we slaughtered enough men for him to believe us?' I noticed a fruit vendor who was preoccupied with another customer and sneakily picked up an apple. We continued walking.

Nichakra's left eyebrow shot up. I spotted a rare smile on his otherwise grave face. It was a little sarcastic, though. Nevertheless, I went on.

'What more shall we do, Nichakra? Does he hate us? Why does he hate us? Well....' I took a little pause to take a bite from that apple before continuing again. 'Well... how could you know? Like me, he hates you too. He does not believe you. Even though he trusts me with a little information, I've noticed that he doesn't trust you at all. It's okay if you're bummed out. It's alright...' Before I could've completed my sentence Nichakra said a couple of sentences that sent a chill down my spine.

'First thing: Don't try to make yourself feel better by saying that he trusts you more than he trusts me.

Second thing: He is in the mid-east to discuss with the allied forces a strategy to force an attack on Chandragarh.' That smile on his face was now mocking me.

I stopped in between while Nichakra didn't mind taking a couple of steps forward before stopping too. He turned back, facing me, and was trying to hide that stupid smile of his.

'I've taken an arrow in my thigh. I've been stuck with a mace and had a concussion so strong that I lost my whole memory of that particular day. I've taken a sword right here.'

I placed my finger on my chest, a little above my heart.

'Just above my heart. I've had many scars and bruises. But believe me Nichakra. Nothing has hurt me more than these words of yours.'

Nichakra burst into laughter and stepped towards me. He hugged me and started consoling me.

'How about we finish our work here in the market and then we'll go to the tavern.' He said, still laughing.

'But the wine is on you.'

'Not a problem for the person who has the trust of Kalki.'

'Will you stop mocking me, you son of a bitch.' I said humorously while pushing him away.

This is how Nichakra is. When Kalki is around or when we are on a significant mission, Nichakra is the most solemn being you'll ever see. He is extremely reticent. In dire situations, you'll get a dire man out of him. But otherwise, he is like any other joyous kind. I enjoy his company, to be honest. During combat, you can rely on him. And while sharing drinks, you can share a laugh with him.

We resumed strolling down the market looking for a strong rope. After searching for it for about a quarter of an hour, my eyes caught the perfect rope dangling outside a store. We bought 5 meters of it and then concluded our night in the local inn. I slept very deeply that night, forgetting what the next sunrise had in store.

The next morning when I woke up, Nichakra was all ready to go meet Hanan and his accomplices. I slowed him down for about half an hour. Now, this was supposed to be a meeting between a group of young guns of Rajkot and us. Hanan and his companions wanted to take major steps in the revolt. They wanted to take measures so drastic and violent that their elders went against them. Even though the elder people of Rajkot wanted to carry on the revolt against the throne, they didn't want to adopt any aggressive practices. But the young blood was a little more vexed with the way they were being ruled. As a result, they came to us to help them fight their battle, against the corrupted. Kalki had accepted the proposal but with certain conditions. The first one that everything will be confidential and untold. Second, they'll only do what we ask them to do. They agreed. They just wanted to express their compulsive anger. Better with us that with their old folks.

We head out for the slightly dense woods in the outskirts. When we reached the spot, Hanan and three other men were already waiting there. Their age band was between 18 and 21. One of them had a small personal blade tucked in his waistband. They greeted us by bowing down and asked about the whereabouts of Kalki. We told them that he had some other important thing to take care of. Questions regarding Kalki were followed by the introduction of the three other men. It was us, who had told Hanan to bring three men with him, the next time we shall meet. They were four and we were two. Six men were enough to carry out the abduction. Increase in numbers will only lead to increase in complexity.

'So what's the plan?' One of them asked. His name was Deval. He was the one with the blade.

'You know the plan.' I answered.

'Yeah… but how are we going to carry out the abduction? And whom are we going to abduct?' Deval asked again.

I looked at Nichakra and signalled him to do the talking.

'Bhadraka and Nrrat.' He said gravely. Nichakra was back to his reticent self. He didn't want the kids to take anything for granted. This was a serious mission and it required all their attention and confidence.

'The head of the food department and the officer of the port.' Hanan said while nodding.

Hanan was facing Nichakra while his other two accomplices, the twins,

Gotam and Girik, were on Hanan's either side. Deval was standing behind Hanan. Nichakra with a tilted head started examining Deval. His head remained tilted for a few seconds and then he was straight as an oak tree.

'Before we discuss anything, I want to ask you, young men, again. Are you sure that you want this?' Nichakra said in his usual heavy voice.

Deval stepped forward and beat his chest.

'We want to do this. Just tell us how and when.'

Nichakra sighed beneath his breath. He turned back towards me. I shrugged my shoulders and gestured that it's his choice.

'Are you aware of the consequences?'

'We'll be hanged, for all I care. Better than living a life of a fool.'

'All right then. Everyone now, listen carefully.'

All four young men leaned in to listen to the plan.

'Annapala Bhadraka and Pattanadhyaksha Nrrat have been carrying the task of treachery for a few years. Earlier when Nrrat was a simple supervisor, he used to take bribe from the smugglers to let them smuggle illegal things in this kingdom. But when he was appointed as the officer of the port, he was also given a power which he ultimately used to cheat the local merchants by imposing fake, increased, import, and export charges. It is an organization where people like Deenabhandwe, Kadamba, Bhadraka, and Nrrat are working together to cheat their people for merely some gold. Even after receiving the warnings, they have carried on to continue their fraudulent acts. These maniacs won't stop from a mere protest. They need to be given a clear and strong message by us, the people who they have been deceiving.'

I glanced at the ignited eyes of these young men. Their countenance was reflecting the spark in their determinant eyes. They were all adamant for immediate vengeance.

'And this message will be given by the abduction of Nrrat and Bhadraka. Both of them are responsible for swindling the majority of the population of Rajkot. The merchants and the farmers. The farmers are not given the right price for the food grains they grow and the merchants have to pay tax which is double the originally stated tax.'

After pausing to examine the frontrunners assembled, he pointed out towards the twins.

'We will carry out this mission in two groups. Gotam and Girik will join me. While Hanan and Deval will work with Aatreyya. We shall take care of the Pattanadhyaksha while you...' Nichakra said while pointing towards Hanan and Deval. '.. shall take care of Bhadraka. Nrrat and Bhadraka's residence is separated by three blocks. The abduction will be carried out a little after full moon..'

Nichakra went on explaining the plan properly to Hanan and his accomplices. When he was done, the sun was above our head and the wind had taken a halt. A beetle caught my attention who was struggling on the ground on his back. He was highlighted by the sunlight which was getting hindered from the leaves of the tall trees.. I bent down and with the help of a fallen leaf helped him get back on its legs. He crawled away as fast as it possibly could. I got up and saw the lot staring at me. I lifted my arms and gestured them to ask what they were looking at. Nichakra waved the awkward air of amusement away and told me that he was done detailing the plan to the young men. I stepped in and asked them to keep this mission confidential and not to include any more people in it. I told them it's not about trust, but about the fact that more people will only jeopardize this sensitive plan. The abduction was to be carried out when the moon was full. We asked them to meet us at the tavern at the full moon. After greeting each other, we all scattered away.

Nichakra and I took to the farms. Nichakra was able to locate an abandoned cabin in the distant edge of the farm line. The farms here have been barren for a long time and hence people weren't seen here easily. The cabin had a deep basement where we will be keeping the elite abducted ministers. I was seeing this cabin for the first time. It was forsaken. Barren and infertile soil could be seen throughout the stretch. A snag and a well were the only two things accompanying the old abandoned cabin. The dead tree's shadow was falling on the well in such a way as if the shadow of its lifeless branches were stretching to get a drop of water from it. I took a peek inside the well which was, as expected, dry. Not a single drop to quench someone's thirst. How futile it is to not be able to do the task you were meant to. I took a panoramic view of the field and sighed. It was a secluded place, just perfect to keep the officials without anyone knowing. Half of the roof was gone. But there was a lot of time to expect the rain. The entrance door was a strong one. All the latches were still intact too. Nichakra opened the latch and gave a gentle push. The heavy door swung open with a squeaky sound. Nichakra has got the cabin clean just a couple of days earlier. Still, significant dust was present on the adjacent shelves and some cobwebs were still visible in the corners. But that wasn't our concern at all. It's not that we have to live there. I followed Nichakra to the corner who stopped before a rug on the floor. He lifted that old rug and a cloud of dust took the visibility away. I swayed the cloud of dust with swift movements of my hand and covered my face. When the visibility was back, I saw a door on the floor. It was the entrance to a basement. Nichakra pulled it open and a staircase appeared. I followed him down to the basement. It was a wooden staircase that was creaking with every step I took. The basement was a tidy one. Ample space to allocate at least a dozen people. A thick pole bisected the basement in the middle. Encircling the pole were three chairs. I threw the rope that we had purchased yesterday on one of those chairs.

'So, what do you think?' Nichakra asked me with a smile on his face.

'It will do.' I replied. After arranging the place properly for our need we went back up. We decided to wait in the cabin till dusk. Nichakra found himself a tidy place to sit and doze off. I walked towards the window and looked outside at our horses which were tied at the front porch. They too were relaxing. My eyes shifted towards the snag and the well. A crow flew over the well and found a branch on the tree to sit upon and launched a series of loud caws. I wondered when was the last time that the tree would have borne fruit, or when the last leaf from the tree was detached and began its inevitable journey of never coming back. The instant cawing of the crow grew more and more exasperating. Eventually, it flew off to vex someone else with its obnoxious voice. I yawned as I looked at the horses for the last time before I too decided to take an afternoon nap.

By the time I woke up, the sun was already half below the horizon and continued descending. Nichakra was in the basement, maybe giving everything a final check. I saw him coming up from the basement and adjusting the rug over the basement door properly.

'Kumbhakaran finally decided to wake up, eh?' he mocked me.

I rubbed my eyes and laughed sarcastically.

Nichakra handed me a bag of water and stepped outside to check on the horses. The last rays of the sun fell on our front porch and entered through the window. Slowly, they started to step out from the window and were eventually gone. I stepped outside of the cabin to stretch and noticed half a dozen of stars twinkling.

'Not much glitter in the sky tonight, is there?' Nichakra asked while tightening the reigns of the horses.

'Since when did you become a vivid admirer of nature?' I asked him inquisitively.

Nichakra opened his mouth to say something but ultimately refrained from speaking. But a smile stretched on his face afterward.

After a few minutes, I asked Nichakra whether we should leave now. Nichakra suggested that we should feed ourselves first and then later we should head to the tavern where we will meet Hanan and others. I placed the latch on the door as we left the cabin on our horses. We were in no hurry. There was still enough time for the abduction to be carried out. We rambled around the fields on our way to the market place. We had supper there and waited until the moon was almost full. After sitting over there for much of the time, the right time finally arrived. I nodded at Nichakra and we were off to the tavern. When we arrived near the local inn, we could see Hanan and the others already waiting there for us. If they have been waiting over there for a long time, a suspicion could arise. I asked them and they reported that they had just arrived there and were afraid that Nichakra and I had already left. We tied our horses near the tavern and after rechecking everything the six of us made our way to our destination. Apart from the half dozen torches igniting outside some houses, the moon's was the only light we could see. A few meters before, we split up into two groups as planned. Nichakra and the twins went their way, whereas I was accompanied by Hanan and Deval. We decided to meet directly at the cabin with our respective officials.

I, Hanan, and Deval strode towards Annapala Bhadraka's house. It was a double story bungalow and the porch was illuminated by two oil lamps. I covered my face with a black cloth and so did my two accomplices. With very light feet we walked at their front porch and assumed a squatted position. I gestured Hanan and Deval to search for any unlatched windows while I stayed in my mean position. After a few seconds, they came back to join me. Deval reported that he found a loosely latched window in the back. With our backbend, we rushed towards the backyard. Deval was right. The window was almost open. Hanan inserted his hand between the gaps and tried to unlatch the double doors of the window. He was successful to do so. The wooden slabs opened wide on their hinges. Deval was the first one to get inside. Hanan followed next and I went in the last. Till now it was going all well planned and to my amusement, these young lads were taking my orders gravely. I was worried especially about Deval, that he would not follow my orders. Anyway, we walked forward in the dark with the only source of light being that of the moon which was entering from the window we just opened. We stumbled upon the staircase. Nichakra had previously told me that the room where his wife and he slept and where their sons slept were on the top. Very carefully, and adamant to not make any sound, we climbed up the stairs. The gallery was lit up with an oil lamp and on its either side were the two rooms. Hanan noticed a little boy sleeping in the right room. He slowly walked towards the door and latched it from the outside. Next, we went inside the Annapala's room. Hanan, Deval, and I assumed our positions. From the little light coming inside from the gallery, we could see that the Annapala and his wife were sleeping, not facing each other. A smile went up on Deval's face. He was becoming edgy and looked at me for an order. I poured some drops of this liquid that Nichakra gave me on a handkerchief and was about to handle it to Deval. I carried out the task of handing him the cloth and tucking the bottle of that liquid in my waist cloth simultaneously. And accidentally dropped the bottle on the floor. The glass shattered and released a resonant sound. Both the Annapala and his wife woke up in a shock. Deval snatched the cloth from my hand and jumped over Bhadraka aiming for his face. He grabbed hold of his neck with his one arm and rubbed the cloth on his face with the other. Even though the light entering the room was faint, it was luminous enough to illuminate everyone's face and their respective brief actions. With numerous strange sounds of shattering and struggle arising from this room, the children had started banging the door from the inside. Bhadraka's wife stunned me. She didn't reveal any hint of screaming or struggle. She just watched her husband getting battered silently, sitting on her bed. And I know that no one will believe me when I say that I reckon I saw a faint smile on her face too.

'Hey, women! Don't make a sound!' Hanan warned Bhadraka's wife. 'Or else, we'll kill your husband.'

'You want me to make a sound to kill my husband? I'll be obliged.' She said.

This time I definitely saw her smile. Hanan and I looked at each other bewildered.

'Are you thieves?' She asked monotonously. 'I warned Bhadraka that a day like this would come. I warned him from indulging into corruption too.' She said while pointing out at Bhadraka who was not struggling now. Maybe he was now under the influence of that liquid. 'Wait a minute. I'll get you the keys to the locker.' She said very casually.

I stepped towards her and raised my hand in front of her gesturing her to stop.

'We're here to kidnap your husband.' These words coming out of my mouth were followed by immense emotions coming out from Bhadraka's wife's countenance.

'Take him! Take him!' She said with a beam of joy stretching on her face.

Deval and Hanan were now totally confused with the situation they found themselves in. They reckoned it to be a struggle. As it turns out. Bhadraka's wife hated him. Deval was standing in front of Bhadraka's numb body, scratching his head and looking at Hanan, asking him what is happening.

'You want us to kidnap your husband?' Hanan asked.

The woman slowly turned her head from me to Hanan. And after waiting for a few seconds began to laugh a clap like and maniac. We hushed her to keep her voice down which she solemnly accepted.

'Oh yes. I want you to take this drunkard baboon away from me. He is good-for-nothing baboon ass. His stupid ass is always fighting with me. Moreover, not once, yes, I repeat, not once has he ever listened to me. He is never home and is always squandering off the money on booze. Take him away. I promise I won't tell anyone.' She removed her earrings and from the adjacent desk picked up her golden necklace. She walked towards me and asked me to take them as an assurance. I was not sure what to do. Deval and Hanan were looking at me and smiling hysterically.

'We must go now.' Deval said in a faint voice.

Deval picked up Bhadraka's body and we swiftly made our way downstairs. To our surprise, Bhadraka's wife sprint past us and headed towards the main door.

'I knew she was playing!' Said Deval. 'She is going to take the streets and cry for help!'

I rushed down and followed her. But tonight, was full of surprises and had us mystified. I saw Bhadraka's wife holding the front door open for us. She had the most joyful grin on her face. Hanan and Deval were perplexed too to see Bhadraka's wife helping us. She waved at us as we walked by her into the street outside.

Deval was a strong young man and was easily keeping us his pace with us while carrying Bhadraka on his shoulders. We swiftly made our way to the tavern. When we reached there, Nichakra's horse was not to be seen.

'They have kidnapped their officials faster than us, eh' I said under my breath.

I hopped onto my horse and Deval placed the drowsy Annapala in front of me. I pulled the reins of my horse and took off. Deval and Hanan scattered and went back to their respective destinations and I rode my horse to the distant secluded cabin. From the distance, I could see the full moon casting its silver vibrating glow upon the small cabin and its companions, a dead tree, and a dried well. In the whole land, those were the only things the eyes could see. Maybe the only things the eyes wanted to see. I could see Nichakra's horse tied up in the front porch. My horse halted in front of the cabin and neighed as I tied it down. I pulled Bhadraka on my shoulders and went inside the cabin. The rug was swept aside but the door of the basement was closed from the inside. I knocked on the door and said my name. Nichakra opened it from the inside and with Bhadraka, I went downstairs. Nichakra had already tied up Pattanadhyaksha Nrrat to the long rigid wooden pole with the rope. Nrrat's legs were tied and were stretched out. His back was supported by the pole and his hands went behind it and were tied too.

'Took you some time, encountered a lot of struggles, eh?' Nichakra asked me while shifting Bhadraka near the pole.

'Not really. I'll tell you about it in the morning.'

'Seems right.' He said with a smile.

Nichakra tied Bhadraka to the pole alongside Nrrat. He double-checked the grip of the rope until he was assured that they were tight enough. We decided to leave the two of them in the cabin alone that night and to return in the morning. Moreover, our horses can't be seen near the cabin anymore. We locked the doors behind us as we left for our old cottage. We successfully did what Kalki asked us to do in his absence. Now, we have to wait until Kalki comes back.

Dissension

By the next morning, the talks of the kidnapping of Annapala Bhadraka and Pattanadhyaksha Nrrat were on everyone's lips. A court meeting was also assembled by the courtiers of the Rajkot palace to study their position. Raja Samrendra was getting anxious and wanted to take matters in his own hands. But his faithful commanders advised him to entrust that responsibility to them. Even though the internal complexity of the palace made it seem like obligatory estimates were being taken to rescue the abducted officials, reality proved that the internal working myth was fallacious. Far from the guileless eyes of the Raja of Rajkot, the entrusted members of the court were worried about the whereabouts of the kidnapped officials, but for their own greater sense of fret about the impregnability of their criminal and crooked enterprise.

Far from the palace, Nichakra and I were accompanied by young Hanan to the secluded cabin in the outskirts, on foot. For most of the part of our excursion, Hanan was seen enchanted with the audacious mission, he reckons, he carried out last night. His enchanted aura was oozing out from his exuberant smile, which he continuously tried to conceal from us. We reached the abandoned cabin and made our way delicately inside. As soon as our footsteps were heard by our crabby guests underneath, a struggle was commenced by them. Poor, people must have been reckoning of us as someone who would help them in their dire need. Nichakra picked up the rug and began to unlatch the door, while a curious Hanan studied everything carefully. As the door was pulled by Nichakra, the sound of struggle enhanced. We all went down the basement, but not before covering our face. Nrrat and Bhadraka gave up on the struggle as they saw three men with their faces covered with black cloth, enter the basement. It was no complex procedure to understand that we were the ones who have kidnapped them. Nichakra removed the bundle of cotton and cloth stuffed in their mouth and united them. Hanan warned them that if they show any resistance, it would prove fatal for them. I placed two plates in front of them to feast upon, while Nichakra pushed an earthen pot in front of them. Bhadraka, longing for a drink, glided towards the earthen pot. With trembling hands, he picked up the ladle and thrust it into the earthen pot. Because of his unbroken spree of shaking, most of the water that commenced its journey to ascend into Bhadraka's throat ended up getting wasted upon his feet. Nrrat was scared stiff and threw a series of questions that we'd already expected.

'Who are you guys? You're the group of vigilantes who gave us those warnings, aren't you? You're Kalki! All of you have committed a grave mistake. All of you are doomed! You are all... AAHHH!'

Hanan kicked him in his groin and Nrrat gave out a loud cry. Meanwhile, Bhadraka who was earlier busy quenching his thirst, came back to true realization when he heard Nrrat's cry. Leaving the ladle behind, he shifted back to his initial position, beside Nrrat.

'Both of you are well aware of the reason you are here' Nichakra said. 'Even after getting a fair set of warnings to drop your illegal practices, you continued to indulge in the habit of looting your people remorselessly. Your actions were profoundly illicit. Your punishments should be substantially severe.'

Nrrat was still moaning while holding his groin meanwhile, Bhadraka was trembling with fear.

'Eat and drink as much as you want before we tie you up again.' Nichakra said as he made himself comfortable on a chair.

Bhadraka ate his food slowly while keeping an eye on the three of us. Especially on Hanan who had just kicked Nrrat. Nrrat, on the other hand, was obstinate enough to not touch his plate. I saw him muttering, cursing, and grumping now and then. Hanan's utterance through his countenance was drastically opposite to the one when we were coming here. His vexed expressions were just too loud to go unnoticed. After Bhadraka had finished eating and Nrrat was done with his cursing, Nichakra tied them to the mast again. Bhadraka showed some struggle while whimpering, but Nrrat was just too stubborn to show any resistance. After that Nichakra walked towards Hanan and whispered.

'These men can't be trusted now. You will be staying here till the next sunrise. I will switch you up then with the twins. Will you be alright with it?'

Hanan showed the shine of his blade by pulling it out a little from his waistcloth.

'Oh. I'll be alright. Don't you worry about me.'

'Alright, then. We shall meet you tomorrow. And remember not to light any lamp or torch in the night. It will invite unexpected visitors.'

'Understood.' Hanan nodded.

'I've tied them quite well and the ropes are strong enough to withstand their resistance. We will put the latch on the doors as we go. We'll see you tomorrow.'

Hanan seemed to have neglected the last words of Nichakra. I could see evil in his eyes. I just hoped Nichakra could too. Nichakra and I ascended above and we latched the door behind us. As soon as we left the premises of the cabin, I confronted Nichakra.

'Are you sure about this?'

'Sure, about what?' Nichakra asked.

'Leaving Hanan behind with the two of them. Are you certain about that?'

'Oh, yes. You're setting his grade of proficiency quite low. He can take care of the two. And if necessary, can take care of himself against the two.'

'No. Not that. Didn't you see how he kicked Nrrat? And don't tell me that you failed to notice his indignant behaviour downstairs. I am not quite sure that we should be leaving him alone with the two. Oh, so you're laughing now. Don't forget, Kalki wants them alive. Leaving those two with Hanan is surely taking a risk.'

'Calm down, Aatreyya. Don't set yourself off with trepidation. Hanan is a responsible kid. You don't need to pull your hair out while thinking of him being alone with those two corrupt pests.'

'Don't come back sulking afterwards. I am warning you now.'

'Don't act like an imbecile now. Come back tomorrow morning and be assured yourself. Now we should go. We've got other work to do. And it's a long way to the town without our horses.'

For the next few hours that we walked, we didn't talk much. I was still vexed about Nichakra not being able to visualize the consequences of leaving Hanan alone in a basement with the people who have looted Hanan's folks for some years now. I reckon we gift wrapped, Hanan, an opportunity to avenge his town by, maybe, mutilating two handcuffed culprits. It was a prospect. He may slay them and flee the next morning, for all I know. Anyway, I swerved those thoughts away and resumed focusing on what lied ahead. Nichakra and I were to collect information about the other members of the sly enterprise set up to loot the naïve. Nichakra took me many places. From the local inn to the merchant's club. I heard the temple tolls and the cries at the cremation. He took me to all the eerie places that evening. But we had our job done. We retired at the old cottage that night and didn't talk much even then. The next morning, we had made up our minds to take the twins, Gotam and Girik, to the cabin. But Deval persisted in taking him instead. And so we agreed upon taking Deval to the cabin. We commenced our journey on foot to the distant cabin yet again. God, was it tedious to walk that far. We might have just hide them somewhere in the town itself. I am quite sure many would volunteer to hide those men in their houses. But then again. It would provoke risk.

When we reached the cabin our monotonous friends, the tree and the well, were, like always, waiting for us. From the front porch, Nichakra and I heard some noise. The noise which baffled him and me. Nichakra looked at me at once and then sprinted inside the cabin thrusting everything on his way. As soon as he opened the door of the basement, he was certain that he had committed a big blunder. He jumped down the stairs and shoved Hanan to the wall. I rushed towards Nrrat who was lying half-dead in his puddle of blood. Every inch of his body was bruised and cut badly. He was not making any movements and initially Nichakra and I were scared that he was all but dead. Nichakra thought of dealing with Hanan later and rushed to my side and checked Nrrat's pulse. It was faint, but it was still there. It was some dire situation that we found ourselves in. Bhadraka, on the other hand, was traumatized by the sadistic and barbarous Hanan. He sat in stupefaction with his eyes wide open and his body trembling vigorously. Deval, still uncertain about everything stood behind us motionless. While the savage Hanan was standing by the wall with a cruel smile, taking proudness from his fiendish method of torture. I offered some water to the baffled Bhadraka, but he was so deep in shock that his mere movements were seized. Leaving Nrrat in the care of Nichakra, I took Hanan by his hands and took him upstairs. He tried to set himself free, but couldn't. In the cabin, I let his arm go. Deval followed us upstairs.

'What were you thinking, asshole?' I slammed him.

Hanan burst into a loud round of laughter. Even Deval was astound to see his companion laughing like a lunatic with blood drops dripping from his raised hands. And then all of a sudden, he stopped laughing and a profound gravity surrounded him. His head was bowed and his long-untied hair was spread all over his face. With his head still bowed he turned towards Deval.

'Do you remember that orphan Kshlok, Deval?' He asked while he slowly caressed his shinning hair.

Deval stepped back a little. He was taken into a deep thought because of that question.

'How did he get orphaned, Deval?' Hanan continued. 'Why did his parents kill themselves? No. Don't swerve your eyes away. Look into my eyes and tell me, Deval. Why did his parents kill themselves? You do remember that, don't you? It was only a year ago.'

'Be… Because… the soldiers burned their house.' Deval replied.

'And why did they burn the house?' His eyes shifted to me.

'WHY DID THEY BURN THEIR HOUSE, DEVAL?' He roared.

'Their crops were destroyed that harvesting season and they couldn't pay their land tax.' Deval replied while he felt a little melancholy.

'Because they couldn't pay the false land tax.' Hanan said while drawing out his curved blade whose edge was dripping blood. 'Because of the corrupt institution set up by these pigs, many of my people have suffered. I will not rest until they all are punished.'

'You, dumbass! What do you think are we doing? We have come to your pity town to expose the illicit activities carried out by these imbeciles. We came here to save you from further thugs. If it wasn't for us, you will still be living a life of a lie.' I said.

'Curse you and your Kalki! Don't we know why you are truly here? You are surely here for your good. You bunch of assholes are just using us for your good.'

'Careful, Hanan. Don't say things you don't mean.'

'Fuck, you! I mean every word that I am saying. Amidst your political war we, the naïve people, suffer. In the grand war between sumptuous classes, we are taken as a ritual slaughter. Your false principles and commandments don't care about the consequences which are always suffered by people like us. Our suffering begins where your spurious claims and reasoning begin. And our suffering will end when the bearers of such claims die!'

Hanan rushed towards me with his blade up above his head. His eyes were red and traces of teardrops were visible on his cheeks. Coming out for me he cried for Deval.

'Are you with me, Deval?' He screamed as he came running in my direction.

Deval, who was sceptical about the current situation, took his steps forward too. Slowly, but he did.

Before Hanan could get an opportunity to thrust his blade into me, I stepped towards him and kicked him in his core. With his face down, he was pushed back. Just as he lifted his head, he saw my rapid fist approaching. He was knocked out and lied on the cabin floor. Deval was confused and had his blade in his trembling hands.

'Don't even try.' I warned him. 'Take your friend back with you. And never show us your face again.'

Blood was oozing out of Hanan's nose, which seemed to be broken. He lied down moaning and twisting with pain. Deval dropped his blade on the floor and picked his bleeding friend up and left the cabin. I could hear his slow fading footsteps as he rushed back. I stepped outside on the front porch just to make sure that they are certainly gone. Watching them disappear, I went inside and opened the door of the basement. Nichakra was cleaning Nrrat's wounds who was now sitting in an upright position. Bhadraka was back to his senses and was gulping water from the earthen pot. I stepped down and placed my hand on Nichakra's shoulders.

'They are gone. They won't be coming back. I ended all associations with them.'

Nichakra was too busy cleaning and covering the open wounds that he let my words go unnoticed.

'We need to take him to a ved.'

'No. We can't. We won't even need to. I can mend his wounds.' Nichakra was becoming hysterical. The last thing we want is for Nichakra to lose his mind. He stood up, ran his eyes at every corner of the basement, scratched his head, and then turned towards me.

'I.. I'll be back. I'll be back in a few moments. Take care of him till then. Get him hydrated.' Saying this he went upstairs. I could hear his footsteps from above as he rushed outside. He slammed the door behind him which was loud enough to hear from the basement too. I stayed back in the basement and got myself a bucket of water which we had brought today. Bhadraka offered to help me with the cleaning of the wounds. We dipped a piece of cloth, turn by turn into the bucket, and with that drenched piece of cloth cleansed Nrrat's cuts and bruises. I tore my waist cloth into two halves to cover two major wounds on Nrrat's legs. After that, we waited. We waited long enough for Nichakra. I was getting restless and so I went outside. The sky turned reddish yellow as I stood beneath the big tree. Birds were flying back to their nests and the sun was setting. I looked at the horizon where the sun was letting out the last rays of the day. And from that light emerged a silhouette. A man was riding his horse at full pace. Nichakra left his horse at the front porch and rushed inside the cabin. I tied down the horse and followed Nichakra. He had brought some ointments, herbs, and bandages for Nrrat's aid. It took him an hour or so to properly fix up Nrrat. After that, he and I helped Nrrat to come upstairs. Bhadraka followed us upstairs. He wanted to ask us something but was just too scared and petrified after today's events. We helped Nrrat to a chair and then, exhausted, Nichakra fell on the cabin floor. He gave a faint cry as he shifted back towards the wall for support. His head was bowed and his spirit shattered.

'I should have listened to you.' He lifted his head upwards. His head was now touching the wall for support and his eyes were exhausted and overcome by adversity. 'I should've listened to you, Aatreyya.'

'Don't say that now, brother.' I tried to console him. 'It's all over now. I've ended our association with them. We don't need to worry now.'

'Oh, Aatreyya. Boy, do you lack vision. Don't you see it? We've provided them with valiant wings. They won't stop now. I saw that fire in Hanan's eyes today. Kalki is going to kill me. He is going to kill me. I've ruined everything.'

It was true that we wanted to launch a riot in the kingdom of Rajkot for many certain reasons. But none of us wanted this riot to take any violent turn. Nrrat who was listening to everything uttered some words which were just audible.

'So Kalki is the name of your leader, not your organization, huh? You both seem to be outsiders. Oh, don't be taken back. I can conclude this by recounting everything that I've listened to coming out from your mouth till now. You have committed a murder. You have placed the youth of Rajkot in peril. Not long before you'll witness their public execution. They will be hanged in the market in front of everyone.'

A chill went down my spine as I listened to those faint words coming out from him.

'We can't keep them here any longer, Nichakra. We should get low and wait for Kalki. We can't jeopardize our work now.'

Nichakra, with his head set back on the wall and his eyes shut, stayed motionless. For the next two hours, the four of us stayed inside the cabin. With every second, the cabin was getting colder and colder. Nichakra finally stood up and turned towards me.

'We'll get them to their home. Tonight. Will you be able to escort Bhadraka to his home safely?'

I nodded.

As we left the cabin with Nrrat and Bhadraka, I bade farewell to the old tree and the well for the last time.

TWO MURDERS

Nrrat and Bhadraka had, as expected, revealed everything about their abduction. Although they didn't see our face, they knew that a couple of young lads and some outsiders were responsible. As a result, some soldiers would come daily to take a bunch of kids to the palace, forcefully, to get any information regarding the matter. Three to five young men were beaten and summoned in the palace in the morning every day. They would return in the evening, brutally tortured and traumatized. Some of them would be too weak to walk and had to take the support of their fellow companions. The twins were also taken in by those soldiers, to break them, to get any particulars or details. But their resoluteness was firm enough to withstand any torture. They didn't break. Hanan and Deval would see those young men return every evening, back to their families. That time of the day would be filled be horror and cries, agony, and anguish. Nichakra and I couldn't help them anymore. Not without any further instructions from Kalki. And now that everyone in the town knew that Kalki was responsible for directing some of their kids towards the path of murder and conflict, I don't reckon we can do much even if Kalki comes back. Anyway, it was almost time for Kalki to return from the mid-east of the country. We just need to stay low until then. We scrutinized the inside happenings mainly from the outskirts of the town. Nichakra, although, once in a while made his visit to the town. It was two weeks after we let Nrrat and Bhadraka flee. The town seemed to have grabbed hold of their normal pace. Just when everything seemed to be neutral and peaceful, a tragedy struck. Something gruesome that Nichakra and I have already anticipated would happened. Two more officials were kidnapped late at night from their respective houses. It was surely the doing of Hanan. The palace became graver and commenced taking paramount measures to rescue the kidnapped officials and punish the wrongdoers. Nichakra came up to me with the news.

'It's Deenabhandwe and Kadamba.'

'This... this can't be good. Everyone in the town knows that we were the ones who exposed Deenabhandwe and Kadamba. They saw us in the market.' It was hard for me to believe that someone like Hanan could come up with such a well-thought plan.

'We have to do something. Or else the whole kingdom will be in turmoil. Hanan will murder them. And when he does, it will be catastrophic for Rajkot.' Nichakra suggested.

Nichakra and I started keeping a close eye on the young fellows of Rajkot for the next five days. We couldn't trace Hanan at all. He must be taking high caution. But on the sixth day, we saw Deval outside the temple premises. He seemed to be nervous and kept looking for someone every time he turned around a corner. He was depicting the deeds of someone who has just committed a crime. We got our lead. We just needed to follow him to get to Hanan. We tread upon the heels, following Deval cautiously on his journey which commenced outside the temple. Deval was continuously checking whether he was being followed. He had his eyes upon his shoulders. He took us outside the local inn, through the crowded main market and then headed in the direction of the palace.

'Why is he going towards the palace?' Nichakra asked me inquisitively.

'Let's find out.' I replied.

We followed Deval until he was at least three hundred feet away from the palace. Then we stopped and saw him go further from behind a banyan tree. He went inside the last right aisle before the gates of the palace and disappeared. We waited for him to come back. After almost 20 minutes, we saw a frantic Deval tracing back as fast as he could, in rapidly taken steps. He was carrying a big sack on his back now. Just as he came out of the right aisle, a couple of men followed out of the same aisle but went ahead along a different path. I advised Nichakra to confront Deval, for we didn't know what was inside the bag. Nichakra agreed but refrained from causing a public scene. So, we waited for the right time to square up to Deval. He squeezed himself past the crowded market again and then headed towards an abandoned barn in the farms. We followed him till there. Inside the barn, he offloaded the sack from his back and swept off the sweat on his forehead with his right hand. He turned back to return but found us closing the door of the barn.

'Why... Why are you here? Didn't you terminate all your association with us?' Deval panicked. With every step we took towards him, he took one step back.

'Why did you kidnap Deenabhandwe and Kadamba?'

Deval saw red as I started questioning him. He stumbled upon a small stack of hay in his attempt to increase the distance between us and him.

'Why is it any of your business? You're just a couple of outsiders interrupting in the working of the governance of our Kingdom. We, the citizens of Rajkot, could take care of ourselves. You... You should return. Yeah… Go… Go back to your place.'

The rage in Nichakra's eyes could be seen clearly. He wanted answers and Deval was giving none.

'Where is Hanan? Tell us and we'll let you go.'

Deval didn't reply. He fell clumsily on the floor as he was retracing back.

'WHERE IS HANAN?' Nichakra raged as he grabbed hold of Deval's neck.

'Someone asked for me?'

I looked at the direction of the voice. Nichakra let go of Deval and turned towards the voice too. It was Hanan and he was accompanied by a dozen people, their age varying from 20 to 40 years. He had created a vigilante group of his own, as it seems.

'What is that you seek, old warrior?' quoted Hanan whose nose was wrapped with a bandage.

'What are your plans, Hanan? And why Deenabhandwe and Kadamba?' Nichakra asked him.

'O, my plans are simple. Just what you and your Kalki wanted. A riot in the town. Nothing big, you see. We don't intend to spill blood if that's what you are looking for. And Deenabhandwe and Kadamba? Don't worry about them. They won't remain in our captive much longer. Tomorrow, they'll be on their way home.'

'I just want you to understand, Hanan. Taking such bold steps could be drastic for you. Maybe even fatal for you and your small club. Don't laugh it off, Hanan. You all aren't warriors. You are all just farmers, merchants, and craftsmen. Don't indulge yourselves into such practices.'

'You don't need to worry about that, sire' said Hanan with a recurring smile. 'We can look after our Kingdom. Dire situations require dire decisions. We have made ours and it would be much better if you don't interfere.'

Nichakra took a deep breath and nodded to Hanan's proposal. Hanan guaranteed us that there won't be any spilling of blood which was all that we care for. So, we agreed to exit. We went past Hanan and there was something I couldn't resist saying.

'What happened to your nose, boy?'

I chuckled as Hanan turned his face away from me.

Just when we were about to leave, Nichakra threw a question towards Hanan.

'What is in that sack, anyway?'

'Nothing that concerns you, sire.'

For the next couple of days, we just watched soldiers marching around the kingdom in heavy numbers. Back-to-back kidnapping could not be taken lightly. The king was getting anxious and had started to doubt his capabilities. He never was fit enough to take the throne. He never was a leader. Always afraid of taking decisions. Deenabhandwe and Kadamba remained kidnapped. There was no news regarding their escape or return from the apparent dungeons of the vigilante group of Rajkot. It was clear that Hanan lied to us about his intentions. He was crafting a bigger plan whose trajectory will ruin not only his puny group but also the people of this town. We couldn't do anything now without revealing ourselves which will jeopardize our cumulative work of the past few years. A bloodless riot is what we actually wanted to ignite in the first place. The pieces were falling perfectly but Hanan took it to another level, of course. A level higher than we ever anticipated. Moreover, there wasn't any sign of that old imbecile. God knows when he is planning to return. Since we have exposed the illicit practices and fraud being carried out in this town, there hasn't been a day that something of high significance hasn't occurred which had its dire consequences. I was suspecting the same today. Two days have gone by without any compound episode of the vigilantes versus the supreme authority.

The next day I woke up to profound and nerve-racking news. Deenabhandwe and Kadamba were found slaughtered in an aisle near their respective residence. Deenabhandwe was missing all his limbs whereas Kadamba's corpse was found without any fingers or toes. They were both naked and had severe lashes and cuts on their body. The worst has happened. Even though these corrupt officials deserved a death penalty by the state, such traumatizing and appalling death is deserved by no one. Moreover, Deenabhandwe had earlier resigned from his post and was living as a retired man when he was abducted. Nichakra and I talked about the severity of this act and the gruesome consequences which may follow next. And so, a piece of critical news did follow. In the evening, the soldiers came up with their drums to announce at the market place.

'The dire and profound state of affairs occurring since the last many weeks has forced Raja Samrendra to take necessary steps. Due to the growing instability of the kingdom of Rajkot, Raja Samrendra contacted Maharaja Brihadratha Akshobhya, the great ruler of the Akshobhyan Empire to seek his help. Yesterday, Raja Samrendra received Maharaja Brihadratha's reply who agreed to send their representatives to restore our kingdom to its rightful glory. Today's unethical and hideous act will be avenged. The criminals of Rajkot will be punished rightfully.'

This news came out to be more shocking and daunting for the corrupt officials of Rajkot than the vigilante group. They were unable to cover up a loophole through which Raja Samrendra's plea for help to Maharaja Brihadratha Akshobhya was sent and hence went unnoticed by them. Now it was their race against the time. They knew that if Maharaja Brihadratha is sending a representative, he will be an unbiased and equitable one, and by no means will they be able to buy his honesty. The winds of change were about to enter Rajkot.

The news brought no change in the criminal activities until an official from the city of Chandragarh arrived in Rajkot. The taxes and revenues rates were not altered neither were the vigilantes halting their criminal offense. In the month that followed the kingdom of Rajkot saw much turbulence. A gatekeeper, accused of bribery, was set ablaze alive in the middle of the day by Hanan and his group. The carriage of the Panyadhyaksha was attacked by armed vigilantes. But because of the bravery and clever perspective of the coachman, no harm was inflicted on the Panyadhyaksha. And as a matter of fact, the latter was one of the few officials of Rajkot who were honest and didn't indulge in fraud. Hanan has gone out to such an extent that for him, everyone is a culprit. Maybe till now, he had forgotten what his true ambition was. Because of that attack, the security forces outside the residences of the officials was doubled. The vigilantes didn't have a plan. They just wanted to destroy and demolish the sins of their city. And with the sins, the sinners too. But the officials weren't mere players. It takes a lot of eminent minds' quick-thinking and clear perspective to commit such a fraud which went unnoticed for almost two years. And even now, with the news of the interference in their working by the Akshobhyan king himself, they were bold enough to continue their malpractices. Either they had surrendered already, given in to their false ideals or they had a master plan. Quite frankly, I didn't reckon there is a way out for them now. They were guaranteed to be doomed.

On the other hand, our objective was achieved. Kalki had made me aware of our aim since our very first day in this city. We wanted to draw Akshobhya's attention to this city. Although Kalki didn't tell me the reason behind it, it makes perfect sense now. Kalki was in the middle-east part of the country to construct an optimized strategy to attack the Akshobhyas. Even if we can draw a little of their attention, away from the potential war, it will only prove to be beneficial to us. And now that they are sending a representative, I and Nichakra were quite sure that it won't be a mere official of Chandragarh. But an important one. Whose absence from the battlefield will shift the tide of the war towards us. But this came at an apparent cost. Blood of the innocent was bound to be shed. Due to the lunacy of Hanan and reserved thinking of his vigilante group, people in Rajkot will be hanged. And the majority of them will be young men.

Reformation

Nichakra and I were among the thousands of others to have assembled outside the palace to see who the representative of the distinguished Akshobhyan Empire was. Thousands of people were standing outside the gates of the palace, beneath the sun, for hours just to catch a glimpse of the potential reformer of their city. By now even Raja Samrendra could be seen strolling back and fro in the palace garden, awaiting his guest. After staging much patience, a swarm of soldiers and a few horsemen were seen marching towards the gates of the palace from the distance. Around 200 soldiers on foot accompanied by 50 horsemen could be seen. Such numbers meant only one thing. That a really important Akshobhyan official was arriving. The crowd began to chant the name of the Akshobhyan Empire. Nichakra and I were the only neutrals in this elevated crowd. As the army came closer and closer, I was able to see the flag bearers bearing the filthiest colours of the vicious Akshobyas. The golden crest shinning on the hue of red made my blood rage. I clenched my fist and ground my jaws. The colours of Akshobhyas grated on my nerves. Nichakra saw the effect it was having on me and placed his consoling hand on my shoulder. As the army came closer and closer the enthusiasm of the crowd became wilder. It was only moments until we could see the man leading the small battalion.

Once the assembled crowd got a look at the man leading the small battalion an exuberant force overwhelmed them. He was the crown prince of the Akshobhyan Empire, Rajkumar Dvij. Son of Maharaja Brihadratha and the future of the Akshobhyas. The reason the crowd could recognize him was because he had visited Rajkot eight years ago with Maharaja Brihadratha and Maharani Drisana. My instinct forced me to grab hold of my blade and step forward into his direction. But Nichakra's strong hands stopped me from going any further.

The highly spirited crowd began chanting his name and started showering him with flower petals. He was given a proper 'prince' status welcome by the crowd. Another young man who seemed to be of the same stature and distinction rode his horse side by side to Rajkumar Dvij's. Neither Nichakra nor I could recognize him. But he looked as an eminent member of the Akshobhyas.

On the other side of the palace gates, Rajkumar Dvij and his associate were welcomed wholeheartedly by Raja Samrendra. Although my field of vision was hindered by the crowd and other obstructions inside the palace gates, I could guess that Raja Samrendra was touched by his emotional side while greeting Rajkumar Dvij. After all, the crown prince was the one who will be helping Raja Samrendra from getting out of the turmoil he found himself in. After all the petals of the kingdom of Rajkot were showered on the Rajkumar, enough to fill the palace grounds with the sweetest of scents, the crown prince and his associate were taken inside the palace to rest.

The young crown prince didn't take much time to recover from the month-long journey from the city of Chandragarh to Rajkot. Like an earnest example, he was back on the streets of the town accompanied by his associate, a palace statesman and a bunch of armed soldiers, the very next morning. He was shown the places where for the following many weeks some of the most dreadful and horrendous acts were executed. The statesman led him to the aisles leading to the residences of Deenabhandwe and Kadamba where their slaughtered bodies were found. He also took him to the heavily guarded residence of Pattanadhyaksha Nrrat where he was recovering from the injuries he sustained, for the last month and a half. The place where the Panyadhyaksha was attacked and where the gatekeeper was set ablaze alive was also shown to Rajkumar Dvij. After taking several notes and studying the cases he and his associate were back on the other side of the palace gates. For the next couple of weeks, the same procedure was followed. Rajkumar and his associate would take down the streets with the soldiers guarding them regularly. And hard work and clever perspective of the prince bore him some definite results. At the start of the third week the abandoned barn where Nichakra and I confronted Deval weeks before, was swept by the army of Rajkot under the supervision of Rajkumar's associate. Dozens of sacks, stuffed with smuggled weaponry, were seized. The swords and blades seized were smuggled out from the palace's defence chambers itself.

Now I could see a clearer picture. That day, the sack Deval was carrying was also one of them, containing swords and blades smuggled out from the Royal defence chambers. Hanan is quite the craftsman of conflict. Only if he could have invested his flair and qualities in the right direction. Nichakra and I were now concerned about our safety too. The way the young prince was unearthing secrets it won't be long enough until he finds out about us too. As a result, we started keeping our eyes open and our heads low.

The week that followed next saw the Rajkumar questioning some officials, recursively. He was adamant to find out the truth. And eventually, the Rajkumar came across the truth. Although Nichakra and I knew that this day would come, it was hard to take it head-on. One early morning a battalion of soldiers of both Rajkot and Chandragarh took on the streets. In separate groups the ransacked the property of 14 men, taking them, forcefully into the custody. Yes, they were the vigilantes and Hanan too was taken into their custody. They were sentenced to a death penalty by public hanging which was scheduled for the next week. Till then they were thrown inside the dungeons of the palace.

The Rajkumar had only questioned the officials of the palace and hence was given a fabricated truth. A truth that didn't reflect any of the fraud details that the corrupt officials have been carrying out for the last two years. The corrupt officials were clever enough to give Rajkumar Dvij the details of only those events which were enacted by the vigilante group of Hanan. But then again, it was the future king of the Akshobhyan Empire that they were trying to fool. Sooner or later, the truth always presents itself.

Rajkumar Dvij and his associate weren't the only ones to arrive in Rajkot during that part of the year. Kalki too finally decided to show up. Nichakra and I were tired and lethargic and were resting back in the sluggish cottage when Kalki knocked on the door. He looked all vibrant and energetic, on the contrary. He was able to succeed in bringing up an optimized plan with the allied forces to take on the city of Chandragarh. But he also happened to miss almost all the major events that occurred in Rajkot. We explained everything to him and also told him about the execution planned for Hanan and his companions the following week.

'It can't be helped. He was too ambitious as it seems. I should have known.' Kalki said. 'You both did what you were asked for. Even though Dvij seems to be taking the right steps to dissolve the riot, it would still take him much time. He won't be back in Chandragarh when we shall attack that place.'

'The Rajkumar is not alone.' I said which drew Kalki's attention towards me. 'He is being accompanied by another young man. A prince, as it seems.'

'A prince?' Kalki asked with his eyebrows submerged deep into his forehead.

'He seems like a prince. Maybe a Rajkumar of some adjacent kingdom. He has been helping Rajkumar Dvij throughout the case. Based on the rumours, it was he who found out about the smuggled weapons hidden in that abandoned barn.'

'That's a plus point for us then.' He said before taking a pause. 'I want to see him, though.'

'He will be present during the public hanging scheduled next week.'

'Alright, then. We'll see him there.'

Nichakra popped up with a question too.

'When are we supposed to leave for the middle-east for the war?'

'I have some errand to run in Ujjain. After a couple of weeks, we will be on our way to Ujjain. Following which, we will head to meet the Shatabdas in the middle-east.'

Nichakra nodded and went back to sleep.

For most of the part of the following week, we had little to do and stayed in the sluggish cottage. Nichakra and Kalki visited the town frequently, though. While I stayed back in the cottage.

The day of the execution finally arrived and the city of Rajkot saw thousands of people take on the streets to see Hanan and his companions hang. There was naturally a towering rage inside the hearts of the people who were not allowed to communicate and share their factual problems with the Akshobhyan representative, but the wise eyes of people like Chandak knew that what Hanan did was wrong too. As a result, soldiers in huge numbers were present to control the displeased mob. Kalki, Nichakra, and I were too present in the crowd in disguise. A total of fourteen gallows, each for a vigilante, were set up in the middle with one hangman behind each of them. The mob became more vexed as one by one the criminals were brought on the suspended stage. They stood near their respective gallows. A statesman stepped on the stage and began to read the crime done by the 14 of them and had a speech prepared for how these vigilantes were harming the integrity of the kingdom. But before we could find out the gest in his speech, the mob reached the ultimate level of their anger and began shouting and cursing which made it impossible to hear what the statesman had in store to say.

'I couldn't see the prince and his associate. Where are they? Weren't they supposed to be here?' Kalki was getting curious.

'They will be here.' I replied.

And just then the prince and his associate ascended on the platform, in front of the culprits.

'There they are. Do you know who that other man is?' I asked while facing Kalki whose eyes were stuck on the stage.

The crown prince gestured the crowd to calm down.

'So? Who is he? Prince of Patliputra? Indraprastha? Sharasvath?' Kalki was still staring at the two young men on the stage.

The crowd listened to Rajkumar Dvij and started lowering their voice and anger.

'Who is it, Kalki?' Nichakra too was getting curious now. He and I were standing on either side of Kalki and were waiting for his answer. But the old imbecile was lost in a reverie. Nichakra, slightly, shook him and he was back to his senses.

'What?' Kalki asked.

'Do you know him?' I asked him again.

'Oh, yes. Yes, I do. I know him.'

'Who is he? A prince, right?'

'No... No. He is no prince. His name is Yugant Yasah. He is a mere friend of the crown prince.'

Something was sceptical about Kalki today. Maybe watching 14 men, who raised their voice against the powerful corrupts, die was something he wasn't handling properly. But we were not capable of doing anything now.

'People of Rajkot.' The Rajkumar commenced addressing the crowd. 'Your anger is justified. No one would like to watch their people receive a grating punishment like such. But my truthful and diligent brothers! I am here to address you and to make you familiar with the barbaric and inhuman crimes these 14 men have committed for the last many weeks. These men have not only carried out the abduction of the officials of your kingdom but they are also responsible for many brutal homicides. They have committed such crimes that can't go unpunished.'

'The corrupt deserved to die! A haunting death, they deserved to die!' A man from the crowd screamed in the defence of the 14 men. Rajkumar Dvij looked a little amazed but didn't let that become a major concern. A huge surge followed that man's defensive voice and the whole crowd was unstable again.

The Rajkumar and his associate were escorted down from the stage and after only a few minutes, the culprits commenced their dangling struggle. But their fight against the inevitable death didn't last much longer and eventually, they left this bittersweet world behind.

In some way, the main culprits, the fraudsters, managed to swerve Rajkumar Dvij's attention from the real case. From the core. But Rajkumar Dvij wasn't one of those people who would be pleased with oneself. He remained in the Kingdom of Rajkot for further inspection because of the words of that common man in the crowd echoed into his conscience. Moreover, even after punishing the culprits, the kingdom didn't seem to stabilize. People's aversion and resentment towards the governing body didn't go unnoticed. The last thing he ever wanted to be was that the people hate the Akshobhyas. He knew he had to adapt himself to a different perspective and had to tackle the problem with a different approach. And this approach would lead to our very first encounter with each other.

The time we ran into Rajkumar Dvij and Yugant Yasah was days after the public execution of Hanan. It was one of the first late spring nights. Kalki, Nichakra, and I, in disguise, were heading towards the local tavern. We sat on our usual booth and ordered our respective poison. The tavern which in most days was a quiet place, not taking into consideration the infrequent brawls among the drunks, was filled with loud in sync chants directed against the palace. A dozen men were surrounding a man who was sitting, in the middle, on a table, responsible for setting up the outburst.

'And so I ask you! Why should we respect the king? Why in the name of the almighty should we not regard the officers with the highest level of contempt?' The man in the middle yelled while gulping on his wine. 'They all deserve a haunting death!''

While another man, amidst the assembled small crowd, questioned his saying.

'Why should we hate our king and the minsters, mate? Don't you know how much money does the King donates? He is the most compassionate and sympathetic ruler Rajkot has ever seen!'

Another man popped up with his opinion.

'The king is blind! Blind with the trust he has in his ministers! See how they have looted us and still, in the presence of the Akshobhyan prince, are looting us! I reckon the young prince is also a member of their illicit scheme! Yes! Yes! Even he is a fraudster!'

'No! No! The Akshobhyan prince is just and kind-hearted! Maybe he has fallen into this sickening scheme as we all did before the arrival of Kalki!' another one said.

Nichakra and I looked at Kalki who was ignoring all their sluggish talks.

'Who is Kalki?' The man in the middle asked. To which everyone assembled there burst into a round of laughter.

'Are you new here, my friend?' One man asked. This question caught the attention of Kalki.

'Everyone knows, Kalki and his small group.'

'Yes! Yes!' everyone yelled in a unison.

'Kalki was the man who came to us like a divine deity, promising to free us from all the lies that we were surrounded by. But in time, he showed his true intentions. He influenced and guided some of our men on a path of violence to fight those bastards. Which eventually led to their execution. God knows where he is right now. But I wish that he is rotting somewhere!'

The image of Kalki in the minds of the people of Rajkot was mutilated because of that twat, Hanan.

'But god, would I pay anything to see those bastards rot in hell! Those corrupt officials! Fooling us for years! Making us pay the taxes which are double than the ones implemented by the Akshobhyas!' One of them said. To which the eyes of the one, sitting in the middle widened. The latter gave a glance to the other person, the one who was taking sides with the king earlier.

'It's them. It's them in disguise.' Kalki said in a slow voice.

'Must be out here to collect further details about the case. Should we do anything?' Nichakra asked. Kalki remained silent for a moment, gulping his wine.

'Let's follow them.' He eventually said.

'What's the need? We have to leave in a few days. Why put ourselves into such a dangerous condition. They won't be returning to Chnadragarh until the war is over.' My questions to Kalki was followed by another moment of silence among us. Kalki watched those men cursing the officials.

'Unless…' I began to continue but was interrupted by Kalki.

'No. We will only follow them. No one will attack them. Is that clear, Aatreyya?'

'Alright! Alright! We have a chance to slay the future of Akshobhyan Dynasty, but alright! We will just wave at the opportunity as it passes by'

Kalki wasn't happy with my way of talking to him and gave me that cold death stare of his.

'I... I am sorry. I understand...' I said with a trembling low voice.

We remained in the tavern for another hour or so. Carefully listening to the two quick-witted men in disguise getting all the information out from the drunkards of Rajkot. Well, that was one of the ways, supposedly. But as the night grew deeper, the crowd diminished. And one by one, everybody started going back to their real world. Rajkumar Dvij and Yugant were the only ones left. After discussing something in low voice with each other, even they made their way out of the tavern. And we followed them.

Oh, how I wish I could stab that son of Bastard Bihadratha. But the old imbecile had made it clear that we shall not use any weapons against them. But why not? This is as rare as it gets! Two young princes of the Akshobhyan Empire, all alone without any fancy army men to protect them, walking in the menacing street of Rajkot, where the indigenous people have committed some of the most horrific homicides in the past few weeks! No one would have even the slightest hint that it was our work. All would suspect the unethical and villainous people of Rajkot as the culprits. But only if there was a real brain inside his skull, rather than a huge pile of cow-dung. Well, maybe he had an intellectual reasoning of not slaying them tonight. But I doubt that we shall have a better opportunity than this.

The two men, instead of heading towards the palace directly, took us on a tour of the kingdom. Through the closed market place, they took us to hear the chirping of the crickets in the farms where the dew had deposited. And then back to the labyrinth of aisles of the upper-class residential area which only made it difficult for us because of the dozens of soldiers marching there to resist any violent uprising. I wish Kalki knew what was happening. I dare not state the reason they were making us chase them to him. But I let Nichakra know that this is not going to end well. Then just before exiting the labyrinth of aisles, they took a left from a house with a wall parameterized around it for protection which would make them invisible to us. We followed them, with me leading upfront. Just as I was about to take that left, a blade headed in my direction. If it wasn't for my quick reflex, it would have gone straight inside my eye sockets, rather than just bruising my temple. It was quite audacious of them to take on the three of us, alone. Quite foolish too. I know I wasn't obliged by Kalki to pick up weapons against them. But I'd be as unreasonable as that old imbecile if I don't even pick up my weapons in self-defence.

'No weapons!' shrieked Kalki.

But I wasn't going to let this chance pass by. I've been thirsty for their blood for so many years and tonight I shall quench my thirst with their blood. A man jumped on me slicing the air with his blade, throughout his reach. I ducked and rolled over to see that my opponent was Yugant Yasah himself.

From the corner of my eye, I saw Kalki defending himself from the rapid blows of Rajkumar Dvij. While Nichakra was nowhere to be seen. Now I had a small window of opportunity. The soldiers were marching just a few blocks away from the place where we were fighting. In no time, they will be here in subsequent numbers. So, I decided to finish this as fast as I could. I leaped in front, thrusting my blade in his direction. He tip-toed his way out of my reach and acrobatically rotated to gain momentum for his second attempt on me. But I wasn't that naïve. I grab hold of his wrist as he came down and kicked him in his chest, without letting him get out of my grip. His blade eventually dropped, but my hold on him didn't. I tried to knock him out by stamping his head with my knee, but he was resolute enough to resist my attack and glided his leg underneath me, making me fall on the ground and making him free of my grip. The black cloth which was concealing my identity came loose as I fell on the ground. Yugnat had a glimpse of my face, just for a moment, before I covered my face with it again. He collected his blade which had fallen a few feet away while I got back on my feet. I could hear the heavy approaching footsteps from the distance and knew that I had less time. As I tried to run towards my nemesis, two horses swept my way. It was Nichakra, sitting on one horse with Kalki in front of him lying almost unconscious while holding onto the reigns of the other horse.

'Get up. Now!' He yelled. I could now see the soldiers rushing towards our direction. The prince and his friend will live on to see a few more days. I jumped on my horse and we took off. Disappearing into the black of the night.

When we approached our old cottage, Kalki was unconscious. I hurried inside the cottage to set up the fire, while Nichakra carried Kalki inside. I could see his dreadful condition now. A blade, possibly of Rajkumar Dvij, was drawn into his chest and was still stuck inside him. Plenty of his blood was spilled and it was extremely horrifying to witness him in such an appalling state. I have been with Kalki and Nichakra for many years now. Over the years we fought against many brave soldiers with exceptional and admirable skills. Nichakra and I have shed a considerable amount of blood. But never have I ever seen Kalki getting, even touched, by his enemy's weapon, nevertheless shedding blood. His fighting skills were unmatched. Many eminent warriors of the greatest nations have fought against him. And not even once has he been defeated. He was the pinnacle of swordsmen ship and was equally good with arrows and spears. But tonight, he bled. He bled because he swore that he won't be picking up weapons against Rajkumar Dvij and Yugant Yasah, tonight. It was incredibly eerie to watch his invincible body bleed. Nichakra swiftly cleaned up his wound and applied proper ointments and medicines while I just stood there, dumbstruck. Watching his motionless body as Nichakra did his work. Was this the end? The end of Kalki?

'What... What is it? Looks like you've seen a ghost.' Kalki said with drowsy eyes as he started to regain his consciousness. I rushed to his side and held his hand.

'Why didn't you attack him? Why?' I asked while trying to control my tears.

'I promise you, Aatreyya. The next time I find myself in front of the Rajkumar, he shall die.' Saying this he closed his eyes and drew a peaceful smile on his face. Nichakra told me that Kalki needs rest and assured me that he will be fine.

The next day I woke up to Kalki's yelp. Nichakra was out, fetching water and that meant I had to attend Kalki, who was in visual pain. He was flexing his hurt muscles which was bound to cause him further distress. The man was resolute to get in fine fettle before the scheduled war on Chandragarh. I saw him outside, on the front porch, trying to wield his sword, which was a heavy one. But after several tries and painful screams he fell on his knees, panting. He threw his sword away in agitation which only caused him further pain. The wound was bound to take more time to heal. Doesn't the old imbecile understand this? He took a blade in his chest last night. How will he able to wield a sword perfectly in just one night? I approached him and told him the bitter truth he already knew. I took him inside and we waited for Nichakra.

Nichakra entered through the front door with an earthen pot. He knew something was grave when he saw us waiting for him.

'What happened?' He asked while placing the earthen pot next to the door. Water splashed out of the earthen pot in this process.

'Sit down, Nichakra. We need to talk.' Kalki said without making any eye contact with Nichakra.

Nichakra sat next to me and waited for Kalki to say something.

'What happened last night, was a mistake. A mistake whose price I shall pay. No matter how much I deny, we know that in my present condition, I can't go on the war against the Akshobhyas.'

Nichakra and I listened to him gravely.

'And therefore, I've decided. Nichakra, you shall go and meet the Shatabadas and represent me in the war.'

Nichakra was taken back as Kalki dumped this huge responsibility on him. But Nichakra was unwavering and determined to take on that challenge too. He accepted Kalki's proposal.

'You will be leaving tomorrow for the middle-east. Aatreyya and I will stay back here.'

The war was pivotal in our path to destroy the Akshobhyas. Years and Years of endurance and effort have led us to this. But now, that our last objective was just in the reach of our hands, Kalki's injury came to us like a blow. Nevertheless, we can't refrain from trying. Nichakra left to see the Shatabadas as a representative of Kalki the next day. While Kalki and I stayed back at the cottage until Kalki was fit enough. The next few weeks were monotonous for me and daunting for Kalki. While I had nothing much to do, all that Kalki did was to dwell on the apparent raging war in Chandragarh. I used to make frequent visits to the town, just to indulge in some activity other than watching Kalki fret all day. The news of the war in Chandragarh broke into Rajkot too. But that didn't influence Rajkumar Dvij's work at all. He stayed committed to his reformation work here in Rajkot while having the utmost belief in his folks at Chandragarh. As usual, he and Yugant carried out their investigation. But within 50 days of Nichakra's departure, a piece of appalling news swept my feet off the ground. I rushed back to the cottage and was scared to be the bearer of this bad news to Kalki.

'The war is lost.' I let it out in low voice.

'The Akshobhyas won. Chandragarh remains invincible.'

Kalki stepped out from the cottage and took a few steps in the woods. Eventually stopping and just staring into the depth of the woods. I knew this would be hard for him. He has been working to bring down the Akshobhyas for god knows how long. Maybe he was the child of the same past. The past that has ruined my and Nichakra's life too. Oh, Nichakra! God knows what happened to him. How bad I wish that he is alright. The news was that the allied forces suffered from heavy causalities. I hope he didn't... I hope he isn't...

'I knew this would happen.' Kalki said with his back on me.

'First, I didn't get them the ASI. Then they must have fretted when they didn't see me there. I should have gotten them the ASI!' He banged his fist into the bark of a tree and made a visible cicatrix.

I stood behind him, watching and wondering. Wondering what ASI was.

He stood there for about an hour, devastated.

The next morning, I was back in the town and found myself amidst a situation that was almost the same as the one that took place some months ago. The soldiers, in huge numbers, took on the streets again. But this time it wasn't the local men who were arrested, but the noblemen. Officials and ministers were taken into custody in huge numbers from their respective residences. The aisles were filled with soldiers marching to take the officials into their custody. Some resisted while some have already accepted their fate. From the gardens of the palace, Rajkumar Dvij could be seen with his hands on the startled Raja Samrendra. Accompanying them was Yugant Yasah, with a wide smile on his face. The Rajkumar and his friend had finally solved the case of the grand fraud. By the afternoon, a total of 22 accused ministers and officials were taken into custody with the charges of fraud and treason against the crown. In the evening an open assembly was organized by Rajkumar Dvij for the people of Rajkot, on the grounds of the palace. Yet again, people in thousand assembled near the palace grounds. The first to address the crowd was Raja Samrendra.

'The people of Rajkot. First of all, I would like to accept my mistake. I entrusted my men to such an extent that it led to the suffering of the people I care for the most that are you all. I would never even in the wildest of my dreams reckon to cause any distress to my people. When my father, Raja Rajendra, on his death bed entrusted me with the responsibility of serving you all I took it as my only ambition in life, and yet I failed to justify my father's words. To justify my ambition. I've failed my people. I've failed you as your king. I've failed you as a fellow resident of Rajkot. Before this deplorable turn of events, you knew me as a compassionate humanitarian because of my regular charity and donations. I was just continuing the tradition my father started. The tradition of favouring the wellbeing of my people above all. But that can't be treated as an excuse for the enormous negligence of duty depicted by me. To sum it all. I find myself irresponsible and incapable of administrating this beautiful and great city of Rajkot. And hereby, I step down from my position of the Raja of Rajkot.'

The whole crowd was sent in a state of shock. The honest words of Raja Samrendra filled with gratitude and apologies were enough for the people of Rajkot to forgive him yet he chose to step down from the responsibilities of a king. The crowd started chanting his name and praising his words and work, to show their support to the king and to show their disapproval to his resignation. The crowd continued to do the same for some time until Rajkumar Dvij took the stage to address the people.

'Honest and hardworking people of Rajkot. I, Dvij Akshobhya the firstborn of Maharaja Brihadratha Akshobhya, arrived here with my friend, Yugant Yasah, on the orders of my father and the king of Bharatvarsh! It was at first difficult to see the whole story when the fraud committing minsters tried to hide the main plot from us, just like they have been doing to you for the last two years. But sooner or later, the truth arrives. It arrives in its true glory and light and shoves the shadows of lies in the distant corner. The true luminous colours of the factual truth may seem to be altered or overcast by the black pitched lies and fiction, but give it a little effort and time for the black clouds to sweep away and you'll ultimately see all the colours of the truth-bearing rainbow. The 22 culprits have been punished. 16 of them have been sentenced to death and the rest are banished for life, not only from Rajkot but from all the boundaries of the Akshobhyan Empire.'

'Long live the prince!'

'Long live the prince!'

'More power to Akshobhyas!'

'More power to Akshobhyas!' The crowd grew wild with excitement.

'And now, about your Raja. A king can't be sentimental or naïve when the question of the administration of your people arises. What your king did was wrong and by no standards does it grace him. His negligence created a void in his responsibilities which has not only imposed questions about the state and working of Rajkot but that of the Akshobhyan Empire too. For this, he shall be punished.'

A dead silence surrounded the boundaries of the palace. Apart from the sound of the gusty wind, nothing else was heard. The silence grew darker and darker with every passing moment. The people were gasping with shock, while Raja Samrendra stood behind the crown prince of Chandragarh with his head bowed, waiting for his fate which he had already accepted.

'Seeing his love for his people and your love for him, by the powers bestowed in me by Maharaja Brihadratha, I appoint Raja Samrendra as your king again.' He looked at Raja Samrendra who was standing behind him and they both exchanged smiles. 'I understand that Raja Samrendra is filled with remorse and shame. And therefore, to right his wrong he shall work harder to win his people's trust again.'

The crowd started jumping in excitement and joy and Raja Samrendra, on his knees, bowed down to Rajkumar Dvij.

'Get up, Raja of Rajkot. Bowing down to a young man like me does not grace you at all.' He said with a saint's smile on his face. He hugged the remorseful king as the rest watched the excited crowd celebrate in the boundaries of the palace.

I came back to the cottage where I found Kalki wielding his sword like his own body's extension and broke the news to him. He continued ghost fighting with his sword while I watched him over, sitting on the front porch. The scene of Kalki wielding his sword was nothing less than a dazzling imperial experience. His moves with the sword would take anyone's breath away. He was a god, while he had a sword with him. I watched him elegantly swing his swords in fast rotations while his body moved swiftly accordingly. His long open grey hair fell on his face and his dense grey beard gave him a majestic look. His tall muscular physique tainted with that scar on his chest only added more royalty to him. For what I know, his body has been free from all the attacks that he bore in his lifetime, except the two. Both of them have left significant memories of them in the form of two scars. The fresh new scar on his chest and the burn scar which stretches from the bottom of his left ear to the bottom of his neck.

After being done with his practice he sat next to me, on the front porch, but we didn't say anything. We just stared into the depth of the forest and listened to those many species of birds making their way across the woods as the sun came down. A koyal bird sat on a nearby tree and began singing in her melodious voice which reminded me of the peaceful times while I was still living in Tosah. I closed my eyes and the spiritual journey begin. Her sweet voice was as peaceful as a morning flute being played by an artist while sitting in the farms of Tosah amidst all that freshly deposited dew. A smile spread on my dry face as I went reminiscing about the springtime in my village. My father and mother taking on the fields joyfully, while entrusting me to my elder siblings. I could feel the tranquillity and stillness that I used to feel while sitting on my mother's lap. No fret of the future. No regrets of the past. Just me, sitting in my mother's serene lap while she slowly caressed my hair with her soft hands. Slowly, I opened my eyes with the smile on my face only getting wider. I saw Kalki who was sitting expressionless and then shifted my eyes back on that Koyal. It flew away with the last rays of the sun. But just as the light of the sun vanished, the light of the forest emerged. The manifest charm of the forest became clearer as the dark woods got illuminated by hundreds of fireflies. Kalki reviled a hint of expression as he saw them adorning the forest with their yellow-green luminesce. I stood up from my place, amazed and radiant as the forest and took a few steps towards them to become one. To become one with the hundreds of fireflies. I stirred among them and started raising my head to watch them all and stopped when the exuberant silver of the moon fell on my rejuvenated soul.

Our 8 months stay in Rajkot was finally coming to an end. We were filled with remorse to our very core. Nichakra's absence added to my misery. Kalki too was seemingly affected by his absence, but years of wrath, salvation, loss, and struggle had made him adaptive to such emotional surges. Yes, our years of struggle resulted in a dead-end. But the only thing we should let our failures teach us is to pick ourselves up from the dusty terrains of defeat and to tackle our problems with more strength and vigour. Sure, the path isn't going to be all flowers and night angles, but that is something we gradually realize while walking on the ever-changing path. And we have been walking on the path for too long to just give in. Since the beginning, we knew that the path we chose wasn't going to be easy. But then again, who loves to accomplish an easy feat? We have bled and shed a lot of or blood and sweat to be where we are now. It's true, the gods have not been pleased with us for so long. They've watched us taste the dirt and maybe clapped when we tried to pick ourselves again and again only to find our nose getting rubbed in the dirt. But that can't be given as an excuse. For god only help those, who help themselves first. Maybe one day, the gods will be pleased. Until that day we, mere mortals, can only try. Yes, we can try. And that is one right that even the almighty can't deprive us of.

Kalki is the most resolute and undaunted man I've come across in my life. He didn't let our great loss get over his ambition. He immediately worked on another scheme and I was going to be a major part of it.

Kalki and I left Rajkot, a little before Rajkumar Dvij and Yugant Yasah. We travelled together till Ujjain where Kalki initiated the first stage of our next scheme. From Ujjain, our paths split up. I took the route to Tamralipti via Sachi to recreate somewhat similar tensions as we did in Rajkot. While Kalki headed towards Indraprastha to talk with the neighbouring rulers of Meerut, Bairath, Topra, and Mathura. It was just the beginning. The beginning of the second great war between the allied forces and the Akshobhyas.

PART 3

Past

'Is he going to come, Mahamantri?'

'Of course, he is.'

'Maybe he was being followed and decided otherwise.'

'Let's just wait a little longer, Yuvan. He will be here.'

It was raining quite heavily tonight. I, personally, never was fascinated by the reinvigorating charm of these rains. I think of them as a poignant reminder by Lord Indra of the many tragedies one has suffered from and the misfortune that followed next. In my childhood, whenever it used to rain, I would be overwhelmed by a deep feeling of grief and sorrow and would usually lock myself in the house. Something just didn't feel right about those memories encapsulated in the falling drops of rain. I would look outside from my window and see those black clouds, above those many quivering trees of the forest dancing with the rapid wind, overtake the bright blue sky slowly. Those clouds would surround me with melancholy just as they would surround the bright sun, which won't seem bright anymore. Such desolation followed me in my adulthood too. These raindrops weren't mere water drops. But individual mirrors. Which reflects individual horrors of the past. Which reflects all the wrong decisions one has taken in his or her obnoxious past. Some say, that the only charm of the past is that it is in the past. But I don't keep the same perspective on this particular topic. I think there is no charm of a rather obnoxious past. The foul memories of the bygone take a void corner in the back of our minds. For me, they show up every time I look at the rain. For some when they see a vague representation of something which would remind them of it. Some are fighting from it every day. Some have already given up.

I peeked outside from one of the ill-formed windows of this cave and saw, vaguely, a rider approaching on his horse from the distance. Just as he arrived at the nearest corner a bolt of lightning struck and his horse, appalled, jumped and neighed. Some pebbles crumbled into the chasm as the horse edged towards the boundary, still on his hind limbs. Nevertheless, the rider gained control of it and continued. Mahamantri heard him from outside, tying his horse and rushed towards the entrance with a lamp in his hand. The gentle rain had turned into a storm.

'Come inside, quickly!' He yelled while illuminating the small staircase, carved from the rocks of the very cave we were in, with his lamp.

The rider came inside, exhausted, and drenched. He was dripping everywhere as he strolled around in the small cave, panting, trying to control his asynchronous heavy breathing. We gave him a minute or two to catch his breath while Mahamantri looked on to him anxiously.

'I am… too old… for this.' He said while still trying to catch his breath. Just when he was about to remove the wet black cloth covering his face, his eyes fell on me.

'Who is he?' He asked Mahamantri Brahmanand curiously.

Mahamantri brought the lamp near to my face. I could sense the heat coming out from it.

'Yashvasin Yuvan. He is my disciple.'

I bowed my head a little in front of him and offered him a brief smile.

The drenched man nodded and removed the wet black cloth covering his face.

He was Prakrant. A secret spy of Mahamantri Brahmanand. He has been in his service for the last 20 years and has been carrying out missions containing high risks for almost the same time. His job usually involved spying some enemy kingdoms and collecting information of any sense that the Mahamantri desired. Prakrant contacted the Mahamantri three weeks ago, asking him to come down in confidence. He has been able to trace a piece of evidence from the recent great war of Chandragarh, which reflects the involvement of one of our very own people, but from the side of the allied armies. Surely it was a grave matter. A matter in which he asked for my appropriate contribution. Because it was a case of national security, no one else was told about this. It was just another field trip for Mahamantri Brahmanand. Just another meeting for him with one of his spies from a multitudinous lot.

'So what is it?' A curious Mahamantri asked.

'An evidence, like I told you before.' Prakrant replied.

'Oh, don't be naïve! What kind of evidence?'

Prakrant went over his satchels, running his hands over half a dozen of them. From one of them, he took out a piece of papyrus and handled it to the Mahamantri. The papyrus was moist from the edges, the effect of the rain.

'I received it from a man who was associated with a commander involved in the latest great war of Chandragarh. He knew the commanding general of the Rudras, one of the three allied forces, as you know.' Prakrant started spilling out the details. 'Now to non-peculiar eyes, it would seem rather a normal message, sent from one allied army to another. But look for the stamp, Mahamantri, if you will. Yes, on the back.'

Mahamantri turned the papyrus around and was shocked to see what was in front of him. An indigenous Akshobhyan stamp.

'The moment I saw it, I was more than assured that one of the members, not an ordinary but an esteemed one having his stamp, was responsible for selling out the details of our army to the enemy. And that is why I contacted you, Mahamantri.' Prakrant said.

Mahamantri handled me the lamp. He brought the papyrus in front of the lamp and started examining the stamp. After carefully running his eyes over it, the solemnity of his eyes, intensified.

'And when you match the content of the message with the stamp, you would know what kind of peril that man was trying to put the city of Chandragarh in. Selling out the information regarding the statistics of our infantry, horseman, and other such things that you would find mentioned in the papyrus.'

Turbulence could be seen in Mahamantri's countenance. He tried to wave that circle of confusion away.

'Is there anything else, Prakrant?' He asked.

'That is it, sir.'

'Very well, then. You may leave now. I am sure you are a busy man.' He said while turning around with his eyes fixed on the stamp.

'Actually, there is one other thing I wanted to discuss with you, Mahamantri' Prakrant said with a nervous smile on his face. He waited for Mahamantri to turn around before continuing. 'You are familiar with my situation, Mahamantri. I have been doing this for you for a very long time now. When I was young, spying on the enemy kingdoms and fleeing when getting caught, in short, putting my life in danger used to be simple and, quite honestly, painless for me. I used to live for these extravagant challenges. But I am getting too old for the field job. It pains me to the core sometimes. Moreover, my wife, Mahamantri. You have met her. She is not so pleased with this job of mine. She constantly asks, alright alright, she constantly shouts at me to take up another job. A job which would pay me more. You see, Mahamantri, she is a family-oriented woman. Even after having our 7th child together last year, she demands more. This is it Mahamantri. I would be pleased if you will look into my matter. A desk job, maybe. Something with the army which would pay more. For all the people, you are most familiar with my capabilities and capacity. If you would please.'

Mahamantri and I exchanged looks. I tried to control my laughter behind the lamp. Prakrant was standing in front of us bearing an awkward smile and rubbing his hands together, juggling his eyes between me and Mahamantri Brahmanand.

'Alright. I will do something.' Mahamantri said.

'Very well, sir. Very well.' Prakrant could not hide his wide smile.

'You should go now. I will call for you.'

Prakrant followed Mahamantri's instructions and took off. But not before covering his face again. I watched him go through the door and then him jumping on his horse through the window. Another lightning struck as he pulled the reins of his horse. The horse picked up pace instantly and just like that, they disappeared into the dark of the night.

I turned towards Mahamantri Brahmanand, not seeing the confusion in his eyes.

'A very fine character you have as a spy, Mahamantri.'

He didn't give much attention to my words. It was then that I remember his change in expression while looking at the stamp carefully, earlier. I saw his eyebrows getting crossed with the same uncertainty.

'Whose stamp it is?' I asked curiously.

'Why do you think that I would know that, Yuvan?' The Mahamantri folded his hands behind his back and looked up to me in a rather compelling way. It seemed like he was taking a test of my skills and my sense.

'That's quite clear, isn't it? I perceived the slight, not very much indeed, change in your expression, Mahamantri, which would consist of lowering of your eyebrows and widening of your eyes when you looked at the stamp carefully. And it took you some time, which means you were recollecting whose stamp it must be and then it just hit to you. Moreover, it has been some time, but it wasn't long enough, maybe 12 years back, when you used to assign the stamps to the officials if I am not wrong. That would also mean someone eminent, of immense importance, must be the one who shared that particular piece of information with the Rudras.' Mahamantri was quite impressed with my answer. 'That being said, I would never force you, Mahamantri, to share any secrets with me. It eventually comes down to trust, isn't it?'

'You know I trust you, Yuvan. That is the main reason why you are here with me.' He said with a smile. 'And yes, I know whose stamp it is. Because I assigned it.' Mahamantri's expression changed once again as he took a deep breath. 'Let me ask you another question, Yuvan. You do know that Maharaja Brihadratha always consults me before making a decision, right? And that he always takes my advice?'

'Yes, I do.'

'Well, that has not always been the case, you see. There have been instances, two instances to be precise, where our Maharaja went against my advice. And both of them dealt with the appointment of two important officers in charge.'

'Mahamatya Acala and Nrchakshu, if I am not wrong, Mahamantri.' I said with a quick flow.

'Yes. You are correct. I advised Maharaja Brihadratha, not to appoint Nrchakshu as the head of his angrakshak panel because of his past. And you are familiar with his history. Not the fabricated one, but his real past. You can understand what influenced my decision, can't you?'

'I can very well, sir.'

'With my years of experience, it becomes necessary for one to judge people according to their past, Yuvan. Every individual gets affected by his past one time or another. No one can escape from its menacing grip in which it holds the individual. One way or another, his actions always get influenced by his history. The same reason why I advised Maharaja not to appoint Acala as the Mahamatya.'

'Is the stamp…?'

'Yes. The stamp belongs to Acala.'

'But why will he do such a thing, Mahamantri Brahmanand? The king trusts him the most. How can one become so devious that making the person who trusts them and puts his belief in them, hurt and vulnerable doesn't affect one's self-being? How can someone be so heartless?' I asked the Mahamantri in dismay.

'Past, Yuvan. In one way or another. Every individual's actions are affected by his past.'

'I am sorry, Mahamantri. But can I ask you about the seemingly bitter truth about the Mahamatya's past that is so affecting his decisions.' I asked.

Mahamantri Brahmanand walked away from the light of the lamp, towards the window and gazed at a tree that had fallen because of the storm.

'What do you think Acala used to do before he was appointed the finance minister of the state?' Mahamantri Brahmanand asked in a grave voice.

'I am not sure, sir. I never was fascinated by Mahamatya's past. I never felt the need to know about his past. But I've heard some rumours. And I found these rumours to be not true.'

Mahamantri turned around and confused me with his smirk.

'The rumours are true. He was a criminal.'

I was staggered by Mahamantri's particular answer.

'I don't get it. How can he be a criminal? He is one of the most prestigious members of the Akshobhyan Empire. I just can't find a link here.'

'It is true, Yuvan. In his younger years, Acala was a criminal. He used to commit fraud and was as avaricious as one can be. From committing pity fraud to making major changes in the financial records kept by Chandragarh's finance office, he has done it all. And all for his lust for gold.'

I was getting confused, trying to match Mahamatya Acala's past self with his present self. There was no connection at all. One of the eminent members of Akshobhyan Empire, a person who manages financial records of not only the state but of all the kingdoms coming under the stretch was a criminal? It was making no sense.

'Then, Mahamatya....' I asked inquisitively. '.... How can a criminal become the finance minister of the most powerful Empire in the whole 'Bharatvarsh'?'

'That is where our King comes in. You see, Acala is a very intelligent man. Yes, that I give to him. His charm, charisma, and his ability to answer with quick and inventive verbal humour outsmarts everyone in Chandragarh. And, one can't deny his ability with numbers and his knowledge about finance. Even back in those days. Yes. A young Maharaja Brihadratha was astounded with his skills. And when the notorious Acala was brought for trial in front of him, the latter impressed Maharaja with his gratified aura. Moreover, it is not that easy to change the statistics in the financial records of Chandragarh in such a way that it goes unnoticed for the whole year. Maharaja Brihadratha, ergo, set him free and also proposed to him. To be the finance minister of the state. And so, he agreed. For who won't want to change his lifestyle in such an extravagant way?'

'But why now, Mahamantri? When he had left his previous lifestyle for good, why to touch that part of the past?'

'As I said, Yuvan. I never trusted him. Neither do I trust him now. No gluttonous slob can win my trust. People like him won't refrain from selling their soul for a few sacks of gold. No wonder he sold such confidential information.'

'I reckon someone else must have used his stamp, to frame him, isn't that a possibility?'

'And that is why we can't tell anyone about this.'

'Does that mean there is still some doubt in your mind regarding Mahamatya's involvement in this subject?'

'No, Yuvan. Not at all. I am all but sure that this is the work of that avaricious Acala. But if we take this case in front of Maharaja Brihadratha now, he would dismiss it by stating the same reason. For he can never accuse Acala of anything this grave. We will need more evidence. Some serious evidence which will all but prove his treacherous intensity. Moreover, don't forget that before he became the Mahamatya, he was a criminal who successfully altered the statistics of the financial records of Chandragarh. Now that he is a Mahamatya, the possibility of him doing the same again can't be ruled out. He can't be trusted anymore. We need to do something. And fast.'

I agreed with Mahamatya. Someone of such calibre and intensions can be very threatening for the state.

'What shall we do now?' I looked at Mahamantri who was shaking his head.

'We can just wait. And hope that a spy of mine comes up with another evidence. Because I have been keeping an eye on Acala's work and till now he has never provided a loophole for me.'

I nodded. A huge gust of wind entered the cave, forcing the light of the lamp to flicker.

'We should go now, Yuvan. This thunderstorm may grow more violent.'

I saw the Mahamantri tuck the papyrus in his waist cloth as we made our way to the palace through a secret tunnel in the cave.

❖

INVITATION.

A soldier approached me while I was in the weaponry chambers talking to a bladesmith regarding the finesse on my new sword. He came up with a message. A message from Maharaja Brihadratha. He has asked for an emergency meeting and so I rushed towards the royal assembly room. When I reached the room, I saw Maharaja Brihadratha sitting on his throne talking to Rajkumar Dvij and Yugant whereas Mahapradhan Ganakarta and Mahamatya Acala were busy in a discussion. After a few moments, Senapati Aagney also arrived, accompanying Mahamantri Brahmanand. When Maharaja Brihadratha noticed that everyone, he asked for was present in the assembly room, he ordered the doors of the assembly room to be closed. It was clear that something of immense importance was to be discussed today. I greeted the Mahamantri and Mahapradhan as I walked towards Senapati Aagney.

'Any idea. Sir?' I asked him in a low voice.

'None. I am in for a surprise too.'

The Maharaja rose from his throne and addressed the small group assembled in front.

'Gentleman, as you can see that you are surrounded by the most important people of Chandragarh, you might have concluded that something of paramount importance is to be discussed here. Important on not will be seen during this assembly meeting. I called for this assembly today at the request of my two young boys. Dvij and Yugant. They have briefly discussed with me their series of anecdotes that took place while they were in Rajkot, working on the reformation of the provincial capital of Saurashtra. I found it rather intriguing and ergo asked for your presence immediately. It is a subject of National security and so I would like you all to present your views on the topic. Now, I will let Dvij and Yugant explain the rest.' Maharaja Brihadratha concluded while gesturing Yugant to take the lead.

'Important people of Chandragarh, when Dvij and I were ordered to travel to the western extent of the Empire we took the orders head-on. But we have to say that the reformation of the provincial capital of Saurashtra was no easy task. The kingdom of Rajkot was in peril and its condition worsened beyond the wildest dreams of Dvij's and mine. The officials of the Kingdom were in constant danger of getting slayed by a group of vigilantes. Before, we arrived 4 of them have been kidnapped. Two of them were released but not before getting tormented. The other two were butchered and their disfigured bodies were thrown in the aisles leading to their respective residences. Soldiers were set ablaze during bright daylight and many ministers were chased with weapons stolen from the palace. Such was the condition of Rajkot when we arrived there. Quite clearly, it required a total reformation. And so, we did. We investigated through and through. We questioned many officials who suffered from the hands of the vigilantes and residents who suffered from the frauds of the corrupt officials. And after we got to the bottom of the case, we successfully carried out trials and punished the culprits.'

'Yes, son. We all know that and we are proud of you two for what you both did in Rajkot. But what's so uncanny about that?' asked the Mahapradhana in his broken voice. Yugant nodded before continuing again.

'When we were investigating the matter, we asked certain questions with one of the survivors of the abduction carried out by the vigilantes. He was the Pattanadhyaksha of Rajkot, Nrrat. He was beaten to a pulp by one of the vicious members of the vigilante group. When we questioned, he provided us with some detailed information, as we expected. The details included the identity of the people who abducted him. There were a couple of young men whom we punished afterwards. But there were two more, three acttually.'

'What do you mean, Yugant?' An inquisitive Senapati Aagneya asked.

'Apparently, there were three men, not indigenous to Rajkot, who were influencing the youth of Rajkot, into adapting a violent touch in their revolt against the palace. Two of them abducted the officials while the third, their leader was away. And the name of their leader was Kalki.'

I noticed something strange about Mahamatya Acala who was taken back a little when he heard the name Kalki. I looked at Mahamantri Brahmanand who was already looking at me. I gestured him towards Mahamatya Acala and he nodded back as an acknowledgement.

'And one late night, when we were returning to the palace after touring Rajkot in disguise the whole day, we were followed by three men, who most probably were the same mentioned. We couldn't see their faces as they were covered. We attacked them the same night. Dvij was able to severely injure one of them before they fled. Now we didn't give much importance to this cause. We thought of them as just another pity vigilante group even though Nrrat cared to mention that these outsiders were no mere simple players but experienced ones. It was last month when in an assembly meeting another uprising was talked about, in Tamralipti. I discussed the possibility of it being the work of the same men with Dvij. We started to think about it gravely and eventually decided to disclose the matter. This is the case, ministers and officials. We think of it as a big case that requires your significant reasoning and advice.' A moment of silence followed after Yugant concluded his speech. Maharaja Brihadratha was the one who broke the silence.

'Is this to be taken gravely?'

Mahamatya Acala was the first to speak.

'I have a question, my prince.'

Rajkumar Dvij stepped forward and gave a nod.

'You said one of them was severely injured. Severe enough to assume his death?'

'I won't say that, Mahamatya. He was a very strong man, physically. Even though he took my blade right into his chest, for a man of that constitution, I don't think that would have proved fatal for him.' The crown prince replied.

'Well, anyway, I think this isn't a grave situation after all. Maybe another small group, like many others the Akshobhyan history has witnessed. If Maharaja Brihadratha wants, he could send a message to the Raja of Tamralipti for better administration or a warning letter, perhaps. Warning them about the potential danger. But I don't see a reason for focusing our attention over there when we have a lot on our plate already.'

Everyone was astounded after listening to Mahamatya's such an honest and straight forward view on the subject.

'I think otherwise.' Said Mahamantri Brahmanand from the back. 'If the two princes reckon it as a grave matter, it shall be. No one doubts Rajkumar Dvij and Yugant's calibre. We are all familiar with their qualities. There isn't one that they meagre in. I think we should take appropriate actions against the matter. Maybe by sending a special task force to Tamralipti.'

Everyone provided their views on the subject. In one way or another, everyone rooted for Mahamantri Brahmanand's opinion.

'What about you, Yuvan? What's your say in this?' The Maharaja asked.

'I share the same opinion as the Mahamatya's, Maharaja. We can't be sure of taking major steps. From what we know they can be a small uprising. Maybe they aren't. But for that, we don't have much information. Warning the Raja of Tamralipti seems to be the most appropriate suggestion that I can provide you now.'

Maharaja ran his fingers on his bushy beard as he indulged himself in grave thinking.

'It is true that we can't be sure of their numbers or intensity because we don't have much information. Maybe the uprising in Tamralipti was the work of someone else. Moreover, the conditions in Tamralipti now are unobjectionable. Even in the time of consequence, their conditions weren't as profound as Rajkot's. It isn't a question about Dvij's and Yuvan's calibre, but the details we have now. Mahamantri Brahmanand, maybe you can ask one of your men to get some information regarding the same. Till then, a warning letter, maybe, will be enough. I'll send one right away.'

Saying this he caressed Rajkumar Dvij's and Yugant's back. After the meeting was recorded and submitted in papyrus to Mahamantri Brahmanad. He kept the record in the cupboard, following the regular procedure. After the assembly was concluded, Maharaja Brihadratha asked for the doors to be opened.

'That's three now, Mahamantri.' I whispered to Mahamantri Brahmanand with light humour.

'Oh shut up, Yuvan. You knew I wasn't giving him an honest answer. I wanted to check Acala's actions and reactions.'

I acknowledged him with a light smile.

'Moreover, our King isn't naïve as the Raja of Rajkot. We provide him with suggestions and advice. Eventually, it's his mind and calibre that does the sorting. There was no possibility of him going on with the advice I provided.'

'Quite right, sir.'

Everyone assembled in the room apart from the royal blood and Yugant, headed towards the opening door. When the doors were completely ajar, we found a soldier standing there. He must be waiting there for the doors to be opened. With a clearer view, I was able to see that the soldier was Nrchakshu. Senapati Aagney was the first to head towards the exit and from a distance addressed Nrchakshu.

'A little late for the assembly meeting, are we?' He said.

'I wasn't invited to the assembly meeting, Senapati.' A calm Nrchakshu replied.

'Oh, isn't that disappointing?' I launched a taunt at him.

Nrchakshu replied with a smile. I smiled back.

'Well, if you will, gentlemen, I would like you to wait for a little.'

'And why is that?' I asked him.

'Just humour me, sir.'

'Aren't you a little down posted for us to humour you?' I tried to provoke him again. But he remained undisturbed and maintained his composure. Maharaja Brihadratha, who was talking to Rajkumar Dvij and Yugant Yasah while sitting on his throne, noticed the little skirmish between me and Nrchakshu and called for the latter.

'What is it, Nrchakshu? I reckon I told you to provide your expertise in training the recruits today. What are you doing here?' He asked in a loud voice.

'I have a message for you, Maharaja. It's from Maharani Drisana.'

'What message?'

'She has asked for your presence in the royal hall, sir.'

'Very well. I'll be there in a moment.'

'She has also asked for the presence of these gentlemen, Maharaja. She seemed quite excited.' Nrchakshu said.

'Well, courtiers, it looks like you have to attend another meeting. It's going to be a busy morning' Saying this he burst into a round of laughter.

We all followed Maharaja Brihadratha to the royal hall where Maharani Drisana was already waiting with the young Rajkumar Adhirohah. Rajkumar Adhirohah rushed towards Rajkumar Dvij and Yugant and stood beside them cheerfully. Maharani Drisana was ecstatic and had a scroll in her hand. The edges of the scroll were decorated with fine gold threads and so we knew that a message from a prestigious kingdom has been received by the Maharani. She walked towards Maharaja Brihadratha's side and handed him over the scroll. The Maharaja commenced reading the scroll. By the time he was done reading, a broad smile covered his face.

'What is this message which has brought delight and radiance to the king and queen of Chandragarh?' Mahapradhan Ganakarta asked with light humour.

'It is an invitation.' Maharaja Brihadratha said with his eyes still fixated on the golden edged scroll. He commenced reading, for us, from it.

'Maharaja Drshkrit, the Maharaja of Indraprastha, solemnly invites the Royal Akshobhyan family to celebrate the festival of Janmashthmi in the colours of Indraprastha.' He took a pause and his smile widened before he resumed reading again. 'Maharani Aarunya and Maharaja Drshkit will be waiting for your arrival.'

The mention of Maharani Aarunya's name was enough to fill the heart of the little prince with a beam of joy. He started jumping around the Maharaja and Maharani. Rajkumar Dvij and Yugant too felt the exhilaration of the invitation. After all, she was their sister. Everybody else's face lit up as they listened to Maharani and the Maharaja with rapture. There was no end to Maharaja's happiness. And so was reflecting from his broad smile.

'And that is why I've asked for your presence, ministers.' Maharani

Drisana turned towards us. 'It's up to you now to convince your Maharaja to take some time off to visit her daughter's in-laws.'

Maharaja's eyes, which were still fixated on the scroll, lost their charm and radiance as Maharani's words fell on his ears. The joyous smile on his face diminished, slowly, into nothingness. A surge of anxiety fell over Maharani Drisana as she saw Maharaja Brihadratha's radiant expressions abate.

We all understood the graveness of the predicament and asked for the Maharaja's permission to leave. Except for the royal family, everybody left the royal hall. Nrchakshu and I were the last to leave.

'You are deluded, do you know that?' I said to him softly. He gave me an inquisitive look as I swiftly went past him. It wasn't long enough until he caught me in the corridors of the palace. He stopped me by pulling me by my arm. As I turned around, with the same hand, I removed my sword from the sheath and placed it on his throat.

'Beware, soldier! Even the Maharaja won't come to your aid if you go on shoving your seniors.' I said with a roar. The empty corridors echoed with my voice as I stayed there placing my sharp-edged sword on Nrchakshu's throat. A drop of his blood oozed out and started ascending down his neck. After seeing much apprehension in his eyes I shoved him back. I watched him grab his throat as I slid my sword back into the sheath. I turned around and continued walking down the empty corridors.

'STOP!' he yelled. But I didn't. I continued walking without looking back. It was the first time that I've witnessed Nrchakshu pass his emotional threshold. I wanted to have more fun. I heard his fast-approaching footsteps and was waiting for him to do something foolish but he went past me only to stop and turned around. I stopped to listen to his words.

'Why? Why do you always do this to me? I've never, even once, quarreled with you. Dam! I've never even had a real conversation with you!'

I smirked and continued walking only to be stopped again.

'No! You have got to answer! Why am I deluded? Why can't I properly serve our Maharaja? Why am I not capable? Why do you do this to me?'

I walked slowly towards him and stopped just a foot before him. I bend forward and whispered in his ears.

'You will know. Soon.'

He bowed his head in dissatisfaction while I stepped back to assume my previous position.

'Now, if you will step aside. I have got a lot on my plate.' I said as I walked past him.

In the evening I was in the company of Senapati Aagney when again we were asked to assemble in the assembly room. We reckoned it was regarding the invitation. Scheduling the voyage of the royal family from Chandragarh to Indraprastha, perhaps. When we got there, we saw the same faces that we saw in the morning in the assembly room with an inclusion of Nrchakhsu. He didn't face me at all during the passage of the meeting.

Maharaja Brihadratha stepped down from his throne to address us once again.

'This assembly meeting is regarding the journey of the royal family to Indraprastha. And I reckon that you all had a subtle hint that I won't be travelling to Indraprastha. As decided, Maharani Drisana, Dvij, Adhirohah, and Yugant will be travelling. Senapati Aagney, I would like you to develop a strong defensive scheme for their travel with the consultation of Yuvan, of course. Nrchakshu and his brave aangrakshak panel will be accompanying the royal family. Mahamantri Brahmanand and Mahapradhan Ganakarta, you both should come up with an optimized route well within the boundaries of our Empire. As we all know that the path to Indraprastha lies outside our boundaries. It will be best to come up with a route either inside our boundaries or within our allies' boundaries.' He took a pause and looked at us all.

'Even a single error or the slightest of oversight in the plans will not be tolerated by me. You all have one week until Maharani Drisana departs with our sons for the Janmashthmi festival in Indraprastha.'

Maharaja Brihadratha was very serious about this matter. And why should he not be? After all, it's the Royal Akshobhyan Family, we're talking about.

❖

Departure

All the preparations for the royal family's journey to Indraprastha were done. I and Senapati Aagney took care of the defence personals to be escorting the royal family while Mahapradhan Ganakarta and Mahamantri Brahmanand came up with a safe route to Indraprastha.

I walked down the palace entrance stairs and saw hundreds of palanquins, embellished with red silk, placed on the palace grounds with thousands of palanquins holders standing beside them. They were accompanied by hundreds of horsemen and thousands of soldiers with dozens of flag bearers. Although, the security of such a degree wasn't necessarily required. The path to Indraprastha was mostly to be covered on the grounds of the Akshobhayan Empire, with halts in Mathura and Bairath. From Bairath they should enter directly into the Kuru Kingdom. The Kuru Kingdom is the paramount ally of the Akshobhyan Empire. It was the army of Indraprastha that provided crucial support to Chandragarh when the Askhobhyan capital found itself in peril against the attack of Maharaja Durajaya of Tamralipti in the absence of Samrat Adhirohah. Hence, it won't be wrong to say that the relation of the Kuru Kingdom and the Akshobhyas goes a long way back. This alliance has only strengthened with time. And with Rajkumari Aarunya's wedding with Maharaja Drshkrit of Kuru two years ago the relation has built up even more. They weren't mere allies now, but families. Good relations between the Kurus and the nemesis of Akshobhyas, Varunyas, and Advaityas, didn't tarnish the shimmering relation between the two. An alliance was indeed set up between the Akshobhyas and their nemesis Varunyas and Advaityas decades ago, the effect of the long war which cost both the sides much loss of men. But hostility and bitterness among the kingdoms remained unchanged. The Kurus were tied with the Varunyas and Advaityas with historical relationships among the members of the respective royal families. And now they were tied with the Akshobhyas with a similar bond.

I accompanied Senapati Aagney to the palace grounds where we found Mahamatya Acala and Mahapradhan Ganakarta waiting for the royal family. When I stood there and gazed at the palace grounds, it was like seeing a small army. Such was the strength of the soldiers accompanying Maharani Drisana and her sons. But it wasn't much of a surprise though. After all, it's the Akshobhyan family. The small army was scheduled to take at least two weeks to reach the summit with the royal family. We all stood there amidst the morning wind blowing mildly in Chandragarh, for a few moments until the Royal family finally arrived. Rajkumar Adhirohah came running down the stairs and chasing him was Yugant. Maharaja Brihadratha accompanied Maharani Drisana and Rajkumar Dvij to the palace ground. The high priest of the temple of Lord Rama near the Ganani River was called upon to bless the family on their journey. He asked the gods to invoke happiness and health to the Royal family by conducting a small havan. After the havan was concluded, the Rajkumars took their parent's blessings. Maharaja bid goodbye to his sons and the Maharani as Maharani's female companions begin ascending into the palanquins. Rajkumar Dvij and Yugant were brought their horses. Maharaja Brihadratha walked with the Maharani and young prince Adhirohah to their palanquins personally. Nrchakshu was leading the soldiers up front. The rest of the aangrakshaks panel surrounded the Maharani's palanquins. On the sound of the conch blown by the high priest, the palanquins were lifted and soldiers assumed the attention position.

I looked at Maharaja Brihadratha and noticed his expressions which weren't profound. Even though his first obligation is towards his kingdom, which requires him to rise above his sentiments and emotion, it doesn't mean that he has become free from all the enticements of life. A definite pain is bound to be perceived by the mortal human body at the time of detachment from one's family. Even though Maharaja remained expressionless except for a smile surfing on his face time to time, I could sense a deep melancholy from his eyes which were already awaiting his sons' arrival.

Nrchakshu screamed instructions from the front and the army changed positions. Finally, they commenced their journey to the capital of the Kuru kingdom. Rajkumar Adhirohah glanced from the curtains of his palanquin and waved in our direction. The joyful prince too realized the soreness of bidding farewell. Even though it was only for a few weeks, the agony could be seen on his face. But he was sure to swerve all these feelings once he reached Indraprastha and meet his sister. Rajkumar Dvij and Yugant were still standing beside us with their horses. Maharaja held their hands and wished them luck.

'Take care of your Maharani and your little brother.' The Maharaja said while letting go of their hands. Both of them nodded and took Maharaja's blessing again one last time. After that, they jumped on their horses and pulled the reins to join the rest who were now exiting from the palace gates. From either side, flowers were being thrown at the palanquins as they made their way to the massive crowd of Chandragarh awaiting them outside the palace gates. Praises of the Maharani and the Akshobhyan royal family could be heard even from the inside. We all stood there behind the Maharaja as he saw the end of the small battalion exit from the palace gates. The gates were eventually closed but the crowd outside was still erupting. They were showering the palanquins with flowers, blessings, and praises. Mahapradhan, Mahamantri, Senapati, and I retreated inside the palace but the Maharaja stood there for a little longer.

The next few days were monotonous. There was nothing much to do. I proposed a hunting trip to Senapati Aagney, but he rejected it, saying he was too busy to squander off the time. That man should learn the importance of enforced leisure. With nothing much to do, I decided to train with the soldiers in the local akhadas which were adjacent to the palace. The soldiers were astounded to see me train with them in the akhadas instead of the royal practice arena. They greeted me as a hero as I walked through them. It was quite nice of them to do so. One by one I took on some soldiers. The rest of them encircled the arena in huge numbers, cheering and chanting. It was fun to test the strength of the soldiers of the Akshobhyan army. They were not easy to fight which was making it more riveting for me. Moreover, their constant cheering of my name made me feel special. Even though I have fought a lot of battles with these men and have remained in their company even outside the battlefield, but practicing with them was as rare as it gets. Maybe I should do this more often. It's fun after all and good for their morale. But after taking on six of them a young boy, a messenger, came running from the palace. He pushed the encircling crowd to make his way.

He was panting when he reached the circumference of the akhada. Everyone looked at him as he stood there trying to catch his breath.

'What's the hurry?' I asked him in a grave voice.

'Mahamantri… Mahamantri Brahmanand' He said in a breaking voice, still trying to catch his breath. I let him breathe whilst wiping the sweat off my body with a cloth. After being the subject of laughter for a few minutes he finally spoke clearly.

'Mahamantri Brahmanand is looking for you. He looked both excited and anxious. He has called for other people too. You should come.'

After drinking plenty of water from the water bag I left the company of the soldiers and followed the messenger to the palace. The soldiers invited me to join them again tomorrow morning as I walked past them. Such an invitation from the people who love you is enticing. But my mind was now focused on the grave situation that awaits me inside. Mahamantri Brahmanand was looking for me in a haste. This can't be good. I took slow steps while climbing the palace stairway. The guard in the front walked towards me and told me that a meeting was called for in the assembly room and my presence was required there. Even though it was another of those emergency assembly meeting consisting of the eminent people of Akshobhyas, I didn't feel like rushing to the assembly room at all. Instead, I strolled towards the destination. My heart was beating fast and drops of sweat rolled all over my body. I saw to it that it took me the longest to reach the enormous closed gates of the assembly room, but I eventually found myself waiting in front of those closed gates. I looked at those two gigantic doors adorned by a collage of paintings depicting a bloody war scene. Half dozens of chariots and dozens of horses with hundreds of men thirsty for each other's blood. The scene was quite appalling for anyone. But I was feeling the intensity of the illustration, in front of me, deeper than ever, even though I've walked past these doors multitudinous times.

The doors were pushed open for me and as they were opened, I could see one by one the same people which were present at the very same spot a couple of weeks ago with, of course, the absence of Rajkumar Dvij and Yugant Yasah. Their respective positions were changed. Maharaja Brihadratha was sitting, as usual on his throne, while below him, beneath the small staircase, stood

Mahamatya Acala, Mahapradhan Ganakarta and Senapati Aagney. All of them were facing Mahamantri Brahmanand who looked like giving a presentation.

'So you're finally here, Yuvan.' The Maharaja said. 'What were you doing? Our men rummage the entire palace, but couldn't find you.'

'Was just trying to lift the morale of our soldiers, sir, by practicing with them at the local akhadas.' I said politely as I made my way inside the assembly room.

'That is very courteous of you, Yuvan.' He said. 'Come on now. Mahamantri Brahmanad has something important to tell.'

I walked past the Mahamantri and stood beside Senapati Aagney. Mahamantri looked tensed and restless. Surely something important was to be discussed today. You don't see the Mahamantri all anxious and appealing every day.

'This is very grave, Maharaja Brihadratha. Very grave.' He commenced in his old heavy voice.

'We are all listening, Mahamantri. Please continue.' The Maharaja said.

'I am afraid, sir. But Rajkumar Dvij and Yugant Yasah were right. Their concern regarding the small vigilante group, the one which was not indigenous to Rajkot, was correct. There is a Kalki. And they aren't merely a small vigilante group.'

With this, he gained our attention. The Maharaja was sitting on the edge of his throne.

'When, your grace, asked me to send some of my men to get correct details regarding the subject, I did. And the news is not good, Maharaja.'

'Speak out, Mahamantri. Conceal no information.' The Maharaja gave his assurance.

'This Kalki. He is an ambitious man, Maharaja. My spies told me that he is plotting something big against the Akshobhyas. His personal information is not much known. Who is he, what he wants and why he wants, is not yet known. But he has a definite association with our enemies.'

Senapati Aagney took a couple of steps towards Mahamantri Brahmanand.

'By enemies do you mean to say...?'

'Yes, Senapati. The Varunyas and the Advaityas.'

The Maharaja stood up from his throne and stepped down the staircase.

'Are you sure, Mahamantri?'

'That's the thing, Maharaja. I don't have much information or evidence to be sure to say that it is true.'

Mahamatya Acala now stepped towards the Mahamantri and threw a series of questions at him.

'On what grounds are you stating that the Varunyas and Advaityas are planning against us?' He said in his usual bold manner. 'Do you reckon that they will break the alliance made by Maharaja Prataparat?'

'No, I don't. That would be very foolish of them if they even consider doing such a deed. But my spies in the capital of their respective kingdoms, which is in Topra and Meerut have gathered this detail. They were able to eavesdrop on some conversations of the officials in each state. That someone named Kalki has been trying to make the two Kingdoms pick up arms against our Akshobhyan Kingdom.'

'And how is he planning to make the two Kingdoms break the alliance? The Maharaja's of Varunyas and Advaityas are not so naïve to even consider the possibility of another great war.' Mahapradhan asked.

'That is what I have asked this meeting for, Mahamatya.'

Mahamantri Brahmanad turned towards Maharaja Brihadratha who was standing with his hands behind his back, head bowed and face towards the throne.

'One of my spies told me.' The Mahamantri continued. 'That a secret meeting is to be taken place between Kalki and the representatives of Varunyas and Advaityas. Where he will try to convince the two kingdoms to rage a war against the Akshobhyas.'

The Maharaja climbed up the staircase and assumed his position on the throne.

'Did your spy tell you the time and location where this meeting shall take place?' I asked him curiously.

'Yes, they did. Their meeting is scheduled to take place three days after the festival of Janmasthmi. In the Indravan.' He replied.

Maharaja's eyes fell on Mahamantri. Everyone was dumbstruck by his answer.

'Isn't that the forest on the boundaries of the Kuru kingdom and the Advaitya kingdom?' I asked as everyone watched Mahamantri Brahmanand in amusement.

'That is true, Yuvan.'

'Are you suggesting something, Mahamantri?' The Maharaja asked gravely.

'You know what I am suggesting, Maharaja. The Kurus can confirm this detail. And if true, they can end the war before it starts.'

A grave silence surrounded us as we wait for the Maharaja to speak.

'What do the rest of you suggest?' He asked while looking outside from the window of the assembly room.

Mahamatya Acala was the first to have his say.

'I reckon it will be imprudent if we do what the Mahamantri suggested, Maharaja. Asking the Kurus to take such a step when even we, the one supplying them the information, are not aware of the factual truth seems idiotic. Involving the Kurus in this while their Kingdom celebrates Janmashtmi is not a clever way to tackle this problem.'

'If not that, we can send our special troops to carry out this mission, Maharaja.' The Senapati spoke up. 'We can discreetly send our men into the Indravan to check on the details. One thing we all agree upon is that we can't let this opportunity to pass by even if we are not completely sure about it. There may be a meeting in the Indravan forest, There maybe not. But if we can confirm this, we shall be able to stop another great war.'

'But that can prove to be perilous. Sending our troops, secretly, in the boundaries of the Kuru Kingdom can prove to be disastrous for our long and strong relations with them. For no one shall tolerate this. We should come up with a way which won't require Kurus involvement and neither shall there be a hazard of jeopardizing the relations between the Kurus and the Akshobhyas.' I suggested.

'What do you suggest, Mahamatya?' Maharaja looked at him from the corner of his eye.

'As we all know, Maharaja, that Mahamantri Brahmanad's spies are rarely wrong with their information. Which only means one thing. That we can't bear to neglect a subject as grave as this. One thing, we all agree upon, is that it needs to be tackled. And it has to be done in such a way that the Kurus are neither involved nor should our relation be jeopardized. I can only think of one way in which it can be done. Rajkumar Dvij and Yugant Yasah.'

'No!' The Mahamantri exclaimed. 'That would be too dangerous.'

Maharaja asked the Mahamatya to continue.

'Rajkumar Dvij and Yugant Yasah shall arrive in Indraprastha in a few days. And they are bound to stay there for at least a month. And assuming that it is the same Kalki whom the crown prince severely injured in Rajkot; it should neither be that hazardous nor dangerous.'

'But their numbers are still unknown, Maharaja. We can't put Rajkumar Dvij and Yugant in such peril.'

'The numbers shall not be a problem, Mahamantri.' The Mahamatya said while shifting his eyes towards Mahamantri Brahmanand. 'We have Nrchakshu in Indraprastha too. Moreover, they can take as many soldiers as necessary to accompany them.'

Mahamantri Brahmanad was still not convinced that this was the best approach. But everybody else, including me, agreed with Mahamatya Acala. We all provided our support and assurance to Mahamatya Acala and Maharaja Brihadratha.

'Mahapradhan Ganakarta, what was the last known location of the army accompanying the royal family?' Maharaja Brihadratha asked.

'They left Mathura for Bairat two days ago, Maharaja.' He replied.

'Very well, then. Yashvasin Yuvan, you shall leave to join the battalion heading towards the Kuru Kingdom immediately. You shall deliver my message to Rajkumar Dvij, in private, and accompany him in the Indravan forest as well. And make sure that you join them before the lot arrives in Indraprastha.'

I bowed and accepted the mission.

'The assembly is dismissed.' The Maharaja declared and without waiting anymore paced his way out. Mahamantri followed him to the doors of the assembly room and called for him.

'I insist, Maharaja, for you to think about it again. I still don't advise you to allow Rajkumar Dvij and Yugant to deal with Kalki and the representatives of Varunyas and Advaityas. It's just too dangerous. It is not the only way.' He said.

'It is the only way, Mahamantri.' Saying this he left the assembly room.

Senapati Aagney confronted me and laid his hands on my shoulder.

'Ready for your next menacing mission?'

'Not quite. I still have to get my sword to sharpen.' I said with slight humour. Senapati replied with a smile too.

We all left the assembly room and I and Senapati Aagney headed towards the infantry chambers for me to acquire things that I will be needing on my voyage to Indraprastha.

It was almost evening when my horse was brought to me. Senapati had come to see me. He was giving me advice when Mahmantri Brahmanad came by. He handed me the scroll with Maharaja's stamp on it.

'Take caution, Yuvan. This is not going to be easy. A simple man won't take it as his ambition to destroy the most powerful empire in the whole Bharatvarsh. He doesn't seem to be an ordinary person. Save Rajkumar Dvij from any possible perils.' He said.

I nodded and jumped on my horse.

'All the best, Yuvan. May Lord Ram protect the Akshobhyan Family.' Mahamantri Brahmanand said.

'Long live the Akshobhyan Family.' I said before pulling the reins of my horse. And then, with full pace took off to Indraprastha.

I travelled for two nights straight, halting only for food and water. I knew it was important, for me to catch up with the rest of the Akshobhyas heading towards the Kuru kingdom before they reach Indraprastha. Or else a suspicion would arise among the Kurus. My journey was back-breaking and wearisome. It has been years since I last went on such a spree of riding my horse without taking any halts. Those were my younger days. I must have been not much older than Rajkumar Dvij when I took that trip. And I didn't feel fatigued at that time. Oh! The jolly younger days.

After forcing my horse to its limits, I reached Bairat on the day which followed after two nights since I commenced my journey. I was welcomed in Bairat after I showed Maharaja's stamped scroll to the soldiers and told them about myself. When I asked them about the small Akshobhyan battalion, I was informed that they left Bairat the previous day, early evening. After calculating the distance and deducing the time it shall take me to catch up with them, I showed some mercy on my exhausted horse and decided to take some time for rest. I placed some hay in front of the horse and tied it up among the other horses of the soldiers of Bairat while I took on the streets. It was a small and happy place if I were to describe it. It was still early morning and the right time for the chirping birds to sit on the trees and look at the scenes of Bairat. After wandering for a while, I decided to sit under the shade of a big tree that faced the main street and behind which were the farms. Large wooden wheels of a bullock cart, being pulled, went over a puddle, formed because of the brisk rain from last night, and splashed the muddy water on either side. Women in several groups, ranging from half a dozen to a full, were going to the well with an earthen pot placed on their waist while the men went past behind me to the farms. A couple of soldiers were marching along the streets. One of them, the same one whom I showed the scroll and gave my introduction, noticed me sitting under the tree ideally and popped up a smile for me. I replied with a smile. I looked at the clouds above from the spaces between the leaves of the tree I was sitting under and saw that they were much grey than blue. After some time, the whole sky illuminated in a shade of grey. The clouds begin to roar like a pride of lions and eventually the drizzling commenced. I didn't feel like getting up from my place because I had become comfortable there. But when the drizzles turned into heavy showering, even the tree was unable to protect me from the cold water drops. I had no other choice but to rush and look for a place to hide. The same soldiers saw me looking for shelter and gestured me to come with them. I paced in their direction and took shelter under a cabin, with them. The shower didn't last much longer and after a few moments, the sun came peeking out. The soldiers invited me to their general mess to have some food with them. I was much obliged by their invitation and decided to join them.

After having something to eat I filled up my water bag and thanked the soldiers for their generous hospitality. Even though I didn't get much time for slumber, I reckoned it would be much better if I were to find and deliver the scroll to Rajkumar Dvij before the sun touches the horizon. And with that determination, I took off once again.

I rode my horse all day with a hope of finding the Akshobhyan battalion, but couldn't. The sun was halfway down the horizon when I left the borders of the Akshobhyan Empire and entered the boundaries of the Kuru Empire. There yet again I showed the scroll and revealed my identity to the soldiers at the boundaries.

'So, were you left behind?' One of them asked.

'Oh, yes. I overslept.' I replied gently.

I rode my horse till the stars and moon became visible in the night sky. And eventually, I stumbled upon my destination. The camps were already set and a double layer of soldiers parameterized the camps. I jumped off my horse and walked the rest of the few meters. The soldiers recognized me and created a break in their parameter to allow me and the horse in. I walked my horse inside and saw the extravagantly lit up scenes. The whole area was lit up with decorative lamps and a joyous aura surrounded everyone. The women were walking with Maharani Drisana to her camp while the soldiers kept their fastidious eyes on everything. Rajkumar Adhirohah was the first to notice me and came rushing in my direction.

'Yashvasin! What are you doing here?' He asked in his sweet juvenile voice.

I squatted to his level and untied a small sack from my waistcloth.

'I am here to deliver you these sweets, my prince.' I said with a smile while extending the sweets to him which I bought from Bairat.

The Rajkumar began drooling and grabbed the whole bag from my hand.

'You are the best Yashvasin!' He said while giving me a tight hug.

Rajkumar Dvij and Yugant Yasah saw the young prince showering his love on me and walked towards us.

'So, who do we have here?' Yugant said.

Rajkumar Adhirohah turned around and lifted his hands showing the sweets to his elder brothers.

'Look! Yashvasin brought me sweets!' He said with a cheerful grin on his face.

'That is very kind of him, isn't it Adhirohah?' Rajkumar Dvij added on.

I stood up and placed my hands on the scroll. Rajkumar Dvij immediately saw Maharaja's stamp on it and placed his hand over mine. Stopping me from pulling the scroll out from my waistcloth. He shook his head lightly before taking his hands off.

'Now, brother, why don't you eat the sweets back in your camp? Yashvasin is exhausted from his long journey. We'll let him rest now.' Rajkumar Dvij said while trying to get Adhirohah away.

The little prince nodded with delight and took off.

'Your presence here with Maharaja's scroll only means something is grave. Let's get out of here, shall we?' Rajkumar Dvij said to me before heading towards the boundaries of the soldiers' parameter.

We walked past the double layer of the soldiers and resumed walking for at least 50 feet.

'Your eyes are drowsy. Travelled without any halt?' Yugant Yasah asked as we stopped under a tree.

'The situation required me to travel continuously. Couldn't risk joining you all after the lot arrived in Indraprastha.' I said while taking the scroll out and handling it to Rajkumar Dvij.

Rajkumar Dvij's eyes which were earlier fixated on me were now curiously looking at the scroll. He opened the scroll at once and begin reading. Meanwhile, I took the liberty to tell them the same.

'You were both right. There is a Kalki and he is plotting something big this time.' I said while gesturing the graveness of the situation with my hands. 'Mahamantri Brahmanand's spies…' I continued. '.. They got some information about a potential meeting that Kalki is most likely to conduct in the Indravan forest, three days after the festival of Janmashthmi. In the meeting, he will try to convince the representatives of Varunyas and Advaityas to rage war against us.'

Yugant Yasah's eyes were wide open. Rajkumar Dvij handed the scroll to him to read the same. I continued with the details of the mission we are required to accomplish.

'The Maharaja has asked you, Rajkumar Dvij, to administrate a search mission for the same in the Indravan, 3 days after the Janmashthmi festival. It is most likely to be in the early morning.'

'This is delicate. Very delicate.' Rajkumar Dvij said while taking the support of a tree.

He came towards me and shrugged my shoulders.

'No one can know about this. You shall tell no one!' He exclaimed.

I nodded. Yugant was finished reading the scroll too. He hid it inside his waistcloth so that no one else could see it.

'We should go inside now. Can't let anyone, not even Maharani sense the suspicion.' Rajkumar Dvij said while patting on my shoulders and gesturing to go inside.

'Tell me properly about it after the Janmashtmi festival. We'll develop a scheme then.' He said to me while we walked towards the parameterized area.

As soon as we entered, we came across Maharani Drisana who was astounded to see me this late at night. We could sense the anxiety on her face as she came walking towards us.

'Yashvasin? What are you doing here? And when did you arrive here?' She asked me in a haste. 'Is everything alright?'

I bowed in front of her before saying.

'Maharani Drisana, everything is fine. I am here….'

Before I could have finished saying, Rajkumar Dvij interrupted me.

'Maharaja sent him here for better administration of the army, mother.' Rajkumar Dvij said. 'He didn't want to take any risks. So, he sent him. Yashvasin has much more experience than Nrchakshu, you see.' A faint smile covered Rajkumar's countenance while he tried to fabricate a story.

'Oh. That was unnecessary, I reckon.' Maharani replied. 'Well, now that you are here, Yashvasin, try to enjoy your stay. Don't fret much about the security. It's my daughter's Kingdom, you see.' She said with a delightful smile.

'Sure, Maharani.' I said as I squatted down on one knee.

Saying this Maharani took off for her camp.

'You must be very exhausted, Yuvan. Have something to eat and I'll see to it that you get a warm tent to slumber beneath.' Rajkumar Dvij said before taking a leave.

It was some worrisome a few days for me. I ate to my delight and then as promised was delivered a tent by Rajkumar Dvij.

The next morning when I stretched my arms outside the tent from the deep slumber, I could see that most of the camps and tents were already packed. I was a little late to wake up but then again, I was entitled to that excuse. I saw Nrchakshu discussing the rest of the route with his subordinates. He saw me and came to talk.

'So, you're here, I see.'

'You could? That is mind boggling.' I said sarcastically.

Nrchkahsu tried not to get carried away and kept control of his nerves.

'Is everything alright?'

'I'll tell you about it later. For now, let's humour ourselves in Indraprastha.'

'Alright.' He replied while trying to kick a stone.

'Oh yes, there is one other thing.' I said. Nrchakshu looked up at me. 'You won't be leading the line now. I will.' I said while mocking him.

Nrchakshu shook his head and left.

It took some time before everything was packed and everyone was ready to go. Indraprastha was not very far from our current location. It was about 50 kilometres march to Indraprastha. A messenger was already sent to Maharaja Drshkrit to inform him about our arrival. I jumped on my horse and went at the start of the line. When everyone was ready, I gave the marching orders and we were off.

After marching for a while, the huge palace of Indraprastha came into sight. We were welcomed in the city of Indraprastha by the people who were standing on either side of the roads. Children were running alongside, gladden, and exhilarated. There were some brighten scenes in Indraprastha. When we joined the main road, which led directly to the palace, soldiers of Indraprastha were seeing standing on either side, after every couple of metres, in a straight line, facing us. The line stretched for two kilometres and went all the way to the gates of the palace. The Maharaja of Kuru Kingdom wasn't stressing out on any detail to welcome his in-laws. We kept on marching amidst the enthusiastic crowd of Indraprastha. Eventually, we reached the gates of the palace of Indraprastha. Just as the enormous gates of the palace were pushed open for us an exuberant shower of flower petals commenced which didn't stop until the whole battalion was inside the palace gates. The palace was decorated as a bride during her wedding night. Fancy torans stretched from every corner of the palace. The passageway, leading to the entrance of the palace, was filled with crushed flower petals of colours taken from the rainbows. Maharaja Drshkrit's court musicians were called to spread the essence of music throughout this charming evening. I gave the halting orders to the battalion in such a way that the palanquin of Maharani Drisana was halted just before the passageway. On either side of the narrow passageway were the Maharaja and Maharani of the Kuru Kingdom waiting to welcome their guests. The battalion stopped and the palanquins were gently placed on the ground. I and Nrchakshu rode our horses to the centre of the lot where Maharani Drisana and Rajkumar Adhirohah's palanquin were. Rajkumar Dvij and Yugant joined us too. We all got down from our horses. I gave another obligatory order for the battalion to bow as Maharani Drisana came out from her palanquin. Maharani Aarunya was enchanted to see her mother stepping out from her palanquin and so were everyone else. Maharaja Drshkrit was the first one to greet and welcome the royal family in Indraprastha. After that Rajkumar Adhirohah rushed towards her elder sister with exhalation and hugged her. A teardrop traced its path on Maharani Aarunya's cheeks as she squatted down to hold her little brother. Everyone was gratified to see the bond between the two siblings. Rajkumar Dvij and Yugant Yasah embraced the Maharaja of Indraprastha while Maharani Drisana held her daughter in her arms. The polite Maharaja Drshkrit joined his hands and bowed a little to welcome the Maharani of Akshobhyan Empire. After that Maharani Arunya was brought a wide gold plate. She welcomed the Akshobhyan family in a proper Hindu ceremonial way. The 'diya' on the plate was waved around them by Maharani Aarunya. After that, she sprinkled holy water on them with the sprinkler and eventually ended the small ceremony by showering them with flower petals. Maharaja Drshkrit then showed them the way to the palace through the passageway decorated with flowers. The Maharaja and Maharani of Kuru Kingdom walked on either side of the passage while the Royal family placed their feet on the soft and colourful path of petals.

The Royal family were taken inside the palace while I Marched the soldiers to the army quarters provided for the army of Chandragarh.

For the next three days, we witnessed the preparations being done for the festival of Janmashthmi in the palace. I and Nrchakshu accompanied Rajkumar Dvij and Yugant to some distant tours of the Kuru Kingdom to come up with a plan to take on Kalki and the representatives of Varunyas and Advaityas if necessary. Even though we were the guests, I always found myself amidst an unavoidable activity or two. These were some very hectic days. Even during the night, Rajkumar Dvij would keep me busy with extensive talks about Kalki, because the night was the only time when we could talk about him without endangering the secrecy of our plan. And as a result, I didn't leave the palace much. And even if I did, it was with the company of Rajkumar Dvij and Yugant. But on the day before the eve of Janmashthmi, when everyone was busy preparing for the festival, I found myself unbounded from everyone. Rajkumar Dvij and Yugant were with Maharani Drisana and Maharani Aarunya while Nrchakshu was helping the Senapati of Indraprastha to secure all the entrances of the palace. Ergo, I decided to take my horse for a brief ride in the Kingdom of Kurus. I got my horse from the army stables and was about to jump on it when a heavy voice called for me from the opposite direction.

'Are we going somewhere?'

My eyes rummaged at the source of the voice. It was Maharaja Drshkrit.

'Just for a little ride in this beautiful city of Indraprastha.' I said with a smile on my face.

'That is unusual.' He said.

'What is, Maharaja Drshkrit?'

'A man of your stature, being free from any responsibility on a day before Janmashthmi festival. Isn't it unusual?' He asked with a smirk on his face.

'It is. Even I find it unusual. But even after thoroughly searching for an opening, I couldn't find an activity to indulge in. Looks like the management of this enormous palace of Indraprastha is honestly accountable for the preparations, sir.'

'HaHa! You are a good orator; I give you that. If I am not mistaken, you are the famous Yashvasin Yuvan, aren't you?'

'Wise eyes know everything! Yes, I am Yashvasin Yuvan.' I replied gently.

'So, Yashvasin Yuvan of Chandragarh, would you fancy to have a conversation with me? Of course, that would cost you your evening trip to explore Indraprastha.'

'You flatter me, Maharaja of Kurus. Why would a king like yourself indulge in a conversation with me? Doesn't your grace has many important things to do than talk to someone of my stature?' I asked.

'Oh, don't underestimate yourself, Yashvasin. Even you know about your legends and stories that everyone has on their lips. I would like to have a conversation with one of the bravest men in this land of Bharatvarsh. But if an evening trip is dearer, I won't stop you from enjoying one.'

'I can't say no to the Maharaja of Kuru Kingdom. Let me have someone take my horseback to the stable.'

Another one of my plans for an evening horse ride in the Kuru Kingdom was ruined. This time by none other than Maharaja of Kurus. I joined Maharaja Drshkrit in the palace gardens after handling my horse to a stable man. We walked for a while before coming across a seating accommodation. Maharaja Drshkrit sat down on the seat while I remained erect.

'Won't you sit down with me, Yashvasin?' He asked.

'I have never sat alongside a Maharaja. How can I now?'

'Oh, Yashvasin. Don't be too polite. You must have shared a table with Rajkumar Dvij. I am not much older than him. And that means you are senior to me in years. Come. Sit alongside me.'

After much hesitation, I sat, sharing a seat with him.

'I've heard, Yashvasin...' He said while looking at me and then to the beautiful scenery in front. '... that apart from being a great warrior, your heart bleeds for poetry. Is that true?'

'I do manage to get time to write some verses, Maharaja.'

'Don't wait then. From what I can see is we have beautiful scenery in front of us and a poet sitting alongside me. Paint me a verbal picture, if you will.'

'My apologies, Maharaja Drshkrit. I don't want to be rude, but I can't.' I said while declining his proposal.

'You can't? Why don't you want to?' Maharaja Drshkrit asked curiously.

'It is not that I don't want to, Maharaja. I can't describe the scenery in verse which is not of my Chandragarh.'

The Maharaja was a little amazed to listen to my answer. I continued stating my explanation.

'I was born in Chandrgarh. And from my tender years, I have walked on the soft grass of that pious land. It has nourished me and has made me the man that I am today. For all my years I've witnessed the serene nature that surrounds the beautiful city. I have walked through the prepossessing sights of the dense Simha forest and have swum in the reverent depths of the rejuvenating water of the holy Ganani River. The inhabitants of Chandragarh are my family and the beautiful land is my mother. I always feel alive while inhaling the cold and vibrant air of Chandragarh. And shall not fret from meeting death if I have to while serving it. I have shed and at times bled for its defence.' I said while describing Chandragarh.

'It is not that I don't want to, but I can't. I can't describe a scene falsely and state that it is better or that I revere its beauty because I can't. Till the end of my years, I shall remain captivated and indebted to the land of Chandragarh. Its beauty shall be the only thing that I'd revere.' I paused when I saw a hint of laughter on the Maharaja's face.

'Think of me as a madman, Maharaja, for you may find it strange to see someone love his land to such an extent. But I can't help it. Chandragarh might not always have given me, it has taken much dearly things from me, so many things which I loved, but how can I despise my motherland? The land where everyone knows my name, where everyone cherishes me. It is not that I don't want to write verses of the beautiful scenes that are in front of me now. The glittering stream flowing over the hill, making its way to emerge like an exquisite waterfall, adorned by a rainbow, encircling which are the white swans. I can't because I can't feel the tranquillity in these forests when I see those trees swaying with every gust of wind they encounter. The colours of this rainbow don't illuminate my heart. Because my heart and my mind are in Chandragarh. What I am and what I will be will always be a part of Chandragarh. I may be just a little part of it, but Chandragarh is everything for me.'

A moment of silence surrounded us for a while before Maharaja Drshkrit finally spoke.

'Chandragarh is fortunate to have a son like you. I know you will state the opposite, but it is the truth. I revere men like you, Yashvasin. I do. The land of Indraprastha lack in men like you. No wonder the Akshobhyan Empire has grown so much over the years. Because it is served by such loyal men.'

I kept staring into the scenery in front of us.

'I could send a message to Maharaja Bridaratha and ask him to grant me your services.'

I looked in amusement at him at once.

'But I know. I know you would be reluctant to leave Chandragarh. But more than you, Maharaja Brihadratha would be reluctant to give your services away.' He said.

Maharaja Drshkrit and I had a diverse conversation in the palace gardens till late evening. When the sunset, he excused himself. Meanwhile, I remained there for a little longer.

The day of the birth of Lord Krishna finally arrived in Indraprastha. Both the royal families of the Akshobhyas and Kurus were ready in fine clothes to visit the nearby temple of Lord Krishna. The temple was filled with devotees coming from all the stretch of the Kuru Kingdom. Busy crowd requires heavy security. The royal families were escorted inside the temple by dozens of soldiers. Maharaja Drshkirt and Maharani Aarunya initiated the 'pooja'. Multitudinous prayers were recited by the devotees. Maharaja Drshkrit donated gold in a huge amount. After the prayers were done, Maharani Drisana led the recitation of Bhagvadgeeta.

I was standing on a distant edge of the temple, few feet away from the crowd of devotional devotees, when Yugant came. He looked concerned and required my presence immediately. He asked me to come with him and said that he'll explain the reason on the way. We stepped out from the temple premises and all I could see was people filling the roads in huge numbers. One couldn't find a space if he tried. Yugant's fastidious eyes were searching the crowd for someone. He held my arm with one hand and had the other placed on his sword's handle, ready to draw it anytime. I couldn't see him this much concerned and eventually asked him what the matter was.

'Do you remember what I told you about a fight I and Dvij had while we were in Rajkot, one late night?' Yugant said while still running his eyes in the crowd.

'Yes. I remember. Very well indeed.'

He looked back at me before continuing.

'The man whom I fought. I saw him. I saw him here, Yuvan.'

'But didn't you say that their identities were concealed?' I asked while stressing on the details that I remembered from that assembly meeting.

'Yes. Their faces were indeed covered. But there was an instance, during the duel where I was able to make him fall. That time the cloth covering his face came loose at once and I was able to see his face. Even though it was dark at that time, I remember his face vividly.'

'We should search the crowd, as fast as we could.' I said before pacing into the crowd.

We searched the crowd for the man Yugant fought in Rajkot. But it was like searching for a needle in a haystack. After spending much time, we came back in vain. We couldn't find him.

'It was a waste of time.' Yugant sounded gloomy.

'No, Yugant. It wasn't. At least we now know for certain, that Kalki and his men are in the city.' I said in an upbeat manner. 'We should go back inside. Our absence will raise suspicion.' I placed my hand on Yugant's shoulders as we walked back.

Back in the palace, a special performance was organized for the Akshobhyan family. Multiple dance performances were done. But what caught everyone's eyes was the play of Rasa Leela. Our very own Rajkumar Adhirohah was dressed as Lord Krishna. The dramatization of Lord Krishna's acts of stealing 'Makhan' from gopiyas was depicted by Rajkumar Adhirohah. Maharani Aarunya cheered her little brother while Maharani Drisana was delighted to see such love between her children. Everyone present was enjoying themselves except Rajkumar Dvij. He seemed to be vexed by the thoughts of the mission that lied 3 days from now. Even though he was able to injure Kalki, the last time they met, a man having an ambition of Destroying the Akshobhyas can't be taken for granted. I, Yugant, and Nrchakshu were anxious and distressed about what lied ahead. But we let our worries get pushed away by trying to enjoy the stage play.

❖

Utkarsh Sharma

INDRAVAN

Three days passed since the festival of Janmashthmi. It was early morning. Nrchakshu and I followed Rajkumar Dvij and Yugant to Maharani Drisana's chamber. Nrchakshu and I waited outside the chamber while Rajkumar and Yugant went inside. It took them some time to come out with Maharani's permission on the hunting trip. But of course, we had to ask Maharaja Drshkrit too. We walked towards the palace gardens where Maharaja Drshkrit and Maharani Aarunya were enjoying the entertaining company of Rajkumar Adhirohah. Maharaja, who was sitting, stood up at once after seeing us all equipped with bow and arrows. We greeted the King and Queen of Kuru Kingdom.

'I've heard that Indravan is home to some wild beasts. Is that true, Maharaja Drshkrit?' Rajkumar Dvij asked while bowing down to his brother-in-law.

'Indeed. Some of the most vicious beasts are to be found there.' He said proudly.

'We were making plans for a hunting trip. Reckoned, should take your permission first.' Rajkumar Dvij stated.

Maharaja Drshkrit burst into laughter.

'You don't need my permission, Dvij. You are free to explore the Kuru Kingdom. Take my horse, if you want, for the trip. One fine stallion, I have.' Maharaja said while twisting his moustache.

'I thank and admire you for your vibrant gesture, Maharaja. But I am well suited for my horse only, you see.' Rajkumar said with a smile on his face. 'We shall leave now. Thanks, yet again.'

'Even I want to go on a hunting trip!' Cried the little prince. To which everyone burst into cheerful laughter.

'Don't you enjoy my company, sweet brother?' asked Maharani Aarunya.

'I do.' He said. The little prince placed his finger on his forehead and went into deep thinking before finally speaking again in his sweet and soft voice.

'Alright. I'll stay. I will ask the father Maharaja to take me on a hunting trip later. And I do enjoy your company, sister.' He said while embracing Maharani Aarunya.

The Maharani turned towards her other sibling and gave him a grave look.

'Dvij, I think it was impolite of you to not ask Maharaja Drshkrit to join you on the hunting trip. He is your brother-in-law after all.'

I, Yugant, and Nrchkashu gulped as we listen to Maharani's proposal.

Maharaja Drshkrit again burst into laughter.

'Don't stress your little brother, Maharani. Let him go and explore the Indravan. Meanwhile, I shall enjoy Adhirohah's company.' He said while lifting Rajkumar Adhirohah.

We all took a sigh of relief.

'Alright then. We shall leave now.' Rajkumar Dvij said as we all greeted the King and Queen again.

We had only walked a few steps away from the palace gardens when we heard Maharaja's call from behind.

'Yes, Maharaja?' Rajkumar Dvij solemnly asked.

'I just want you all to follow caution. Indravan is what divides Advaityas from the Kuru Kingdom. Even though we have wholesome relations with them, they won't like the crown prince of Akshobhyas roam around in their boundaries. So don't wander around carelessly. Is that clear?' Maharaja said gravely.

'Yes, Maharaja,' replied Rajkumar Dvij.

'Very well then. Enjoy your hunting trip.'

We watched Maharaja walk back towards the palace gardens. We all knew that this meeting will take place in the Advaityas occupied Indravan. And so we had to go behind the enemy lines.

The Indravan forest was 25 kilometres away from the palace of Indraprastha. It stretched for about 50 kilometres in both length and breadth. We rode our horses till the Indravan came into view. Rajkumar Dvij halted our small troop to discuss the scenario one last time.

'Listen carefully. We don't know for certain what lies inside the forest. We don't know their numbers, their intentions, or anything near. All we know is that inside somewhere is the beginning of the potential war and we have got a chance to finish it before it starts.' The Rajkumar had a dazzling spark in his fearless eyes. Later he asked me to lead. And so, I did.

'We shall lead in two groups.' I said. 'Nrchkashu and I will lead. Whereas Rajkumar Dvij and Yugant will see the back. Our first motive is to confirm that the information that Mahamantri Brahmanand provided is true. This situation is very delicate and hence we need to confirm it first. Because our carelessness inside the boundaries of Advaityas can also lead to war. From what we know, Kalki is the one behind all this. We have to go to him. Because his death will ensure that the plan never lived.'

We confirmed the details before jumping on our horses and riding inside the Indravan. The Indravan was not as denser as the Simha forest. Riding our horses here was easier. The boundaries of the Kuru and Advaitya Kingdom were divided by a large wooden plaque, stating the same. On either side of the plaque, the name of the Kingdoms was written. Both the armies had an agreement to keep the forest free of any security measures and so not even a single soldier was seen guarding the boundary line. Still taking measurable precautions, we hid our horses back behind a dense bush where they couldn't be seen. Now, we just need to search the forest carefully. We rummaged through the forest, looking for any suitable clue.

'What are we exactly looking for?' Nrchakshu asked while slashing the bushes ahead of him with his blade.

'Anything that indicates the presence of humans.' Yugant replied from the back.

'And what exactly are they?'

'A fire, maybe a cave. Look out for the footprints. It is easy to trace footprints during rain.'

It took us some time before we spotted dense smoke coming out to our direction from a chimney of a nearby hut. We hid behind the bushes to take a clearer look. A man was guarding the front door. We were facing the back of the hut which was about 60 meters away from us. From a small window in the back, we could see dense figures. We needed a clearer look and so slowly and cautiously walked towards the hut. We hid behind it among the horses of the men tied. Rajkumar Dvij and I took a glance from the window. There were eight men inside the hut who were talking discreetly. They stood surrounding a table on which a map was spread. All of them had their faces covered, which signified the extent of confidentiality of this meeting. One of them, old but tall and heavily build, was guiding them by highlighting different places on the map with his hand. He had a big scar on his chest from what I saw. Rajkumar Dvij pulled me down, below the window.

'That's him. That's Kalki.' Rajkumar whispered.

'Their faces are covered. How can you be sure?' I asked in a low voice.

'Did you see that big scar on his chest? He got that from an injury he sustained from our duel in Rajkot. I am sure of that.'

'What should we do now?' Yugant asked.

Before I could have suggested anything, Rajkumar Dvij took the lead.

'They are eight. And we are four. We need to take them by surprise. One thing we can be sure about is that Varunyas and Advaityas won't be sending mere soldiers to represent them here. These men inside will be tough to defeat. We also need to make sure that they are not able to flee. It means we have to scare their horses away. Yugant and I will attack them from here with arrows. Nrchakshu and Yuvan, remain at the edge of the hut. The guard will come back when he will hear the scared horses. Take him and then take down anyone who leaves the door.'

Nrchakshu and I nodded before going forward, sticking to the edge.

It was happening. It was finally happening.

It all happened in a brief moment. Yugant cut loose the horses and scared them away. Rajkumar Dvij was ready with his bow and arrow. The noise of the appalled horses caught everyone's attention. The guard came looking back and saw Nrchakshu slit his throat. From the inside, I could hear the cry of men getting shot with arrows. Their bodies fell on the floor of the cabin with a thud. Nrchakshu tried to take the remaining men, coming out from the front door, all by himself. But I stopped him from doing so. And he was furious about it. A total of five men came outside of the hut alive. While I was holding Nrchkashu's arm from going any further, Rajkumar Dvij and Yugant came sprinting forward to take on those men. Yugant was facing Kalki. While Rajkumar Dvij was surrounded by the four others. I let go of Nrchkahsu's arm but not before telling him to help the Rajkumar, while I joined Yugant.

Our opponent was a brawny man. Every essence of his aura and structure said that he was a warrior. Yugant went for him, all out. He launched multiple strikes of his sword at him, but Kalki defended himself with ease. I watched the two from the back while I stood in position. Yugant was resolute to slay Kalki for once and for all. He brought his sword above Kalki's head. The latter tried to pull himself back from Yugant's reach. But Yugant proved to be faster for him. Just as Kalki pulled himself back, Yugant jumped forward and kicked Kalki on the face. Unable to balance himself, Kalki stumbled and fell on the ground, revealing his face in the process.

'Is…. Is this true?' I heard Yugant whisper while he stood, dumbstruck, gazing at the fallen enemy.

I took charge and came in between Yugant and Kalki whose hands went swiftly to his face to conceal his identity. He stood up and began running in the opposite direction. I ran behind him, leaving my surprised companion behind.

After chasing Kalki till a certain distance someone thumped the pommel of his sword on the back of my head. I stumbled and fell, face first, on the ground. Another man helped me pick myself up. It was Nrchakshu. I saw the attacker join Kalki in fleeing. Nrchkashu and I continued chasing them.

We chased them for some time. The heavens opened their gates and what followed after a majestic thunder was heavy rain. Eventually, they both stopped. They stood above a small steep hill. We were panting at the foot of the same hill. My head was spinning. I touched the surface of my head where I was hit, only to find out I was bleeding. 'That bastard will pay for it.' I said beneath my asynchronous breath. The two had brought us to a secluded area in the forest, far away from our other companions.

'You both should go now.' Kalki said gravely.

But before I could have said anything, Nrchakshu rushed towards Kalki and went all out on him. Their swords clashed with each other, matching the thunderous sound of the storm.

'Stop it!' I cried. But Nrchakhsu didn't listen.

'If you want to fight, we shall fight.' Kalki said accepting the challenge.

Kalki cut through the air to reach Nrchakshu, who too stormed in front. Kalki swiped through his feet, but Nrchakshu was fast enough to jump. He then brought his sword down on Nrchakshu who was just able to defend himself. The strong hands of Kalki were providing much thrust. His attacks were just too heavy for Nrchakshu to defend against. Moreover, the wet, slippery land made it difficult for Nrchakshu to keep his balance.

'What are you looking at? Want another thump on your head?' That bastard caught my attention. Nrchakshu had pushed Kalki away from his companion. I started climbing the steep hill. Forgetting the situation, we were in, I pranced towards him. I dropped my sword in between. I wanted to feel his blood on my hands. He glided his sword in front of me, I ducked and, in an instant, thumped his face. One blow and blood came dripping out of his lips. He slashed the air in front of me yet again. I moved aside and punched him on his temple. He was pushed aside but was able to keep his balance over his trembling legs. I kicked his hand and his sword fell on the ground. Multiple blows on his ribs and he began coughing blood. But that bastard kept smiling which stirred my blood even more. I kicked him in the core. He fell on the edge of the hill. He went downhill, rolling. I followed him down and stood over him. I stamped his face repeatedly until his hideous smile was concealed with blood and mud.

'Next time choose your opponent wisely!' I yelled as I spit on his face.

Kalki and Nrchakshu's fight caught my attention again. Nrchakshu had sustained multiple cuts and was bleeding badly. I rushed towards them. I couldn't bear to see Nrchakshu helplessly getting beaten by that man. Nrchakshu fell on his knees, exhausted and drenched with sweat, blood, and the rain. Kalki saw me from the corner of his eye and retreated from hurting Nrchakshu furthermore.

It was over. Kalki and I stood near each other's companions who were beaten down to a pulp. We exchanged looks and walked towards each other to exchange our places. My head was spinning wildly. I was having a problem looking straight, forcing my eyes to not shut. The rain wasn't making it any easier. But I had no problem seeing Nrchakshu get up and run towards Kalki. I cried his name and asked him to stop. But maybe it was too late. Kalki turned around and saw Nrchkahsu approach him with a sword. He stepped aside and an exhausted Nrchkahsu lost his balance and fell from the hill. He rolled down and stopped a few meters in front of me. He tried to get up, but in vain and fell, unconscious. He was lying in a puddle of his blood mixed with mud. Kalki took out a bow and an arrow from his back satchel. The world was spinning right before my eyes. It was getting harder for me to concentrate and see. But I could, yet again, clearly see Kalki aiming for Nrchakhsu's head.

'NO!' I cried. 'You won't kill him!'

Kalki stopped and glanced at me.

'If you kill him it's all over between you and me!'

I looked at him with aggression and shook my head slightly, gesturing him not to proceed. He retreated from killing Nrchakshu but his arrow was still extended. He merely changed his aim. He aimed his arrow at me now. I wasbetrayed and vulnerable but these dizzy spells made it difficult for me to care. His arrow missed me by a few inches. Well, at least that's how it looked like at first. I looked back and saw Rajkumar Dvij lying on the ground, motionless, with an arrow sticking out from his throat.

'He kept his promise! He kept his promise!' That beaten-up bastard cried as I closed my eyes for a little while.

❖

REMORSE

I woke up in a lightly illuminated room. A surge of pain reminded me of the injury I had sustained. I swept my hand over my head and noticed that I have been patched up. I looked at my hands and saw that my knuckles were bruised, from beating up Kalki's companion.

He kept his promise! He kept his promise!

I tried to stand up but felt weak. Nevertheless, I stood up by taking support from the adjacent wall. My legs were shaking feverishly. God! I felt so weak! But a faint sound caught my attention. I could hear the cry of a woman from the corridors. An inquisitive surge forced me to walk towards that faint cry and so I did. With every step that I took towards the cry, it became shriller. I swept the curtain of the door hastily and stepped outside of the room. The aching pain forced me to retreat, to lie down on the bed, but the shrill cry of the women sought solace from me. I could see that I was brought back to the palace of Indraprastha. A soldier saw me in distress and approached to help me. I swerved him away, without even looking at him, and just followed the voice. I felt dizzy yet again. God curse that bastard for giving me this headache! The walls of the palace felt like an illusion. Everything was inconsistent. The visions came and went. For once, I could see the walls adorned with portraits. I blinked and they were gone. For once, I could see a fancy pot upon a decorative table. I blinked and there was nothing. But the women's helpless cry remained consistent. I felt like I was going back in the darkness. But I didn't want too. Not again.

The shrill cry of the woman filled the palace with the utmost horror. It was the only voice I could hear. It echoed in my ears, overcoming my every impulse, and filled me with misery, sadness, and severe despondency. Something was so dull and uninspiring about her voice. I was not able to make out whose voice was this, yet it felt so similar. It felt like I've known this intrusive voice for ages. It has been sitting in a distant corner of my consciousness the whole time. It kept echoing in my ears. I tried to speak to her but couldn't hear my voice. The women's cry was all that I could hear. I felt helpless. I tried to scream. I cried with all my strength but only her voice reached my ears. It became so depressing that I wanted it to stop. I prayed for it to stop but its intensity just kept on increasing. I fell on the ground, my hands covered my ears. Everything seemed to be unclear. Everything seemed to be a blur. I opened my eyes and, vaguely, could see dense figures approaching, to rescue me. At that very moment, happiness ceased to exist. I was overcome by the deepest sense of melancholy. My mind was playing tricks on me. I wished my mind was playing tricks on me. All of a sudden, I felt nostalgic and tried to overcome this melancholy by remembering my pleasant past. Oh! The sweet past, if there was any. My childhood appeared in front of me, in my mother's arms. Her soft hand brushing my hair as I lay on her lap. How sweet she smelled. She smelled like hope. She smelled like home. Her enchanting countenance was in front of me. I could see her and tried to embrace her but my hands felt short. My reach just wasn't enough. I tried hard, multiple times. But I kept missing her. She began to fade. I tried to remember her countenance again, but it was all blurred out. A cloud of mist-covered her face. This cloud grew denser and denser by every passing moment. It took all shades of grey before turning into smoke. A cloud of smoke coming out from a fire. Fire! Fire! All the memories of my obnoxious past came hunting back. I tried to keep them at bay but they hustled their way in.

It was dark and I was standing behind a tree, at the end of a forest, and was watching people scream as they ran for their life. I watched them get slayed. I watched them get set on fire alive! Such an annihilation. Such daunting deaths. The scream of the burnt crept inside me like an excruciating horror. I wanted to do something. I wanted to be of some help. But I was paralyzed with fear. I felt weak and my legs trembled. I was already appalled, scared to death after witnessing such a painful end of my people. But nothing was as painful as listening to the blood-curling scream of my mother. I saw her running while shielding an infant close to her bosom. She was torched from the back but kept running. Her cry! Her scream! Her shrill cry sought solace from me. My heart couldn't bear her screaming. My heart couldn't bear to see her in such agonising pain, and so I ran. I forced my paralyzed body to make a move. But I had no control over my limbs anymore. The struggle of making the move was sore and futile. I fell on the ground. I saw my mother fall on the land, filled with corpses. Filled with death. I tried to crawl towards her and extended my arm for her to grasp. But I was too far. My mother kept on crawling away from a man wielding a sword. A sword meant to protect people, to save them from distress and harm. I cried for the man to stop. I cried so hard. But no sound came out. I cursed myself for being so weak and naïve. For not being able to help. For not being able to do anything as that man brought his sword down on my mother's burning body. For not being able to do anything as the Maharaja of Chandragarh brought the ASI down on my mother's burning body.

When I opened my eyes, the dreadful scenes of the past were gone. But I could still hear a woman crying. Some soldiers helped to get me back on my feet. They were pushed away by Yugant, who has come to see me. I took his support and slowly made my way to the source of the voice. He took me to the veranda of the palace, where a small crowd had gathered. I could see Maharaja Drshkrit standing in the middle, from the back. I let go of Yugant and pushed my way to the front of the crowd. I saw Maharani Aarunya crying over the dead body of her brother. Rajkumar Dvij's lifeless body lied in the middle, covered from the neck to down with a white blanket. Maharaja Drshkrit was standing behind. Maharani Drisana was sitting next to Maharani Aarunya but didn't show any expressions. She was shocked to the core. Not a single tear was shed by her. She just stared at Rajkumar Dvij's face. I felt weak again. All the scenes of Indravan came rushing back to me. I remembered watching an arrow sticking out from Rajkumar Dvij's neck as he lied on the moist green land of Indravan. His eyes were open. Yes, I remember even the smallest of the details. I started trembling again. Yugant came from behind and held me again. I never meant to harm Rajkumar Dvij. I would have saved him from Kalki. I could have defended him against Kalki if it was required. God his real name isn't even Kalki! Why do I keep saying it? I was filled with remorse and shame for not being able to defend my prince. For not being able to save him. But I did save one life. A life that was more precious to me than anything. Or did I? I turned towards Yugant and grasped him with all my strength.

'Where is Nrchkahsu?' I tried to scream but words came out in a broken whisper.

'He is fine. He'll make it.' Yugant told me.

I took a sigh of relief. I thought about Maharaja Brihadratha and how deeply will the death of his son affect him. But I couldn't care less about him. I searched for the little Adhirohah. He was nowhere to be seen. They must have taken him somewhere else, where the news of his brother's death won't reach him. I asked Yugant to take me to Rajkumar Adhirohah. I pleaded him multiple times. And he eventually took me to Rajkumar Adhirohah's chamber.

The chamber was guarded by two soldiers. I went past them. Yugant was not able to face the little prince and so remained outside. As soon as I went inside, Rajkumar Adhirohah came running and hugged me. His soft cheeks were moist with tears. I squatted down and held him. He cried his heart out. I didn't realize his small cries would pain me to such an extent.

'What happened to the elder brother, Yuvan?' He asked me sobbing. 'No one is telling me what happened to him. Please, Yuvan. Please tell me. Is elder brother…?'

I didn't say anything but nodded to his question. It was tormenting to see his small eyes shed big teardrops. He grabbed me tightly and I let him sob. In all these years, I never realized that I have become so attached to Maharaja Brihadratha's sons. I held Rajkumar Adhirohah closely to my heart until the little prince cried himself to sleep.

The next day Rajkumar Dvij's body was cremated on the banks of Yamuna River. Rajkumar Adhirohah and Yugant Yasah provided flame to his cold corpse. Maharani Drisana had still not shed a tear. She just stood there and watched as her son's body was burnt to ashes. She didn't utter a single word, a single cry. It was horrific to see her gone into such a deep state of shock. I stood behind the crowd, with a little help from a couple of soldiers. Something was so wrong inside me. I never reckoned I could conjure such affection towards the princes of Chandragarh. Maybe watching them grow, helping them over the years had made me care about them. Moreover, Rajkumar Dvij was never meant to die, neither was Nrchakshu meant to be beaten so close to his life. Someone had to pay for Rajkumar Dvij's death. And I'll make sure that he does.

QUESTIONS

We arrived in Chandragarh with the late crown prince's ashes in an urn. The news of Rajkumar Dvij's death had already swept throughout the Akshobhyan Empire. The whole city of Chandragarh mourned over the one who was destined to be their future Maharaja. But destiny is a cruel thing. We never know what our destiny is until it arrives. There was no joy in people's eyes to see the royal family return. There was no happiness. And why should there be any?

When we arrived in the palace of Chandragarh Senapati Aagney, Mahamantri Brahmanand and Mahapradhan Ganakarta were present to welcome us. Maharaja Brihadratha was nowhere to be seen. When asked, by Maharani Drisana, Mahamantri Brahmanand told that the Maharaja has not left his chamber ever since he heard the news of his son's untimed demise. Senapati Aagney helped Nrchakshu to walk to his chambers, while Yugant helped me walk to my room.

Yugant was saddened to his heart about Rajkumar Dvij's demise. He was too moved to his core. Even though they weren't related by blood, they have had a brother's bond between them. They have grown up together, learned together, fought together and both were supposed to be the future of Akshobhyas. But now he was left alone. He was left alone with his memories and thoughts. Thoughts that were going to stir a wave of complications and shall rise differences in Chandragarh. Multiple secrets were going to be unearthed. Yugant knew whom he saw in Indravan. There was no doubt in his mind. That day he saw a person he had least expected to see. He too felt betrayed and he needed answers. Answers that only Maharaja Brihadratha could provide.

Yugant escorted me to my room, even though I asked him to leave and that I was fit enough to walk on my own. But he needed to talk to me, alone. He wanted to ask me something to which he already knew the answer.

'Was he him?' He asked me.

'I… I don't know what you're talking about, Yugant.' I replied, trying not to look him into his eyes.

'Yuvan! You've been here for almost 25 years now. You know what I am talking about.' Yugant was getting furious. 'You fought him. I just want to know. Is Kalki really…?'

'I can't remember, Yugant. I've had a concussion. I only remember that day in Indravan in bits.'

'You remember watching Dvij die but you can't remember the real face behind that black cloth?' He asked in huge exasperation. 'I need answers, Yuvan! If I am not getting them from you, I know the exact person who shall provide me with them. I am going to the Maharaja.'

'Don't, Yuvan.' I said. 'Maharaja is not in the right state of mind, to talk to you now. He is suffering from severe shock. Your questions will only make things worse. Let him get over Rajkumar Dvij's death. Then you shall have all your answers. Till then just wait.'

'I can't, Yuvan! If I wait any longer, I'll go mad. I just can't wait.' Saying this, he stormed out of my room. I, with a limp, followed him.

I was not sure if Yugant will be able to handle the truth. Neither was I sure that Maharaja Brihadratha would want to remember his past. Yugant was so profound with his resoluteness that he attracted Mahamantri Brahmanad's attention. He stormed towards Maharaja Brihadratha's chamber while Mahamantri Brahmanad and I followed him, asking him to stop. There was heavy security outside Maharaja's chamber. A dozen soldiers were guarding the premises. Maharaja wanted to be left alone. The soldiers blocked Yugant's way. Yugant was furious and impatient. He wanted to meet the Maharaja anyhow. And so he did the unthinkable. He drew out his sword on his men. He was ready to chop off anyone's head that would come in front of him.

'Let him go.' A voice said from behind.

We all looked at the direction of the voice. It was Maharani Drisana's voice. She was standing behind us and has seen everything. She has known

Yugant from his childhood, has showered love on him like a mother. She knew that no one could stop a resolute Yugant.

'Let Yugant through. No one shall stop him.' She said again.

Yugant immediately drew his sword back into its scabbard and bowed down to Maharani. Maharani Drisana didn't wait long and went on her way after providing the permission.

The soldiers scattered away from the doors of the chamber. Yugant went ahead and gave a gentle push. But the door was locked from the inside. He started pounding the door with all his might until the latches from the inside came loose and the door was pushed open. What we saw in front of us was disheartening.

All the curtains of the room were drawn in. The only hint of light that came inside was from the slight opening between the curtains. The light fought for its existence from the black pitched darkness which constantly kept pushing its hope to spread or live. Maharaja Brihadratha was sitting below a somewhat same curtain-drawn window, on the floor, perpendicular to the door through which Yugant entered. His legs were widespread and his right arm took the support of a nearby chair, through his elbow. His long hair was spread all over his face which was overcome by lassitude. The Maharaja of Brihadratha was nearing his 50th birth anniversary, but by his looks, he looked like a much older man. Maharaja's uttariya had come loose and was dangling from his other hand. With the opening of the door, a ray of light entered the room and fell directly on Maharaja Brihadratha. He tried to block the light with his left hand.

'Who is it?' He yelled at the man for violating his order of not disturbing him.

It was probably the first ray of light that had entered his eyes in so many days. His vision was bound to be vague. From the very bright light entering the room, he saw a dense figure, a shadow approaching him. He reckoned he knew who it was.

'Dvij? Is that you?' He called his son's name while trying to stand up. He fumbled, dropped a few glasses off a nearby table in his vague attempt to get back on his feet.

With his left hand still blocking the light falling on him, he tried to run towards the shadow which was growing bigger and denser with every step that he took forward. He stumbled just before the dense figure and fell near his foot. He lifted his eyes but could only see a blurred image of the figure's face. He rubbed his eyes over and over but could only curse his failing vision.

'Dvij? Please talk to me, son! Is that you? I can't see. I can't see!' He cried.

After getting much frustrated he just let it all go and grabbed hold of the shadow's legs and began crying. He cried his heart out. For a brief moment, his cry was the only thing that was heard in the whole palace. It echoed into the depths of both the palace and our hearts. Yugant finally reached out for the man crying over his legs. He picked Maharaja Brihadratha up from his shoulders.

'I am not Dvij. Dvij… Dvij… He is gone.' He said with much hesitation and gently shaking Maharaja's shoulders.

The Maharaja lifted his head again. This time he could see Yugant.

'Yugant.' He said while feeling Yugant's face with his hands. 'My son. You've come back. Yugant, you have come back.' He said before embracing Yugant firmly. He kept repeating the same words over and over again. Even though the Maharaja of Chandragarh was in shock of losing his one son, he was, at the same time, grateful for another son to come back without enduring any injuries. But Yugant Yasah didn't feel the same for the Maharaja.

He gently pushed Maharaja Brihadratha away. The Maharaja was bewildered to see Yugant doing so. He was trembling, anxiously.

'You are not my father.' Yugant said with his eyes fixed on the perplexed Maharaja.

'Don't say that, son. For god's sake, don't say such things.' Maharaja Brihadratha said who was shivering now.

'You are not my father. You are not my father!' Yugant yelled. His resolute red eyes were sending the shivering king in a state of nerves.

'Why would you say that, son? The Maharaja said in a low trembling voice. You may not be related to me by blood, but not once have I treated you anything less than my son. You know it is true when I say this. I have loved you the same as Dvij. I have always been true to you. Please don't say such tormenting words. I can't handle another shock. I am not capable.'

Seeing Maharaja in such a terrible state, Mahamantri Brahmanand went inside the chamber to stop Yugant from causing furthermore distress to the Maharaja. I followed him.

'You lie. You lie when you say that you are true to me. My whole life has been a lie. You kept me in the shadows of a lie.' Yugant said.

'Yugant. Stop it now.' The Mahamantri said while holding onto his arm. 'Can't you see you are causing further more distress to the Maharaja? Stop it now, for god's sake!' Yugnat gave him a cold stare and pushed Mahamantri's hand away from his arm.

The Maharaja tried to console the agitated man.

'That is not true, Yugant, you know. Why would I possibly lie to you? I have never lied to you.'

'You said my father was dead!'

A chill went down Maharaja's spine. He was white with fear. His trembling intensified and his legs began to lose their strength. I rushed and grabbed hold of him, preventing him from falling. He shook his head in disbelief.

'Ya... Yayati? How do you...?' He whispered.

'I know because I saw him. I fought him in the woods of Indravan. You said my father had died in a war. You lied! You lied! You call yourself my father? What father tells such a lie to the son he loves? You kept me in the dark for so long. How could you? Didn't you feel anything after pushing me away from my father? Why would you, huh? You are the great Maharaja of the mighty Akshobhyan Empire. The great Maharaja with a heart as black as coal. You are not worthy of any respect. I am not your son! Do you hear me? I am not your son!'

Yugant bashed his way to the gates of the palace. He took his horse and went away.

The Maharaja was devastated after hearing such allegations from Yugant. He knew he had done the crime of not telling Yugant about his father but there was a definite reason for that. The Maharaja didn't take it well at all. He fell extremely sick and was bedridden for the entire day. A dozen *veds* remained by his bedside watching his every breath, every pulse. One could say that dark times have arrived in Chandragarh.

Yayati Yasah

It was still early morning; the sun had not come up yet. Rajkumar Adhirohah came to see me. I was astounded to see the little prince awake this early. Sadness was reflecting from his face and so I took him to the palace gardens for a morning walk to cheer him up. He was thinking about what had happened all of a sudden to his family. One of his elder brothers was dead and the other one stormed out of the palace after having a huge argument with his father. The little prince was thinking way more than his age.

'I feel sad for father Maharaja.' He said as we walked on the soft grass, barefoot. 'I wish I could do something for him.'

I felt sad for Rajkumar Adhirohah. I hated how much affect his tears had on me. I couldn't tell him that the one responsible for his father's ill condition was his father himself. His past immoral deeds are coming back to haunt him. And little did Rajkumar Adhirohah knew that it was just the beginning.

'You should see him, my prince. He will feel better.' I suggested.

The little prince looked up to me in confusion.

'But he needs rest. Don't you think? He will be disturbed because of my presence.'

I wonder when he got so matured.

'No, Rajkumar. I reckon the Maharaja will feel much better after seeing you.'

The little prince ran this thought around his head for a little while before asking me to escort him to the Maharaja's chambers. And so I did. The chamber was, as usual, heavily guarded. But the guards, without any arguments, paved path for Rajkumar Adhirohah, as if he was already expected by the Maharaja. He held my hand and asked me to come with him. Inside the chamber, I saw a couple of veds making some ayurvedic medicines for the Maharaja who was lying on his bed asleep. Beside him sat the Maharani. As it turns out she was sitting there all night. The Rajkumar let go of my hand and took small steps towards his father. Maharani's eyes fell on him. She extended her arm for him, with a smile on her face even though she was overcome by lassitude because of being awake the whole night. The little prince stopped a foot away from Maharaja's bed and with his soft voice called out for his father. His words fell on Maharaja's ears like an aid. Like a helpless ant, drowning in a river grasp for a leaf to survive, Maharaja Brihadratha too tried to grab his last hope to live. He slowly opened his eyes and saw Rajkumar Adhirohah standing in front of him, enforcing a smile while wiping out his tears.

'Adhirohah?' He said while trying to get up.

The little prince helped his father to fix his back on the headboard and made his place next to him.

'It will be alright, father Maharaja. I will always be here for you. I promise.'

The Maharaja couldn't be prouder to witness such resoluteness from his son. He embraced his son whilst shedding a few tears. I left the family alone and walked out. I had another business to take care of. The misunderstanding between Maharaja Brihadratha and Yugant has given me an advantage. There is no one else Yugant loathes more than the Maharaja of Chandragarh. And this would make it easy for me to persuade Yugant to join our cause. With him, on our side, our power shall increase manifold.

The biggest benefit I've got over the years for being gentle and respectful towards all these important people of Chandragarh is that they all share things with me. These things can be anything important. Secrets, lies, truths, feelings. Oh! Feelings. How badly can one manipulate the other if he knows what his feelings are? In the case of Yugant, I knew where he goes to find solace in dire times. And I knew he goes there alone. Perfect opportunity for me to gain the upper hand. I took my horse and headed towards the Simha forest. In the east, quite deep into the forest, there is a pond. It is all plain there, short grass, no trees, and a few rocks to sit upon and stare. Yugant once took me to that place. It was a long time back. He was depressed then and he was depressed now. I knew he'll be there.

It took me some time to reach that particular spot. But I was surprised to see that he was not there all by himself but was rather having a company. I noticed two horses tied up to a tree, from the distance and yes, the horses were familiar. One was owned by Yugant and the other by Senapati Aagney. Senapati Aagney's presence here could be disastrous. I knew he was here to talk some sense into Yugant. Which was the last thing I wanted right now. I tied my horse a few meters away from theirs and tip-toed my way towards them. They both came into my view. They were sitting on a rock, near the pond. Senapati Aagney was talking to Yugant and the latter was busy throwing pebbles in the pond. To eavesdrop on their conversation, I went around and pushed myself against a nearer tree.

'You should come back and apologise, Yugant. Maharaja is dis-heartened because of you.' Senapati said.

'And why do you think I care?'

'Don't be so obstinate, Yugant. Don't forget he was the one to adopt you when...' Senapati paused after realizing where he was heading.

'When what, Senapati? When what! When my father didn't die and the man who pretends to be my father kept me away from him?'

'Don't say this, Yugant. You don't know why he did so.'

'Alright. I won't say.' Yugant stopped tossing the pebbles in the pond and looked at Senapati. 'Tell me why he did it and I won't say anything.'

'It is not that easy, Yugant. We were made to take an oath. An oath that abides us from talking about it.'

'All of you are liars. Why are you even here? To make me realize my mistake? Was it my mistake that I remained in the shadows of a lie? Was it my mistake to react the way I did after getting to know that my real father is alive? 21 years, Aagney, 21 years! 21 years ago I was told that my father was killed in a war. Even though it was hard for me to believe that my father, whose praises and songs of bravery our men sing, could get injured, let alone get killed in a war.

My father was no ordinary soldier, Aagney and you know it well. You were his disciple, for god's sake! But I made myself believe that my father, the bravest warrior of Akshobhyas, was no more. He died in a war. I made myself believe. For 21 years I was an orphan...'

'You were not an orphan. Maharaja Brihadratha...'

'I was an orphan! For 21 years I thought I was an orphan. But then I fought my father. I made him bleed, Aagney. I made my father hurt.' He stood up in anger.

'That man was not your father.' Senapati Aagney said gently.

'He was my father. Yayati Yasah was...'

'Yayati Yasah was not your father!' Senapati Aagney lost his patience. 'You call that man your father? Alright. I will tell you what happened. To make you realize your mistakes, I shall break my oath. For I can't let you take Maharaja Brihadratha's name in disgrace.'

While I remained hidden behind the tree, I realized that I have lost the opportunity to turn the tides.

'There is no doubt that your biological father was one of the bravest and greatest warrior the land of Bharatvarsh has ever seen. Maharaja Sarvyoni, during his later years, was fortunate to have him leading his invincible army. He was a loyal man. He led the army of Akshobhyas to several victories. Maharaja Sarvyoni, on multiple occasions, received many general and costly gifts from the lands beyond our boundaries to get the services of your father. But your father was a devoted man. He was devoted to the land and the Maharaja of Chandragarh. But more than him, Maharaja Sarvyoni was devoted to him. No treasure, no pleasure of the world could get Maharaja Sarvyoni to part ways with him. Legends say that the true power of the Akshobhyas lies within the ASI. But the true power of the Akshobhyas lies within those many loyal and brave souls that have, in their time, served this distinguished Kingdom. One of them was your father, Yugant. He was the pinnacle of perseverance and intelligence when it came to army strategies, there is no denying that. But his loyalty towards the crown wavered a few years after Maharaja Brihadratha took the throne. I know it is hard for you to believe but this is the truth. Senapati Yayati had his reasons. The compassionate, intelligent, and equitable Maharaja Brihadratha we know of now wasn't always the same. You have to take into consideration the fact that when Maharaja Brihadratha ascended the throne, he was merely a boy. The responsibility of administrating the greatest kingdom in the prestigious Bharatvarsh was too massive for a boy of 22. Even he acknowledges, that some decisions he took back then were not so considerate. He took some time, but the results are in front of you. He proved to be one of the greatest Kings of the Akshobhyas. In the beginning, everyone thought that Maharaja Sarvyoni, on his death bed, went against the paramount rule in the Akshobhyan history. The rule to prefer deeds over birth. Everyone thought that the ailing king made his son as his successor because he was captivated in his son's love. But they all failed to see the true potential of Maharaja Brihadratha. Eventually, they all accepted their mistake and accepted Maharaja Brihadratha as the ruler of Akshobhyas wholeheartedly. But your father, Yugant, failed to see the same. He was impatient and never considered a young man suitable for ruling this illustrated Kingdom. After a series of events, differences began to grow between Senapati Yayati and Maharaja Brihadratha. He became untrue towards the crown of Chandragarh.'

Yugant was shocked to learn the truth. And this one, I can guarantee, was not fabricated.

'One day, your father decided to not take it anymore.' Senapati Aagney continued. 'He stormed an assembly meeting where all eminent rulers of Bharatvarsh were assembled and foolishly questioned Maharaja Brihadratha's capabilities in front of everyone. Maharaja Brihadratha could have had the rogue Senapati Yayati in chains and have him thrown in the dungeons for dishonouring him in front of everyone instantaneously but he let your father state his concern. Senapati Yayati launched a series of blames towards the King and accused him of poor and unjust administration before ultimately asking him to prove his worthiness towards the throne of Chandragarh by challenging him for a duel. Everyone was shocked by the extent to which your father had fallen. They were shocked even more when Maharaja Brihadratha accepted his challenge because everyone knew that your father was invincible. He was yet to taste the sourness of defeat. Everyone feared that Senapati Yayati would kill the last male bearer of the royal Akshobhyan blood. But Maharaja Brihadratha yet again proved everybody wrong. You know how brave your father was, Yugant. You watched him train every day. I have been in many wars with him and have seen many great warriors of different kingdoms bow down to him on the battlefield. Your father was majestic with the sword, Yugant. But that day, Maharaja Brihadratha was untouchable. And don't have this false perception of him wielding the ASI. He used a sword given to him as a gift by the then Maharaja of Indraprastha, the very same day in the same assembly. I never watched your father fail so horribly, Yugant. But that day, even your father realized that he was defeated. And that was no mere defeat. It was a defeat of arrogance. Your father was imprisoned for showing disloyalty towards the crown. For picking up a weapon against the Akshobhyan blood to kill. Your father was imprisoned for being a traitor. And don't let me remind you of the severe punishment for the traitors, Yugant.'

'Death of the traitor and his whole family.' Yugant murmured in broken words.

'The moment your father picked up his sword against Maharaja Brihadratha his death was guaranteed and so was yours. But why are you alive, Yugant? Why are you still alive after you questioned Maharaja Brihadratha's intensities just like your father did 21 years ago?'

Yugant's head was bowed down. He had realized his mistake. He had a panic attack and sat down on a rock but Senapati Aagney, nevertheless, continued.

'Mahapradhan Ganakarta read the charges against your father that next day. Your father was supposed to be sentenced to death and so were you. Everyone in the assembly room agreed with the severe punishments your father deserved. Except for Maharaja Brihadratha. This was one of the decisions he took by going against the laws of Akshobhyas. As I said before. He was young and some decisions he made were not rightful. This was one of them, Yugant.

'Letting you live was wrong in the laws of Akshobhyas, Yugant. Letting you live was wrong!' Senapati Aagney yelled above Yugant who was sitting holding his head.

'When everyone asked the king to kill your father and you, Maharaja Brihadratha decided otherwise. He sentenced your father to live in banishment, away from the boundaries of the Akshobhyan Empire, and allowed him to take you with him. But do you know what your father said to this? Do you?'

Senapati Aagney took a little pause and looked down on Yugnat.

'He said that his child will be a burden to him, Yugant.'

Yugant was astounded and looked up at Senapati Aagney with astonishment.

'Yes, Yugant. You heard it right. Your father abandoned you.'

Senapati Aagney's words echoed in Yugant's ears.

'Your real father left you all alone because you were a burden to him. He left you in Chandragarh where you were nothing more than a traitor's son. But Maharaja Brihadratha went against the law one more time. He took you as his son. Maharani Drisana was pregnant with Rajkumar Dvij at that time, making you the eldest of his sons. And it was no mere sympathy that he showed that day. You know how you were treated while you were growing up. Like a true prince. Not only that, but you were also considered as a worthy candidate for being the crown prince of Chandragarh. But Rajkumar Dvij was more capable than you and ergo was appointed as the future Maharaja of the Akshobhyas. And tell me, Yugant. Did you, even once, heard anyone referring to you as a traitor's son? Oh please. No one ever treated you anything less than a prince. And because of whom? A man you call a liar. For whom you have lost all your respect. I pity you, Yugant. For not realizing what you have done to dishonour Maharaja Brihadratha. Maharaja Brihadratha made everyone take an oath to not let you, in any way, know about that very day. Why do you think that Senapati Yayati's picture still adorns the walls of every important building in Chandragarh? Why would they let a traitor's picture hang on the walls alongside some of the most loyal members in the history of the Akshobhyan Empire? Because Maharaja Brihadratha cared for you. Because he looked down at you as his eldest son. You are so wrong about our Maharaja Brihadratha, Yugant. So wrong. And if you have even the slightest of doubts about the factuality of the truth, I have told you, you know the path to the Advaityas. You can go and ask for yourself about the truth from your traitor father who now roams around with a different name but the same ambition.'

Senapati Aagney shook his head over the helpless Yugant and left him alone. He jumped on his horse and went back to the palace. My presence too was futile now. Now that Yugant knows the truth, persuading him will be impossible. Without making much noise, I tip-toed my way back to my horse and headed towards the palace leaving Yugant alone with his thoughts.

When I reached the palace, the sun was half above the horizon. Everyone was awake by now and were ready to head towards the Ganani River for depositing the ashes of Rajkumar Dvij. Rajkumar Adhirohah was sitting on the staircase in white clothes and was waiting for everyone else to arrive. Senapati Aagney was walking back and fro on the top of the staircase. He was seemingly anxious about the little conversation he had with Yugant. I felt I saw Nrchakshu too peeking from the edge of the entrance. But after a clearer look, I reckoned otherwise. I greeted Rajkumar Adhirohah as I went past him to join Senapati Aagney. We talked for a few moments until Maharani Drisana, Mahamantri Brahmanad and Mahapradhan Ganakrta arrived. To my surprise, Maharaja Brihadratha was able to join us. He was assisted by a few soldiers. But it was surprising to see that the man who was ill and was bedridden was now standing on his feet and was ready to walk to the Ganani River. Much determination was shown by him. Maybe I wasn't the only one who gets influenced by Rajkumar Adhirohah's tears.

The lot marched towards the pious Ganani River. It was a dull walk, as expected. The high priest was already waiting for us on the banks of the Ganani River. A small havan was conducted for the late Rajkumar's soul to find peace and solace. Eventually, the time came for the deposition of Rajkumar Dvij's ashes. Maharaja Brihadratha was overcome by a concern. He thought Yugant at least would be present to scatter the late Rajkumar's ashes.

'We should wait.' He murmured to Maharani Drisana. The Maharani shook her head slowly and persuaded the King to deposit the ashes in the river with Rajkumar Adhirohah.

But the Maharaja was sure that Yugant will arrive. And he was right. From the crowd emerged a guilty Yugant. His head was bowed as he came forward. Maharaja was seemingly happy to see him. Maharaja, Yugant, and Rajkumar Adhirohah scattered the ashes of the late Rajkumar into the Ganani River. After the ceremony was concluded, a remorseful Yugant asked for forgiveness from the Maharaja. And the Maharaja, forgetting everything that had happened, embraced Yugant Yasah.

❖

ACALA

'Come with me, Yuvan. I can't wait anymore. I have to tell him.'

'Maharaja's health has only just improved. Are you sure this is the right time?'

'I can't wait for the right time, Yuvan. Rajkumar Dvij is dead!'

'But you said no one would believe, let alone the Maharaja if we present our case without any grave evidence.'

'I remember what I said. But this can't wait. Come with me at once.'

Mahamantri Brahmanand was profoundly obstinate. He failed to see that accusing Mahamatya Acala isn't going to be easy. But for him, the Mahamatya is the real culprit. The real traitor who sent Akshobhyan military details to the Rudras. It will be nice if he can persuade the Maharaja to believe the same.

I accompanied Mahamantri Brahmanand to the assembly room. Maharaja Brihadratha was sitting on his throne, all alone. He was mixed up in his thoughts when we came in and was surprised to see us is such haste. Well, the Mahamantri was in haste. I have been patient for the last 25 years. I could have waited a little longer. Maharaja Brihadratha rose from his throne and seemed to be in much better physical condition now. Mahamantri took a few steps towards the Maharaja before speaking up.

'Years ago you didn't take my advice, Maharaja. You didn't listen to me while appointing Acala as the Mahamatya. I told you that a man with a past like that couldn't be trusted. But you made the mistake of trusting him anyway.'

'What are you talking about, Mahamantri? I hope you have a valid reason for accusing your Maharaja of committing a mistake.' The Maharaja said gravely.

'I don't wish to humiliate your majesty's reputation. But appointing Acala as the Mahamatya was a grave mistake. A mistake that took our crown prince away from us.'

'Beware, Mahamantri, about what you speak!' The Maharaja roared.

The Mahamantri had gone berserk to accuse the Maharaja of Chandragarh of killing his son. I wish I wasn't here to witness this. Seeing me accompany the Mahamantri will only harm my reputation in front of the Maharaja.

'I know you have always loathed Mahamatya Acala. But this is just taking it too far, Mahamantri.' Maharaja Brihadratha said loudly.

'You know the reason for my hatred against that pretentious Acala, Maharaja. But this time I am not the only one to say this. Yashvasin Yuvan agrees with me.' The Mahamantri said while pointing towards me.

I cursed the Mahamantri for dragging me into this. All these years of effort and endurance to be recognised by the King was in danger now. The next few lines that I say shall determine whether the Maharaja would trust me anymore.

'What do you want to say, Yuvan?' The Maharaja asked while giving me a grave look.

'It happened one night, Maharaja. Days before the invitation from the Kurus arrived. I was accompanying Mahamantri Brahmanad to meet one of his trusted spies.' I said while remembering to be gentle and calm. 'The spy gave us a papyrus scroll, Maharaja. The scroll was sent to a commander of an army that we fought back in the Great War months ago. It contained the information about our army's strength and other confidential details that could have brought us in peril. That scroll had Mahamatya Acala's stamp on it.'

The Mahamantri took out the scroll and handed it over to the Maharaja for him to have a closer look.

'The Mahamantri told me that it was Mahamatya's as he was the one who assigned him that particular stamp.' I said while the Maharaja was giving the scroll a closer look.

'What does it mean to you, Yuvan?' The king asked.

'I believe there are high chances that the scroll was sent by Mahamatya Acala himself. It is very difficult to forge a stamp like that, Maharaja. Moreover, the stamp remains with the owner almost all the time..'

'Almost.' The Maharaja highlighted. 'Almost with him at all times. Is that right, Yuvan?'

'Yes, sire.' I replied.

'Mahamantri, I would advise you to stop wasting your time on proving Mahamatya as the enemy of the state and focus your time on looking for a potential spy in our palace who has committed this crime of forging.'

'Acala is the spy, Maharaja. Why can't you see that he is not innocent? There is every right to believe that he sent information which resulted in Rajkumar Dvij's death. Acala is as avaricious as it gets. He'll do anything for a pot of gold.' The Mahamantri said.

'Mahamatya Acala is not the spy, Mahamantri. Neither is he a gluttonous man as he used to be. Stop judging people by their past. People change. Mahamatya Acala is a loyal man. He is loyal to the crown.'

'So was Senapati Yayati, Maharaja.'

'Mahamantri!' The walls of the assembly room echoed as the Maharaja yelled. 'Remember your limits. One more word and I shall forget who you are. I won't differentiate you from the prisoners in our dungeons.' Saying this the Maharaja stormed out of the assembly room.

Mahamantri Brahmanad was disappointed. His downcast eyes reflected his distressed. He walked towards me and patted me on the shoulders before going past me. I too followed him till the exit of the assembly room.

When I turned right from the assembly room, I saw Nrchakshu, and this time I was certain. He was coming in my direction. But when he saw me, he turned his way. This time I was certain that Nrchakshu was trying to avoid me. Something was wrong with him and I wanted to know what. I followed him to the artillery chambers which he locked behind him. I knocked on the door a couple of times.

'Who is it?' He asked from the inside. I remained silent and kept on knocking.

He opened the door eventually. I rushed in and locked the door behind me.

'What are you doing?' he asked.

'What are you doing by trying to avoid me?'

'I... I... wasn't.'

'Don't lie, Nrchakshu. You have been avoiding me since we came back from Indraprastha.'

'Why does it even matter to you?' He asked while shoving me off and unlocking the door.

'If you have any questions, you may ask.' I said to him as he stepped out of the chamber.

He paused and sighed. Then he turned back and closed the door again. He sat down on a stool that was behind the door.

'Is Kalki really...?'

'Yes. Kalki is the former Senapati of Akshobhyan army. Yayati Yasah.'

'You knew him, don't you? I mean personally.' Nrchakshu asked.

'Yes. When I joined the army Yayati Yasah was the Senapati. We had multiple interactions. Enough for us to get familiar with each other.'

Nrchakshu lost eye contact with me and lowered his head.

'Maybe that's why he didn't kill me. When he saw you, he just stopped and moved away from me.' He said in a low voice.

'You remember that?' I asked curiously. He looked up again.

'Yes. That and the instance when I rushed towards him with my sword. After that, it all went black.'

'Yes. That was something idiotic to do.' I said with a hint of humour.

Nrchakshu smiled for a while but then became upset again.

'I never thanked you for it.' He said. 'For saving my life.'

'That is what we are supposed to do, aren't we? To help our companions.'

'Yes. But I failed to do so for Rajkumar Dvij. I wasn't strong enough to fight Kalki. Only if I was more capable. I could have saved Rajkumar Dvij.' Nrchakshu felt devastated.

'Don't blame yourself. It wasn't your fault.' I said while trying to cheer him up.

'But why would Yayati do such a thing? It is so inhuman of him to harm the empire he once served.'

'Yayati Yasah has his reasons.' I said. 'Maharaja Brihadratha has not always been the 'ideal' king. Of all the people you should know that.'

'Maharaja Brihadratha has always been fair and kind to me. Why would you even say such a thing?' Nrchakshu asked in a rather blunt manner.

'You don't know anything, Nrchakshu. Maybe you should start asking the right questions about your history. To quote Mahamantri Brahmanand: 'your past defines you'.'

'What do you mean?' Nrchakshu was getting giddy.

'Wrong question.' I said with a smirk.

Nrchakshu stood up from his seat, agitated. I didn't give him much attention furthermore. I unlocked the door, stepped outside, and walked away in an indefinite direction. Nrchakshu called out for me a couple of times but I didn't turn around.

I had nothing much to do. So, I thought I'd go for a ride on my horse. When I commenced descending the staircase, I noticed a soldier taking a scroll inside the palace. It was a rather shabby one. By the looks of it, it was meant for someone of low prestige and I wondered who that might be. I asked the soldier to stop.

'For whom is the scroll for?' I asked in a heavy voice.

'Mahamantri Brahmanand, sir.' He said to me.

His answer made me intensely inquisitive. An old filthy scroll addressed to Mahamantri Brahmanand. I had a little idea from whom it might be.

'Hand me the scroll. I'll see to it that Mahamantri Brahmanand gets this.'

'I was asked to deliver the scroll directly to the Mahamantri, sir.' The naïve soldier said.

'I said I'll see to it that it is delivered to the Mahamantri.' I hardened my tone.

The soldier gave me the scroll and walked away. I previously had my doubts about the confidentiality of the scroll. It seemed to me that it contained something of immense importance. Something classified, perhaps. And I was proved right when I opened the scroll. The message was written in a historical language, presumed to be extinct. The Akhzariyan. I, then, immediately asked another soldier, one of my trusted men, to deliver the scroll to the Mahamantri.

'Tell him you received it directly from a man at the gates of the palace.' I said as I handled the scroll to him.

I took a sigh of relief as I watched him go back inside the palace, heading towards the Mahamantri's chamber. I remembered I was heading for a ride before but decided otherwise.

The night that followed was long. I couldn't sleep and so I roamed in the corridors of the palace, waiting for the right time to come. I stopped at the passageway which overlooks the Simha forest, from the back of the palace. I stood there and gazed the moon as it looped over the lightly swaying trees. It wasn't a full moon. But in some time, it will be. I was blocked by a Column from his sight as Mahamantri Brahmanand walked towards me.

'Greetings, Mahamantri.' I said. Surprising the old man who wasn't aware of my presence.

'It is you, Yuvan.' Mahmantri said. He was taken back a little. Maybe he didn't expect me to be here at all.

'Having trouble sleeping?' I asked as the silvery moonlight illuminated my face.

'Yes.' Mahamantri said with a smile.

'It is going to rain tonight.' I said while gazing at the clouds around the moon. I looked at the Mahamantri again.

'Well, I wish you a good night, Mahamantri.' I said before walking away from him.

❖

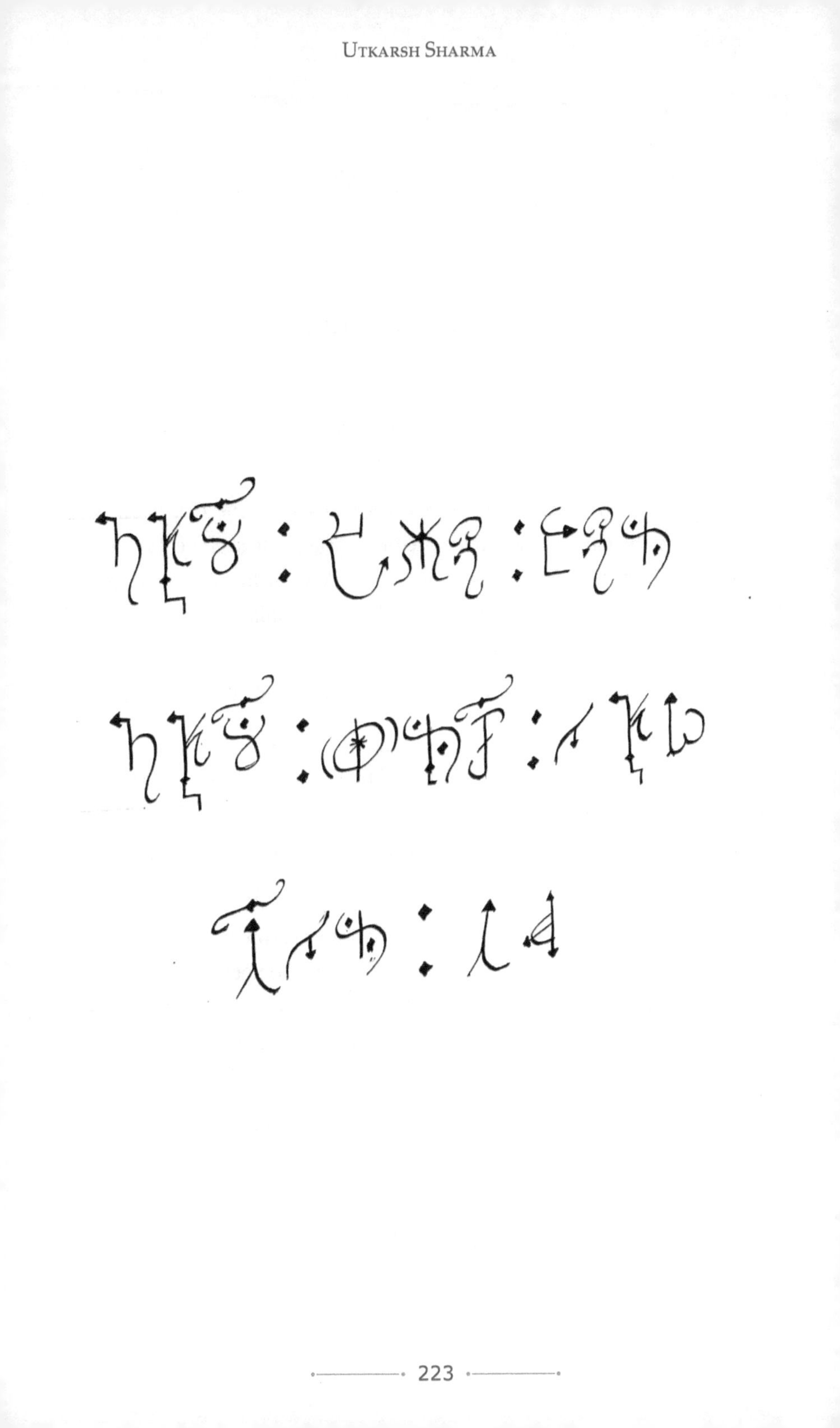

'I apologies for being late, Prakrant.' The Mahamantri said as he approached the cave, stamping on the puddles formed.

'I couldn't take the secret passageway to come here.' He continued. 'Yuvan was walking in the back of the palace premises, where the secret entrance of the passageway starts. I couldn't risk it and so walked all the way here, instead. Don't worry I am all alone. No one will notice you. I didn't even ask any of the soldiers to escort me here. You need not worry.'

The Mahamantri began to dry himself as he stood at the entrance of the cave.

'Why isn't the cave illuminated, Prakrant? You sure like working in the dark, don't you?' He said humorously.

The Mahamantri walked into the cave and stood a few feet away, facing Prakrant.

'It is raining quite heavily today. Maybe a storm is on its way.' Mahamantri Brahmanand gazed outside the window for a brief moment before continuing again. 'I received your scroll in time. So my doubt was right, wasn't it? So tell me, is he involved with Acala? I knew they both were working together. I knew it. Are they working for an organization or just for some gold?'

The impatient Mahamantri, who was eager to know the truth, threw a series of questions at Prakrant. But the latter didn't reply.

'Why aren't so saying anything?' The Mahamantri tried to look at Prakrant's face from different angles which was not visible because of the dark.

'Are you still upset about what I told you last time? Be mature, Prakrant.

I guaranteed you a desk job. But it will take a year. That is the time I require to replace you with someone equally capable. Don't test my patience now. Answer me. For whom are Acala and Yuvan working for?'

The Mahamantri still didn't get any answer from Prakrant.

'Prakrant? Are you alright?' The Mahamantri walked towards his spy and placed his hand over his shoulders. He tried to have a clearer look and unintentionally pulled Prakrant.

Mahamantri's spy fell on the floor of the cave with a thud. The Mahamantri was appalled to see him fall. He tried to bend a little to have a closer look at his body. A bolt of massive lightning struck outside and illuminated the scenes inside the cave. The Mahamantri stumbled and fell backwards when he saw a headless body of Prakrant. With a heavy breath, he tried to crawl backwards, with his eyes still fixated on his spy. Another lightning struck outside. This time illuminating my face which was covered with blood. The Mahamantri looked at me, frightened. He was horrified to see my bloody smirk, as I walked towards him. He resumed crawling backwards, this time at an increased pace. His back slammed on the walls of the cave. I kept walking and stopped a few inches away from him. I took my sword and with one swift move cut his chest. He gave a loud cry and tried to stop the flowing blood with his hands. Meanwhile, I ignited a lamp and placed it in a corner. The old man kept delivering multiple cries as I gazed outside from the window.

'You were wrong, Mahmantri.' I shifted my eyes towards him. 'The storm has already arrived.'

The Mahamantri still couldn't believe that I was able to outsmart him.

'Don't' worry, Mahamantri. I didn't cut your vitals. You won't die instantly. The night is still young. We'll have a nice conversation.' I said.

'I knew you were working with Acala. I had my doubts when you were the only one to agree with him in the assembly room, days before Janmashthmi. You disloyal bastard!'

'Using abusive words does not grace you, Mahamantri. You should know that.' I burst into laughter.

Mahamantri Brahmanand looked at my laughter with utter degradation.

'Oh, poor Mahamantri. Do you still think Mahamatya Acala is involved? No, Mahamantri. It is all me. Open your eyes! Think! Think!'

'That stamp…' Mahamantri whispered.

'You loath Mahamatya Acala to such an extent that even after knowing that his stamp could have been easily misused by someone else, you chose to believe otherwise. Sometimes, I reckon you don't hate Acala because of his past, Mahamantri. You hate Acala because of your arrogance. Maharaja Brihadratha went against your advice and that hurt your self-esteem. Because it was the first time, wasn't it? That, someone, decided to not agree with the sagacious Brahmanad.'

The Mahamantri was perplexed to see his ignorance and realized his grave mistake.

'It was me, Mahamantri. All the time it has been me! The scroll was never sent by Mahamatya Acala to the commander of any army. It wasn't even sent before the war. I used that opportunity to wave your much increasing attention away from me. It was I who went through this struggle of finding the appropriate moment to use Mahamatya's stamp without his knowledge. Oh, Mahamantri, you won't understand my endeavour to get his stamp. But the Jaitharas and Shooras helped me with it. Yes, Mahamantri. You remember that case, don't you? I remained in the courtroom after the case was concluded. The courtroom was all empty. There was no one but me. And after a couple of minutes, in which I forced Mahamantri's stamp on that scroll, which he had left in the courtroom, unknowingly, I too made my way to the exit.'

The Mahamantri sat on the floor of the cave wondering how merely he was fooled.

'But… But why did you do it, Yuvan? Maharaja Brihadratha trusted you, we all did. The Akshobhyan family gave you everything. Recognition, trust everything. How can you be so heartless, Yuvan?' He asked.

The smile on my face ceased.

'Past, Mahamantri. In one way or another, every individual's actions are affected by his past.' I said gravely.

'Don't be sad, Mahamantri.' I said while regaining my smile. 'At least you are defeated by your disciple. Isn't that right, Mahamantri? Your disciple, who turned out to be a spy?'

The meaning of my words came as a bolt from the blue for Mahamantri Brahmanand. He could sense that more secrets were going to be unravelled tonight.

'Your doubt is valid

Your disciple is a spy

Meet me at full moon'

'This is what was encoded in the scroll, wasn't it?'

Mahamantri Brahmanand was shocked to his core. He was astounded to know that I was able to decode an extinct language.

'How do you know this language?' He asked.

'You are not concentrating, Mahamantri. Think, Mahamantri, Think!'

The Mahamantri was finally able to assemble all the pieces of the puzzle correctly.

'You said your actions were affected by your past. And you know the Akhzariyan. The language which was presumed to be extinct when the last clan that used it was wiped out from existence.' Mahamantri Brahmanand said slowly.

'Yuvan. It's not your real name, is it?'

I shook my head slowly, in agreement with the bleeding old man.

'Yuvan was a made-up name, to conceal your real identity. So Nrchakshu isn't the lone survivor, is he, Yashvasin Yudhvan?'

'See, Mahamantri? All you had to do was concentrate. Alas! Only if you were able to concentrate earlier.'

'You killed Dvij! You, weasel!'

'Oh, no. I didn't kill him, Mahamantri. I would never harm the Rajkumars. The arrow that Rajkumar Dvij took in his neck was of Kalki or, as you now know, Yayati.'

'You work for Yayati? How much can you fall, Yashvasin? Don't you have any pride? Selling your services to a traitor like Yayati.'

'Yayati isn't a traitor and you know that Mahamantri. Of all the people, you know what the Maharaja did in his early years of ruling the kingdom. You were the one he came for advice. One can say, you are equally responsible for his acts of foolishness. And to talk about working for Yayati.' I took a pause and chuckled before continuing again. 'Again, you are drawing the wrong picture, Mahamantri. Losing our concentration, are we? As I said before. It is all for me. It has always been me.'

My laughter echoed in the small cave before I took another pause. The Mahamantri was bewildered to see this sinful side of me. A gentle, biddable, and benevolent disciple turned out to be an immoral man. It was bound to be quite a shock for him.

'I watched my entire clan get slaughtered that night, Mahamantri. I watched my sister and my father burn. I can still feel the heat coming out from the flames that covered their bodies. Do you know how tormenting that is? Your past reminding you of all the pain you have suffered. There hasn't been one night when the nightmares didn't haunt me. Do you know how that feels, Mahamantri? When each night you try to sleep but the scenes of your mother getting brutally killed flashes in front of you? Do you know how that feels when you have to serve that man who, with his own hands, has slayed the women who gave you birth? Yes, Mahamantri. The night I swore to seek vengeance was the same night I saw Maharaja Brihadratha slay my mother.'

The Mahamantri was losing sight. His eyes were flickering. The blood loss was taking its toll.

'We had to take that step, Yashvasin. I don't reckon you know it but the reason behind it was…'

'I know what the reason was!' I raged.

'But slaying the entire clan? What kind of justice is that, Mahamantri? A Maharaja slaying the people he was meant to serve. It is anti-poetic, isn't it?' I said while noticing Mahamantri's drowsy eyes.

'It doesn't make much difference now.' I continued. 'Akshobhyas annihilation is certain. No one can stop me, Mahamantri. I will steal the ASI.'

'You don't know where the real ASI is. The sword in the basement is a fake. You'll never get your hands on the real one.'

'Do you still think I am so naïve, Mahamantri? Look at yourself. Who put you in this condition? Who outsmarted Mahamantri Brahmanand, the man who is known for his intelligence and wit not only in Bharatvarsh but in the land that lies across the great seas too? I will get my hands on the ASI. It is true, I don't know about its actual whereabouts yet. I don't know where it is hidden. But Maharaja Brihadratha knows. And so, will his Aangrakshak panel.'

'You won't use Nrchakshu as your pawn!' Mahamantri Brahmanand said with the last ounce of spirit he had in him.

'I am not so heartless. I won't use him as my pawn. He is the last surviving member of my clan. I am just going to tell him about his past. I will fill him with blind hatred until I can see the same wrath and indignation in his eyes for Maharaja Brihadratha. Whatever he tries to do next is his choice. Believe me, I won't force him to join my cause. But it seems uncertain that he won't.'

I looked at the Mahamantri whose eyes were now closed. His breath was still there. But he was close to death.

'Quite a conversation we had here, Mahamantri Brahmanand. But it is getting late now.'

I walked towards the Mahamantri and squatted down to get to his level. He opened his eyes and stared at me.

'Well, I wish you a good night, Mahamantri.' With this, I shoved my sword inside him. My sword penetrated him three times, just to make sure that he is gone.

The rain made it difficult to drag the bodies of Mahamantri Brahmanad and Prakrant. The blood on my face, when interacted with the rain, took the form of small streams that went through my arms and chest, before finally getting washed away. The rain washed my sins away. I'd like to think about that. I rolled their corpses into the chasm. It will be years, not in my time, when their bodies will be discovered. That is if they are not eaten away or don't rot.

I noticed the sun rising above the horizon. The rain had also become less violent. It was time for me to get back to the palace and meet Nrchakshu.

Through the secret passageway, I returned to the palace and waited for the right moment.

Mahamantri Brahmanand's absence didn't go unnoticed. Mahapradhan Ganakarta was the first one to ask about his absence. The situation became grave when the news broke to the Maharaja in the evening. Maharaja Brihadratha last saw the Mahamantri with me and so asked me to meet him.

'Is he on one of his regular trips to the distant regions of the Empire?'

'Yes, Maharaja. He left last night. Said it was somewhat important. He received a scroll from one of his spies based in Suvarnagiri. Here, he left a message for you too.' I said while extending a forged scroll to him, stating the same in Mahamantri's handwriting and with his stamp. 'I escorted him till the Ganani River, where one of his men was already waiting for him with a carriage.'

'So he went to Suvarnagiri, huh?' Maharaja Brihadratha said while reading the scroll. 'He'll be gone for months, it seems. That is fine, though. You may leave, Yuvan.'

I bowed in front of the Maharaja before leaving. In the corridors of the palace, I saw Nrchakshu, from the distance, calling out for me. I took no notice of him and went on my way. This cycle continued for a few more days. He would try to confront me but I would just ignore him and test his patience. I knew he will break one day. And that day arrived soon.

It was afternoon. I was in my chamber, going over the weapons statistics when Nrchakshu decided to pay a visit. I expected him to be agitated. But the lad got too far. He swiped the papyrus records from my hands. I stood up.

'What do you think you are doing?' I yelled at him.

He forced me to a wall. My head banged on the surface and I fell. He picked me up by my neck. I resisted him and pushed his hands down, eventually shoving him away.

'You don't realize the gravity of your crime, Nrchakshu. You'll pay for it.' I said and stormed towards the door. But Nrchakshu came in between.

'You are not going anywhere without answering my questions.' Nrchkashu was enraged.

'You are out of your mind!' I exclaimed.

'Am I?' He asked in sarcastic wonder.

'Let me go.' I said gently.

'Answer me and then you shall leave. You wanted me to ask the right questions, didn't you? Alright. Here it is. Why of all the people should I know that Maharaja Brihadratha was not generous and kind in his past? Is this the right question?'

'Nrchakshu, you are not in the right state. You are not thinking it straight. Go now. We'll talk later.' I tried to calm him down.

'No!' He exclaimed. 'I want the answers now. I want to know why you are always trying to get the better of me. I want to know about Maharaja's past. I want to know about my past!'

I was surprised to hear Nrchakhsu's choice of words.

'But you told Senapati Aagney that you don't want to be bothered by your past. Now, all of a sudden you are curious about it? You are not making much sense here. I am asking you again to go back. We'll talk later. '

'I know what I said that day to Senapati Aagney. But it's tormenting. I know I am the last surviving Yudhvan. I know about that night of the massacre. But you keep on mocking me, torturing me. You keep on saying that I don't know about my past. I want to know the rest. What about my history is so ridiculous that me not knowing it makes me an imbecile in your eyes?'

'Why do you care what I think?'

'I don't. I don't care what you think. I care about the missing pieces of my bygone days. I fear that my past will define who I am and who I become. This lack of knowledge is agonizing. Just tell me already. Please, I beg you. I can't live in the constant fear of my past coming back to haunt me one day.' Nrchakshu fell on his knees. He was overcome by lassitude. I picked him up and made him sit on a chair.

'25 years, Nrchakshu. I have waited for this moment for 25 years.'

Nrchakshu looked up at me with confusion.

'You are not much different from Yugant. Both of you have lived most of your respective life in a lie.'

'What do you mean?'

'What Senapati Aagney and Mahamantri told you about that night of the massacre was a lie. It was a conspiracy. A deceitful scheme to slay the Yudhvan clan.'

'A conspiracy? What are you saying, Yuvan?' Nrchkahsu asked in a shaking voice.

'The army of Zeerat didn't attack Chandragarh on the commands of Raja Sahasrajit. It was Maharaja Brihadratha and Mahamantri Brahmanad who made it look like this. They were the ones to come up with this plot of wiping out the entire Yudhvan clan from the face of the earth.'

Nrchakshu stood up in astonishment.

'How do you know all this?' He asked while giving me an inquisitive look.

'You are not the only survivor of the Yudhvan clan, Nrchkahsu.' I replied.

Nrchakshu's eyes widened. He was completely baffled.

'My real name is Yashvasin Yudhvan. And you are my nephew.'

THE NIGHT OF THE MASSACRE

My last words startled Nrchakshu. His eyes were wide in incredulity. He couldn't believe what he was listening to. Maybe he didn't want to. His reactions were justified. After all, the things I was telling him were life-altering.

'This can't be true.' Nrchakshu muttered under his breath.

'It is true. I know these facts have got heartfelt gravity with them, making it difficult for you to believe. But it is true. Your mother was my elder sister. And it is also true that she was killed on Maharaja Brihadratha orders.'

Nrchakshu looked at me with dissatisfaction.

'My mother?' He asked in a low voice.

'Your mother was not a simple Yudhvan woman, Nrchakshu. She was the wife of the last leader of the Yudhvan clan. Nishprabh Yudhvan. Your mother and father were one of the most powerful people in Chandragarh. It is so ignorant of you for not knowing that. You should have asked more. You should have asked the right questions.'

'But why would Maharaja Brihadratha slay my parents?' He asked with uncertainty.

'Maharaja Brihadratha was a coward, that's why. Instead of facing the problem like a true Maharaja, he decided to uproot it altogether.'

I walked a few steps in the other direction of Nrchakshu. It wasn't easy for me either. Every time I had to remember that night, a part of me would die. But Nrchakshu needed to know.

'I don't understand. What forced the Maharaja to do such a horrid act?'

'No one forced your Maharaja, Nrchakshu. It was solely his decision.

You want to know why? I'll tell you why.' I turned around before continuing again. 'Your father and Maharaja Brihadratha were friends since their childhood. One was born in the oldest clan of Chandragarh. The clan of the eminent warriors. Yudhvans. While the other was born in the most powerful royal family in the whole Bharatvarsh. The Akshobhyas. But their difference in birth never became an issue in their friendship while they were growing. One can say that they shared the same relationship as Rajkumar Dvij and Yugant Yasah. They were that close. They also treated each other as their arch-rival. They were immensely competitive and always tried to outsmart each other. In this small competitive game of theirs, they both became splendid warriors. But their friendship took the test of time when they were both burdened with their respective responsibilities. Maharaja Brihadratha was the first to take this test. The untimely demise of Maharaja Sarvayoni saw Maharaja Brihadratha take the throne of the Akshobhyan Empire. His appointment as the Maharaja of Chandragarh commenced a reign whose early stages can be said to be the worst in the history of Chandragarh. A dark period which was concealed, from the world and the future generations, with the help of deceiving lies. As I said, the Yudhvans were the oldest clan in Chandragarh. That would also mean that they were the biggest too. Our increasing population made it difficult for us to accommodate our aboriginal land. We asked the Maharaja to grant us the adjacent piece of land. But instead, he relocated us to the most distant area of Chandragarh, near the Simha forest. The decision was not welcomed by us, but eventually, we had to agree. The demise of the leader of the Yudhvan clan followed next. After acknowledging your father's capabilities, he was made the leader of the clan by the other Yudhvans. One other view taken into consideration that made your father more eligible for the post was the fact that Nishprabh Yudhvan and Brihadratha Akshobhya were childhood friends. But this didn't prove to be instrumental at all in decreasing the formidable void between the Yudhvans and the Akshobhyas. The Maharaja of Chandragarh took a series of impetuous decisions against our clan. The most adverse of them was the removal of the Yudhvans from higher posts in the army. This was deplorable and strong condemnation was done by the leaders of the Yudhvans. No clear reasons were provided by the Akshobhyans for their harsh actions. Our clan members feared that if such grievous acts continued against them, there will come a time when the Yudhvans will be subsided from Chandragarh. And so, the

Yudhvans planned to do what they have been doing for ages. War. They planned to attack the Akshobhyas.'

Nrchkahsu stood from his place in surprise. He was staggered to know that his clan could start a riot.

'The Yudhvans raged war on the Akshobhyas?' He asked.

'Yes. It was a shocking decision, even for me. I was 14, mere a child, that time. But big enough to understand what was right and what wasn't. I knew the gravity of the decision and was totally against it. That night, hours before the massacre, I decided to talk some sense into my brother-in-law. But my father restricted me from doing so. I was depressed to notice that my clan members were filled with so much apprehension against the throne that they failed to see that raging war against the mighty Akshobhyas would only have one outcome. Annihilation of the Yudhvans. We could take them by surprise and hurt them a little, but there was no way that we could have defeated the greatest army in the whole Bharatvarsh. But my father, just like many others, failed to see the same. I was called a traitor by my father. He said that I'd sold my soul to the Akshobhyas. I was upset with this accusation and so, I ran away deep into the woods. My mother tried to stop me, she asked me to not go. But I didn't listen. In the forest, I tried to console myself and decided to visit Nishprabh and my sister in the morning. But little did I know that that morning would never come. Mahamantri Brahmanad had his spies deployed everywhere. One such infiltrator was within the Yudhvan clan too. Mahamantri Brahmanand had already discussed the scenario with Maharaja Brihadratha and had come up with a scheme to stop the Yudhvans. Instead of acting like a Maharaja and solve the problem, that Bastard Brihadratha slayed our entire clan.'

'But what about Raja Sahasrajit and his son Akshaj? There was an involvement of Zeerat, right?'

'It was an act, Nrchakshu. A well-written act. Raja Sahasrajit of Zeerat was taken seriously ill days before. The veds checking on him told his family that the Raja had only a few days to live. Therefore, his son, Akshaj was declared as the new Raja of Zeerat in secret. And I reckon you are aware of his avaricious intensities. Maharaja Brihadratha was made aware of this news and his wicked mind came up with this plan. He waited till Raja Sahasrajit was dead, which wasn't long. After that, he shared his immoral scheme with Akshaj who was easily convinced with a few sacks of gold. The army of Zeerat was ordered to attack the Yudhvans late at night and they made it look as an uprising from the late ruler of Zeerat. Whole blame was driven towards the late Raja Sahasrajit who lived his life serving Zeerat and the Akshobhyas loyally. This is what you get when you serve the deceitful Akshobhyas with all your heart. You either get evaded or killed.'

'But why would Maharaja Brihadratha do this?'

'ASI, Nrchakshu. ASI.'

'What does the ASI has to do with all this?' Nrchakshu asked.

'History tells us many things about the ASI, Nrchakshu. Most of them are how the ASI has brought peace and power to the Akshobhyas. But history has also concealed many truths. From the founder of the Akshobhyas, Samrat Mahadhyata, growing ambitious to the present ruler, Maharaja Brihadratha getting drunk with power, the ASI has influenced them all. What do you think the curse of ASI is?' I asked while pointing towards Nrchkahsu.

Nrchakshu was taken back for a while.

'That it only serves its holder?' I asked to which Nrchakshu nodded slightly.

'No, Nrchkahsu. That is not even close. The truth about the curse of ASI is much more horrid than that. Why do you think Maharaja Nagbhushana cared to build a separate chamber for the most powerful weapon? Because he knew the real curse of the ASI. The ASI captivates its holder, Nrchakshu. It bewitches them. It has affected everyone that has wielded the sword, for longer than it is meant to be. Maharaja Nagbhushana had seen his ancestors getting influenced by the power of the ASI. He knew the impact that it has on his wielders. It makes a person ambitious. It makes the person zealous. It makes him hungry for power. Even the greatest ruler in Akshobhyan history, Samrat Adhirohah wasn't able to control the ASI. Because it is the other way around. The ASI controls its wielder, Nrchakshu. The ASI, in its strange ways, has dominated the Rulers of Chandragarh. Every ruler since Maharaja Nagbhushana has taken caution. Except for the wars, where the ASI is meant to be used, the ASI has not been held by any ruler of the Akshobhyas. Except for Maharaja Brihadratha.

During the reigns of Maharaja Nagbhushana, Maharaja, Prataparat, and Maharaja Sarvayoni, the ASI was kept in the secret chamber in time of peace. But Maharaja Brihadratha was obsessed with the power of the ASI. The ASI kept in the chamber now is a fake.'

Nrchakshu was mixed up with his thoughts. I had a little idea about what he might be thinking.

'You know where the real ASI is, don't you?'

Nrchakshu looked at me, surprised.

'It has been the ASI, Nrchakshu. The ASI ruined your childhood. It made you an orphan. The ASI deprived you of a happy and joyous life. It killed your parents, my sister, and everyone else that shared the same blood with us. The ASI took our families away from us.'

Nrchakshu was shaking vigorously.

'The ASI, Nrchakshu. It slayed our entire clan.'

'STOP!' Nrchkashu exclaimed.

'Stopping me won't change the past, child.'

'You could be lying.' Nrchakshu was becoming hysterical. 'You are lying! Till yesterday you used to mock me. You used to get on my nerves, constantly trying to provoke me. And today, you say you're my family? No, I refuse to believe you!'

I tried to calm him down. I place my hand on his shoulders but he shoved me away.

'I know it is hard for you, Nrchakshu. I have witnessed Yugant suffer from the same cause. Both of you have lived in the dark for most of your lives. Moreover, it is natural for you to not believe me. If you don't believe me, you can ask Maharaja Brihadratha yourself. I hardly think he will lie to you after what has happened between him and Yugant.' I took a pause and slowly placed my hands on his shoulders.

'But don't forget. Maharaja Brihadratha and ASI are the reason that you are an orphan.'

Nrchakshu cried and pushed me away. I fell on the ground and he stormed out of the room. I followed him.

Nrchakshu paced towards the palace gardens in exasperation. I kept my distance while I followed him. After some time the destination came into sight. I saw Maharaja Brihadratha strolling in the garden alone. He was in his evening clothes. The area was secluded. The Maharaja had ordered the soldiers to leave him alone for a while. Good for us. I followed Nrchakshu till the last massive columns which would hide me while I listen to them.

The Maharaja saw Nrchakshu coming towards him from a distance. He was curious to see Nrchakshu advance towards him with such graveness. With his hands behind his back, he questioned Nrchakshu.

'You seem a little tense. What is the matter?'

'I want to know about my parents.'

Nrchakshu's statement took Maharaja out of the blue.

'Your parents?' asked the Maharaja who was left stupefied.

'Yes. I want to know who they were and how they died. And I want to hear the truth.'

'The truth?' Maharaja asked with a faint smile.

'Yes. The truth.'

'What is truth, Nrchakshu? Everyone has their version of the truth.'

'Please don't play mind games with me, Maharaja. I just want to know what happened that night, 25 years ago.'

'I knew these days would come, Nrchakshu.' The Maharaja said while turning away and taking a few steps. 'I knew they would come back to haunt me. My past mistakes. First Yugant and now you. I will tell you the truth.' He turned back towards Nrchakshu. 'And I would tell it in the version you would find most appropriate.'

The Maharaja of the Akshobhyas took a deep breath before carefully uttering his next set of words.

'I ordered that massacre to take place. I am responsible for your parents' death.'

Maharaja's words fell on Nrchakshu's ears like a bolt of lightning. He was dumbstruck. A teardrop rolled over his cheeks.

'I am responsible for your clan's massacre.'

'Why?' Nrchakshu asked in a low voice.

'To maintain peace and integrity in Chandragarh. The Yudhvans were dangerous to Chandragarh's peace. As a Maharaja I had to take that decision.'

'As a Maharaja you were supposed to protect your people!' Nrchakshu cried.

'What kind of king are you? You slayed the people you swore to protect. Aren't you ashamed?' Nrchakshu threw a series of blames on the Maharaja.

'No, Nrchakshu. I am not. I am neither ashamed nor do I feel remorse for that night. It was one of the decisions that I had to make as the Maharaja of Chandragarh. I was young when I ascended the throne. It was difficult for me to accustom to all the responsibilities all of a sudden. Dire times require tough calls. The Akshobhyan Empire became vulnerable after the demise of father Maharaja. I had to make tough calls to make sure the integrity of our empire remained intact.'

'But he was your friend!' Nrchakshu exclaimed.

Maharaja Brihadratha was surprised to know the Nrchakshu already knew so much about his past.

'So you know. I wonder who told you that. But Yes. It is true. Your father, Nishprabh Yudhvan, was my friend. We grew up together and fought battles together too.'

A smile popped up on Maharaja's face as he remembered his old friend. The brisk nostalgia took him away from the present.

'We used to be inseparable and always tried to compete with each other in every aspect. Those are the days I treasure. But everything changed when we were forced with the responsibilities we didn't ask for. I had to take the throne to serve my people and your father was asked to administrate his people. It was unanticipated by us. We never looked up for such big responsibilities. We were living our days, being immature, and all of a sudden we were asked to serve and fight for our men. It changed everything, Nrchakshu. Everything.

Nrchakshu looked at Maharaja in distraught.

'I am surprised by your knowledge of your past. I don't know who told you about it. But as you may know, your father…'

'But why leave me? Why did not you kill me with the rest of my family?' He interrupted the king.

Maharaja Brihadratha took a long pause. He looked at Nrchakshu with a lack of certainty before coming to understanding. Nevertheless, he continued.

'I was asked by Mahamantri Brahmanand to not witness the bloodshed. He feared that I, still a young sentimental man who cared about his people, would be moved because of the heart-wrenching scenes near the Simha forest and would order the army to restrain. But I went down, anyway. To witness the dark reality of becoming a Maharaja. To witness the graveness of my decision. I saw people in huge numbers getting slaughtered. Even today, those scenes come back flashing in front of me in the form of nightmares. Men and women being set on fire. The sheer horror of their cries. It is torturous to even remember those scenes. But one of them was just too distressing. Among those scenes, I saw an elderly woman who was set ablaze from the back. She was running and crying in pain. My heart could not bear to hear her excruciating cry and so I approached her. She fell on the ground and was crawling, screaming, and was agonized. I decided to relieve her from all the pain in the world and thrust the ASI into her. She was gone, instantly. Just when I thought I'd had enough and decided to go back into the palace, I heard a cry. A cry of an infant. I looked for a child but couldn't see one. After carefully listening to the cry, I moved the now-doused body of that elderly woman. She was shielding a child from the attack of my soldiers. I instantly recognized who the child was. It was you, Nrchakshu. I had been to your father's home a couple of times after your birth. Your mother, a very kind woman, always welcomed me with a warm smile. I had even held you before that night. And so there was no doubt in my mind that the child was the son of my friend. I decided not to annihilate the entire Yudhvan clan. I decided to let you live.'

'Why did you take the ASI out of the secret chamber?'

This question was unexpected by the Maharaja.

'Why do you ask?' Maharaja Brihadratha asked.

'Are you familiar with the true Curse of ASI?'

'I am the Maharaja of the Akshobhyan Empire. I am familiar with a lot of things that are more confidential than the ASI and its curse.'

'And you still decided to remove the ASI from the secret chamber.'

'That is something I don't have to explain to you.' Maharaja replied gravely.

'You removed it because you were obsessed with its power.' Nrchakshu accused the Maharaja.

'I removed it because of a theft attempt that took place days after I took the throne.'

'You are lying!' Nrchakshu yelled.

'You have always lied.' He continued. 'That is what you are best at. Not properly administrating your people. But lying. That is what you have done with Yugant and that is what you did to me.'

'I don't reckon I have to explain anything more to you. I told you the truth you wanted to hear. And I don't regret the decision I made that night 25 years ago as the Maharaja of Chandragarh and the Akshobhyan Empire. Moreover, I am happy that you know the truth now. Keeping Yugant in the dark made me realize the graveness of my lies. But it was his nobility to forgive me and to accept me for who I am. I don't expect the same from you, Nrchakshu. Yours was a greater loss.' Saying this Maharaja turned his back on Nrchkashu. 'I want to be left alone. You may leave now.'

Nrchakshu ran his eyes around the palace gardens and then gave a slight nod. He turned around and in small steps made his way back to the palace. It was difficult to judge where he was heading as he stood over the entry staircase and thought for a while. Then, all of a sudden, he turned around and paced back into the palace. He was heading towards a particular direction now. I watched a dozen soldiers salute him as he went inside the Maharaja's chambers. After a brief moment, he came out with something in his hand, covered with a big red silk cloth. He rushed to the royal stable to get his horse. I commenced following him but remembered to keep my distance. Nrchakshu headed deep into the woods of the Simha forest. He was riding his horse at a high pace. For a little while, I even lost him in the woods but was eventually able to trace him. He eventually started to lower his pace. The part of the forest seemed familiar. Yes, it was. From a distance, I could see an engraved stone sign set up on the orders of Maharaja Nagbhushana. It was the place where the two founders of the Akshobhyan Empire used to perform Sadhna. Nrchakshu stepped down from his horse and loosened the entity, wrapped in a red cloth, which was tightened to the horse's saddle. He walked towards the two rectangular stones and sat on one of them. He stared at the covered entity for a little while. The sound of the cuckoo bird made me realize that we weren't alone in the forest. I wished Nrchakshu did what he had to a little faster. But he remained there, seated. And kept on staring at the entity which he held in both hands. After some time, he took a deep breath and stood up. He placed the entity on one of the stone and pushed the other massive stone for a couple of feet. He then dug up a hole, four feet wide and a couple of feet deep. And then threw the entity inside the hole and covered it with dirt before pushing the stone to its previous position. He dusted his hands off his clothes. Then he jumped on his horse and took off. No one saw Nrchakshu for the next three days.

DECLARATION OF WAR

We were called for an important meeting to discuss the news that broke out in the morning. The city of Chandragarh was in a state of emergency. As usual in the case of emergencies, we were called in the assembly room to discuss our next step. Except for Nrchakshu and Mahamantri Brahmanand, everyone else reported.

'Gentlemen....' Maharaja Brihadratha addressed us. 'You all must be aware of the rumour that broke out in the morning. It saddens me to tell you all that it isn't merely a rumour. Indraprastha has been captured. The Varunyas and Advaityas broke their alliance with the Kurus by shocking them with an unexpected attack to seize the palace of Indraprastha. They have also declared war against us, the Akshobhyas. I received a secret scroll from the Maharani of Kurus, my daughter, which makes me believe that some people of the Kuru family were able to survive. Maybe they are counting their days in a hideout. Maybe they are already dead. But the predominant fact is that the Varunyas and Advaityas have broken their alliance. Not only did they attack the Kurus who have always come to our aid, but have also committed the grave mistake of breaking the alliance with us. They deserve retribution.'

Everybody present in the assembly room was overcome with passion and enthusiasm. Maharaja Brihadratha's words had pumped up all.

'Years ago, former Senapati Yayati Yasah committed a treacherous crime of turning against the crown. That time my error in judgement saw him leave the Akshobhyan boundaries alive. He has come back. More traitorous than ever. More treasonous than ever. With a plan more fatal than ever. This time there won't be any error in my judgement. He shall pay for his crimes. With Yayati the rulers of Varunya Kingdom and Advaitya Kingdom shall also pay. We are in a state of war. And this war will end when I'll see the Akshobhyan flag hoist high in their capitals, Topra and Meerut.'

'Long Live Chandragarh!'

'Long Live Chandragarh!'

'Long Live Chandragarh!'

He exclaimed and everyone repeated with him.

Senapati Aagney and Yugant Yasah were ordered to prepare the army of Chandragarh for the war whereas Mahapradhan Ganakarta was ordered to send messages to the vassal kingdoms to send their army to Chandragarh. The first message ordered to be sent was to the Raja of Patliputra. The courageous and valiant army of Patliputra was famous nationwide. Maharaja Brihadratha wasn't taking any chances. The army of Chandragarh wasn't big enough for both the armies of the Varunyas and Advaityas and he was aware of Yayati's expertise in the battlefield. He has seen Yayati win wars for Chandragarh since his childhood. He won't take Yayati so lightly. After all, the army of the enemy was going to be administrated by him.

Senapati, Yugant, and the Mahapradhan left the assembly room to work upon their given task, leaving me and Maharaja Brihadratha alone. The Maharaja and I had a little conversation.

'I hear Nrchakshu is missing too.' He said.

'You heard right, Maharaja.' I replied.

'First Mahamantri and now Nrchakshu. Their presence is required in Chandragarh more than ever.' Maharaja said with a hint of anger.

'Yuvan, I want you to send your best man to Suvarnagiri. He should reach there faster than the news of this war. Ask Mahamantri to come as fast as he could. And send the rest of your men looking for Nrchakshu.' He said.

I bowed to him in acknowledgement. I noticed something strange about Maharaja Brihadratha and didn't hesitate to point it out.

'I am sorry, Maharaja. But it looks like you forgot to bring your sword today.'

Maharaja's eyes met mine awkwardly. His face was white as if he was trying to hide something from me, which was strange given he was the Maharaja of the Akshobhyas who should fear nothing.

'I have given it to the bladesmith. Won't be futile to sharpen it in such dire times. Who knows, maybe I'll have to enter the battlefield too.' He said trying to wave the air of uneasiness away.

'That won't be required, sir. Entrust that responsibility to us. Permit me to leave now.' I said while bowing down to him.

I walked out of the assemble room, leaving Maharaja Brihadratha alone who was staring outside the window. A strange run of misfortune he finds himself in. First the death of his eldest son. Then the fall out between him and Yugant and Nrchakshu. Now the capture of his daughter's kingdom. All his past mistakes were coming back to haunt him. Lying to Yugant and Nrchakshu. Letting Yayati live. All these mistakes were taking their toll.

I was heading towards the palace grounds where my men had assembled. But my legs hindered their movement as I walked past Mahamantri Brahmanand's room. It was latched but not locked. A cobweb could be seen on the latch surface. I looked around. Everyone was in a rush. The declaration of war had taken free time out of everyone's life. I wonder if anyone was looking at me. I ran my eyes around but found everyone busy in their preparation of the war. I walked towards the door, slowly, and unlatched it. It opened with a creak. I pushed the doors ajar. There was hardly any space for the light to come in. The heavy curtains were drawn in. The opening of the door illuminated a short path in the room which led to a chair covered with dust. An impulse asked me to be sure and I swiped the handle of the chair with my finger. I rubbed the dust between my finger and thumb. Then I started examining the room. Some portraits adorned the wall on the right side. It was difficult to guess who they depicted. On the left was a huge book rack. Many scrolls and books were placed on it. Some scrolls were coming loose from the rack. I was inquisitive about the books he read. A particular section caught my attention. Seven books were tightly adjusted into it. I tried to get one out of its place but couldn't. I pulled with all my strength until one of them came loose. But one accompanied another and then another joined in. One by one four of the books fell on the floor creating a big cloud of dust. I coughed before picking them up to put them back. Just when I was trying to put them in again, I noticed an old book, half stuck behind the other three that remained inside. It looked like some royal record, but an old one. Its cover was beautifully embroidered. I pulled it out before inserting the fallen books inside that particular section. I ran my hand over it. The red embroidered cloth covering it depicted royalty. I wondered what records were kept inside it, what secrets were hidden. I was about to open the book but a familiar voice made me drop it.

'What are you doing in Mahamantri Brahmanand's room, Yuvan?' Senapati Aagney asked curiously.

I was unable to come up with an excuse and just kept babbling some noises. It was awkward.

'Nrchakshu has come back. Quit doing what you were and come outside at once.' He said and rushed away.

I took a sigh of relief and picked up the book. The book aroused my interest and so I decided to keep it with me. It's not that Mahamantri will be mad now if I mess with his belongings.

When I stepped outside, I saw Senapati Aagney holding onto Nrchakshu with his arm while the latter pled to be excused once again. I walked over to examine the situation more clearly.

'Please let me go. I will be gone only for a brief moment.' Pled Nrchakshu.

'I told you we are amidst war and now you want to leave?' Senapati Aagney raged over him.

'Try to understand, sir. I will be back. It is very important. I have committed a mistake. I just have to make things right.'

'Let him go, sir.' I said from the back.

Senapati Aagney was amazed to see me support Nrchakshu at times like this.

'Are you out of your mind too, Yuvan? This man left the palace 3 days ago without noticing anyone and now that he has return and Chandragarh is in a state of emergency you want me to allow him to leave again?' Senapati grumbled.

'He said he'll be back in a moment. It is not that he has a main role in the preparation of the war. Let him go. We don't require his assistance at this moment anyway.' I represented my opinion.

It took some time but Senapati Aagney eventually permitted Nrchakshu to leave. Nrchakshu without wasting any time took his horse and paced towards the Simha forest.

'Now if you shall excuse me, I have some orders to follow.' I said before leaving Senapati's company myself.

Nrchakshu was perplexed when he couldn't find the entity wrapped in the red cloth. He dug deeper but still, nothing. He dug a dozen such holes around the same one, with the hope of finding it. But all in vain. He was out of breath and was sitting with his back on one of those pairs of stones, disheartened and anxious.

'Looking for this?' I said.

He turned around at once and was scared stiff to see me wielding the ASI. I held the ASI over my head, mesmerized by its glory as it shone over.

'How did you get it?' Nrchakshu said while getting up in a haste.

'Oh. Just found it lying around.' I said sarcastically.

'Give it to me, Yashvasin. I must return it to Maharaja Brihadratha.' He said while taking small steps towards me.

I, still bewitched and enraptured by the ASI's beauty, stood still as he walked towards me.

'25 years. For 25 years I kept searching the ASI. I always thought the Maharaja had it removed to another secure location. How can an entity be insecure if it is never away from your sight? Of course, it was always with Maharaja Brihadratha. His sword has always been the ASI. How much doltish could I be?'

'Don't be foolish, Yashvasin. You know the ASI bewitches its holder. Give it to me. I must return it to Maharaja Brihadratha.' He kept coming towards me.

I pointed the sword towards him, gesturing him to stop.

'And why do you reckon you must return it to the Maharaja?'

'You know that, Yashvasin. Yayati has captured Indraprastha and had declared war on Chandragarh. Chandragarh is unsafe. We must return it to the Maharaja at once.'

I burst into a round of laughter after listening to Nrchakshu.

'You want to make that man invincible again? That man slayed your mother and father. He vanquished your entire clan. And you still want to hand the ASI over to him.'

'Yes, I do. Even after knowing what he did to my clan, I want to give him back the ASI.'

'And why is that, if I may ask?'

'That night Maharaja Brihadratha did what he had to as the protector of peace of Chandragarh. I know the Yudhvans were not treated without prejudice but those matters could have been solved without an uprising too. Attacking the palace was never an option and you of all agree with that.' Nrchkahsu replied.

'That was a foolish decision, that's why I agreed. But what kind of Maharaja annihilates his people?' I asked with rage.

'So, what do you want to do, Yashvasin? Fight in the battle with ASI?'

'Yes. I will fight while wielding the ASI.'

'You must ask for Maharaja Brihadratha's permiss...'

'But not for the Akshobhyas.' I interrupted.

Nrchkashu was taken back by my answer.

'Now that you know everything about your past, Nrchakshu. It is time for you to know something about me too. This scheme of persuading the Varunyas and Advaityas to rage war against the Akshobhyas? Yes. Yayati didn't come up with it. It was me.'

When Nrchakshu listened to my revelation, he was so out of the blue that one could have dropped him with a feather.

'And the great war of Chandragarh a year ago? My plan too.'

'What... What are you saying, Yashvasin?' He asked feverishly.

'You heard it right, Nrchakshu. Every word is true. I am the brains behind all the misfortune the Akshobhyas are stuck by in the past year.'

'You bastard!' Nrchakshu leaped onto me.

He threw a series of punches on me, but I managed to glide away from them every time. He got his sword out and sliced the air in front of me but I blocked his attack with the ASI. I was able to move the ASI with unbelievable speed and with great ease. Before he could have drawn his sword back to attain momentum for his next attack, I cut him from his waist and then kicked him on the back of his thigh. He fell on his knees. He was already tired with the digging and now he wanted to fight me while I held the ASI.

'You used me as a pawn, didn't you? You used your nephew as a pawn. You immoral bastard!'

'Your words hurt me, Nrchakshu. Do you reckon I'd like to wait 25 years to get the ASI? I could have obtained it much earlier than that. It is true I have always wanted the ASI, for I knew the Akshobhyas couldn't be defeated with the power of gods residing with them. But child, you misunderstood me.'

'So why wait 25 years?' Nrchakshu screamed while few blood drops dropped out of his hand clutching his waist.

'For you, Nrchakshu.'

'You lie!'

'No, I am not lying. You are the only family I have. I could not have left you alone with these slayers. I knew I have to be closer to you to make sure you were safe. I waited to tell you the truth until you were mature enough to understand what is right and what isn't. But it dampens my spirit to see that you are still not able to differentiate between the two clearly.'

I swung my sword multiple times, for fun, as I walked towards him.

'I will ask you one more time. You can come and work with me and Yayati on our plan to burn the Akshobhyas to the ground. And from their ashes, we shall flourish a new Chandragarh which will thrive and prosper with justice or you can go back to Brihadratha who would most probably kill you for stealing the ASI.'

'I will never work for the enemies of Chandragarh.' Nrchakshu said.

'Well, you already are.' I said and thumped his head with the pommel of the ASI.

Nrchakshu moaned as he fell on the ground face first. I slid the ASI into its sheath and jumped on my horse.

'And tell your Maharaja that he should not wait for Mahamantri Brahmanand. I took care of him. We will meet again, Nrchakshu. On the battlefield.'

I pulled the reins of my horse and paced towards Indraprastha.

TAKEOVER

My horse jumped on its hind-limbs as some soldiers tried to agitate it by poking their spears into him. Nevertheless, I forced my way inside the gates of the palace of Indraprastha. The flags of Varunyas and Advaityas were fluttering at the top of the palace. I left my horse in the palace ground and stormed inside, furiously, to find Yayati. A squadron leader tried to stop me but I couldn't care less.

'You can't go inside. Stop at once!' They all yelled. But I continued on my path.

An arrow went pass me, bruising my elbow pad. I saw an archer straight ahead lowering his bow. A couple of men came slashing their swords on me. I shifted my balance accordingly to escape the sharpness of their swords. Soon at least a dozen of those soldiers, each bearing a sword or a spear, came and surrounded me. I was already enraged because of Yayati. These soldiers only made me more violent. I couldn't get a better opportunity to test the reliability of the ASI. And so, I slid it out of the sheath. I felt a surge of energy being transferred from the ASI to my arms. Something felt so right while I wielded it. Three soldiers came on me at once. I was able to escape their attacks quite effortlessly. Not only was I able to move the ASI without any difficulty, but I was also able to change my position without much effort too. They kept on coming towards me in a group of three. But every time I found myself with enough time to slit their throat or pierce their body. One by one, corpses started falling while I slowly made my way inside the palace. I cut the last soldier in such a barbaric way that the others became appalled and couldn't get themselves to fight me. Giving everyone one last stare, I started ascending the staircase. I could see Yayati looking down on me from the above floor. He knew the reason for my rage. No one tried to stop me on the stairs. The soldiers cleared my path while I walked past them with the ASI in my hands and death in my mind.

When I reached the floor above, I noticed that Yayati was enjoying some esteemed company. Maharaja Jatsaya Varunya and Maharaja Vira Advaitya, the current rulers of the Varunyas and Advaityas were standing alongside him, with a glass of wine in their hands and an insinuation of concern in their minds. Certainly, Yayati had not told them about me. I reckoned I'll show them my calibre first. The introduction can be provided later.

Out of fear, the two rulers ordered their Aangrakshaks to attack me. The Aangrakshaks hesitated first, seeing my vicious deeds on the palace grounds, but their duty compelled them to pick arms against me. I was in no mood to spare lives today. After weeks I was finally able to confront Yayati. I was in no mood of showing them my placid side. I was unperturbed about what my first impression shall reflect. The first soldier came and slashed his sword on me. I ducked, escaping his reach, and kicked the second soldier approaching me. Then I turned around and pierced the first one. The next one gave me some blows to defend but his efforts were futile. I launched a series of attacks and pushed him to the edge of the veranda. From there I lifted and threw him down on the stairs beneath. The rest of the soldiers were too afraid to even make a move. They stood there, shivering with fear. The Maharaja of Advaityas was courageous enough to draw his sword out against me, but I gestured him to stop and so did Yayati. I turned towards Yayati and choked him against the wall with my left hand. Slowly, I started to lift him. My action proved to be a source of amazement for the two rulers. An unknown man enters your palace and slays dozens of your men and then tries to kill the person who is supposed to command your army. How would you feel?

'Why did you kill Dvij?' I whispered while staring into his flickering eyes.

'He was supposed to die in the war anyway.' He said in a breaking voice.

I turned to my right and noticed a tall, dark soldier about to attack me. But before he could bring his sword down on me, I sliced his whole arm off with the ASI. He dropped down on the floor and started rolling in pain. With a clearer look, I noticed he was the same man who I'd beat up to pulp in Indravan.

Kalki was starting to show some resistance now and held my arm, chocking his neck, with both of his hands, and tried to loosen my grip. But it was pointless.

'One thing I asked you not to do. One thing, Yayati!' I raged. 'I told you not to harm the Akshobhyan Family, except Brihadratha and yet you slayed Dvij.' I lifted him more.

'I... I am sorry.' He pled in a hoarse whisper.

I loosened my grip and Yayati dropped on the floor on his knees. He started panting heavily, while the two rulers stood there dumbstruck with what they had witnessed. I placed my hands on the railings of the veranda, overlooking the palace grounds, in frustration, and saw thousands of soldiers, assembled, staggered after all that they witnessed on the veranda. I realized I had made a mistake of overstating my power against their commander, Yayati. But their morale will increase manifold once they know that I'll be fighting from their side.

'So that is the power of the weapon of the Gods, huh?' Yayati asked, still panting.

'I could kill you with a mere blade any day.' I stared deep into his eyes.

I was getting vexed from the moaning of that guy whose hand I'd cut off. Vira Advaitya ordered the soldiers to take him away.

'Is that the ASI, Yashvasin?' Yayati asked again.

Maharaja Vira and Maharaja Jatsaya couldn't believe what they heard.

'ASI? So you were able to get the sword out of Chandragarh?' Jatsaya asked.

I slowly ran my eyes over the ASI. Not a single drop of blood adorned its edge. Dozens of men slayed a moment ago and still, not a single drop of blood could be seen. I cut my thumb from its edge and let the blood fall over it. Drop by drop, all of it got absorbed within the double-edged Khanda. Its lustrous intensity remained intact.

'Yes. It is the ASI.' I replied while sliding the sword back into its sheath.

'See gentlemen?' Yayati addressed to the two rulers. 'I promised I'll get the ASI out of Chandragarh, didn't I?'

'Does that mean, this brave warrior is with you?' Vira asked.

'Oh, yes. I think a formal introduction is pending.' Yayati said, trying to wave away the air of awkwardness.

I was still infuriated and was looking at Yayati with extreme rage. But I reckoned it won't make much difference now. The prince is dead. It can't be helped. I walked towards Yayati and stood beside him.

'He is Yashvasin Yudhvan. The actual intellect and architect of the plan to take down the Akshobhyas. We have been working together for a long time.'

'Yashvasin? Do you mean the famous Yashvasin of the Akshobhyas? I have heard of him a lot. His tales of bravery and valour are well known. But isn't his name Yuvan?' Jatsaya Varunya asked.

'Yuvan was the name that I used while I worked for the Akshobhyas to conceal my actual identity.' I replied. 'Now that I have got the ASI and don't need to work for them anymore, I reckon there is no reason to do the same. My name is Yashvasin Yudhvan. One of the last few surviving members of the Yudhvan clan.'

'The great Yudhvan clan of the mighty warriors whom everyone feared to face in the battles? But weren't they all annihilated?' Jatsaya threw up another question.

'A handful survived, Maharaja of Varunyas. I reckon this much information is enough for now. The only thing you need to know is that I'll be helping Yayati Yasah command the allied armies of the Advaityas and Varunyas. But before that....' I turned towards Yayati. 'Where have you kept the royal family of the Kurus?'

A moment of silence followed. Everyone tried to avoid eye contact with me.

'I asked for something.' I said with much strain.

'Maharaja Drshkrit was slayed in the battle. He killed many of our men, ergo I had to kill him.' Said Yayati hesitantly.

I sighed heavily to his reply.

'And what about the rest?'

'We found the women and children hiding in a secret passageway. They are now kept under house arrest in late Maharaja's chamber.'

'Get the palanquins ready. Tomorrow morning, they shall leave for Chandragarh.' I said.

My decision was not entirely welcomed by the two rulers. They tried to raise their voices but Yayati gestured them not to, while I saw them from the corner of my eye.

'Yayati, I want to talk to you alone now.' I said and looked at the two rulers.

They were seemingly sent into a rage because, of course, they weren't used to taking orders. After much struggle with their self-esteem, they left with their remaining Aangrakshaks.

I watched the crowd gathered in front of me, looking at me with utter horror and shock, while the heavy footsteps of the two stout rulers faded away. I looked around the huge palace ground filled with thousands of soldiers all awaiting me to address them.

'My name is Yashvasin Yudhvan.' I said in a loud voice as I addressed them. The whole army of soldiers burst into a gush of whispers, confirming with each other whether the name they heard was right.

I raised my hand to calm down the impatient crowd.

'Many of you might know me as a warrior of the Akshobhyas. But that is something I had to be to achieve my ambition. All of you, the Varunyas and the Advaityas, are assembled here because of my firmness of purpose. Your rulers have joined hands to take down the Akshobhyas on my request. I am not an Akshobhya. Neither am I an Advaitya or a Varunya. I am a man with one and only one purpose. The purpose of taking down the Akshobhyas and wipe them out from the face of Bharatvarsh. This purpose may seem to be too ambitious or beyond the bounds of possibility considering the rumours which state that a weapon, made by the gods themselves, reside in the capital of the Akshobhyan Empire, Chandragarh. Which is true. The Akshobhyas are invincible until that weapon resides in Chandragarh.'

The soldiers again became restless and began talking about their chances against the ASI. I raised the sword above my head and the whole army went still and silent.

'This is the reason why my name remained associated with Akshobhyas for the past many years. This is the feared weapon of the gods which I was able to get out of Chandragarh.'

The whole army was frenzied over my words. They began chanting and cheering wildly. I was again required to raise my hand to calm them.

'But this alone doesn't guarantee our victory against the mighty Askhobhyas. I have lived with them for many years and one thing I know is that they don't rely on this weapon to ensure their excellence for the years to come. They have many great warriors to ensure the required.'

A dead silence surrounded the crowd whose moral went down crashing.

'But the reason I worked hard for this alliance between the Varunyas and Advaityas for so many years is that not for a single moment have I doubted the ability and calibre of their armies. The Akshobhyas fear you all the most and that's why ensured their safety years ago by binding all the kingdoms down with a fake understanding and alliance. And that is why I stand here to ask you, the valiant and bravest men in the whole Bharatvarsh. Will you lend me your support to overthrow the unethical and immoral army of Chandragarh?'

'Yes, We Will!' The whole crowd roared.

'Will you let me command you to the victory over the Akshobhyan Empire?'

'Yes! Yes!'

'Then we shall have the whole Bharatvarsh.'

The palace of Indraprastha lit up with the energetic and dynamic roars of the army. They were filled with a tireless passion to add their name in the history books.

I took some joy by running my eyes over the massive army that I was able to form after so many years. Then I turned around and looked at Yayati with grave eyes.

'Just because I am not seemingly enraged right now doesn't mean I have forgiven you. Every time you go against my decision you attract misfortune. When I sent you that scroll, while you were in Rajkot, asking you not to interfere in Dvij and Yugant's business you decided to do the opposite, and ergo jeopardized our plan. I would have slayed Brihadratha a year ago if it wasn't for you. You got injured there and the morale of the allied forces came down crashing here in your absence. One more mistake, Yayati, and you'd wish you were dead.'

Yayati's head remained bowed the entire time.

'Let the preparation commence. The Royal Kuru family has to leave by tomorrow morning.'

Yayati nodded and walked away.

'One more thing.' My voice made him stop and turn around.

'Here. Take this.' I said while handing him the ASI.

Yayati Yasah was surprised to see me handle him the sword of the gods.

'Why will you even think of giving it away?' He was astounded.

'I am not giving it away. I am giving it to you. You are the only person I could trust right now. And the only person I need to trust. I know with you wielding the ASI, our army will dethrone Brihadratha with much ease.' I said while handing him the sword.

'You won't regret this, Yashvasin. You can put your trust in me.' Yayati said.

'Moreover, there is a reason that the sword is famed for the curse associated with it, not the blessing that it grants, among the Akshobhyas. I won't like to get bewitched by this sword. And neither will you, perhaps. You are the only one here who knows the curse, apart from me, which will help you to understand how and when to use the ASI. Don't let it get to your mind, Yayati.'

Yayati nodded with much joy.

'You may go now. Get the preparations started.' I said.

The next morning, I was out there shedding sweat beneath the early morning sun while training with our soldiers. Only a few days remained until we march to the land of Chandragarh. It won't harm if I can encourage and influence the army a little more.

When the sun was way up high and the palanquins were ready to escort the royal Kuru family, I led the members from their captivation to the palace grounds. Maharani Aarunya eye's reflected pure hatred for me.

'Don't be so displeased with me, Maharani. Maybe you won't if we'd meet under different circumstances. But right now, we find ourselves in a cycle of vengeance. What happened to your husband on my orders was required to keep this cycle running. Your father commenced it. And don't worry. My quest for vengeance won't stop with just your husband's death. Because what your father did to me is far more indignant. He shall reap what he has sown. And with him, his family shall suffer too. It's not something I want. But something you shall all get for being related to him.' I said with a calm face.

'Then why are you letting us go? Haven't you already committed enough sins to fall from everyone's grace? Slay us now. It shall only add a few ounces in your lot of sins committed. You have fallen the furthest. A few deaths of children and women are not going to furthermore degrade your reputation.' The Maharani said in high dudgeon.

'If I kill you now, then my acts won't differ from your father's. It is a waste to explain it to you now anyway. You can ask your father about it when you reach Chandragarh. I bid you goodbye, Maharani.' I said. And with this, I turned my back on her and commenced walking away from her.

'You shall rot in hell, Yuvan!' She yelled.

I turned around with a smirk and shook my head in disagreement.

'I guess it's futile to correct you now. Anyway…' I said while walking towards her. 'Here. Give this to Maharaja Brihadratha, if you will. You won't regret to handle this to your father personally.' I said while handing her a scroll. Then with a gentle smile, I walked back into the palace.

From the large veranda of the palace, I saw the palanquins exit the palace gates. In a few days, they will reach Chandragarh. And we shall follow next.

War Commenced

The day before we marched to Chandragarh, I discussed the war strategy with the infantry unit leaders, who shall lead their respective units in the war under my and Yayati's command. Yayati was by my side all the time. After the meeting was concluded, the unit leaders bowed before us, asking permission to leave. It has been a hectic and restless a few days for me, working with the soldiers on their tactics and swordsmanship. But it was necessary. Because in the war, the greatest strategy is to trust your commander with your life. And I was assured that I had done enough to charm my way into their hearts and minds. So, I thought of having a quiet evening in the palace gardens, overlooking the serene view, to rest my mind. But the tranquillity of the moment was short-lived when the two rulers arrived. I was sitting with my eyes close, listening to the sounds of the birds and the gushing of water in the waterfall at the distance, when their heavy footsteps knocked their way inside my consciousness.

'Greetings, the commander of our army. Would you fancy our company?' Vira Advaitya said while gulping down his wine from a gold cup, adorned by some precious stones, he held in his hand.

I nodded gently, with a grin, and gestured them to join me.

'Isn't this a lovely place to take your mind off from the upcoming war, Yudhvan?' Jatsaya Varunya asked.

'Indeed.' I replied.

'Especially for you, Yudhvan, for you have been working hard since the last few days to win the trust of our men.' Vira Advaitya said with a pretentious smile on his face.

'Does that concern you, Maharaja of Advaityas?' I asked.

'That is why I am here, Yudhvan. Should it concern me?'

'Well…' I said while facing them both. '… Now that you have disturbed my tranquil evening. I shall give you your answers, Vira.

'I don't think that is the appropriate way to talk to your Maharaja, Yudhvan.' Vira Advaitya said sternly.

My smile ceased. I looked at Vira Advaitya with a stern face. After taking a few footsteps towards him, I stopped. He was shaking with hesitation.

'I don't think it is healthy for you to talk to me like that, Maharaja of Advaityas.' I said while he slowly took some steps backwards.

'You can't threaten us, Yudhvan. You don't even have your ASI with you.' Said Jatsaya Varunya with a mixture of hesitation and terror in his eyes.

I mocked them with a smile.

'My abilities don't cease with the ASI, neither do they increase with it. If you still doubt that in your puny minds, you can always ask the countless men I have slayed or if that is not feasible, your men with whom I have been training recently.'

'Don't forget, Yudhvan. We have provided you our army. You should be thankful to us, instead of trying to steal our men by influencing them.' Jatsarya said with a trace of rage.

'You make me laugh, Maharaja of Varunyas. You make yourself feel as if you are doing a noble deed. Like charity. But don't forget about your own greater greed that forced you to accept my proposal in the first place.' I turned around and gazed at the scenery again. 'And you need not worry about the army. I am not trying to win them over you. Only if you had ever lead your respective army, rather than dumping the responsibilities over to your officials while you yourselves enjoy an extravagant lifestyle, you would know, how important it is to have your men's trust.'

I heard the two royals mutter curses behind me.

'Everything shall remain as planned. We win the war. I get my vengeance and you get bits of the Akshobhyan Empire. And let me warn you. Your fear might come true if you interfere in my state of affairs ever again.'

Jatsya Advaitya slammed his glass of wine on the soft grass beneath before making his way back inside the palace along with Vira Advaitya. I closed my eyes and took a deep breath to clear out the disruption caused by their arrival. When I opened them I noticed Yayati standing beside me, overlooking the serene view in front of us.

'I shall stay here.' He said.

I looked at him inquisitively as he turned around. He had a smile on his face.

'After we win the war, I will come back and stay here, in Indraprastha.'

'That is strange.' I said. 'I thought you were faithful to the land of Chandragarh.'

'I still am. I am faithful to the land of Chandragarh I once knew. It isn't the same now. And you know that quite well. Brihadratha has befouled Chandragarh. Each unit of that land is tainted with his sins. It is not the same pious land of Chandragarh I once knew.'

'We can work together on that.' I tried to reassure him.

Yayati raised his left eyebrow and was rather intrigued.

'I reckon you promised the two rulers the crown of Chandragarh.'

'Well…' I said while trying to conceal that sly smile on my face. 'I make a lot of promises, Yayati. Just a few days before his death, I promised Mahamantri Brahmanand to accompany him on his journey to the holy city of 'Prayag'. We both know that it is not going to happen now or is it?'

Yayati looked at me for a moment while I patiently waited for his reaction. After some time, he shook his head sideways, slightly, before bursting into a round of laughter.

'What I want to say is simple, Yayati.' I continued. 'If it wasn't for you, my dream of a perfect vengeance would have remained only a dream. We both have made this possible. And if you want the throne of Chandragarh or any other kingdom, be it Indraprastha, I shall see to it that you get it.'

'I'll think about it later, Yashvasin.' He said as he laid his heavy hands on my shoulders. 'I'll leave you with your thoughts now. A big day lies tomorrow.

Make sure to get some rest.'

I watched Yayati get disappear behind the large columns. For a while, I stood alone in the palace garden. I watched the sun come down and the moon, in all its glory, take up the dark sky. It was covered with a yellowish shade tonight. The stars glimmered a lot less too. Only a couple of them accompanied the yellowish moon. I stood there, with my eyes closed, as its silvery luminance sank me into oblivion.

The next morning as Yayati and I took to the palace ground, we were cheered by the thousands of soldiers ready to rage war on Chandragarh. Hundreds of war elephants and hundreds of thousands of horsemen, archers, and infantrymen stood, awaiting the marching orders. I let Yayati take the podium and address the men. Vira Advaitya and Jatsaya Varunya held on their wine glasses in the back. I heard them mutter curses as usual. After Yayati was done, I allowed the two rulers to address their men for a brief period and to give the marching orders, eventually. The new allied army with the Asi was ready to take on the invincible army of Chandragarh.

The Second Great War of Chandragarh

The Kingdom of Bairat and Mathura were seized by one of the most powerful battalions of our army three days after we captured Indraprastha. They tend to crumble easily. Maybe because the Akshobhyas were giving much attention to the war after they got the news of the fall of Indraprastha and the declaration of war on them by us. Passing through them was no problem. But we reckoned we might face inconvenience while passing through the neighbouring towns and villages of Chandragarh. But it wasn't much of a struggle either. They were abandoned, as we found out, on the orders of Brihadratha. He is trying to minimize the extent of their upcoming annihilation. But no matter how hard he tried now. Blood is bound to spill. And that's too in huge amount.

We set up a camp in the nearest town of Chandragarh. It was about 3 kilometres away from the battlefront. Like the other neighbouring towns and villages, Bindutva was abandoned too. Several signs showed that the inhabitants of this small town left in a haste. Bindutva had a comparatively smaller spread than other towns it was surrounded by. Several huts and cottages, long stretching farms, and cattle sheds were the main elements in the scenes here. A temple was erected in the centre of the town. The light from the jyoti placed in front of the idol of the monkey deity, Hanuman, showed that the inhabitants had just left.

'What about their reinforcements, Yashvasin?' Yayati was concerned.

'Their most powerful allies, The Kurus, are no more. The only help will be from the vassal kingdoms. The kingdoms they have captured. The valiant forces of Pataliputra will be a headache. But you don't need to worry about that. It will take them a week or two to arrive. The other major forces are of Sanchi and Ujjain. And they'll never reach the battlefront on time.'

I took some steps towards Yayati and pulled out the Asi from its sheath.

'Moreover, you are capable of defeating the whole army of Chandragarh just by yourself.' I said while running my eyes along the sharp edges of the Asi. I put the double-edged Khanda back into its sheath and patted Yayati's shoulders a couple of times.

'But that won't be required. The Varunyas and Advaityas are known for their barbaric infantrymen not only in Bharatvarsh but the lands that lie beyond too.'

Yayati gave a brief smile.

'That bastard, Aagney won't go down easily. And even if he does, Yugant will take his place…' The echo of my words penetrated my senses a little too late. But when I noticed Yayati, his attention was unaltered. Still, I wanted to be assured.

Yayati saw my disquiet.

'I took that decision 21 years ago, Yashvasin. And I stand firm on it.' He said trying to reassure me.

I nodded.

'Aagney and Yugant are the two pillars, which remain, supporting the architecture of the Akshobhyan dynasty. With me gone and Mahamantri Brahmanand and Rajkumar Dvij's demise, their strength is already halved. I want you to deal with Aagney. Leave Yugant for me.'

'But that is alright with me…' Yayati tried to explain himself but I asked him not to.

'I believe you, Yayati. I know your hands won't quiver when the time comes. But let us divide our responsibilities for now.'

Yayati showed his agreement with a brief nod.

'But what about Nrchakshu?' He asked.

'Nrchakshu is the least of my concern. His unforgivable act of stealing the ASI has already put him in jeopardy. Brihadratha forgiving him is the last thing that I expect. But even if he does, Nrchakshu won't be much of a problem. Worst comes to worst, I'll order anyone from Vrishank and Bhagiratha to face Nrchakshu in the battlefield.'

'Will they follow your orders, Yashvain? You might have made your place, big enough, in the hearts of the soldiers for them to follow your orders. But won't it be difficult to persuade the commanders of Varunyas and Advaityas? Their loyalty still leans towards the rulers of their respective kingdoms who, if it has escaped your attention, don't like you... at all!'

'You don't need to fret on that. I know how to get a favour from someone or how to win someone's trust. If it has escaped from your attention, I have been doing it for a long time now.'

Yayati chuckled under his breath.

'It is confirmed then. Tomorrow we shall avenge our land, our ancestors.' Yayati sounded determined.

'For the last time, run our war strategy for tomorrow with the leaders of our army. You may then retire with the army. For tomorrow we need our full attention and potential to be with us.' I said.

Yayati acknowledged with a nod and a smirk before exiting my camp.

I stood by the window of my camp, overlooking a wide black drum containing a fire, beside a big tree. The flames rising from it stretched upwards to several feet. They were twisting and dancing with every gust of wind that hit upon them. A couple of soldiers were shouting nearby. Some were laughing and others were in deep slumber already. There weren't many stars in the sky tonight. The moon was not visible from my camp. Pupils of my eyes moved with every slight movement of the yellow flames crackling. They took the shape of my conscience. Yayati is an emotionally strong man. Over the years he has accepted his son as an enemy. Yayati and Yugant both were given their respective choices. Yayati chose his path and Yugant chose his own. They both will try to slay each other if the situation asks for it. They won't waver from picking up their swords against each other, even though they share a bond. A bond that was much pious than many others. Tomorrow we will face the weakened, but yet an invincible army of Chandragarh. All of our concentration will be required tomorrow. After being ready for so many years for vengeance I stand here asking myself whether I am. 25 years ago I lost my family, my clan. I lost all of them but one. My blood. My nephew. But avenging my family would mean destroying it completely. I have waited for so long. But now I wish I had more time. I wish I had some time to get Nrchakshu to our side in this war. For I am not Yayati who has risen above. Much above from all the enchantments of life. Tomorrow I shall have my revenge but at what cost?

With the first light of the sun, we marched towards Chandragarh. Hundreds of thousands of soldiers, who looked gallant in their shinning armours, and thousands of elephants and horses lift the atmosphere with a vibrating intensity as they marched in unison. I along with Yayati Yasah and the two rulers led our massive army to the battlefront of Chandragarh. My heartbeat matched with the deafening sound of our army men's heavy footsteps. Everything that I'd dream of since the age of 14 was about to become a reality. Brihadratha crying for mercy before I slit his throat is all I want.

We found the Akshobhyas waiting for us as we slowly took the battlefield of Chandragarh throughout its stretch. Their army's strength looked almost half, compared to ours.

Not even a year, since this barren land witnessed the massive bloodshed when the invincible Akshobhyan army fought the allied forces. That was a futile attempt. Because of Yayati's idiocy, we lost that war. He was fortunate that I didn't slay him for ruining my years of patience and effort. But he redeemed his folly. And here we stand now, stronger than ever, in front of the most fearful army in the whole Bharatvarsh. But without the ASI they are nothing more than a toothless tiger.

The strongest and most fearsome warriors in the land of Bharatvarsh were once again ready to take arms. There was nothing but death in their mind. Their eyes were covered with flames and their thirst could only be quenched by their enemy's blood.

I, Yayati, and the two rulers, in our respective chariots, went forward. A couple of carriages and some horsemen from their sides strolled in our direction. Both parties met in the middle of the dusty land. It was the last month of the cold. A cool breeze blew from the east and swept the dust with it, scattering it on our faces, in the attempt. But the hindered visibility didn't stop me from noticing the tightened fist and displeased countenance of Senapati Aagney.

'You back-stabber bastard!' He yelled through the cool dusty breeze.

'Beware, Aagney!' Yayati rushed to my defence. 'You are talking to the representative of the allied army.'

Amidst this skirmish, I couldn't help but notice the calmness in Brihadratha's eyes. Our eyes met and from that point, I neither blinked nor did I look anywhere else. It was killing me, to see him remain so still and act unaffected. I wanted to see him in agony, distressed. But he remained calm as an undisturbed pond in the middle of an enchanted forest.

Brihadratha turned towards Vira Advaitya and Jatsaya Varunya.

'You both have committed a grave crime of breaking the alliance set up between our respective Kingdoms by our ancestors. You have disgraced them. Surrender yourself and your kingdom or face vicious punishment.'

The two rulers exchanged glances before bursting in a round of laughter.

'Yeah, right? That is why we have brought our massive army with us. To surrender.' Jatsaya Varunya said.

Yugant's eyes were wide open as he remained seated on his horse. He was bewildered to see his father not giving him any notice. Yayati, not once, looked at him.

'It is decided for you then.' Brihadratha said in such a grave manner that the laughter from the face of the two rulers ceased at once.

He finally turned towards me.

'For you...' He begins. 'Death is the punishment for traitors.' He said while taking a quick look at Yayati. 'For committing a crime towards the crown and murdering the crown prince and the Mahamantri of the Akshobhyas, you shall be hanged. I order you to surrender and hand back the heritage of Akshobhyas that you stole.'

Yayati placed his hand on the handle of the ASI sticking out from its sheath. He made this heavy action to catch the opposition's attention and to mock them.

'You order?' I asked Brihadratha. 'Just like you ordered for the slaughter of my clan?'

Brihadratha remained calm as a lit candle, in a dark and damp room, unaffected by wind.

I sighed before continuing again.

'The only way you are getting the ASI back is by winning this war.' I said with a smirk.

'Seems quite difficult now, doesn't it? To win a war without the ASI.'

'We can settle that without the war and unnecessary bloodshed, Yashvasin.' He said before shifting his eyes towards Yayati.

'Remember how, 21 years ago, I humiliated you in the open assembly, Yayati?' He aimed for Yayati's nerves and hit the bull's eye. 'You have your chance now, to settle the score for once and for all. You and I. Right now. The winner wins the war.'

Yayati's wish for vengeance escalated. He gripped his fist around the ASI.

'I won't need the ASI for that. Let's have it right…' I interrupted him before he could have accepted the proposal.

'No, Maharaja of Akshobhyas. Although your proposal is enticing and it would please my heart to see you die, it shouldn't be quick, you see. I have waited for 25 years. And I want to see you break. Slowly and painfully. I want you to see your Kingdom fall before you can rest your eyes.'

Senapati Aagney was on the verge of losing his nerves.

'War it is then.' Brihadratha declared. It was still hurting not to see him reflect any emotion.

Both the parties turned around. I watched Yayati finally catching his son from the corner of his eye. Our chariots were once again placed ahead of our army. And with the blow of the conch, the war began.

Within an instance, the soldiers of either forces clashed in the middle of the barren land. Shield striking, swords slashing the air, men yelling, men screaming. This type of atmosphere wasn't new for the battlefield of Chandragarh. Many men have sacrificed themselves for the city of Chandragarh. The capital of power in Bharatvarsh. They have shed their blood as an offering to this land. But even after receiving this contribution which not at all meagre, the unfertile land remains discontent.

I, Yayati, and the two rulers remained in the back with a battalion and overlooked the war amidst the clouds of dust rising from everywhere. Yayati had provided Bhagiratha and Vrishank with the orders earlier. It was early in the war for us to step in. Even though our vision was hindered to some extent, the activities in the battleground remained clear to our eyes. It was a skirmish. Neither Yayati nor Aagney were using any vyuh. But then again, the war has just commenced. Maybe they were trying to see if either of them has learned something new, to capitalize upon it. The two rulers remained seated in their chariots like a couple of indolent and deplorable baboons. With a glass of wine in their respective hands, they were sharing laughter. I wondered how are their kingdom not yet obliterated. Both the kingdoms must be utterly unfortunate to have them as their kings. We watched the men fight for us till the sun decided to take some rest. There was an equal number of causalities for both sides. After the sunset and no one remained thirsty for their enemy's blood, the bodies of the martyrs were taken back to their respective camps so that their brothers could give them final rites.

The same process continued for six days. Either side was able to cancel out the effect of the battle formation of their enemies. Both sides were equally matched and at the end of the day suffered from equal causalities. But this was until the reinforcements from Pataliputra arrived. After that, the war took a drastic turn.

JATSAYA VARUNYA

'They will be too tired to perfectly concentrate on the war. They are joining the war directly after weeks of travel.' The ruler of Varunyas tried to wave away any wind of concern.

'It is the army of Pataliputra that you are talking about. How can you be so naïve as not to take them seriously?' I raised my voice.

'Believe me, Yashvasin. There is nothing worry about.' He said in a low voice.

His negligence towards the potential of the army of Pataliputra made me vexed. With every word he spoke, I felt like ripping up his head open, more and more. I ground my jaws in anger. I closed my eyes, tried to dissolve every emotion into nothingness, and then shifted my position towards Vrishank.

'Any other information regarding the tactics that might be used by the Maharaja of Pataliputra and his commander?'

'No news about the tactics as of now, sir. But there is one thing which might concern you.' Vrishank said.

'What it is?' I asked quickly.

'Raja Ijay of Pataliputra is not joined by his commander in the war. Their commander, Hridyansh, has stayed back to protect the kingdom from any attacks while their king fights with the Akshobhyas. In his absence, Hridyansh's son, Anns, a young man, not much older than the crown prince of Akshobhyas ever was, has joined in. He is trusted with commanding the audacious army of Pataliputra. I, myself, find this quite intriguing, considering his immature age.'

'See?' Jatsaya Varunyas burst from behind. 'One more reason to stress less.'

I turned around and stared at him.

'Trusting a young man with such a responsibility. Isn't that horrendous? Brihadratha must be getting frenzied seeing his end near.' He continued.

'Get out.'

Jatsaya's eyebrows were raised in surprise.

'What did you say?' He asked while stepping closer to me.

'Get out.' I raised my voice by a decibel.

'How dare you? How dare you…' Jatsaya Varunya stopped in between, after witnessing the red in my widely open eyes.

He took a few steps back.

'You will pay for this, Yashvasin.' His words came as a warning.

Jatsaya Varunya stomped towards the exit. But turned around right at the end and glared at Vrishank, gesturing him to join him away from us. Vrishank looked at me, requesting for permission.

'This is my war, Jatsaya. And these are my men now. Try, once again, to insult me in front of them, and you won't have a throne to sit upon, neither a kingdom to rule.' I warned.

Jatsaya stormed out in humiliation.

My eyes went from Vrishank to Bhagiratha and finally landed upon Yayati.

'What is your say?'

'Raja Ijay of Pataliputra rules over several brave men. Men who are equally capable of winning the war with their intellect as they are capable of with their dauntless bravery. If their commander has not joined the war, it still provides the Raja with several options, for there is no shortage of brave men in Pataliputra. The fact that he chose the young lad, Anns, over all of them is a warning for us. It warns us that we should not take that child lightly.'

Vrishank and Bhagiratha nodded in agreement.

'That is true, Yayati. We should stick with the plan then.'

I turned around to the two commanders and ordered them to spread the information throughout their infantry.

'Tomorrow we take the war to the next level.' I said to conclude the meeting.

Yayati and Bhagiratha left my camp instantly. I caught Vrishank, still, assuming his position.

'You are allowed to leave now, Vrishank.' I said once again.

His eyes met mine and he showed some hesitation.

'What is it that concerns you?' I asked gently.

Vrishank finally spoke up.

'I have heard about you a lot, Sir. You are known in the entire Bharatvarsh for your unmatched swordsmanship and bravery. But the thing that graces your reputation the most is your incessant love for your motherland, Chandragarh. If I were honest, I'd like to say that I admired you the most for that. I am not trying to insult you in any way. This soldier dreads for forgiveness if, in any way, I have disgraced you. For that is not my purpose. But now, that you are raging war against your motherland, the fact states the otherwise. It seems like the never-ending love has finally ceased. It is still unclear to me why would a man like you take this step. I am a mere soldier. And my whole purpose is to take orders without asking questions. That's why my knowledge about you is limited.'

'Does this concern you, Vrishank? A concern like this, during such an important phase of the war, in the eyes of a prestigious commander can take the war away from us. There are only two solutions for it, then. First, you either leave the war. Distracted minds lead to downfall. Second, or I should help you increase your knowledge about myself. I'd like to opt for the second choice. Because I recognize your importance. And only a fool would let go of you.' I said while drawing the curtains of my camp.

'Your words make you bigger than mere beings, sir. While working with you, I have known why the army of Chandragarh sing praises for you, why you were a local hero in Chandragarh, why they all loved you. But the lack of knowledge is not my concern, sir. It has been years now. I have adapted to taking orders without questioning my superiors, Maharaja Jatsaya to be precise. The reason I admire you the most is that I share the same love for my country as you do for yours. And it eats me to the core knowing that someone like Maharaja Jatsaya sits in the throne of Varuya kingdom. My concern should not be confused with my loyalty, sir. My forefathers have been loyal to the throne and so am I. This loyalty is an heirloom. But it still concerns me to see someone as ignorant as Maharaja Jatsaya sitting upon the throne. He drinks and drinks all day and runs away from any grave responsibility. My people suffer because of his discourteous behaviour, which is least expected from a king.'

'But there isn't much we can do about that, can we?' I placed my hand on his shoulder.

'I wish someone like you ruled the Varunya kingdom. You would make a great king, Sir. You try to reach out to people's hearts. Be it, soldiers or farmers. Your gratitude towards them is honourable.'

'I am no king, Vrishank. I am not here for the long haul either. But I know, after seeing men like you that the Varunya kingdom is in right hands.' I smiled at him and he smiled back.

Vrishank bowed in front of me before making his exit. It was going to be a long night. I indulged myself in the many papyrus charts that spread in my study.

The next day I noticed that my words, last night, penetrated deep inside Jatsaya Varunya's heart. Or maybe it was his arrogance that I hurt.

'I want to lead the army today.' He said to me early morning.

Yayati insisted to let him lead for once and so I permitted him to lead the army on the battlefield.

The scene of the opposite side of the field was appalling. The Akshobhyan army had increased in number, now that the proud army of the Pataliputra had joined them. The conch was blown and the battle began.

Jatsaya was determined to prove me wrong and, so, began by going fully into the army of the Akshobhyas. He led the army in the sarbatomukhi dand vyuh. This formation requires the best warriors to form a circular formation in the front alongside their respective battalions. Behind the circle, the rod-shaped formation keeps supplying the front with men or any other requirements. Jatsaya along with Bhagiratha, Vrishank, and other battalion leaders led their battalions to form a massive circle and began butchering anyone that came in contact. It was intriguing to see the Maharaja of Varunya use such a strong formation to annihilate the opponents. The damage was seen. The Akshobhyas began losing men in huge numbers. Our army was suffering a minimum loss of men. And even those were replaced by the men in the back. The tide was with us. But then the drumbeats emerged from the back. The Akshobhyan Army changed position. Senapati Aagney must have come up with a formation to counter the sarbotomukhi dand vyuh. The strong troops of the Akshobhyan army, capable of holding the powerful circle of our army, came in front to draw some time for the rest of their men to attack at the rod-shaped formation, in the back. It was clever of Senapati Aagney. If the reinforcement line is cut, the circular formation in the front won't be able to cover up their loss. It took some time for Senapati Aagney to penetrate the formation and it costed him much of his men too. But once through, he began to cut short the reinforcement line. The soldiers in the back found it difficult to continue to provide help in the front, as they fought the enemy in the back themselves. The appropriate thing to do was to regroup the army and come up with a new strategy. But Jatsaya Varunya was obstinate. He refused to change his mind and kept going with the compromised sarbotomukhi dand vyuh. Our men began to fall in big numbers. The rod formation in the back began to shrink. When the connection line between the circular head and the rod-shaped end was finally broken, it gave Jatsaya Varunya no other choice. After much resistance, he ordered the army to regroup and the formation was broken.

The bloody battle went on with a steady, but treacherous, pace. Once, Jatsaya Varunya was assured that he could afford to fight with a different strategy he ordered the infantry leaders to change formation. This time he opted for a defensive approach. Our army took the formation of Mandala Vyuh. It is a semi-circular shaped formation and is usually very hard to penetrate. The Maharaja of Varunyas took charge himself. He took the lead on his gigantic elephant and surrounding him were different groups of army men led by their respective leaders, in a semi-circular formation. Even though it was courageous of Jatsaya to keep himself in the open as he led the formation, the two commanders, Vrishank and Bhagirath, followed him closely with the best infantry and horsemen they had. Mandala Vyuh proved to be frustrating for the Akshobhyas. As their men came in contact with our defensive formation, slowly, their bodies began to fall. One by one they came closer with only two options with them. The first to fight the Jatsaya and our best men surrounding him, second to try and penetrate the walls of the vyuh. Anything they tried, was futile. Jatsaya was enjoying himself now. He was free from the swords of the enemy's as he remained seated top of his huge elephant. Moreover, Vrihsnak and Bhagirath were there to protect him. Jatsaya got the best view of seeing the Akshobhyas get slay. But this formation was far easier to break for Senapati Aagney. I did warn Jatsaya earlier, to not underestimate Senapati Aagney. As a disciple of Yayati, he had learned from the very best. The faith of the Akshobhyan army men, within the distance of a few hundred yards to our army, was set. But the ones away, regrouped to the sound of the beats, yet again. To counter Mandala Vyuh Senapati Aagney went for the Vajra Vyuh. One of the most offensive formations an army can use in a battle. Senapati Aagney, Yugant Yasah, Raja Ijay, Anns and battalion leaders, and some other horsemen were surrounded by multiple layered walls of infantrymen from four sides. Jatsaya Varunya was a little too late to realize his mistake. As soon as the Akshobhyan army in the formation of Vajra Vyuh came in contact with our army, Jatsaya Varunya gave a run for his life. He ordered the two commanders to accompany him. Jatsaya Varunya was successfully able to go behind his wall before the Akshobhyans could get a chance to slay him. Now the Mandala Vyuh was a defensive approach and was difficult to penetrate. But the multiple layer formation of the Akshobhyas began to attack our wall layer after layer. They concentrated their power in one section of our formation. When the walls came loose, Senapati Aagney, accompanied by another leader, went head to head with our men who were trying to hold the line. The result? Massive annihilation. Our army had to retreat.

The following night, back in the base camp, Yayati and I were waiting for one of my trusted soldiers.

'Where is he?' I asked the soldier.

'He is in his camp, sir. And drunk.' He replied.

'Ask Vira Advaitya to join us there.'

The soldier bowed, asked for permission to leave and left.

'How are you going to do it?' Yayati asked.

'Watch me.'

On my command, the camp of Jatsaya Varunya was surrounded. Dozens of armed soldiers stood encircling the tent. I walked towards the tent. The men made space for me and Yayati to walk inside the restricted circular area. And once we were in, closed the gap.

We walked inside and were least surprised to see the Maharaja of Varunya seated on a chair, by the window, with a glass of wine in his hand and a huge jug, containing the same, kept on the table in front.

'Came here to criticize me?' The drunk king sensed our presence.

'That could have happened to anyone.' He continued. 'We have still got the weapon of the gods.' He said, pausing for hiccups now and then.

'You fled.' My comment forced Jatsaya Varunya to look at me. 'My men died.'

Vira Advaitya appeared from the front door of the tent, all tensed. Bhagiratha and Vrishank followed him in.

'What is happening…?'

'Your men?' Before Vira Advaitya could have finished his sentence, the drunk king rose his voice.

'Your men?' He continued. 'You half-witted bastard! How dare you call them your men?'

Vira Advaitya was shocked to see Jatsaya Varunya raise his voice in front of me.

'They were my men. When I don't give the least of thought on whether my men live or die, who are you to fret upon them? They are my slaves. And they'll do whatever I ask them to do. You mind your own business, you son of a bitch.' He threw his empty glass of wine towards me. But before it could have hit me, Yayati caught it in mid-air. I didn't move an inch.

Vira Advaitya gasped at Jatsaya Varunya's stupidity. He rushed towards him, held him from his shoulders, and kept asking whether he was out of his mind?

'What can this bastard do, anyway? He isn't a leader. He doesn't even have a country to live in. His people want him dead!' Jatsaya Varunya burst into a round of laughter.

Yayati walked towards the Maharaja of Varunyas and slammed the empty glass of wine, he had caught mid-air, on the floor.

'You are crossing your limit, Maharaja Jatsaya.' He said while holding him from his left arm.

Jatsaya shrugged his arm and made it free from the tight grip of Yayati's hard hands.

'Ask your representative to back off, then. We still have the ASI. With the ASI we are invincible. I am invincible. If a few men die, then let it be. It is a sacrifice they have to make to see me take the throne of Chandragarh.'

'Shut up, Jatsaya!' Vira Advaitya yelled. 'Don't insult Yashvasin. Have you forgotten…?'

'I don't fear him! He is a pretentious man with no real identity. Yuvan? Yudhvan? Hell! He doesn't even have a name! He should have died with his miserable clan!'

I walked towards Jatsaya Varunya. Two feet away, I drew out the ASI from Yayati's sheath and with one swift movement slit open Jatsaya's throat. He fell on the floor, on his knees, and with both hands grabbed his neck in a futile attempt to stop the flow of blood.

Vira Adviatya's face was white, except for the few blood drops of Jatsaya Varunya that covered his face, diagonally. He was visibly trembling with fear. He looked at Vrishank and wondered why Jatsaya's commander didn't come for his aid. But Vrishank stood still, looking at the wall of the tent in front of him.

I pulled Jatsaya's sword out from his sheath and extended it towards Vira Advaitya.

'Congratulation, new Maharaja of Varunyas. I hope you are a better king than your predecessor.'

PRIDE OF PATALIPUTRA

The new Maharaja of our army led in the battle. Vrishank and Bhagirath accompanied him. Yayati insisted on joining the war, but I asked him to wait a little longer. When asked when we shall take the field, I replied, until sufficient damage is done.

Vira Advaitya's excellence in statecraft and battle strategies was overshadowed by his, lately, indulgence in oblivion which he achieved through alcohol. But after witnessing what happened to Jatsaya Varunya, he took matters gravely. He ran us through his ideas of leading the war, last late night. We agreed with him. He didn't want to go for the stack at once but wished to take them out stick by stick. The army of Pataliputra was causing much distress to our men. Vira Advaitya aimed for them.

He began the war by inducing fear in the Akshobhyas by leading the army in the Krauncha vyuh. This formation is highly aggressive and requires agility and strength in massive amounts. The formation represents a heron with an outstretched beak and large wingspan. Vira Advaitya led the army from the beak while the two commanders took care of either wing. The other battalion leaders strengthen the formation by the edges. Last night, Vira Advaitya had talked me through with his plans. And he had everything encapsulated under one scheme. No wonder he kept me awake all night to increase his knowledge about Senapati Aagney.

The Akshobhyan army was bewildered to counter our army in such belligerent formation. But Senapati Aagney's experience in war would come handy for them. The commander of the Askhobhyan army, shortly after the encounter, ordered his army to regroup in the Garuda Vyuh. Just like Vira Advaitya anticipated. The *Garuda Vyuh* might look similar to Krauncha Vyuh in appearance. But the swoop of the Garuda Vyuh nullifies the posture of Krauncha Vyuh. However, Vira Advaitya led his army head-on into the Akshobhyan army. With a sly scheme in his mind, of course. Senapati Aagney and Yugant Yasah were positioned at the eyes of the formation, while the King of Pataliputra led his side of the army through the right-wing. The young Anns was at the neck.

Capitalizing on the plan, while the two armies were amidst butchering each other, a big chunk of our army, led by Vira Advaitya and the two commanders, drifted towards the right. We had the advantage of having a comparatively larger army. This is how we planned on using it. The right wing of the Akshobhyas was now filled with our involvement. Raja Ijay led the right wing for the Akshobhyas. Raja Ijay, our focus for today. While the other soldiers held the line for us, our best men, accompanied by Vira Advaitya and Bhagiratha and Vrishank came face to face with Raja Ijay, who was left alone with his battalion. After much slaying of their men, the right-wing of their Garuda vyuh began to shrink. The bird's right-wing was shot with an arrow. But before Senapati Aagney could understand what happened, Raja Ijay and his left-out battalion found themselves inside a strong Chakra vyuh. It is a multilayer formation in the shape of concentric circles. The Chakra vyuh we formed was of five layers. Roughly, a thousand remaining soldiers of Pataliputra found themselves enslaved in a prison formed by tens of thousands of our men. Outside the *Chakra vyuh*, the Akshobhyan army was held by the rest of our men in numbers stretching to tens of thousands. Even if the Akshobhyas were able to go through them, penetrating the *Chakra vyuh*, won't be easy. One by one, the soldiers of Pataliputra, inside the circle, met their death. When Raja Ijay was the only one left, Vira Advaitya and the two commanders walked to the centre. The exhausted Raja of Pataliputra was upbeat. He swung his swords at the three men who laughed at his failed attempts while dodging his strikes. The three men encircled him and began moving around him. Difficult to concentrate, Raja Ijay went for the man he faced in front of him, Vrishank. But Vira Advaitya kicked him from the back and the Raja of Pataliputra fell, face first, into the dusty terrain. While the three men fooled around the lone enemy, a section of our line, outside the vyuh, erupted by the wild forces of men led by Anns. He moved like a fast gust of wind through our soldiers. Slaying and butchering everyone who came in front of him. As it happened, he went ahead of his infantry and found himself alone at the circumference of the Chakra

Vyuh. He looked at his struggling men behind him. And then began penetrating the vyuh all by himself. His agility and movement with the sword showed his maturity which was beyond his age.

At the centre, Vira Advaitya was making sure that the death of Raja Ijay was slow and painful. Raja Ijay, wounded and covered with blood, struggled to even stand up without wagging feverishly. It seemed like the two of them had some problems from their very past of reconciling.

'How does it feel now, you swine?' Vira Advaitya yelled.

'You deserved what happened to you that day, Vira.' Raja Ijay said with drowsy eyes. 'You were young and foolish. You deserved that.'

Vira Advaitya revolved his sword, and with the momentum gained, thrust the sword in the lap of Raja Ijay. The latter's scream filled the atmosphere with utter horror.

'Is that what you think?' He yelled over Raja Ijay's squatting and bleeding body.

'And that is why you shall die!'

With this, he propelled his sword to penetrate the armour of the fallen Raja of Pataliputra. But before he could have killed Raja Ijay, Anns, using the uplifted shield of a soldier in the last layer of the *Chakra Vyuh,* launched himself towards the men in the middle and, with the pommel of his sword, shoved Vira Advaitya as he landed. The Maharaja of Advaityas and Varunyas rolled over the ground. He dusted himself off as he stood up and spit up the sand he took inside in the process. The latter was bleeding from his mouth, result of the impact of Anns's strike. With the back of his hand, he wiped the bleeding. Meanwhile, Anns was horrified to see his Raja in such an appalling state. The fallen man was almost unconscious.

'Jatsaya Varunya was a fool to underestimate you.' Vira Advaitya said as he was joined by the two commanders.

Without saying anything more, the three men launched themselves towards the young Anns whose sole purpose, now, was the protection of his king. He couldn't allow the men approaching him to slay his king. But what chance did he stand against the mighty warriors of our army?

He blocked the first two strikes of Vira Advaitya and Vrishank. But Bhagirath caught his forearm by the sharp edge of his sword. But what he showed next, was an excellent display of skill and vigour. Vrishank, with all his might, landed heavy blows on his enemy. But the young soldier of Pataliputra, wielding his sword with one hand, got away without a scratch. Brihadratha jumped over him but Anns was fast enough to block his attack. He moved quickly to get away. Anns was playing defensively. He knew he couldn't attack the three of them and get away alive. He was waiting for his men to penetrate the Chakra Vyuh. Till then, he had to stop his opponents from coming onto Raja Ijay.

It was Vira Advaitya's chance now. His first attempt was to sweep off Anns from his feet. After indulging the latter in successive blows, he went for his legs. But Anns used his greatest skill, his speed, to his advantage and jumped away. The three men knew, taking Anns down, individually will take much time. And time was our enemy at the moment. They knew that their *Chakra Vyuh* was meant to stop the enemies for only long enough it might take to slay Raja Ijay. So, they gathered around their young opponent to end things for once and for all.

Bhagirath was first to attack the encircled lad. But Anns was quick enough to dodge him and also scratched his attacker's waist. Bhagirath screeched in pain for a moment. Vrishank took notice of Anns's dangling concentration and leaped forward. He got Anns with a sudden attack around his core and his armour came loose. Vrishank, giddy with his first success, went for another attack. Anns bowed down to escape Vrishank's reach and then swiped down at his feet. Vrishank fell on the ground and saw Anns coming down on him with his sword. Vira Advaitya, lurking for a clear moment, saw this as an opportunity and slashed his sword from the back. A massive cut stretching from Anns's left shoulder to his right side of his waist was made, on his unarmoured back. He screamed in pain as he tried to get away from the three men. But his effort bore fruit.

All men in the middle turned around to the hustling sound. One large section of the Chakra vyuh was forced open by Yugant Yasah and his men. Dozens of Akshobhyan infantrymen came oozing inside from the opened section. Seeing this, our subsided soldiers joined their leaders.

Anns shouted at Yugant to take the unconscious Raja back to safety. Yugant knew his men won't be able to keep the opening intact and that everything that had to be done should be done as fast as possible. The two parties began a brawl inside the circle. Few of Yugant's men were able to reach Raja Ijay first and began to escort him as the rest stood against our soldiers. But they began to fall quickly. Escaping Yugant came into sight as he tried to carry Raja Ijay outside the nearest concentric circle. Vira Advaitya removed his bow from his back sheath and stretched an arrow. After getting an aim of Raja Ijay's head, he released it. But Anns came in between and took the arrow in his chest. Yugant, perplexed rushed towards Anns's aid but was forced to move back by Anns' cry of helping Raja Ijay instead. The three leaders broke away from the few remaining Akshobhyan soldiers fighting in the middle, leaving them for our infantrymen to deal with. But their attempt to catch Raja Ijay and Yugant was hindered by the injured, but determined, Anns who stood royally with a sword in his hand and an arrow sticking out of his chest. Whilst seeing the glimpse of the afterlife, he fell on the three leaders as a storm. He halted them for long enough to see Yugant escape the mighty grip of the Chakra Vyuh with Raja Ijay. Vira Adviataya was furious to see his failure. And when his rage met the smiling face of drowsy Anns, the end of one was confirmed. The detached head's eyes were closed, but the smile remained intact.

The conch was blown as the sun came down. Vira Advaitya and the two commanders led the army back to the camp. I, Yayati and our battalion which oversaw everything joined them.

'The injuries Raja Ijay sustained were severe. He won't be able to pick up a sword for the rest of the war that is if he does not die.' Vira Advaitya said.

'You did what was planned. You delivered a splendid job.' I said.

'But that kid. Men like him, don't deserve to die so young.' Vira sounded disheartened.

'War does not see who deserves and who does not. War only sees that it gets what it wants. War wants death. And it shall have it one way or another.' I said reassuring him.

Vira Advaitya was crestfallen to realize the cruel reality of the war which he has realized previously on many such occasions.

'Pataliputra is fortunate to have such men serving it. Men like Anns are the true pride of Pataliputra.' Vira Advaitya said as the last light of the sun fell on his face.

Back at the base camp, in Bindutva, Yayati came in knocking in my tent while I studied war statistics from the multitudinous papyrus records spread on my table.

'Is much damage done now?' He ran his eyes on the records too.

I looked up, away from the study, at him, and gave him a gentle nod.

'Does that mean…?'

'Yes.' I said before he could have completed his sentence.

A cunning smirk spread on his face. The war just got more exciting.

MASTER AND STUDENT

With the leaders of Pataliputra not available to fight and the massive loss of infantrymen yesterday, the tide of war shifted to our side. Vira Advaitya's intellect and warfare knowledge excelled for us. The Akshobhyas were vulnerable. The reinforcements arriving from Sanchi and Ujjain will only help them to force time to delay their inevitable annihilation. It was time for me and Yayati to join the war. And Yayati, with his new sword, couldn't be happier.

With, Yayati leading, our army showed an extravagant enthusiasm. Yayati's aura, which changed as he stepped in the battlefield with the ASI, was transited throughout the army. This aura was divine. Not in its sereneness but like the wild zest which could be traced in the war of the gods. I have not seen the ASI being used in a war before. Maharaja Brihadratha had never stepped into the battlefield to fight. A need never occurred. With the excellent administration of the army set up by Yayati Yasah and now Senapati Aagney, the wars always belonged to the men of Akshobhyas. But now that the two Senapati's face each other in this historical war, the outcome may differ. And it will.

At first, I was concerned when I saw the focused and centralized Yayati dazzle with supreme verve. But with this, he brought a thorough change in the army, so I subsided the concern. The army knew the power of ASI. From the very inside of their mother's womb to the day before the war began, they have heard the myth. They have been inquisitive to confirm the reality of the godly weapon. But when the legend of ASI was forced to them as a reality, they knew they'd become invincible as a singular force. The last stage of the war had commenced. It was time to hurt the Akshobhyas to their very core.

Senapati Aagney led his army in the Ardha Chandra vyuh. In the formation, in the shape of a half-moon, Senapati Aagney placed himself upfront. He shone like the pole star who, like the Ursa Major and Ursa Minor, formed a link between the Akshobhyan and Pataliputra armies. Of course, he had to lead defensively. Senapati Aagney, in his royal six-horse chariot, was accompanied by Yugant Yasah, in the right end, while the other infantry leaders spread across the curves.

Yayati ordered the drums to be beaten in the synchronization of the Makra Vyuh. In the shape of a crocodile, this formation requires a massive army which we had. Yayati stayed in the position of the eye. I was not far from him. Vrishank and Bhagiratha were on either edge of the body and Vira Advaitya stayed back at the tail. Vira Advaitya was required to see that Askhobhyan horsemen were slayed today in big numbers. We wanted to take away their agility. The two armies collided and the battlefield lit up to the sounds of swords clashing, shields banging, and the injured screeching. This field wants blood. And it will get what it needs.

My Chariot rushed into the Akshobhyas, many getting butchered from the sharp spikes poking out from the four wheels. I aimed for the Akshobhyan horsemen coming from all directions. The pointed end of my arrows met them all. The high decibels of the war were deafening. Stamping of the thousands of horses and chariots caused much annoyance. Blood was everywhere, accompanied by limbs, somewhere, and heads, somewhere else. A couple of horsemen, one with an arrow pointed at me and other ready to slash my head off, came rushing towards my Chariot. The archer led the two. He released his arrow and I ducked to miss the impact. Now it was my chance. I launched two arrows at the same time. He tried to dodge the first one by shifting to his right and found the second arrow in his chest. He fell on the battleground and I saw his companion's horse crush his skull with one of its strong hind limbs. The next one drew his sword, but not on me. He took my coachman's head with him, as he went by. With no one to guide my horses, my carriage took a hit from an abandoned carriage, missing a wheel which lied ahead. The weight shifted to one side. I was able to jump before the carriage took multiple spins and killed a dozen soldiers, ours, and theirs. The same horseman turned around and rode towards me. I dusted myself off. My helmet was gone and I was bleeding from my right temple. To my adjacent lied a wheel of the same abandoned carriage.

With all my might I picked it up from one end, by the spokes. As the horseman came, with his sword extended to my side, I swung the wheel, with the help of my body weight. The other end of the wheel got suspended in the air. After two rotations I gained enough momentum to throw it at the horseman. The wheel crushed his ribs. He coughed blood as he fell on the ground with the wheel above him. The lone horse still came running towards me. I caught him by the reins and jumped on him.

As I went riding the horse into the heart of the Akshobhyan army, I noticed Vrishank in a sword fight with Yugant Yasah. Yugant was not fooling around. He was delivering sharp blows to Vrishank. I noticed Vrishank without a shield to defend. Yugant forced him back with the help of continuous attacks. Vrishank was out of breath. He dodged the last attack and kicked Yugant Yasah on the right ribs. A couple of hits and Yugant's shield fell on the ground. He was pushed back by Vrishank. But Yugant caught his balance again. He fixated his eyes on Vrishank's legs and was able to understand his movements. Capitalizing on that detail, he was able to touch his opponents' shins by his sharp sword. A touch was enough to force Vrishank on the ground. Vrishank's end seemed near. I took out a small blade, tucked inside my waistcloth, and threw it at Yugant as he began to bring his sword down on the fallen Vrishank. But Yugant was quick. He stepped on the shield, on the ground, by the edge. The shield flipped a couple of times as it got suspended in the air and took my blade's hit. Yugant was distracted for a moment. And that was just the time Vrishank required to escape. He caught a pole in the corner of a Chariot of one of our infantry leaders and forced his way in. Yugant glanced at me, as I went by. It was too early in the day to kill a prince. And so, I didn't indulge myself in a duel with him.

I went ahead, slashing everyone who came in front. After drenching my sword with the blood of 20 men, I found myself in a daunting predicament. A dozen of archers stood in front. With their arrows aimed at me. They were led by Evyavan, the leader of the archers' squad. I increased the pace of my horse. Two arrows went by, missing me. Three came in, successively. I took out my shield and defended myself from them. The fast horse was making it difficult to keep the shield study. The arrow which came next bruised my arm pad. I was getting closer to them. Another arrow was launched. This time, it bruised my shoulder and created a flesh wound. I lost my shield. The rest of the archers loosened their grip simultaneously. I couldn't dodge them. The only option? I jumped off the horse. The horse went straight, stamping and injuring many of those archers. Half of them were able to step aside in time. I rushed towards them. They tried their luck with a few shots, while the distance between them and me decreased. But now, that I was on the ground, it was easy for me to dodge the arrows. I blocked a couple of them with my sword. They realized it was futile now and drew out their swords. In no time, I was in a sword fight with six of them and Evyavan. I could see the horror in their eyes. After all, they knew me well. I was one of them not a long time ago. They gave a fight, but it was futile. The first found his guts dangling from his opened stomach. The second one made me defend myself. After defending three attacks I thrust my sword into him. Then half rotated, pulled my sword out, jumped, gained altitude, and pushed the sword in the shoulder of the soldier, from the top, that followed, as I came down. Three more to go. They came all at once. I ducked and one of them went behind. The next one came slashing the air, I stepped aside. Then chopped off his right arm and kicked him on the back. The first one came back but couldn't match my speed. I pierced my sword into his right eye socket. The last one was appalled but had to fight. His head rolled on the ground and stopped at the feet of Evyavan.

'I used to respect you, Yashvasin.' He said while drawing out his sword. 'Who could have thought a trusted member like you would turn out to be a traitor? I pity you, Yashvasin'

'Traitor, back-stabber, or renegade. Call me whatever you want. But don't pity me for knowing the dark secrets of your Maharaja Brihadratha. You should know about the person you serve. Show some interest there. I laugh at your heedlessness.'

'I'll laugh too. Over your dead body.'

Evyavan and I indulged ourselves in a brawling duel. It took me a while to notice that Yayati was fighting a few feet away from us. He was butchering all his opponents in the most barbaric way. The ASI shone as if it was a light source. It looked like Yayati was enjoying slaying them. The ASI was, slowly, taking over him. I could sense it. I couldn't fight Evyavan with all my attention. Something about Yayati was intriguing. I have seen him fight a few times before.

But never have I seen him fight with such zest. No. It was something more than mere zest. There was a hint of evil in his eyes. But it didn't concern me as long as it ensured Akshobhyas obliteration.

'Where's your attention, you spineless bastard? Fight me with all your strength!' Evyavan yelled as we clashed our swords.

I shook my head. Gained my concentration and went for him. Evyavan, an excellent archer and a skilled swordsman, was difficult to fight against. Our duel intensified. He was able to make his sword taste my blood when he went for my core. From the waist, I bled. But that was it. Apart from that, he wasn't able to touch me. I cut his calves and was able to do substantial damage on his arms. Soon he was out of breath. A few more strikes and he'd be done. But then, my concentration wavered again. In the time, I fought with Evyavan, Yayati had single handily slayed an entire infantry squad. A hundred soldiers were slayed in minutes. But nothing less was expected from Yayati. The Akshobhyan leaders sensed his danger. They knew if Yayati continued this slaughtering spree, the war will be over soon. I wasn't surprised when Senapati Aagney stepped in.

The master and the disciple found themselves facing each other in dire circumstances. The past and present of Chandragarh looked in each other's eyes. Yayati Yasah's smile faded. He was grave now. On the other hand, Senapati Aagney displayed a cunning smirk. It seemed as if the latter was waiting for this moment for a long time.

'I didn't wish to fight you under such circumstances, Aagney.' Yayati remarked.

'But somehow, here we are, master.' Senapati Aagney said while spinning his sword in a continuous circular motion. 'I'd always wanted to fight you. Without you holding down yourself.'

'Here is your chance now.'

'Maybe you could opt for another sword. It won't be a fair duel, after all.'

'You know I can't do that. You have to test your faith against the ASI.'

Senapati Aagney's smile grew wider. He looked at his feet for a few seconds.

'So let it be.' He said as he lifted his head.

The two rushed towards each other and stopped at the sharp sound of their clashing swords. It was a high-speed duel, which came as a shock considering their respective age. Blink, and you'll miss a strike. Senapati Aagney and Yayati were the best swordsmen that I know. I have been to the furthest corner of Bharatvarsh and have fought and known many great and skilled swordsmen. But Senapati Aagney and Yayati Yasah were the best among them.

I wanted to watch their duel but Evyavan was making it difficult for me to focus. Who would want to miss the best sword duel in ages? I had to deal with Evyavan first and that too fast. But the archery leader was not going down easily. He was cut from many places and was bleeding too. But somehow, he was still standing on his feet. I wonder how strong those legs were. I ran towards him and forced my sword in front but he stepped aside and tried to kick me in the stomach. I caught his leg and turned him around. That bastard used that moment for his gain and punched me in the mouth as he turned around. I was pushed backwards. My lips felt swollen and numb. When I graced my mouth with my other hand, I drew blood. Evyavan stood a few feet in front with his hideous smile.

'You… I underestimated you, Evyavan.' I said as I rubbed my hands with my blood.

'You underestimated the power of Akshobhyas without the ASI.' Evyavan said.

'No. That I didn't.' I whispered.

Evyavan, with the little confidence he gathered with that punch, came rushing towards me. A mistake he won't be able to regret.

I walked slowly towards his direction. After a few seconds, we found ourselves in another brawl. I dodged his attacks with slight opposite movements. When he brought his sword down, I turned to the side. When he slashed his sword horizontally, I moved back. When he tried to sweep me off my legs, I picked up my nearest foot and stepped back. He looked exasperated. His breath was highly asynchronous. But he kept on coming. He tried and tried but missed every time. He was overcome by lassitude. Last of his blows were highly tiresome and dull.

He gave a final attempt and, with his body weight, brought down the sword. It was easier to dodge him now. I shifted to one side and he, not having control over his body anymore, took a few steps ahead. I pierced him from the back. But he turned around, with my sword still in his back. He swung his sword a couple of times before falling on the ground. I pulled my sword from his back.

'One stubborn son of a bitch you were.' I said over his dead body.

I shifted my attention towards the adjacent fight. Yayati Yasah and Senapati Aagney were fighting with the same quickness as before. For all I could see, the intensity of their fight had increased. Senapati Aagney had taken one hit. A small cut on his neck. A drop of blood poured down on his sword as he swung it towards Yayati. Yayati, on the other hand, was clean. He looked vibrant, even after slaying hundreds of men. The blood that adorned his armour was not his. He was hardly out of breath. Their duel, anyhow, was stirring for me. I wish the war would halt for a moment so I could see them fight without any interruptions. Their mere movements around each other were thrilling. The way they moved their swords, with the motive to kill and defended themselves was nothing short of an art. But the outcome was inevitable.

'You were difficult to fight then and you are difficult to fight now.' Yayati said with pauses.

'I learned from the very best.' Senapati said in one go as he forced himself towards Yayati. He went for his head and was quick. When Yayati embraced in a position to defend himself, creating an opening at the bottom, Senapati Aagney changed his aim and went for his legs. Yayati unable to properly defend himself stumbled and fell on the ground. Aagney leaped forward and tried to attack Yayati as fast he could. But Yayati was able to block the attack by drawing the ASI above his head. He kicked Senapati Aagney, forcing him to take a few steps back which was enough for him to get up and dust himself off.

The battle was becoming interesting by the passing moment. Even with the ASI, Yayati was finding it difficult to defeat Senapati Aagney. Akshobhyan soldiers, now and then, were hindering my view and concentration from the historical duel being fought a few feet away. The sun was coming down. Only a brief amount of sunlight remained in the sky. I knew what had to be done.

Slaying and pushing away the Akshobhyan soldiers I made my way next to Yayati Yasah. He was, at first, a little disappointed to see me fight with him to defeat Senapati Aagney. He reckoned I doubted his calibre. But he was fast to realize that we should not squander away precious time. The more damage we could do early, the better.

'First ASI and now two against one. Is that even fair?' Senapati Aagney remarked.

'You know the old saying.' I said and slashed my sword on him. He blocked my attack and kicked me. I was pushed back on my knees. Stepping on my bend back, Yayati jumped and landed on Senapati Aagney with the ASI. Aagney tried to block him, but the thrust was too much. He took the hit. His left arm was sliced. A few inches of his skin, peeled off, remained attached to the arm by one end. He cried in pain.

'No!'

I turned towards the source of the sound. It was Yugant. I looked at the sun and not much time remained. I had to stop Yugant. I launched a series of strikes for Yugant to defend while, in the back, Yayati dealt with the injured Senapati Aagney.

Senapati Aagney's movements were slowed down. His left arm was covered in blood. Drops of blood dripped from the tips of his fingers in a continuous flow. Yayati wasn't toying around. He cut Aagneya from his vital areas. After a few moments, Senapati Aagney could fight no more. He bled from his arms, neck, legs, and everywhere, where the armour didn't hide the injuries.

'I wished for this to end differently. But it can't be helped.' Said Yayati.

Senapati Aagney had given up. He fell on his knees. Taking deep breaths, he forced a smile on his face. The mixture of blood and dust on his face made the smile hideous.

'I wished for you too, master. I wished you'd give up evil. But that can't be helped either.' Senapati Aagney spat out blood.

'You were my best student.'

Yayati Yasah thrust his sword in Senapati Aagney's stomach three times.

The latter coughed blood as he fell on the ground.

I was able to push Yugant away. A few of our soldiers came on him. I and Yayati left the scene on our horses. After a while, the conch was blown.

Brihadratha Akshobhya

The dead bodies of the fallen soldiers were aligned over the stack of sandalwood. I helped the soldiers to do so. Hundreds of our soldier, gone. Thousands of Akshobhyan soldiers died. Yayati, Vira Advaitya, and the two commanders watched over from a distance. I gave them a dispassionate look. Vira Advaitya turned around and headed for his camp. After the preparations were done, the cremation ceremony began.

The stars twinkled less tonight. The huge flames, rising, overtook the responsibility to shimmer up the night sky. Such nights are the part of the horrific reality, the war brings with it. Lifting the morale of the soldiers, after they arrange the death bed of their brothers, is always a difficult and overwhelming task. You can't cheer up your soldiers if you are surrounded by an air of melancholy. For most of the days that follow after such nights, I have filled my men with the greatest enthusiasm. No problem arises when I try to uplift my men's morale. But this time, it was difficult on my part. Senapati Aagney's death was pivotal in the war. But for me, it was hurting. I have shared most of my life in Chandragarh with him. We have trained together. We have been in wars together. We have bled together for the safety of our motherland. But that didn't stop me from scheming his death. And that was hurting.

I walked towards Yayati who was expressionless. He was dejected too. After all, he slayed his student. But war demands death. And it shall get it. We went for a stroll under the moonlight. Some soldiers were retiring to their camps, others were up for the night watch. They all greeted us as we went past them.

'With Senapati Aagney dead, the Akshobhyans will have no other choice.' I discussed.

'Brihadratha will lead his army tomorrow.' Yayati said.

'The war won't go long. Two days. That is all.'

'You amaze me, Yashvasin.' Yayati stopped walking. 'For so many years, you have worked for Brihadratha. Still, you underestimate him.'

'Without the ASI he is nothing.' I said.

'He defeated me in a duel without the ASI in an open assembly.' Yayati whispered harshly, remembering the events of that day.

'I won't change my opinion.' I replied gently. 'Our army hasn't suffered much loss. Vira Advaitya is doing great. Vrishank and Bhagiratha are doing a splendid job too.'

'That won't ensure us a quick victory. I hate Brihadratha with my very heart. But even I won't subside the fact that he is a brilliant warrior.'

'Yugant and Brihadratha are the only two great leaders left in the Akshobhyan army. The remaining battalion leaders are good. But the best ones are already dead.'

'What about…?'

'Nrchakshu has disgraced Brihadratha.' I said sternly. 'If Brihadratha was to forgive Nrchakshu, we would have seen him on the battlefield.'

'So where is he now?' Yayati asked.

'I couldn't care any less.'

Back in the battlefield, Akshobhyas were helped by reinforcements coming from nearby smaller kingdoms. But that didn't make much difference. Our treacherous army continued with their barbaric feats. But the death rate of the Akshobhyan soldiers slowed down with Brihadratha leading them. Smaller, but defensively strong formation helped them to keep themselves in the war. But we had plans to counter the scheme. Vira Advaitya's job was to keep Yugant Yasah busy. So that he won't interfere when the time is wrong. I and Yayati were fighting together. Yayati, as expected, was slaying the infantry and horseman ruthlessly. I aimed for the war elephants. They had caused the greatest number of deaths in our infantry. The Akshobhyan wild enormous elephants, when tamed, could prove to be beneficial in such wars.

I opted for a horse today. The chariots are royal and advantageous in most occasions. But I had to be agile. Many tried to hinder my horse's movements but met the sharp edge of my sword. My horse's legs were covered with dust and blood. Blood not of its own. After riding for many yards, I stumbled upon a line held by a group of gigantic war elephants. The Mahavats sitting on the top were trained archers. I pulled the reins and kicked the horse and tried to make my way past the line. An arrow was launched but missed. I kept ongoing. Right in front of the elephants, my horse lost control. The elephants began to trumpet and my horse, scared, stood on its hind limbs. I struggled to get the horse under control. After dodging multiple arrows and pulling and kicking the horse, it finally admitted to my orders. From the little opening in the wall of the war elephants, I made my way past them. Our archery squad was not far behind. There were almost a hundred of those godly animals. I signalled for the archers' leader. And with his permission, arrows filled the skies. The Mahavats were dead after one round. But war elephants were not affected by one round of tiny arrows. A dozen rounds of arrows and some courage from our infantry were required to bring them down. The loud trumpet cry of the elephants was ear-splitting. In their suffering, they killed several of our infantrymen. But even after so much death and agony, five of the elephants remained. And they had gone mad. They charged towards our army and caused a massive stampede, killing hundreds in the process. These five elephants, the mightiest I have ever seen, seemed to be indestructible. Many tried to stop them but in vain. Something had to be done and fast.

Yayati came to the scene. I decided to join him. He went for three elephants that remained in one group. Two others were causing mayhem distinctly. I ran towards one of them.

I stopped at its monstrous foot. It had caught two of our soldiers within the grip of its 12-foot long trunk. It was one huge war elephant. It threw the soldiers many yards away. I asked for a spear from a soldier. He threw one in my direction. Not only did I catch the spear, but I was also able to catch the elephant's attention too. The eyes were red and the left tusk was broken in half. A scar zigzagged its way on its forehead. A foot long. The elephant swung its trunk in my direction. It all happened in a blur. I was able to bring my shield between its trunk and me. But the impact was hard. The shield broke in half and I was tossed a few yards away. There was no time to search for the injuries.

When I looked up, a black round mass of darkness covered the sky above me. I crawled away. A few inches from me he forced his foot down and a cloud of dust covered me. I stumbled, fumbled, and got up in a haste. It was time to get a grip on reality. I noticed that a huge wound popped out on its back. The elephant was tall and the wound was out of my reach, even with the spear in my hand. I had to get over it. The Howdah, that it was carrying, was broken in pieces. Several arrows were sticking out of the howdah and the elephant too. I puzzled my way behind the elephant and caught its tail. I poked it from behind. The elephant became vexed and gave a trumpet whilst standing on its hind limbs. When he landed, the land trembled beneath him.

'What a godly beast.' I whispered.

I ordered the infantry to form several layers of circular parameter around the elephant. I called for the drum beaters to scare the beast. The elephant was becoming perplexed and that's what I desired for. The soldiers in the back formed a platform from one big shield. I ran towards them, jumped on the shield and they launched me high enough on the elephant. I thrust my spear into its back and it gave a cry and was back on its hind limbs again. I balanced, somehow, and prevented myself from falling. The elephant was scared. It was time to free him from all its miseries, courtesy of us humans. A repeated procedure of pushing a spear in and out of that one massive wound was enough to bring the elephant down. The soldiers cheered as I got down from the dead beast. But it wasn't over. Another elephant was causing havoc nearby. I looked at Yayati. He had slayed two of the three elephants without much help.

A familiar being came into view. There was no doubt. It was Balrama, Brihadratha's ride on hunting trips. He must have been forced into the war. The biggest creature I have ever seen. The maddened elephant stared at me for a moment. Maybe he remembered me. I remember him for sure. But as a peaceful and lovingly creature. I was familiar with Balrama's nature. It was Mahapradhan Ganakarta, perhaps. His potion and herbal mixtures can make a sane man go berserk. In huge amounts, it can turn a tranquil and calm elephant into a disastrous weapon of war. His eyes reflected dense greyish shade. They showed a glimpse of black clouds amidst a thunderstorm. The area around his eyes was rubbed with an herbal mixture, perhaps, of deep sunset shade. After a few moments of realization and reminiscence, Balram charged at me. He picked an enormous tree log, from the stack of many, and threw it at me. I almost took a hit when I dived to my right, missing by inches. He hurried towards me. I tried to calm him down with the usual gestures, like in those old peaceful days, but it was pointless. This time, I took a hit. He pushed me away with his trunk. I fell on a small bed of arrows. My armour provided much protection. But one sharp end of an arrow pierced into my right bicep. I pulled it out and ran towards Balram. He swung his trunk with all his might. I jumped and watch the trunk whirl around only to come back again. He missed it again. I ran behind him and tried to stay there. Balram was filled with vexation. Several horsemen were throwing spears at him. The gigantic beast wasn't going to come down with puny spears. He caught hold of one of the horses with his long trunk. The horseman jumped in time. He flung the horse towards our infantryman and many were rolled under it. Poor animals were fighting the war of humans. That's the tragedy of the reality of the world we live in. There was no way I could jump, somehow, on his back. Putting a ladder on the back of such an animal was illogical. Balram was no ordinary elephant. He had already slayed hundreds of our men. I started slashing at his legs from behind. But that was just another futile attempt. He kicked behind and I was tossed several feet away. Balram turned around. I watched him come towards me, as I lied with a dozen corpses. I reckoned this was it. He stopped in front of me and gave me a loud trumpet. Then he brought his gigantic trunk on me. I noticed something lustrous from the corner of my eye. The next thing I know, the thick and muscular trunk of Balram was cut in half. It was Yayati. The blood spill from the trunk covered me and the cut out of trunk fell to my right. Balram's cry covered the atmosphere. There is nothing more daunting I'd heard. Yayati lent me his hand and I caught it. Yayati had slayed the three other war elephants and has come to my aid. Without wasting any time, he ran towards the elephant who was in tremendous pain. Yayati wanted to do this quickly. He slashed Balram's legs with the ASI. First, his hind limbs forced him on his buttocks. Then his forelimbs forced him to lie on one side. Yayati ran above Balram and changed the way he gripped the ASI. With both hands, he thrust the ASI into Balram's head.

Yayati glanced at me, as I stood a few yards away pressing the injured arm to my body, and then took off. I loosened my waist cloth and wrapped it around my arm tightly. Such injuries are inevitable in war. I stepped on to my chariot and decided to fight, for the rest of the day, from there. My aim was not as precise as it is. But it was precise enough to take the soul out of the Akshobhyan soldiers. Pulling the arrows proved to be a little painful. But I had to deal with it. I was dejected but adamant. A certain part of me wanted to go and see Brihadratha agitate over the loss of his soldiers. I thought about the happiness I would get when I see the downcast eyes of Brihadratha, when I see him hopeless and wretched. I asked the coachman to turn the Chariot towards Brihadratha's direction.

I never fought Brihadratha Akshobhya. Neither have I seen him in an actual duel. The morning practice sessions were the only place where I would see him pick up a sword. But that was practice. He was good. But war brings out the very best or worst from the people.

By the time we reached the area where Brihadratha was fighting, my stack of arrows was almost empty. I flexed my bicep, took my sword, and jumped out of the chariot. In an instant, I was surrounded by dozens of soldiers. But that wasn't the thing that concerned me. I noticed Brihadratha sitting on a rock formation. He sat there royally as if he was assuming the Chandragarh throne. I found it queer. The Maharaja of the greatest kingdom in the whole Bharatvarsh, sitting ideally, with a little smirk, on a bunch of rocks between thousands of men who wanted his blood on their hands. He was staring in one direction. I shifted my eyes in the same direction. Vrishank and Bhagiratha, on their chariots, were approaching him. A few yards away, they asked for their chariots to be stopped and stepped out. Vrishank had a maze with him. It was a heavy golden maze, with sharp pokes sticking out from it. Bhagiratha was equipped with a sword and an axe. A few of the Akshobhyan soldiers went head to head with them. Vrishank and Bhagiratha slayed everyone in their path. After walking towards Brihadratha for a while they stopped and stood 10 yards away from Brihadratha whose smile remained intact. Brihadratha stood up from his place. He removed his sword and threw the sheath away. He assumed his position and let his smile grow wider.

A few of our soldiers joined me against the dozens of Akshobhyan infantrymen that surrounded me. Even though I was fit enough to be at their throat myself, I reckoned a little help won't be a bad idea after all. Because, now and then, my concentration would waiver.

Our two commanders rushed towards Brihadratha at once. Vrishank leaped forward with his heavy maze. Brihadratha ducked and the rocks behind him crumbled from the force of the spiked maze. Bhagiratha came slashing his way on Brihadratha. A left strike with the sword. A right strike with the axe. But Brihadratha defended himself well. Bhagiratha's gift of being ambidextrous provided him an upper hand in the battles. Brihadratha spun around and pecked him, on his back, with the pommel of his sword. Now that is something I'd never imagine. Brihadratha's movements were highly agile. His balance was perfect. The way he spun around on one leg in the exact amount he needed so that he'd be at the right place, was applaud worthy. Both our commanders were astounded too. And their fight had just begun.

An Akshobhyan soldier's sword, inches away from me, forced me to sweep my eyes off from Brihadratha. A spear flew from the right and entered his temple from one side and came out from the other. I nodded at my fellow soldier.

Brihadratha carefully moved around. Bhagiratha and Vrishank had him in between them. Brihadratha's fastidious eyes were watching every movement of his opponents. Baghiratha was the first to attack. He swiped his axe horizontally. Brihadratha showed great flexibility. Forcing his other hand on the ground for balance, he curved back. When Vrishank came running, sensing Brihadratha to be in an uncomfortable and clumsy position, the Maharaja of Akshobhyas did a handstand, with the same hand. Vrishank was shocked by the unexpected move. Brihadratha, with his legs above, came down on Vrishank and caught the latter on the head. Vrishank fell on the ground, face first. That was a dirty hit he took. His head began to bleed. It all happened in a heartbeat. I wonder when the Maharaja of Akshobhyas would use to practice something like that. Brihadratha stood next to the fallen Vrishank. His attempt to slay Vrishank was ruined by Bhagiratha's flying axe, which when he dodged formed a crack in a massive rock behind and got stuck.

Three soldiers, equipped with spears, came in view. It was difficult to fight them because the range required with a sword is less than the range needed to fight with a spear. A lot of my soldiers accompanying me were killed. I had to move around quickly a lot. I slayed one of them and took his spear. After that, it was an easy job. But more and more Akshobhyan soldiers kept on coming. Later, something staggering caught my eyes.

Vrishank was back on his feet. He was collecting his maze, which had fallen a few feet away, while Brihadratha and Bhagiratha were indulged in a sword fight. Vrishank had been substantially bleeding. One side of his head was covered with blood. He looked lethargic but was adamant to carry on. After shaking his head vigorously for a while, he was back in the fight. Brihadratha was aware of his recurring presence. Vrishank took on Brihadratha, giving Bhagiratha needed time to pull out his axe from the crevice of the rock. After a while, Brihadratha was, yet again, fighting our two commanders at the same time. It was bewildering to watch Brihadratha fight with such ease. Not only was he successfully defending himself, Vrishank and Bhagiratha suffered multiple cuts and bruises.

Reinforcement came. With more men fighting with me, the Akshobhyan soldiers began to fall rapidly. I wanted to join the fight against Brihadratha. I let my men take the front and rushed, myself, to the adjacent fight. Halfway there, I stopped and, for a moment, was appalled.

Brihadratha moved like gushing water in a stream. His feet were more graceful than a dancer's. And his sword skills were of the highest quality. Vrishank and Bhagirath were on either side of the Maharaja of Akshobhyas. Bhagiratha was exasperated. Not once was he able to touch Brihadratha with his sword. I noticed a smile on Brihadratha's face. A smile that mocked Bhagiratha. Full of rage, Bhagiratha lost his mind and, hence, the fight. He yelled with frustration and threw his axe towards Brihadratha. With only a distance of eight feet between them, he was sure that Brihadratha couldn't escape unharmed. But he was wrong. Brihadratha moved just a little, as much was required. The axe got stuck in Vrishank's chest. Brihadratha, just in front, pulled out the axe, swung around, and cut off Bhagiratha's head. It happened so fast that it was hard to believe. Even after witnessing it with my own eyes, I found it untrue. It was a trick. It must be a deceiving lie. For how could the Brihadratha Akshobhya I knew came up with such unimaginable abilities?

Brihadratha saw me, gaping at his incredible feat. His smile was lost soon after. We were separated by more than fifty yards. He threw the axe at me. I was not thinking straight. I was perplexed after what I had just witnessed. A group of soldiers came running in front of me. One of them took the axe on his helmet, which submerged deep into his head. The pain in my arm brought me back to the right senses. I couldn't fight, let alone win, against Brihadratha in my current situation. And so I turned around. Borrowed a horse from one of my men and left. Brihadratha Akshobhya had kept his excellent swordsmanship qualities hidden for so many years. I wondered what other secrets were about to unfold.

An Unexpected Warrior

Yayati Yasah's stare was insulting me.

'Will you stop it?' I said sternly.

Yayati remained silent.

The oil lamp on my desk was losing its light. I asked a soldier to pour more oil into it.

'For all the time I spent in the palace of Chandragarh, Brihadratha never showcased even a hint of his actual abilities.'

Yayati's silence was mocking me.

The oil lamp was illuminating my desk again.

I sighed and accepted my fault.

'What should we do next?' I asked Yayati.

'Our army suffered more causalities than the Akshobhyas today.' He said firmly.

'How is that possible?' I was shocked. 'I thought our loss was limited only to the southern end of the battlefield where Brihadratha was.'

'In the north, along with Yugant, their reinforcements were able to do much more damage.'

'But the reinforcement was nothing!' I stood up. 'How can four thousand soldiers do such damage?'

'Their reinforcements keep on coming, even if it is in small numbers. They can cover up for their loss. But we can't do that. It pays in positive for ruling over a major extent of Bharatvarsh, you see?'

'What do you suggest?' I asked.

'It's simple. Kill Brihadratha.'

'Help me recollect what we have been trying to do for so long.'

'I'll face him tomorrow. I have an Intel on where he will be leading the army tomorrow.'

'Anything that you find appropriate.' I said while applying an herbal mixture on the stitches on my arm.

'But he will be surrounded by a lot of men.'

'You think?'

'Be serious, Yashvasin.'

'It's not me. It's the medicine the ved made me drink half an hour ago. Stronger than the strongest wine I've had.'

'I want you and other leaders of our army to accompany me. We can't let Brihadratha get help from others.'

'Do you realize the gravity of your statement? If we concentrate our leaders at one place, the soldiers placed elsewhere won't have someone to direct them and therefore…'

'We'll lose a lot of our men. I understand.' Yayati said. 'But that is the risk we have to take. We are losing our men, anyway. And with no reinforcements, we won't be able to stand long. Akshobhyas are playing a game of endurance. We can't win that game. Attack them with all our might. We have to end it soon.'

I got up, felt a little dizzy. Yayati lent me his hand.

'I can't counter that. Let us do it your way. Tomorrow, we'll slay Brihadratha.'

By the next morning, the pain in my arm subsided. I was feeling a lot better and I needed to do. Yayati was addressing the army. Asking them to fight with all their might.

On the battlefield, Yayati led our army in the *Trishul Vyuh. In Trishul Vyuh,* the army is divided into three separate sections. Brihadratha was leading his army from the centre. And so we focused our strength in the middle. The other sections were led by two battalion leaders each. All the other great warriors were encapsulated between the infantry in the middle section of the army. But the Akshobhyan army had other plans. The two sides clashed and the spree of slaying begun. And from the beginning, we got to see the sly nature of the Maharaja of Akshobhyas.

A battalion of the Akshobhyan infantry, covered with four walls of horsemen reached the depth of our army. They slammed the *shehnais* and destroyed our *nagadas,* making us unable to instruct our army when in need of a change in formation. This was very clever of Brihadratha. Now, if we want to change formations, we had to reach out to the army through messengers on horses to each battalion. Not only would that take much time, but the enemies could also easily counter our formation, now that we can't encode the message through drums and trumpets. That Akshobhyan battalion was slayed soon after, but the damage was done. But a scheme bigger than this followed. Brihadratha had read our mind-set and was capitalizing. He was ready to sacrifice his men in huge numbers. It was no secret that our biggest weapon and hope to win this war was Yayati Yasah wielding the ASI. It was impossible on their side to force Yayati on giving up the ASI. Hence, Brihadratha replicated the strategy of Vria Advaitya of slaying the paramount leaders of our army. Vrishank, Bhagiratha, and half a dozen of our battalion leaders were dead. I, Vira Advaitya were the ones remaining.

A little while into the war and Yayati Yasah found himself in a massive ten layer *Chakra Vyuh.* No, slaying Yayati was not a part of their scheme. But delaying him was. Yayati had saved me and other members of our army on multiple occasions in this war. Brihadratha's army wasn't taking any more chances. Even for a warrior like Yayati who wields the ASI, penetrating a chakra vyuh was bound to take some time. The time was limited and so they sent their best warriors to slay me and Vira Advaitya. I was leading a thousand soldiers and one hundred horsemen. My chariot stopped when I encountered Yugant. He was leading a battalion of hundreds of men and a group of archers. The archers did their damage and then our infantry found themselves fighting the Akshobyan battalion. Yugant stepped out of his chariot and challenged me for a duel.

'Afraid to pick up your sword, you traitor?' He yelled. 'Don't. I won't be fighting you with my spear.'

'Oh please do. I insist.' I chose a spear from the stack and stepped out of my chariot.

Yugant gave a smile back and stepped back into his chariot to exchange his sword with a spear.

'Anything to keep you from stealing my sword.' He mocked me.

'I asked your father to face you today. He replied by saying that you're not worthy of his time.' I shrugged my shoulders.

I saw the change in his countenance. He threw two spears at me, back to back, out of rage. I dodged the first one and lifted my shield to defend myself from the other. It penetrated my shield by two inches. I laughed at him. And once again, Yugant and I found ourselves in a duel. I remember that fine morning. A little before Nrchakshu kicked me into unconsciousness, Yugant and I had a duel. First with the spears then a sword fight. But this time, it wasn't mere practice.

Yugant and I, with our spears aimed at each other, were moving around each other, in embraced position, waiting for the other to initiate the fight. I did the required. I forced my spear at his head. He leapt forward, countered my attack by swerving my spear away, and raised his leg to kick me in the face. I stepped aside and nearly lost my balance. But was fast enough to regain it though. For a long time we fought, till the sun shone above our head. I only defended myself from the ruthless attacks of Yugant. We were both exhausted. But Yugant had a rather deeper effect.

'Out of your breath already?' I tried to reach out for his nerves.

He kept on coming. He even got me a couple of times. But my patience gave up when I saw Vira Advaitya, in a distance, fighting for his life from Brihadratha Akshobhya. I caught Yugant out of the blue as I commenced a spree of offensive attacks. I increased the pace of our fight. But somehow, the exhausted Yugant Yasah kept up. I was searching for the right time to provide that final blow and it came soon. I watched for his movements. But they weren't following a fixed pattern. I had to improvise. He swung and slashed his spear horizontally. I blocked his attack by forcing my spear on his, vertically. He tried to knock me out with his elbow but I caught it and pushed him away. He leapt again, this time aiming for my legs. My calves were hurting, but I carried on. He was aware of my injury and tried to waiver my concentration elsewhere so that he could get an opening on my arm. I did what he wanted. He eventually went for my right arm. I let go of my spear. With one hand, I caught the pointed end of his spear. Blood oozed out of my hand. I pulled him closer to me and slashed my forearm, of the other hand, on his spear. It broke into two pieces. Yugant was shocked. After punching him three times in the face, I thrusted the pointed end of the spear, still in my hand, deep into his left thigh. He cried in excruciating pain. He lied flat on the ground, trying to get the spear out. I walked back and, from my chariot, equipped myself with a bow and a stack of arrows and began to rush towards Brihadratha. But Yugant's painful cry sent a giddy feeling down my spine. I began walking towards him as he struggled to get the spear out. A few soldiers came to his aid. I aimed for their heads and my arrows found their way. Yugant's cry halted as I stood over him. From the stack, I took two arrows and thrust them in his hands, crucifying him to the ground in the process. His cry intensified. Then, slowly, I pushed the broken spearhead, deeper into his thigh with my right foot. It amused me to hurt him. The war had made me a sadist.

'Stay here and wait for your king to die.' I said and left the scene.

Vira Advaitya was crawling away from his death. Brihadratha walked behind him, closely. Brihadratha caught me from the corner of his eyes and diverted his concentration from the half-dead Vira Advaitya whose half-closed, drowsy eyes took my notice too. His bloody hands reached out for me, asking for help.

Brihadratha turned around and looked straight into my eyes.

'There are many questions, Yashvasin. Killing time for answers.' He said as he walked away from the fallen Maharaja of Advaityas and Varunyas.

'Not that the answers would make any difference now.' A couple of Akshobhyan soldiers came at me. I punished them for their interference and took their lives as a token of apology.

'It might seem sorted for you, Maharaja of Akshobhyas. Vira Adviatya almost dead. Jatsaya Varunya gone. You preach power. Maybe you can get the intact Bharatvarsh to rule upon now.'

Brihadratha walked and stopped four yards away from me. It was weird. Here we stood, in a brief silence. Having a conversation now and then in the break of the quietness whilst our men died around us. Some of our men encircled Vira Advaitya and took him back to safety. Brihadratha saw it all but didn't try to stop them.

'You have caused me a lot of pain, Yashvasin.' He said gently.

'So have you.' I held my sword between my hands firmly and was ready to fight.

'I didn't have many options that night, Yashvasin. You should know that. Your clan was planning to destroy the integrity of Chandragarh. I could not allow that.'

'Butchering the people you swore to protect is never the solution.'

I leapt towards him. Our swords clashed sharply.

'Not one day passes by when I don't think about that unfortunate night. I have spent countless sleepless nights thinking about ways I could have prevented that unfortunate incident.' Brihadratha Askhobhya said while pressing his sword against mine.

'Profound words from a heartless being. That is something new.' I forced his sword to one end and punched him in the face. He was pushed a few feet back.

'Careful, Maharaja of Brihadratha. You'll lose your throne if you're not careful. For I don't think to be modest with someone ostentatious like you would grace one's self-being.'

'All right then, Yashvasin Yudhvan.' He said before the fight got intense.

While I fought the only man subjected to my hatred, all I could think of was Yayati captured inside the *Chakravyuh*. I found it strange. For all the years I sweated beneath the blazing sun, tortured myself through the vigorous routine of training and shed ounces of blood courtesy of those multitudinous bruises and cuts, all I had wanted was a chance to avenge my family. A chance to slay and destroy the Maharaja who butchered and burned my entire clan, who killed my mother. This was my chance. After years of hardships, failures, and a little success I stand here. Looking straight into his eyes. The eyes which have daunted me for all the years that I stayed in the royal palace of Chandragarh. These eyes mocked me.

'So close and you still can't even touch me.' The eyes would say and then burst into laughter.

Now that I needed the most from myself, for I can slay and destroy him completely in the next brief moment, I wasn't myself. Maybe I never was the man I dreamt of who would kill Brihadratha Akshobhya. I asked this question for the very first time yesterday when I saw Maharaja of Akshobhyas slay our two commanders with such ease. Watching him fight once was enough for me to scale myself with him. I despised myself for being so cynical. For thinking that I'd won so many fights, taken so many souls, put myself through horrendous pressure for only to lose today, when I ought to win. This was unwanted.

Brihadratha landed a strong punch on my face and broke my nose. But I felt nothing. Blood drops started dripping on the dusty barren land. One drop. Falls on the ground. Gets absorbed. No trace. Another drop falls. The cycle repeats. Another punch on my face. This time my lower jaw came loose. I felt nothing again. Another punch. This time he caught my eye. It was swollen. But yet I felt nothing. I looked at Brihadratha Akshobhya from the other eye. My vision was hindered. But I could see his face. That countenance. Not much had changed since that night. The same king. In the same armour. With the same expressions. I was seeing images. Maybe because of the three punches. They were blurred, not clear. But seemed familiar. Same night. Same boy, paralyzed with fear, reaching out for his mother. That was enough.

With hindered vision, broken jaw, injured arm, and stiff muscles, I returned Brihadratha's blows. Our swords clashed. I used my balance to my advantage and made the attacks a little acrobatic. Brihadratha came slashing the air in front. I did a windmill and stepped aside. I felt so light. He continued his flow of attacks. I ducked once, back flipped the other time, and ultimately scratched the right part of his face with the sharp tip of my sword. A huge scar formed on his face. Apart from the scar, I noticed a hint of amusement on his face. For how could a man this bruised and damaged still fight? Our swords met again. But this time, Brihadratha's sword was shaking just like his confidence. The fight was to get into each other's head. I had established my presence in his which he was finding hard to believe. He kept on coming at me. And each time left with a cut or a knock. But he didn't give up. Keeping up with Brihadratha's movements was tiresome. Outsmarting him was exhausting. The throbbing pain in my head asked me to stop. My heart, pumping wildly, asked me to take some rest. The burning cuts over my body asked me to give up. But physical pain didn't affect me now. I had an emotionally strong barrier keeping the excruciating physical pain at bay. I was not going to give up and neither was the Maharaja of Akshobhyas.

Brihadratha Akshobhya was finding it hard to balance himself. He took the support of his sword, now and then, just to approach me. He had crossed his threshold. Anything he did was many times harder on his body. So, he used his brain. He tried to come from my left, every time. My left eye was swollen badly and anything coming from there was not visible to me. I tried to defend myself against his attacks. Most of the time, I was successful. But more than a couple of times, I took some serious hits. My left hand was bleeding badly. A stream of blood, which began from the shoulder, was joined by many tributaries originating from various openings on my arm and descended on the ground in the form of blood drops.

'You don't understand, Yashvasin.' He said in pauses between taking heavy breaths. 'You were too young to understand that night and too blinded with hatred to understand it now. I know you tried to talk your clan out of that scheme. Because you too knew the consequences of their actions. I didn't propose to slaughter your clan. But it was the only way. I had to accept his proposal.'

'His hood is tainted with innocent blood as much as is yours. What he did that night showed his cowardness. I was out there, hours before the massacre. I was out there, resolute enough to kill him.' I said with aggression.

'He decided what was best for the city of Chandragarh. He was right about the Yudhvans. Your clan was a plague. A plague which was meant to be annihilated.'

My eye strained. Brihadratha's last words acted as a source of energy for me. I stormed towards him and brought down my sword on him. He tried to defend, but I had forced my sword just too hard. Brihadratha Akshobhya was forced to his knees. I thumped him in the face with my knee. His sword came down. I again ascended my sword to bring it down on the kneeling Maharaja of Akshobhyas. He tried to get his sword up to defend himself. Our swords clashed. But yet again the force was too heavy for him to stop. His sword, below mine, cut deep through his shoulder. The Maharaja of Akshobhya shrieked in pain. I enjoyed seeing him suffer. I pressed more, and his shoulder oozed out blood like an earthen pot overflowing with water.

'The Akshobhyas are a plague, you son of a bitch!' I said as I took a few steps back.

Brihadratha Akshobhya was down on both knees. His eyes were closed and he was swaying lightly. A light gust of wind would have been enough to make him fall on the ground. He was breathing heavily. His chest pumping and relaxing in extreme cycles. Blood was everywhere. On his face, arms, legs, and what remained of his armour. His sword remained, horizontally, inside the two-inch cavity in his left shoulder. No energy remained in him to even express the pain he was suffering from.

'Yes! Yes, it was imprudent of my clan to not see what they were getting themselves into.' I found it hard to get words out of my system because of the burning sensation in my chest. 'I tried to stop my father. I tried to stop them all! But was labelled as a traitor by my father. A traitor for seeing it through. I hated them for that. I hated them all!'

Brihadratha Akshobhya's eyes opened a little.

'But that still doesn't make wrongs right, does it Brihadratha? Do you think your father Maharaja Sarvyoni would have been proud of you? Do you think he would have liked this impromptu decision of yours? You could have talked it through with us. But no. You didn't. Instead, you labelled us as terrorists. The Yudhvans. The oldest clan in Chandragarh, who fought and bled for the safety of this land. You labelled us as a danger for our motherland. And how did you counter that? You killed my clan. You became an arsonist. A terrorist. You burned them all. Burned them all right in front of my eyes! And for what? To prove that you were right. Because you were the King. A King has to be right. But guess what Maharaja of Akshobhyas? You were wrong!'

Brihadratha Akshobhya forced a smile on his face as I ran towards him with my sword. It enraged me even more. He looked up in the sky and closed his eyes. I pulled my sword back to gain some momentum. A couple of feet away from him, a couple of feet away from achieving my vengeance, I slashed my sword at him. But was still too far. An arrow swirled from the distance. It penetrated my wrist, went all the way through, and emerged from the other side. My sword fell on the ground. Brihadratha opened his eyes to the sound of my sword hitting the ground. We both looked at the direction from where the arrow came. And both were equally surprised to see Nrchakshu.

The Last Duel

I dared not to pull the arrow out. I cut it from both ends. Four inches of wood remained inside my wrist. The blood vessels were badly cut. I couldn't curve my hand to grab my sword with it and so had to pick it up from my left hand. Nrchakshu had another arrow aimed at me, just in case I tried to attack his king again. He took little steps towards us and joined his kneeling Maharaja at his side.

'What are you doing here?' I asked Nrchakshu.

A group of Akshobhyan soldiers a little over a dozen gathered around Nrchakshu and Brihadratha Akshobhya. They carefully removed the sword penetrated in his shoulder and wrapped the wound tightly with a cloth. Then they picked up their king and started to take him away to safety. All this happened whilst my nephew had an arrow aimed at me.

'You know I can't allow this, Nrchakshu.' I said as I watched the soldiers take away the unconscious Brihadratha. I took a step towards them.

'Don't!' Nrchakshu yelled. I stopped.

'You know I can't.' I said.

'Then you won't leave me any option.'

'Do what you are required to do then.'

Exhausted, I started running towards the fleeing soldiers. An arrow went past me. A warning by Nrchakshu. I grabbed one of the soldiers from his shoulder and pulled him back. Using my left hand to wield, I thrust my sword in him. As I pulled out the sword, an arrow pierced my back. I looked behind. Nrchakshu pulled another arrow at me. I turned around and began the struggle of slaying the soldiers helping Brihadratha. After thrusting my sword in the neck of one and the head of two other soldiers, Nrchakshu shot another arrow. This time, I took a hit in the back of my left thigh. But I kept ongoing. A few of our soldiers came to my aid. They began to fight the Akshobhyan soldiers. Only two remained by Brihadratha's side. I forced myself, somehow, towards them. I was just a couple of feet away from them when I took another arrow. This time on my left calf. I fell on the ground with the rest of our soldiers who came to my aid. Nrchakshu came running as I watched the two soldiers, joined by some archers, flee away with their King.

'Don't make me do this.' He said with a trembling voice. With the little energy I had left in me, I crawled, intending to decrease the growing distance between me and my vengeance.

'Why are you doing this, Nrchakshu?' I said in broken words. 'He slayed our family. How can you not see.'?

'I do see. But I see something beyond. That you can't see because your vision is hindered by your quest for vengeance.'

I looked at the direction of the soldiers taking Brihadratha Akshobhya to safety. A comforting smile stretched on my face. Nrchakshu was puzzled to see me smile.

'Vision hindered by my quest of vengeance or not. I see what pleases me.' I stretched my finger in the direction. 'Save your king if you can.'

Nrchakshu looked in the same direction. Brihadratha Akshobhya lied on the ground while the Akshobhyan soldiers gave their lives, fighting Yayati, to protect their king. It took him some time, but Yayati was finally able to break free from the chakravyuh. And now, he stood inches away from slaying Brihadratha Akshobhya. Nrchakshu rushed for his King's aid. I forced my severely injured body to crawl and join him but couldn't. A group of our soldiers surrounded me from all sides. I made myself comfortable in a rock formation and stayed there. When I ordered the men to join Yayati and help him slay the Maharaja of Akshobhyas, they refused kindly stating, they care about me more. I cursed them over and over again only to give up, eventually. I was in no condition to exceed the limits of my body. Maybe I'd form a stronger bond with these soldiers on the training ground. But I needed their protection. I was in no condition to defend myself anymore. The soldiers tried to take me away to safer ground. I refused. I wanted to witness Brihadratha's death.

Yayati butchered the Akshobhyan soldiers in the most gruesome way. He was accompanied by a huge battalion of our soldiers. The Akshobhyan soldiers fell like dry twigs on a windy evening. But the more they were slayed, the more soldiers came to take their place. But Yayati had smelled Brihadratha's blood. Stopping him now was beyond the bounds of possibility. Soldiers came between him and the unconsciously lying Brihadratha only to meet their death. When no one was left between him and the Maharaja of Akshobhyas, he looked down at Brihadratha Akshobhya. A smile stretched on his wizened face. Brihadratha moved a little. It was difficult to see what his light actions were. But it made Yayati vexed. I thought that was it. When Yayati pulled the ASI, with both hands, above his head, I thought that was it. But the gods were apathetic towards us. They had, through various agents suggested their disapproval. This time that agent was once again Nrchakshu. Nrchakshu was comparatively on the higher ground when he jumped and kicked Yayati in the face, to stop him from slaying Brihadratha. In this war, till now, apart from the late Senapati Aagney, no one came close to even graze Yayati's hair, let alone provide him a knock. Because of the impact, Yayati's face shifted towards his right. He watched his helmet roll on the ground for a few feet. His long grey hair came loose from the left. With the ASI, still in his hand, he caressed his hair and then tied them carefully. I noticed a small cut on his upper left cheek. He didn't look pleased.

Nrchakshu stood between his Maharaja and Yayati Yasah like a dam protecting villagers from a treacherous river. But how long would the dam stand for? The rescue of Brihadratha Akshobhya resumed. Yayati turned around the direction where they were taking the Akshobhyan King, took a step forward too but found Nrchakshu's sword in front.

'No!' Nrchakshu yelled. 'Don't even think.'

'Go away, kid.' Yayati grumbled. 'Don't you remember what I did to you the last time we met?'

Nrchakshu remained silent and kept his sword, erected, pointed at the man wielding the ASI. Yayati couldn't wait longer. After getting a last glimpse of the fleeing soldiers, Brihadratha was lost to him in the battleground. He couldn't find him. With every passing moment, he was getting anxious and so stepped towards the last direction he saw the soldiers take Brihadratha Akshobhya. Nrchakshu swept his sword at Yayati. Yayati blocked the attack with a frenzy of anger.

'Last warning for the nephew of Yashvasin Yudhvan. If you weren't related, you'd be long dead.' He warned.

But the service-bond Nrchakshu launched a brief series of attacks. The clanging of their swords sounded as one intact sound. Such was the pace of Nrchakshu's attack. Yayati lost his patience eventually.

'Alright then. I shall pave my path to Brihadratha over your dead body.'

Nrchakshu and Yayati's duel was one of the last things I'd wanted. Nrchakhsu's stubborn nature and Yayati's fierce ambition would only lead to one thing. Last time I was able to stop Yayati in Indravan. But this time, now that the war demands blood, stopping Yayati won't be rational.

Nrchakshu's attacks weren't clean. His mind was preoccupied with something other than the war. Maybe a sense of guilt still lingered in his mind. The guilt of, somehow, using my nephew to my good lingered with me for days. But that wasn't my paramount concern, so subsiding those thoughts weren't difficult. In Nrchakshu's case, it was different. He was fighting against the man who held a sword which he helped, even though unknowingly, to smuggle out of the Chandragarh palace. But even though his attacks weren't properly executed, he let them out in quick succession. Giving a lot for Yayati to defend. Nrchakshu was playing it securely. Not many openings were given by him to his opponent. Now and then a few soldiers would distract the two warriors with their interference. But before those soldiers could try to enact the main plot of slaying the hero, the denouement of their actions would be called for by the two warrior's swords.

Yayati Yasah was impatient and wanted his duel with Nrchakshu to end as soon as possible. For a moment I thought Yayati glanced at me. A quick glance. As if he wanted to tell me his intention of killing my nephew. I didn't want him to slay him. But if that is something that lies between me and my vengeance, I'd do it myself.

Of all the soldiers and warriors Yayati fought with the ASI, Nrchakshu proved to be the toughest to fight against. Yayati was still looking for an opening to land the perfect blow on Nrchakshu. Our soldiers, fighting near Yayati were a little shocked too to witness their lead commander have such a hard time fighting back. Nrchakshu's actions were not only quick but were rigid too. I watched him land two successive heavy blows, with his sword, on Yayati. On the impact of the second, Yayati almost lost his balance. But, somehow, held on. After a while, Nrchakshu and Yayati found themselves inches away from each other with their swords clung onto each other. Yayati was vexed to see himself suffer against someone who he thought was an amateur fighter. He shifted his sword, and hence Nrchakshu's balance' towards his right and then while uttering a loud cry kicked Nrchakshu with all his might. Nrchakshu was forced back. He stumbled and rolled three times before stopping amidst the dusty dense cloud that rose with his fall. On his fall, Nrchakshu's face suffered from the impact of a few rocks. His face was scratched badly and blood came spurting out from what looked like a broken nose. Watching him bleed ushered Yayati to the much-needed confidence and credence of Asi's power yet again.

I was feeling much better and so tried to stand up after taking the arrow out from my calf and covering the wound with a cloth. Just then, a group of Akshobhyan soldiers attacked the soldiers guarding me. The soldiers defended me well. But one Akshobhyan soldier broke loose from their defensive wall and came at me. His eyes were wide open and so was his mouth. He was yelling at the top of his voice. Looked like he was exasperated with me. But then so was most of the Akshobhyan soldiers. His sword was inches away from my head. I removed a dagger from my waist cloth with one hand. From the other, I caught him from the back of his neck. Then, I pulled myself down and rolled him over me. As his head came down, I pushed the blade into his throat. By the feel of the impact, I was sure that I'd crushed his Adam's apple. Because his head was over me and I didn't have much energy to make sudden and powerful movements, the blood that gushed out of his neck drenched my face. I pushed him back behind whilst I lied on the ground, panting, covered with blood. The soldier guarding me, after finishing off the soldiers who attacked us, feared that the blood I was covered with was mine. They bent beside me and looked for some serious injury on my head. I assured them that the blood wasn't mine and then tried to stand up again.

The balance of the duel wasn't one-sided anymore. Yayati's confidence increased manifold. He was no longer just defending himself. Nrchakshu was able to guard himself against the sharp edges of the ASI. But was finding it hard to defend himself from those strong punches and kicks of Yayati. Nrchakshu swiped his sword, horizontally, at Yayati's head. Yayati ducked and caught Nrchakshu by his neck in the grip of his right arm. Forming a fist with the other he punched Nrchakshu on his ribs. A massive crack appeared on his armour. Another punch and Nrchakshu took a deeper impact. His armour broke open from his left. Yayati got ready for a third successive punch. Nrchakshu knew that if he took another hit, continuing fighting would get much difficult. He threw his sword a few feet away towards his left. Then, he grabbed Yayati's arm, holding him from the neck, with both his hands and bend down, pulling Yayati over him. Yayati's feet were off the ground. Nrchakshu curved much deeper. Yayati rolled over him and was thrown, on the ground, on his back. Nrchakshu, free from the strapping grip of Yayati, rushed to pick up his sword. After picking up his sword he brought it down on the fallen Yayati. Yayati rolled to his side and Nrchakshu's sword hit the ground. Another attempt was launched by Nrchakshu to slay Yayati. This time Yayati, still on the ground, kicked Nrchakshu's sword away. Then he grabbed Narchakshu's arm, with which was holding his sword, and pulled him down. He picked his legs up and pushed Nrchakshu in the air behind him. Nrchakshu was suspended two yards above the ground and fell four yards behind Yayati.

'Fucking amateur.' Yayati remarked as he stood up.

I wanted to have a clearer view of the duel. Along with the soldiers on my side, I started walking towards Nrchakshu and Yayati. The soldiers were worried to see me walk in such a horrid condition. But I was feeling much better now. Halfway there, we encountered a hindrance to our summit. It was Yayati's estranged son.

Yayati and Nrchakshu's fight was undergoing the test of time. They were fighting for a long time now. In the previous days of this war, Yayati didn't show any signs of lassitude. But a certain glimpse of lethargy was reflecting from his face now. This fight demanded more effort from him than his fight with Senapati Aagney. I noticed Yayati struggling against Nrchakshu again. His right arm was cut deeply. Our soldiers fighting near him were startled to witness him vulnerable against the attacks of Nrchakshu whilst he held the ASI, the weapon of the gods. Yayati was panting and clenched his right arm, just above the deep cut he sustained.

'I accept my mistake. I misjudged your level of perseverance.' Yayati said.

Nrchakshu remained focused. He didn't reveal any hint of gratification. Instead, he looked for an opening and leaped at Yayati. Yayati's breath was asynchronous and so was his movements. Nrchakshu and Yayati's swords clashed above Yayati's head. Yayati had to do a half squat to get the required time and strength to block the Nrchakshu's attack. After the clash Nrchakshu, in rapid movement, went a little ahead and brought his sword back, trying to catch Yayati by his left leg. Yayati blocked that attack immediately too. But Nrchakshu's next attack on Yayati's other leg strained the latter's miserable movements. He cut the calf of his squatted right leg. But again, he didn't waiver his focus. Instead, he increased the distance between him and the screeching Yayati. As Yayati took and endured those attacks, our soldiers were losing their attention, confidence and it felt like, for a moment, the war too.

Yugant didn't leave his chariot. He was in a condition much worse than mine, courtesy of our last fight. He ordered his men to march and kill me. Hell broke loose as my men commenced a skirmish with Yugant's soldiers. Yugant launched an arrow. But it missed me by more than four feet. The holes in his hands, I made with the arrows, were making it difficult for him to get a clear aim at a six and a half feet man standing just forty yards away from him. I laughed at his vague attempt and became the reason for a vein to pop in his forehead, a sign of an increasing rage. I wondered why he was still on the battlefield. He was as useless as chariot missing a wheel. Moreover, he was putting his men's life in jeopardy as they remained around protecting him in this violent war. Then I looked at the only shiny reflecting surface of my sword which was only a couple of inches clear of the blood all over and got the answer. Yugant looked at me furiously. But his expression changed and so did mine when we heard a heartfelt loud cry which symbolised pain and nothing but pain. Yayati was down on his knees.

Everyone in a diameter of 100 yards from Yayati Yasah and Nrchakshu stopped. A sudden chill went down my spine. An eerie silence surrounded us.

The noise of swords clanging, shields banging and men crying a hundred yards away still knocked our ears. But the intensity of the noise decreased to such an extent that it felt unnatural. This silence was seen with reverence. It gave us time to look into ourselves. For what we found ourselves in. The blood in our hands and death in our minds. We weren't the royal soldiers of our land who needed to be revered after the war. Just a bunch of savages butchering each other to our heart's content. The depth of this silence was something I feared falling into. Not now. Not just now.

I looked at Yayati. He looked miserable. His armour was gone. Broken, it lied a few yards away from him. His hair was messy and spread all over. He was out of breath. Now and then the long hair spread across his face, covering his mouth, would wave as he exhaled deeply. The scar on his chest, about which Rajkumar Dvij told me in Indravan, came into view. In his waist, a dagger was half dug. A drop of blood made its path visible as it descended from the dragger to the ground. The deep wound on his arm, a gift from Nrchakshu, hideously smiled at our soldiers. He lost his armour, shed much blood, and looked like his confidence and belief had departed to an unknown place. But the ASI remained inside the firm grip of his hand. Nrchakshu, on the other side, still stood in a stance. He was exhausted too. His armour pumped up with every breath. The look on his face depicted that he was finding it hard to believe that a wielder of ASI was down on his knees in front of him. But he was not carried away. He stood, blocking any openings, believing that his duel with Yayati was just not over. But that is not what the soldiers inside the hundred-yard circumference thought of. But soon their thoughts were going to reconcile.

ASI

I started walking towards Yayati. I didn't care if any Akshobhyan soldier came after me with their swords. Seeing Yayati fall I was crestfallen. Seeing the ASI fail, I was sure my vengeance shall remain incomplete. Through the many still standing soldiers, I knocked my way towards the centre.

'Won't you kill me?' Yayati said with evil but tired smile on his face.

Nrchakshu tightened his grip on his sword.

'No.' He said quickly. 'Even though you are a traitor to the crown of Chandragarh and Akshobhyas, a revered warrior like you don't deserve to die through the hands of an Aangrakshak. You shall be taken as a captive. Maharaja Brihadratha shall decide what to do with you.'

Yayati Yasah's head bowed. His lips were moving. At first, I thought his lips were trembling, with fear or fever. I was not sure. But at second look, it seemed as if he was mumbling something. I pushed the soldiers aside and stood at the edge of the parameter in which Nrchakshu and Yayati were fighting. Nrchakshu walked towards Yayati steadily. He knew that his opponent still held the ASI. Listening to him carefully, I was able to hear what Yayati was mumbling. It felt like a prayer. A prayer to the creator of the ASI.

'Lord Brahma…' He prayed. 'Let the true power of this godly weapon flow through me. Let the world witness its true power. Curse me with the dominance of the weapon of the gods.'

Nrchakshu was still a few feet away from Yayati when the latter lifted his head, looked at Nrchakshu through the gap of his long grey hair, and popped up a wicked smile. Nrchakshu stopped. The smile changed into a sinful smirk. Then, he turned his head, looked at the soldiers who were staring at him, and stopped at me.

'The true curse of the ASI, Yashvasin...' He whispered.

He looked at the sky and began to laugh. Soon the laughter turned into a roar. Nrchakshu was frightened and took a few steps back. Everyone was confused seeing Yayati laugh at his shameful defeat. But the words he said to me echoed in my ears. Was it time for this generation to witness the power of the ASI?

A cold breeze blew on the battlefield, making the soldiers shiver. I sensed a change in surroundings. I lifted my head and looked at the sky. The blue sky which was clear and bright a moment ago was being covered with a dark greyish shade. The sun god, who was exhilarated to watch the outcome of this war, decided to hide behind those dark dense clouds. Now not only the soldiers in the hundred-yard parameter were confused and scared, but the ones all around. It has been weeks since the last drop of rain fell in Chandragarh and decades since this barren land bathed in the divine reverential rain. In this cold month of winter, no one was expecting to see black clouds take the sky. Soon they started to roar. Yayati still laughed like a madman. In the dark pitch silence, the only sound was of the grumbling of clouds and laughter of Yayati Yasah. Every other soul stood in the battlefield scared stiff. Soon the thunder rumbled and lighting flickered its way into the battlefield. And then, the thing that never occurred in the past hundred and fifty years happened. Whilst I looked up at the growling clouds, a raindrop fell on my forehead. Soon heavy rainfall ascended on earth. The water was cold. The tap of the drops felt like a tocsin. Alarming us about the upcoming annihilation.

Yayati's laughter finally stopped. He dug the ASI in front of him. Using it as a support, he picked himself up. Nrchakshu's eyes were wide open in shock. The man who was incapable of standing still now stood as if he was unharmed from any injury. Yayati's wounds were still deep. The blood still flowed from his waist. But the way he stood, looked like he was new. New as he was during the first day of the war. He had this grand look on him. He was vibrant and seemed to be full of energy. He lifted the ASI and pointed it at Nrchakshu. His bulging biceps, broad chest, and the strong core, adorned with the loosely let hair, which danced with the flowing wind, and the dragger which still popped out of his waist suited him right. It made him look like the warrior he was. I was dazzled by his looks. To me, he resembled the great Grandsire Bhisma. I've read about him in the holy books and have seen him only in my imagination. But the resemblance was so similar that it baffled me a bit.

The scenes were enlivening. It looked something out from a historical book's war scene. Yayati standing royally, pointing the ASI towards Nrchakshu. While, in the back, the shrieking saddened sky cried in pain, shedding tears like rain.

'It will be the other way around, kid. I'll decide what to do with your Maharaja Brihadratha.' Yayati's voice was stronger than ever.

Nrchakshu gulped with trepidation.

'But before that, you shall die.' Yayati said.

A powerful bolt of lightning, illuminating the petrified faces of the soldiers, descended from the dark heavens and stuck on the battlefield, inches away from Yayati Yasah. The brilliance of the dazzling strike was blinding. Everyone was forced to cover their eyes. When the effect subsided, which wasn't for so long, the war gave us another reason to be astounded. Yayati stood behind a massive black spot, a little dug from the force, and seemed to be unharmed. On one hand, he had the ASI. In the other the dagger which he might have pulled out amidst the brightened scenes, which still dripped blood. He loosened his grip on the dragger and it fell on the ground, just beside his foot.

One last time, Yayati looked in the sky. We were all drenched, so was he. He shook his head vigorously. Water splashed out in the form of shinning flickering bands. He looked at Nrchakshu and leaped at him. There wasn't much change in his way of fighting or the intensity. The only thing which enhanced was his confidence. And confidence was enough to break down Nrchakshu. The previous scenes were daunting. Most of the soldiers still stood baffled. But they were brought down to reality when Yugant's rapid arrow was caught by Yayati Yasah by his left hand. A couple of Akshobhyan soldiers, seeing this, rushed inside the parameter to test their fate, or to put it in a better way, to know their fate. This let out a massive surge among the other Akshobhyan soldiers. The war was initiated again. But the outcome didn't change. The little fear, which remained inside them, proved to be beneficial for us. Yayati was breaking at them like a storm. Butchering them with much more ease. And so were our soldiers. Soon after, Nrchakshu and Yayati were facing each other again.

'You can't beat me.' Yayati flowed with confidence.

He glided his sword and brought it down on Nrchakshu. The young Aangrakshak was forcefully thrown back to play defensively. An attack followed another and then another. With each attack, the thrust from Yayati's sword increased and made it difficult for Nrchakshu to defend. He was taking his steps back after each blow. The wielder of ASI was giving no chance to his opponent, who seemed to have lost belief in himself. Yayati was losing his patience. He held the sword with both hands and picked it up as high as he could. Then with lightning speed, brought it down on Nrchakshu, cutting the air in between. Nrchakshu picked up his sword to defend himself but his grip on the handle was not as firm as it should have been. He lost his sword, which fell a few feet away. Yayati gave him no chance to pick up the sword. He began to bring the ASI down on Nrchakshu once again. Nrchkahsu stumbled on a shield. Curved down, on his one knee, and held the shield to his defence. The ASI cut through the shield and got stuck in there. He pulled the shield as hard as he could intending to disarm Yayati. But in vain. Yayati was pulling his ASI with greater force. His knees bent a little in this tug-of-war. Nrchakshu, capitalizing on the situation, whirlwind to his right, stepped on Yayati's thighs and kicked him in the face with his right foot. For the first time in this war, Yayati's grip on the ASI came loose. He was tossed to his right. The ground beneath was now muddy due to the first rain. Nrchakshu couldn't balance his landing over the slippery ground. He skidded on his landing and the shield, with the ASI in it, got away from him. Nrchakshu struggled to stand up. He was helped by the ferocious Yayati. He picked Nrchakshu from his chest armour with one hand. Nrchakshu's legs were suspended a couple of feet above the land, fluttering in a struggle. Yayati, with the other hand, punched him in the face. But the next attempt was stopped by Nrchakshu when he forced his knee into Yayati's core. His grip came loose and Nrchakshu landed on the ground, this time not slipping. A fistfight commenced between the two.

The ASI lied, stuck in a shield, a few feet away from the two brawling men. Little did it struck anyone's attention. I wanted to take the ASI in my hands, save it from any misfortune until Yayati was done with Nrchakshu. But in my present condition, I was the one who needed to be saved. The soldiers guarding me were busy fighting the Akshobhyan soldiers. Now and then an opposing soldier would come, storming his way, towards me. Taking on a puny soldier or two wasn't a difficult task even in my present condition. But I knew I required help when I noticed three Akshobhyan soldiers' fantasy stuck by the ASI. They stood surrounding the weapon in a dilemma, as to who should pick the godly weapon first. I looked around, looking for any of my men to aid me to reach the ASI. But everyone was indulged in exchanging blows and attacks with each other. I ordered one of them, anyway, to assist me to rescue the ASI. He swept his eyes away from his opponent for a second to acknowledge the order. His head rolled down the inclined battlefield the second later. Growing impatient, I hurried towards the three men. The pain was unbearable but little choice did I had. One of them stood watching the other two struggle to separate the ASI and the shield. I brought my sword down and the shield shattered into multiple, broken, pieces of wood. The ASI came loose and I was quick to pick it up. The three Akshobhyan soldiers, dead serious in their eyes, stood against one gravely injured opponent wielding a revered weapon. It was unwise to do so, but I closed my eyes and let my ambition flow through my mind once again. Giving it up, when I stood so close, wasn't an option. After inhaling deeply, I opened my eyes only to find the three running towards me. The surge of power wasn't like the one I felt while I stormed the gates of Indraprastha palace and slayed dozen of soldiers on my way to Yayati. I felt nothing. But somehow, I was able to fight them off together. One of them fled while the other two fell on the battleground with their eyes wide opened, not blinking.

Nrchakshu, as expected, was beaten badly by Yayati. The latter, on the other hand, looked quite lethargic too. He saw me standing with the ASI and walked in my direction. I had some doubts but ultimately tossed the sword at him. He looked at me as if asking for confirmation. I knew what he was asking for. I looked at Nrchakshu who was struggling to stand up. I adored his level of perseverance. Beaten up so badly, still wanted to go on.

'It needs to be done.' I nodded.

Yayati Yasah walked slowly towards Nrchakshu with the ASI stretched out.

'You are a warrior. A true heir of the Yudhvan clan. Your father would have been proud if he could have seen you fight with such vigour.' Yayati said to Nrchakshu.

Nrchakshu looked at me. I, cowardly, tried not to look him in the eyes.

'That being said…' He continued. 'It's time for you to die.'

Nrchakshu was on one knee when Yayati commenced slashing the ASI horizontally. But maybe the fate of Nrchakshu or this war was not to be ceased just yet. An Akshobhyan shield came whirling, from a distance and stuck Yayati on the head. The sharp edge of the shield, rotating with much momentum, formed a deep wound on his face. Stretching from his right temple down to his cheeks. Yayati was forced to his left. His expressions were hidden. Courtesy of the long hair spread all over his face. I could tell it was a hard hit. He eventually lifted his head and looked at the direction from where the shield came whirling. In a distance, the ruler of the Akshobhyas sat crouched with one hand on the ground for support. The deep wound on his left shoulder seemed to be mended by a ved and was properly covered. He was surrounded by a squad of soldiers and was panting heavily. They were standing on higher ground. Beneath them were dozens of big, pointed rocks poking out of the muddy land. Of all the people, Yayati was shocked the most. I was startled too. To see the man who was unconscious moments ago back on the battlefield was the last thing I expected. Nrchakshu was too hit by a bolt from the blue. But he was scared stiff more than he was shocked. His Maharaja was in no condition to fight anyone. But I doubted that. The way he threw the shield at Yayati was no easy task. What else could one expect from the Maharaja of the greatest empire in the whole Bharatvarsh?

The soldiers guarding me joined me again. Some of them were missing. But I didn't expect anything less from this war. I wondered what went inside Yayati's mind. He was vexed. His eyes were burning red with rage. His grip over the ASI tightened. Then I looked up at the water pouring grey sky and tried to reckon for how long we were fighting. The dark of the clouds was stretched throughout the sky. The light of the sun was being blocked for so long that thought never crawled inside someone's mind that the sun might have set already. But maybe I was overthinking. Every minute in this cold battlefield felt like a lifetime. I wondered whether the bright vibrant light of the sun still shone above those gloomy clouds.

'Your king is as persistent as you!' Yayati exclaimed as he addressed Nrchakshu.

Nrchakshu still struggled to get up. His breath was heavy and much of his blood had already shed. His face was almost unrecognizable because of it. I felt sad for him. But if this is what has been written by the almighty, I shall not try to cause a ripple.

'Even skinning you alive won't be marked as a 'daunting death' on you. No. But watching your king die before your eyes, being unable to save him. To feel so helpless. That would be formidable.' Yayati whispered near Nrchakshu while feeling the fresh wound on his face.

He squatted down near Nrchakshu. He grabbed the latter by his hair and pulled his head up. An arrow was launched at Yayati Yasah by one of the soldiers standing near Brihadratha Akshobhya. Yayati had no problem blocking it. In fact, he pulled Nrchakshu's head even more until his eyes could see his king standing at a distance.

'I'll kill him first.' Yayati whispered in Nrchakshu's ears before letting him go.

I wanted to accompany Yayati to Brihadratha's death. But my guards decided otherwise. Brihadratha was sure to be guarded by the best Akshobhyan men. And it was true. After all, the only thing that stood between Brihadratha and his death was a wall of best Akshobhyan warriors. After much debate, I was able to persuade my men to join Yayati Yasah and to make his job easier.

Yayati picked up a massive shield, lying over a huge rock. He blocked a sequence of arrows, launched by archers standing behind Brihadratha, with much ease. The Maharaja of Akshobhya took a few steps ahead as his eyes raged with vengeance and wrath for his old Senapati. But the Akshobhyan soldiers pled him not to take matters in his hands, provided his current state of health. Yayati began to climb the rocks, carefully as to not injure himself from their sharp edges. And as expected, one by one he slayed the Akshobhyan soldiers who stood as a hindrance between him and his quest. Even though he was in a condition worse than mine, Brihadratha Akshobhya stood strong, even though only briefly, against the wielder of ASI, after all the Akshobhyan soldiers near him were slayed. The injuries he sustained while having a duel with me were too grave. His movements were weak. His control over his sword was loose. One kick in the core from Yayati was enough to make him lose his balance and to make him take the knee.

Yayati raised his hands in victory. He bent a little, over Brihadratha Akshobhya to proclaim his win over him.

'Do you see this, Brihadratha?' He asked the fallen king as he gazed at the scene of the Battlefield. The Akshobhyan soldiers were being outclassed by our men. Their cry and horror screams seemed to be pleasing Yayati. The smell of their warm blood mixed with dirt and mud tingled his nostrils as he inhaled. He squatted before Brihadratha and overlooked the agonizing scenes of death and misery with him. He swayed his hand over Brihadratha Akshobhya's injured shoulder.

'Do you see this, Brihadratha?' Yayati whispered near his ear this time, increasing the pressure over Brihadratha's wound. The latter gave out a painful cry. For a moment I could hear nothing else but the harrowing scream of the Maharaja of the Akshobhyas. Watching him in excruciating pain brought a joyous smile on Yayati Yasah's face. I knew he hated him from his very core. But to enjoy torturing a being was not like Yayati. His smile, anyway, short-lived. He stood up to have a clearer look at the soldier ascending the rocky terrain. It was his estranged son. Yugant Yasah.

Yugant's injuries were profound too. The cuts in his calves hindered his movement. Blood still oozed out of his arms. The holes in his hands were hidden behind layers of bandages, allowing him much grip and less need of folding them as to hold his spear.

'You don't need to do this.' Yayati said as Yugant approached near.

Yugant, with his spear pointed at Yayati, was able to walk him away from his Maharaja.

'The outcome of this war is all but certain. You, no more, need to follow him. His cruel reign is over. You are free to join me now, son.'

'I am no son of yours!' Yugant exclaimed. 'My father is my king. And I, unlike many, am loyal towards my king.'

Yayati chuckled in amazement.

'I can understand. Over the years, this heinous Brihadratha has inculcated his false ideals in you. You are blinded with false knowledge.'

'It's true.' Yugant replied. 'I was blinded for a while. I was blinded with hate towards my king when I came face to face with the truth. I loathed him for not telling me about you. Now I can see why he did that. Yes, now I see everything clearly.'

Yugant, hastily, suspended his spear in Yayati's direction. Yayati was quick enough to shift aside.

'You are an imbecile!' Yayati enraged. 'Alas, the diminutive brain of yours shall never understand. Leaving you behind all those years ago does not look like a mistake now.'

Yugant threw a series of attacks on Yayati. But they were all loose and lacked accuracy. Yayati was about to answer back his estranged son's attacks when he saw an unexpected warrior. Nrchakshu, using his sword as a stick for support, came near them. He stood near his Maharaja and helped him get back on his feet. I could see three warriors, fighting for the Akshobhyan cause, bloody and battered, stand up against the wielder of the godly weapon, over higher ground with rocky terrain.

I could hear the neigh of horses behind me. One of our infantry leaders brought me a carriage. I was quick to get into it but refused to leave without knowing the outcome of the fight over the higher ground.

Yayati was outnumbered. But still, he had the upper hand. His opponents were finding it difficult to even balance themselves properly. This fight could have been the one with a quick end. But Yayati decided otherwise. He wanted to play. It began as a tedious fight. Yayati dodged the attacks while he laughed over their futile attempts. Yugant pushed his spear as hard as he possibly could at Yayati. But his movements were slow and predictable. Brihadratha Akshobhya was wielding his sword with only one hand. Because of his injured shoulder, he couldn't make his arm to even hold a sword. Nrchakshu was exhausted and was drenched with a grimy mixture of sweat, blood, and mud. But after multiple failed attempts, the trio began to trouble Yayati. The Maharaja of Akshobhyas was the first to land a successful attack. The three, steadily, increased the pace of their attacks which was quite surprising to watch. Being on the top of an uplifted land, half of the battlefield could see them fight. With every blow they landed on Yayati, the tide shifted. Here the three increased their pace and there their soldiers' confidence multiplied.

Brihadratha landed another successful attack. This time scratching Yayari's waist with his sword. Yayati soon realized that he could no more take it lightly. He gave out a booming roar. Vexed, he walked towards Brihadratha. Nrchakshu and Yugant came in between but were shoved away by Yayati, who had nothing but blood in his eyes for Brihadratha. His sword was twice blocked by Brihadratha, who was slowly backtracking. The strength of the blows could not be completely blocked by him. The third attempt saw Brihadratha lose his sword. Yayati grazed the ASI on his left thigh and once again, Brihadratha was on his knee. He lifted the ASI to pull it down one last time, to end this war but found Yugant in his opposition once again.

'I'll deal with you for once and for all!' Yayati exclaimed.

Another dual commenced on the higher ground. As expected, Yugnat showed difficulty matching his opponent. The dual lasted briefly when Yayati punched Yugant on the face and he went down swirling a couple of meters.

'Do me a favour and change your name after this war that is if you even survive. Let my clan name die with me. You are a disgrace to our family name. I'd rather let the name die, into extinction than letting you become the flag bearer of this esteemed clan.' Yayati said in exasperation.

He was about to turn around and walk towards Brihadratha when he heard Yugant dust himself up from the ruins.

'Whatever pleases you. With your death, I'll end this war and your clan name too.' Saying this, he rushed towards Yayati with the little strength he had in him.

But Yayati was just too strong for the injured and bleeding Yugant. He was of no match to his biological father. Brihadratha, weak and feeble, watched from the back as his adopted son took a massive beating. His expressions were too profound to not be felt. With his eyes reflecting pain, I could see his lips moving.

'Give up.' He seemed to be saying. 'Give up and go back. You can't win against him.'

A drop of tear rolled over his wrinkled cheeks as he watched Yayati thrust his sword into Yugant. The ASI went in his stomach and emerged from the other end. An inhuman smile bloomed over Yayati's face as he watched Yugnat gasping for air.

'And you thought you could beat me?' He whispered.

A saint-like smile spread over Yugant's face as he tried to say something out in broken words.

Curious, Yayati leaned in.

'No. But he can.' Yugant said.

Yayati's eyebrows raised. He tried to pull out the ASI from Yugant's body. But the latter was holding on to it with all his might. Blood came dripping through those multi-layered bandages. Yayati tried with all his might but his attempts were futile. His eyes widened when he caught a glimpse of Nrchakshu, from the corner of his eye. Nrchakshu had jumped in the air and was bringing his sword down. Yayati was dumbstruck. His frightened eyes caught the resolute eyes of his son.

'The curse dies now… with you.' He said before a bright beam of light covered the battlefield.

The intensity of the light was painful to naked eyes. For a brief moment, the war stopped. The sound of the war was gone. Everything took a halt. It was oblivious.

When the light subsided, everyone looked at the source of the light. Nrchakshu had aimed for the ASI. The invincible weapon was broken in two. Dead silence surrounded the battlefield. Everyone stood dumbstruck. The unthinkable had happened. Nrchakshu, panting, was forced to a distance by the outburst of the light and energy from the ASI. Yugant and Yayati had sustained visible burns. Yayati was frenzied and was unable to give in to reality.

'How is this possible?' He whispered.

His eyes were wide and pale. He was trembling with fear. He took small steps back, stumbled upon a rock, and halted.

'How is this possible?!' He exclaimed.

Yugant pulled out the other half of the sword from his trunk with a loud cry.

'Maybe the gods weren't so pleased with you, father.' With this, he pushed the broken edge of the sword deep into Yayati's throat. Blood started to stream out. Both Yayati and Yugant fell on their knees, face to face. Yayati had horror in his eyes. In his last moments, all he could do was wonder how the weapon of gods failed him. He fell on the ground. Yugant stared at Yayati's lifeless body before closing his eyes.

THE CONCLUSION

The darkness above subsided. From the broken holes in the grey blanket of clouds, the vibrant sunlight came busting in. The grey mist curled and burnt. Soon, every inch of the sky was clear again. Enough natural light of the day remained.

Every human soul on the battlefield witnessed the defining scenes above the rocky terrain. Our soldiers saw the death of their commander-in-chief, Yayati Yasah. The Akshobhyan soldiers saw the courageous act of Yugant and Nrchakshu which uplifted the curse of the ASI. The fight between four men changed the outcome of the war of hundreds of thousands. The tide shifted. Our soldiers were bewildered with Yayati's death. They were assured that with the failure of the weapon of the gods, the almighty had suggested his reasoning and has taken the side of the Akshobhyas. The Akshobhyan soldiers thought the same. I tried to take command.

'Fight back, you idiots! The war isn't over. We still have the upper hand!' I tried to stop them from fleeing back. But their confidence was broken beyond repair.

Apart from my trusted soldiers, no one showed a will to fight.

'The outcome is decided, sir. You must leave too.' One of them said.

'I won't!' I yelled. 'I'll fight till my last breath. I'll rip Brihadratha's head with my own hands!' I said as I tried to step out of the chariot. But they stopped me from doing so.

'Let go of me! That's an order!' I exclaimed as I tried to jostle my way out of their grip. They jumped up in the chariot and its wheels began spinning in the opposite direction.

Tears rolled down my eyes as I watched our soldiers flee the battlefield. It was heart-breaking. Being so close to my revenge. But yet so far. The Akshobhyan soldiers chased us to the very end. They were resolute to not let any of us live. A dozen of horsemen chased our chariot. Archers aimed for us, but we defended ourselves with the shields. One of the horsemen threw his spear, aiming for the wheel and hit the bull's eye. The chariot broke down and took numerous spins before taking a halt. Most of the men in the chariot died. I crawled my way out of the wreckage. One of the soldiers grabbed me from the back and pulled me towards a horse. He made me sit on it and patted on its back. The horse took off.

'Don't stop until you have reached a safe place.' He yelled. I looked back to see him for the last time. Our eyes met before a spear pierced his chest, from the back.

It all happened in a blur. I still couldn't believe any of it. But when I saw the large blanket of Akshobhyan soldiers on our tail, I realized it was all real. We had lost the war and now we're on the verge of losing our lives. My horse was fast enough to help me escape. But not all of our soldiers were fortunate. The majority of them died. The others fled. The Akshobhyans remained invincible.

The Book of Secrets

• ◉ •

Back at our base camp in Bindutva, the news of the lost war had already spread like a wildfire. Everymen was in a haste to run away from the upcoming annihilation, coming in the form of the Akshobhyan soldiers. And it didn't take them long. The Akshobhyans followed us closely. They began slaying every man they saw. Ours were too afraid to even give a fight. Tents were burned, men were butchered. It was a chaotic mixture of blood and fire.I was right at the end of the camp. It would have been easy for me to not look back and run away. But I did look back. To see the result of my quest for vengeance. I found myself with ample time to take a bird's-eye view of the burning camp in ruins. My tent caught my attention in the end. An urge raised within. It asked me to go back inside the camp, risking my life. And so I did. Amidst the death that surrounded the base camp, I made my way to the tent. Near the entrance, I hopped down from the horse and took a look at the wide shelter. The top half was set ablaze and the flames were descending rapidly. I rushed inside without reckoning upon the consequences of my action. The visibility inside was hampered because of the sooty smoke that surrounded everything. I knocked my knees on some tables, dropped some earthen pots before ultimately banging my head on the old dusky wardrobe. With all possible haste, I opened it and grabbed hold of a satchel. After tying it around myself, I rushed back outside where I was welcomed by an Akshobhyan soldier's sword. I dodged to the other side, almost fell, and found myself without any weapon. He forced himself on me. Using his force to my advantage, I was able to push him inside the burning tent. He came out, covered with a blanket of fire, crying for help. I jostled him away and released him from the burning sensation by using his sword to penetrate his chest. Sensing the increasing danger, I jumped on my horse and pulled the reins. An arrow bruised my shoulder but soon I was out of danger.

After a long day, witnessing uncountable deaths, the sun began to retire. Soon the last hue of the day was gone too. I needed some rest too, but was running out of time. I decided to ride all night and the other day too to reach Indraprastha before the Akshobhyans. With the remaining soldiers in the palace, we could regroup and possibly come up with another plan. My eyes were heavy and every part of my body was throbbing with pain. I had sustained multiple bruises and cuts and enough blood has already been shed. I started to hallucinate and, at times, would lose consciousness. But a sudden jerk from the horse would wake me again. My body needed to rest. But I couldn't stop. On the second morning, my horse stopped outside the city of Indraprastha. The city was still at some distance. Exhausted, I was asleep on my horse. When I woke up, I realized the horse had stopped to drink some water from the nearby pond. Poor soul. Putting strain on my self was my right. But completely forgetting about the horse's wellbeing was not justified from my side. I, somehow, managed to climb down the horse. I was worn-out to my very core. After gulping down the cold water of the pond for some time and washing my face and my wounds, I felt better and decided to head inside the city. Little did I know, another surprise waited for me in the vicinity.

The city of Indraprastha was in ruins. At the entrance of the city, I was welcomed by a gut-wrenching scene. Two large masts were erected on either side of the narrow passage which led to the city. A flag, each, fluttered atop the posts. Both of them bored the colours of the Akshobhyas. But that wasn't the obnoxious part. The poles were hammered with several massive nails. From the nails swung the heads of the soldiers, tied with a string, we left behind to guard the city. A dozen heads on either post were to send a message. The leader of the Akshobhyas would never command such atrocity. It wasn't the work of the Akshobhyas. For I was sure that no Akshobhyan soldier passed by me in the two nights I rode for Indraprastha. I tied my horse behind a dense bush, a little far away, and walked towards the city to douse the fire of curiousness within but not before covering myself with a ragged blanket as to not catch unwanted attention.

After walking for a while, I stopped at a barricade. Another Akshobhyan flag swirled with the slightest disturbance of the wind on a pole nearby.

'Who are you?' A voice called from behind the barricade. A tall, dark soldier wearing an armour that didn't belong to the Akshobhyas came forward.

'With what business do you approach the gates of this city of Indraprastha?' Another one came from behind. He was short and had a round belly.

The Akshobhyan colours were all around the city but the soldiers bore different. I knew that they were the soldiers of some kingdom that came under the rule of the Akshobhyas. But which one?

'Oh, great warriors of the noblest cause! I was a resident of this divine city until the treacherous alliance of the Advaityas and Varunyas drove me out of its gates.' I said trying to gain their sympathy.

The taller one glimpsed at the cuts on my uncovered arm.

'Those devil's merchants raped my wife and daughter and slayed my friends in front of my own eyes! When I tried to fight back, the weak creature that I am, they beat me to pulp and threw me out of the city to die alone from the injuries I'd sustained.' I sobbed. 'I was content that I'll meet my family in the afterlife, but witness my misfortune, O' mighty soldiers! The gods didn't even let me die! Such was the fate of many other people like me.'

After witnessing the look on their face and finding them properly matched with the ones I had in mind I continued.

'I heard that their evil alliance was defeated and uprooted from the very core. And so I came back to see and thank the valiant soldiers who restored my motherland to her foremost glory.' Impressed and content with my little act, the fat one walked towards me.

'Rejoice, poor soul!' He said while placing his hand on my shoulder. 'You have been liberated by the blessing of Maharaja Brihadratha of the Akshobhyas.'

I clenched my fist with vexation, which caught the eye of the guards. Alarmed by the situation I tried to keep calm.

'I am sorry, brave warriors of this land. But didn't the Akshobhyas win the war with a whisker recently? Moreover, I've previously had the great luck to dwell into the exquisite scenes of the Akshobhyan soldier's march in their splendid brilliance. I have seen their armour. And yours don't match.'

The two soldiers chuckled as they exchanged glances.

'We are the soldiers of the Gandhara Kingdom.' The said. 'Our kingdom answers to the commands of the Akshobhyan ruler. Maharaja Brihadratha sent for us before the war.'

That Bastard Brihadratha sure knew the art of war.

'That's the best news I've heard for a long time!' I said with a fake sense of exhilaration.

The implacable soldiers of Gandhara weren't the ones I'd be pleased to face in the present scenario. They were known for their barbaric acts on and off the battlefield. I could not have risked getting involved with them. And so I decided to leave silently now that only two soldiers gave the guard.

'I shall go and inform my companions, who suffered from the same dreadful fate as mine, about this delightful news right away.' Saying this, I turned around.

I'd only taken a couple of steps in the other direction when one of the two called out for me.

'Stop!' He exclaimed. I turned around and faced him.

'What is it, valiant warrior of Gandhara?' I asked in a low voice.

'Your legs…' He pointed out. A hideous cut surfaced on my calf. 'It looks nasty.' He continued. 'Let us take you to a ved. Meanwhile, tell us about the location of the hideout of other people of Indraprastha. We shall go and rescue them ourselves.'

'Oh, these injuries given by the ruthless and immoral enemy is nothing compared to the joyous hope you brave soldiers have provided me with. Moreover, don't fret over the rescuing of my companions. You have just won a great battle. I am sure you require rest. Moreover, the hideout isn't far away. I'll be back before you know it.' After giving a reassuring smile, I turned around and commenced taking rapid steps.

Cold sweat took me over when I heard their approaching footstep. The sound of their drawing sword was not assuring at all.

'Stop!' They yelled. 'Turn around and don't move.'

I stood there in utter silence.

'Turn around I said!' The fat one yelled again.

I could hear him walk towards me. He placed his hand on my shoulder and it was the last thing I wanted.

I took a quick step forward and turned around. The fat soldier was left with my ragged blanket. From one of the holes in it, he saw my foot approaching his face. But it was too late for him. He fell on the ground with a thud. After picking up his sword I thrust the metal into his chest. The taller one ran towards me and kicked me in the ribs. The impact was strong. He then punched me in the face. I coughed some blood. I knew this had to be dealt with quickly. He swung his sword at me. His reach was longer. But I managed to dodge and with all my might swung my sword at his face. His movements meagre in speed. Next thing I knew, his head was rolling on the ground.

After picking up my blanket I hastily hopped towards the other direction. From behind the bushes I jumped on my horse and charged away from the city of Indraprastha. For everything seemed to be lost now. The last hope was shattered. I decided to go north.

I wandered for three days. Stopping only to drink and eat. Danger was everywhere. The boundaries of the Akshobhyan ruled Bharatvarsh were vast. And so I had to take every decision with utmost care and precision. I could not put myself in peril of being getting recognised. Being a renowned member of the Akshobhyas first and then their foremost enemy had its hazards.

On the fourth day, I arrived at a small peaceful village called Alpagarh. It was a distant village, miles away from the nearest city. People were cheerful and hardworking. I walked beside my horse, with its rein in my hand. The people who passed by greeted me with their warm smiles. I felt welcomed. Exhausted as I was, I noticed a banyan tree, not gigantic neither young, near the local well and decided to take some rest. I tied my horse nearby and made myself comfortable beneath the tree's cool shade. The climate was de-stressing. The women of the village would come to the well and get their earthen pots filled with its cold water. The clouds in the blue sky were gigantic and white. I tried to form some images with them but my mind was too stressed. The chirping of the birds, which like me came to repose under the shade of the banyan tree, was the only sound around. And it was soothing. It has been some time since I last witnessed such peace. I closed my eyes for a brief moment. In this brief moment, I felt detached from the earthly worries. I was not dead, but being alive didn't feel like this. I could have just stayed like that forever. After an enjoyable moment of respite, I opened my eyes and looked around. I stretched my hands and it was then I remembered about the satchel. The same satchel for which I risked my life at the base camp in Bindutva. I opened it and a red velvet caught my eye. I picked it out and studied it under the daylight. It was the book, I stole from Mahamantri Brahmanand's library. I was intrigued just as I was when I first held the book. Having much time to waste now, I opened it.

'The book of truth' It read in the Akhzari dialect.

My eyes became grave and I leaned in. I was in for another surprise. With every line I read, my eyes began to engross more and more into the book. After a meticulous moment of reading, I closed the book. My heart-beat had increased and my breath became heavy. I looked around feverishly and rushed to my horse, untied it, and rushed out of the village.

I never thought I'll see him again. But it was necessary now. After so many years it was time again. It was time to meet Nishprabh.

About the Author

The author is a software engineer working in a multinational professional services company based in Mumbai and has also worked as a guitar instructor.

Fascinated by stories and music, the author shuffles his time between reading and strumming chords on his Hofner and Cort guitars. And at least once in a year goes on a solo adventure across the country.

Apart from fiction, the author often finds mental repose in reading and writing poetry and has a blog where he expresses his thoughts in the form of verses.

His blog is https://poemsandfiction.blogspot.com/

The author resides with his family in Navi Mumbai.